*She thought she knew
all there was to know about love...
until he showed her
the meaning of true ecstasy.*

D0375502

Dear Friends,

I have always loved legends and myths, and stories of noble, larger-than-life heroes and magic. So, once upon a time, I took one of my favorite legends—that of Arthur and his knights—put my own spin on it, and called it *Believe*. Originally published more than a decade ago, *Believe* has now been updated and tweaked a tiny bit, but the story is the same—a story of white knights, myths, and magic.

It's long been one of my favorites and I hope it becomes one of yours.

Enjoy the magic!

All my best,

Victoria Alexander

By Victoria Alexander

BELIEVE
THE VIRGIN'S SECRET
SEDUCTION OF A PROPER GENTLEMAN
THE PERFECT WIFE
SECRETS OF A PROPER LADY
WHAT A LADY WANTS
A LITTLE BIT WICKED
LET IT BE LOVE
WHEN WE MEET AGAIN
A VISIT FROM SIR NICHOLAS
THE PURSUIT OF MARRIAGE
THE LADY IN QUESTION
LOVE WITH THE PROPER HUSBAND
HER HIGHNESS, MY WIFE
THE PRINCE'S BRIDE
THE MARRIAGE LESSON
THE HUSBAND LIST
THE WEDDING BARGAIN

Coming Soon
DESIRES OF A PERFECT LADY

VICTORIA ALEXANDER

Believe

AVON

An Imprint of HarperCollins*Publishers*

This book was originally published July 1998 by Dorchester Publishing Company, Inc.

AVON BOOKS
An Imprint of HarperCollins*Publishers*
10 East 53rd Street
New York, New York 10022-5299

Copyright © 1998, 2009 by Cheryl Griffin
ISBN 978-0-06-172883-9
www.avonromance.com

First Avon Books paperback printing: December 2009

Avon Trademark Reg. U.S. Pat. Off. and in Other Countries, Marca Registrada, Hecho en U.S.A.

HarperCollins® is a registered trademark of HarperCollins Publishers.

Printed in the U.S.A.

10 9 8 7 6 5 4 3 2 1

*This book is dedicated with all my love
to my husband, Chuck,
who has always believed in me,
always been my white knight,
and always wanted a book of his own.
He deserves one.*

Chapter One

". . . *So* even though it's a charming story, it's a myth, a legend, with no more substance than a fairy tale." Tessa St. James favored the class with her superior I-am-the-instructor-and-therefore-I-know-what-I'm-talking-about smile and waited for the inevitable question.

She didn't wait long.

A perky brunette in the second row raised her hand. "But couldn't it be real?"

Tessa bit back the impulse to roll her eyes toward the ceiling. After all, questions from students were good. Part of the learning process. She just wished they'd learn a little faster.

"No, it couldn't. As I said earlier in the hour, if Arthur existed at all, he was a fifth- or sixth-century Celtic chieftain. The stories about Camelot and the Knights of the Round Table and everything else are straight from the fertile imagination of men like Geoffrey of Monmouth and Thomas Mallory."

"But what about the search for the Grail?" a skinny long-haired kid said with an insolent challenge in his voice. She knew the type. They were a campus subculture. Raised on computers and *Dungeons and Dragons*, these unique individuals never let the high-tech nature of one passion overshadow the fantasy of the other. More than likely, all he knew about the Grail came from *Monty Python*.

"The Grail search is, of course, an integral part of the Arthurian legend. But it's almost more a necessity, a technique really, to make the entire story work." She pulled a deep breath. Wasn't this class over yet? "If you have a bigger-than-life hero you need a bigger-than-life quest. What's more noble and heroic than the search for the cup of Christ? It's the stuff myths are made of. And that's exactly what we're dealing with here. A myth. Nothing more."

"How then do you explain the many and varied landmarks throughout Britain that mark the life and death of Arthur and his knights?" A tall, distinguished-looking gentleman leaned against the wall in the back of the classroom.

Tessa narrowed her eyes. Who was this guy? And when did he pop in? She sure hadn't noticed him earlier in the hour. He looked suspiciously like a visiting professor. His accent was slightly British, his jacket was traditional herringbone, his silver hair short and his steel gray goatee trimmed to perfection. All in all, he bore a vague resemblance to Fred Astaire. Definitely a professor. Damn, the administration was supposed to let you know when you had another instructor auditing your class. Tessa wasn't at all fond of guests, expected or otherwise, in her classes. Especially this class.

"It's not uncommon for ancient legends to leave their mark on a landscape. The prime example is Mount Olympus in Greece. There is no question the mountain was never the home of the gods but—" The bell that signaled the end of the hour in undergraduate buildings clanged, cutting her off. Too bad. She was just warming to her favorite subject. Students surged from their seats and headed toward the door amid the usual bedlam of changing classes and she yelled after them in the futile hope of being heard. "Next week, we start the section on Norse mythology. Check your syllabus for the required reading."

She sighed, scooped her books off the desk and remembered the visiting professor. Who was he and why was he in her class? She scanned the room and the remaining students flowing toward the door. Great, he had already left. She strode through the doorway and glared up and down the hall. Nothing. Well, she'd probably hear about him sooner or later. Hopefully much, much later. Her goal these days was just to last to the end of the semester and Christmas.

Tessa made her way through the packed corridor to the tiny office allotted her as an assistant professor. It could have been worse. It could have been a grad student's cubicle. She dropped her books on the already littered desk, sank into her chair, leaned her head back and closed her eyes.

Three more weeks. The words repeated themselves over and over in her head like a mantra and for the first time today, a smile creased her lips. Three more weeks and she'd leave the snow and ice of the Midwest behind for sunny Greece. The ancient home of Aphrodite and Apollo. The mythical location of Atlantis itself. A legendary playground for modern man.

Her smile widened. Oh sure, she'd be doing research during her six-month sabbatical for her book on the origins of Greek mythology but she wouldn't be spending all of her time in dusty old libraries. No, delving into the legends of that historic land meant real field work. In the most wonderful fields on earth. Small, whitewashed villages that hugged the shores of the sapphire blue Aegean . . .

"I'd know that smile anywhere. You're not in Kansas anymore, are you, Dorothy?"

Tessa laughed at the familiar voice but refused to open her eyes. "No way. Kansas was never like this."

"You're in Greece again, right?"

"You got it." Tessa snapped her eyes open. "Three more weeks."

"I know, I know." Angie Whitcomb sighed with ill-concealed envy. "I'd kill to go with you. But right now, I'll settle for lunch. Oh, here." The short, chunky graduate student thunked a large box down in the middle of the debris on Tessa's desk. "This came for you in today's mail."

Tessa eyed it curiously. "What is it?"

"Beats me. I didn't open it. I didn't even shake it." Angie pushed tendrils of dark hair away from her face. The haphazard ponytail she habitually wore was never up to the task of imprisoning her unruly hair. "I think I deserve a reward for that."

"For doing what you're supposed to?"

"Well, sure." Angie shot her an indignant look. "It's not sealed well. I could have peeked right in and no one would ever have known. It took a great deal of willpower not to check it out."

Tessa grinned. Angie's curiosity was legendary around the classic literature department. "I'm impressed. What fortitude, what strength of character, what—"

Angie plopped down in the only other chair in the cramped office. "It's from your mom."

"I thought you said—"

"I read the return address." Angie shrugged. "Shoot me."

"I wonder what it is?" Tessa studied the box idly. Her mother was always sending her odds and ends she thought would interest her.

"Probably a Christmas present. Something for your trip maybe. Tanning oil, sunglasses," Angie grinned wickedly, "a tiny little bikini."

"Angie, I'm going to work and that's all."

Angie snorted her disbelief. "Right."

"Really." Tessa's protest sounded weak even to her own ears. "I am."

"You've been writing that book for two years now. You and I both know there's no need to go to Greece to finish it up."

"And your point?"

"My point is—it's a scam, Ms. St. James. Plain and simple." Angie crossed her arms over her chest and leaned back in the chair. "You can call it research or a sabbatical or whatever you want but I'm saying you're planning on mixing a whole lot of pleasure with a little bit of business. And I'm also saying the Greek gods you're looking for won't be entirely mythical."

"Angie!" Tessa should have been indignant at Angie's far-too-perceptive assessment of her plans, or at least defensive, but the very idea of how close Tessa was to the trip—no—the adventure of a lifetime tempered any possibility of annoyance. "I admit, I'm planning on having a ball. I've dreamed about going to Greece most of my life. And if a god or two gets in my way, well," she shrugged, "I'm certainly not going to pass up the chance for a little fun on the other side of the world."

"Love on a Greek island." Angie sighed. "Sounds like a movie title."

"Wait a minute, pal." Tessa leaned forward and stared at the younger woman. "Sure, a Greek god sounds like a good time but I'm not looking for love." She shrugged. "I've given up believing in love."

"Everyone believes in love," Angie said firmly.

"Not me. It doesn't exist in my case."

"Why not?"

"Simple. I grew up with two loving parents in a wonderful relationship. That's how I thought my life would be." Tessa shook her head. "But every time I fall in love, and I have experienced that unstable emotion on a number of occasions, thank you, every single time I offer my heart to some man, he crushes it. It's not going to happen again. No way, no how. Love is as big a myth as the gods on Olympus. Which is, in case you were wondering, a ski resort today."

"Hey, everybody's heart's been broken at least once. It's part of the game. You know, the emotional equivalent of no pain, no gain." Angie studied her. "I don't see why anyone doesn't believe."

"Oh, I believe all right." Tessa grinned. "I believe in tall, handsome Greek gods. I just don't believe in mortal men." She picked up a pen and aimed it at her friend. "But I'll believe that dreams come true if I can just survive the next three weeks."

Angie smiled sympathetically. "You still hate that class, don't you?"

"It's not bad enough that I had to take it over in the

middle of the semester but I missed the sections on Greek and Roman mythology, Mediterranean legends . . ." Angie's long-suffering expression pulled her up short. Tessa wrinkled her nose in chagrin. "You've heard this before, haven't you?"

Angie's eyes twinkled with amusement. "Just about every time you have to teach that class. Thank God it's only two days a week. I still don't get it. I can see why you'd prefer hot-blooded Greeks frolicking with lowly peasants to Norse gods in the land of ice and snow, but who in their right mind doesn't like King Arthur and Lancelot and all that good stuff?"

"Me, that's who. Think about it, Angie." Tessa tapped the pen on the desk in an authoritative manner. "First of all, it's set in medieval times. A disgusting, crowded, filthy, smelly period. Full of plague and pestilence. Even if you had money and power and lived in a castle, life was primitive at best."

"Okay, so it doesn't sound as good as Greek gods cavorting under the hot sun beside a sparkling sea wearing nothing but a toga and a smile."

Tessa laughed at the image. "Sure, but what does? The Middle Ages can't compete. Have you ever seen a suit of armor?"

"Yeah," Angie said grudgingly.

"Would you really want to wear cold, heavy metal? Let alone cuddle up next to it? Well?" Angie looked distinctly uncomfortable at the thought and Tessa pressed her point home. "Or better yet, throw yourself in the arms of a man who's been encased like a canned ham all day? Not my idea of a good time."

"I'll give you that one, but what about love? It's a terribly romantic story." Angie compressed her lips into a stubborn line. "Arthur and Guinevere and Lancelot."

"Love?" Tessa scoffed. "More like infidelity, betrayal and disillusionment. At least when love enters into a Greek legend it has a purpose. Explaining the change of seasons or whatever. Arthurian myth doesn't even have a great moral other than, maybe, don't trust your best friend with your wife."

Angie shook her head. "You are positively sick, Tessa St. James."

"I am not." She laughed. "I simply believe the Greek legends, and the Roman ones too for that matter, are classic, and Arthur and his pals are just plain grubby. Besides, it's make-believe. It's not real."

"Neither are Greek gods, but that doesn't seem to bother you."

"Okay, I admit it. None of these gods or kings or people ever existed. Period. Now." She rose to her feet and considered the package on her desk. "Let's see what goodies Mom sent. There should be a pair of scissors here somewhere."

Angie dug through the odds and ends cluttering the desk. "Don't you ever clean this mess up?"

"Sure. At the beginning and the end of the year."

"Got 'em." Angie presented the shears with a flourish. "My Lady Tessa, your sword."

"Very funny." Tessa ran one blade of the scissors along a long strip of mailing tape, opened the box and pulled out fistfuls of crumpled newspaper.

"Very nice," Angie said, "a little light reading for your trip."

"My mother has always been a fanatic about packing boxes. She doesn't think anything shipped should be allowed to move around." Tessa cleaned out the last bit of newsprint and smiled. "Well, look at this. Mom's been bargain hunting again."

"What is it?" Angie strained forward to peer into the box.

"Books. Old books."

"Books?" Disappointment rang in Angie's voice. "That's it? No Christmas cookies? No peanut brittle? No homemade fudge? Just old books?"

"Yep, sorry. But not any old books." Tessa pulled out the top book and studied it. "Children's books. Old children's Christmas books. I've been collecting them for years. Take a look at this, especially the illustrations."

Tessa handed the volume to Angie, who flipped it open and paged through it. "It is kind of neat."

"Isn't it?" Tessa excavated three more books from the apparently bottomless box. "It looks like these are from the twenties or thirties. They were mass produced but, even so, I think the quality is much better than today."

Angie grabbed another book and flipped through it. "I like the old-fashioned style of the drawings. It's kind of innocent."

"I know. Mom must have found these at garage sales. She's a bargain hunter from way back. I grew up with her dragging me from one sale to another on Saturday mornings. Now, whenever she runs into something she thinks I would like, she picks it up and sends it to me. Oh, good, here's a note." Tessa fished out a folded sheet of monogrammed stationery.

"So, what does it say?"

"Well." Tessa scanned the note. "She's still pissed

I'm not going to be home for Christmas, even though we are celebrating together on the day before Christmas Eve."

"Understandable. My mother would have a fit that would last through Easter if I wasn't home for Christmas."

"But she does understand a bargain. And she can't argue with the great air fare I got by flying on Christmas Eve. It also says, 'Everybody needs a bit of magic.'" Tessa shrugged. "Whatever that means."

"Maybe she knows you don't believe in love and hopes at least you believe in magic."

"Wrong on both counts." Tessa stared into the box. "There's another book in here." She reached in to grab it. "It's jammed in kind of tight. If I can get my fingernails . . . Hah! Got it." She pulled out the book, stared at the lengthy title and broke into a grin. "You won't believe this." She handed the volume to Angie.

Angie glanced at the gilded title gleaming dully on the cover and laughed. "She doesn't know you very well, does she?"

"She knows me very well." Tessa retrieved the book and studied it carefully. "This is really intriguing. The cover looks like it's maybe a hundred years old or so. It's still fairly easy to find works from that era." Carefully she opened the book. "But the pages seem much older. I wonder how that happened?"

"Maybe somebody replaced the cover at some point?" Angie said helpfully.

"I suppose . . . Still, it's strange." Tessa turned the pages slowly. "This looks really, really old. Take a look at that print."

Angie glanced at the page. "It's a cursive style, like

handwriting instead of block print." Her gaze met Tessa's. "So what?"

"I don't know. Since the cover's been replaced it's probably not terribly valuable." Tessa pulled her brows together. "But it is interesting."

"Interesting?" Angie clapped her hands to her cheeks in an exaggerated expression of surprise. "Why who would have thought, our very own Ms. St. James would have found that particular subject interesting in the least little bit."

"Knock it off." Tessa laughed. "It's the book I find interesting not the subject." She laid it gently on the desk. "I'll look at it later. Let's go get something to eat."

"It's nice to know you believe in something." Angie stepped to the door.

"Oh, yeah? What?"

Angie tossed her a smug smile. "Food."

"You've caught me. I'm a believer. Now let's go." Tessa pushed her out the door in a good-natured manner. She'd examine the book more closely later today. It was weird though, this particular volume arriving when it did. Probably no more than a bizarre coincidence. Still, like a song she couldn't get out of her head, the book's title throbbed in the back of her mind:

My Life and Times
The Story of Merlin
Wizard Extraordinaire and Counselor to Kings

Tessa arched her back and stretched her hands over her head in a vain effort to relieve some of the stiffness in her joints. It seemed like she'd been sitting here forever. Alone. Exactly why she loved the stacks in the old wing of the university library. People rarely came into this area and, since Tessa had a tendency to talk to herself out loud when she concentrated, this was the perfect place for her. There were no windows back here, nothing to really mark the passage of time and it was easy to focus on whatever work was before her She glanced at her watch and straightened in surprise. It was nearly eight o'clock. She'd been here all day.

"And what have we managed to get accomplished? Not much." Tessa stared ruefully at the array of books scattered across the broad expanse of the scarred, ancient oak table. She'd pulled almost every reference the university had to offer on dating antique books. *The Story of Merlin* defied them all and through the course of the day, the mystery had become an obsession.

She was fairly confident about the age of the cover though. It dated to the late 1800s at the earliest. There was nothing particularly special about it except that it was in remarkably good condition. A little wear around the corners seemed to be the extent of any damage. No, it wasn't the cover that fascinated her.

She flipped open the book and turned the pages one by one. The paper was like nothing she'd ever seen. It bore a striking resemblance to a very fine parchment. Tessa had examined books that dated back five hundred years before but that parchment was brittle and fragile and stiff with age. The pages in this book were supple and flexible as if they were new. But of course that was ridiculous. Even in the 1800s no one used parchment. Beyond that, after more than a hundred years, parchment too would lose its pliant properties.

The pages themselves weren't half as intriguing as the words printed on them. At least she thought it was print. It could well have been actual handwriting. She shook her head in frustration. That made no sense at all. She ran her finger lightly over one page. If this was written, no matter how old, there would be a difference in the feel of the page, with subtle ridges and indentations in the surface, as compared to a sheet of mechanical printing. As far as she could tell, it was flat.

But it was the illustrations that took her breath away. In a style that seemed more realistic than the nineteenth century, the colors, vibrant and alive, defied any test of time. Each depiction was more glorious than the last. Here was a painting of a knight pitted against a dragon, so evocative she could almost feel the heat of the dragon's breath on her face and shiver with the fear of the valiant knight. There was a court scene, a great hall draped in the banners of the king's men with the laughter of a hundred lords and ladies echoing through the chamber. She turned another page and caught her breath. How had she missed this picture? It was the most stunning illustration yet.

A knight knelt in prayer before an altar, his hands clasped, his gaze turned toward the heavens. He wore some kind of tunic, with a massive sword in a scabbard at his waist. A red jewel glittered in a ring on his little finger. A single shaft of light from a window that was little more than a slit in the wall illuminated his upturned face. His hair was dark, nearly black, the color of night. His profile was classic: a straight, noble nose, lips firm and full, a touch of defiance in the set of his chin, eyes deep and lit with a burning passion. She couldn't really tell from the picture but somehow she knew his eyes were blue and nearly as dark as his hair. He seemed to fill the tiny chapel with his presence. Strapping. That's what he was. Strapping. She drew a shaky breath. Wow. What a hunk. And what a shame he belonged in the one legend she didn't particularly like. Of course, somebody like this could change her mind. She grinned. "Too bad he isn't real."

Reluctantly she turned a page. Strange. This had to be the fourth or fifth, or maybe the fiftieth, time she'd gone through the book today. Yet, she seemed to see something new each time she leafed through it. Like the picture of Sir Hunk. She laughed, the sound unnaturally loud in the quiet of the stacks. He really wasn't her type, anyway. Now if he were a Greek god . . .

She flipped back to the beginning of the volume. She'd already tried and failed to find a single page with any kind of copyright date or publishing information. Maybe she'd just missed it. She seemed to be overlooking quite a bit in this little book.

The title page opened before her and again she read:

My Life and Times
The True Story of Merlin
Wizard Extraordinaire and Counselor to Kings

Nothing there. She turned the page and her hand froze.

The True Story of Merlin

She flipped back and stared. There it was. It did say *True*.

"I must be getting tired," she muttered. "I could swear that word wasn't there before." She rubbed her eyes and turned the page. Again, she stared in disbelief.

Here was another picture she'd obviously skipped right over. Although how anyone could was amazing. Piercing, imperious, black eyes stared out at her from beneath a blue wizard's conical hat. White hair curled around his head and a long beard lay in waves on his chest. His robes matched his hat, a deep royal color with gold planets and stars dancing across the fabric. She glanced at the caption at the bottom of the page: *Merlin, Wizard Extraordinaire and Counselor to Kings.*

"And modest too, eh pal? But what do you expect from a myth?" Tessa laughed softly and bent forward for a better look. The eyes of the image drew her closer. A glimmer of amusement lingered there. Funny. Her initial impression had been one of hauteur not humor. The old guy kind of looked like someone she knew, too. Short of Santa Claus, she didn't know anybody who even vaguely resembled this guy. Her gaze drifted down the page to the caption at the bottom: *I am not a myth.*

Tessa gasped, jerked her gaze away and bolted upright in her chair. "I didn't see that."

She tried to fight it but couldn't resist the compulsion for another quick peek.

You did too.

"Whoa!" Tessa slammed the book shut and jumped from her chair. Panic surged through her and she struggled to stay calm. She drew three deep breaths. "Okay, relax. There's no problem. I'm just tired, that's all. I've been here way too long, staring at small, tight print, in bad light, and my eyes are going." She glared at the innocent looking volume. "Or my mind."

Tessa quickly gathered up the research materials scattered across the table. "I'll turn these in, go home and relax. Yeah, that's the ticket."

By the time she'd finished methodically stacking and restacking the library's reference books, the beat of her heart and pace of her breathing was nearly normal. Merlin's book sat on the table untouched. Her reluctance to pick it up again was ridiculous. She simply hadn't read the captions correctly, that's all. There was nothing more to it. Add to that the end of a long day, her growing excitement over her upcoming trip, even her mother's whimsical note about magic, and it was no wonder she was seeing things.

"Don't be an idiot, Tessa." She nodded sharply and reached for the book. Her hand shook and the volume slipped from her grasp, tumbling to the floor to land with its pages spread open and flattened, its cover facing up. "Damn."

No matter what else this book might be it was obviously old, possibly valuable and deserved to be handled better. She picked up the ill-treated volume, ignored a strong desire not to look at it, and flipped it over.

The book had opened to the illustration of the knight in the chapel. Once again, the vividness of the picture struck her. The skin tones of the knight were so warm and real, she almost thought she could reach out and touch the pulse throbbing in his throat. The coolness of the stone walls and the deep serenity of the room itself was so well portrayed it seemed to seep from the picture to envelope her. The brightness of the sun streaming through the window was nothing short of lifelike. The brilliance captured her and held her mesmerized. Dust motes danced in the light. The beam itself grew more and more intense. She raised her hand against the blinding ray but couldn't seem to turn away.

What was going on here? She couldn't wrench her gaze from the picture that pulled her inexorably closer although she never took a step. Fear clutched at her stomach and she fought against whatever force held her in its grip. What was happening to her? Dimly, in the back of her mind she likened the sensation to a classic movie technique. A pan-zoom, she thought it was called. The camera moved forward while the lens moved back, creating a disorientation of space and distance. The effect had always made her dizzy on screen, but caught in its grasp here and now, nausea swept through her. She hurtled toward an image that swelled until it encompassed her vision, her senses and, finally, her world. Tessa struggled against a shock that stole her breath and stilled her heart. She covered her eyes with her hands and battled to regain control. Abruptly, the turbulent atmosphere encompassing her quieted, as if an off switch had been thrown.

She kept her hands pressed over her eyes. What in the hell was that? Was she sick? Dead? Had she had some kind of attack or seizure?

She stood unmoving for a long moment. Her heart thudded in her chest. She couldn't remember ever being scared like this in her life. Oh, she had known fear now and then but never sheer, unadulterated terror. At least not aside from an occasional nightmare. But terror gripped her now. What would she see when she uncovered her eyes? Once more she sucked in a deep breath. Whatever else she was, Tessa St. James had never been a coward and she was not about to become one now. She dropped her hands and stared at the vision in front of her.

A knight knelt in prayer before an altar, his hands clasped, his gaze turned toward the heavens.

Chapter Two

❦

"Holy shi—"

"Now, now, my dear, your language. This is a chapel, you know."

Tessa whirled toward the voice. An older gentlemen leaned against the stone wall in a nonchalant manner. His accent was slightly British, his jacket was traditional herringbone, his short hair silver and his steel-gray goatee trimmed to perfection. She gasped. "You! You're—"

He broke into a perfect step-shuffle-ball-change that would have gladdened the heart of her third-grade tap dancing teacher.

Tessa stared in confusion. "Fred Astaire?"

"Nope." He executed a few more perfect steps. "But people tell me" —he finished with a flourish— "ta-da. I look like him."

Her eyes widened with disbelief. Between Sir Hunk over there and the Fred Astaire look-alike obviously expecting applause, this had all the makings of a nightmare. "Somebody pinch me, I must be dreaming."

At once pain shot through her upper arm. "Ouch!" She clapped her hand over the affected limb and glared at the Fred Astaire impersonator. He hadn't moved an inch but Tessa had no doubt he was responsible. "That hurt!"

He shrugged. "You said to pinch you."

"Well, I certainly didn't mean it!"

"If you didn't mean it, you shouldn't have said it."

"It's just one of those things you say. You know, like don't cry over spilt milk or don't lock the barn door after the horse is gone or," she narrowed her eyes, "crazy as a loon." Once again pain twinged through her arm. "Hey!"

"Sorry." He favored her with a pleasant smile. "I slipped."

"I'll bet." She rubbed the spot of his slip in a vigorous effort to ease the ache. "Who are you anyway?"

He crossed his arms over his chest. "I daresay, I should be quite offended you don't recognize me."

"I recognize you, all right. You interrupted my class this morning."

"Come, come, my dear, it was hardly an interruption. I did nothing more than ask a simple, and quite pertinent, question."

"Fine. Maybe it wasn't an interruption." She aimed an accusing finger at him. "But you weren't supposed to be there. The administration is expected to notify instructors of any outside visitors. Those are the rules. That's what the university has conceded as part of the collective bargaining agreement."

He raised an insolent brow. "I'm not part of any collective bargaining agreement. And the only rules I adhere to," his eyes sparkled, "are my own."

"I don't care!" Damn, this man was annoying. On the other hand, her irritation had displaced most of her fear. "All I care about is the answer to my question. So one more time, Fred, who are you?"

He sighed. "Are you certain you don't recognize me?"

"Yes!"

"Positive?"

"Yes, yes, yes!"

"Perhaps I need a little help on the public relations front," he murmured.

"Perhaps," she ground out the words through clenched teeth, "you need to put your ego away for a moment and just answer the damn question!"

"Tessa," he said softly. "Remember the chapel."

"I don't care about the chapel!"

"That's rather rude of you."

"Rude?" She choked with indignation. "Rude?"

"You said that, my dear." His tone was as patient as if he dealt with a small child.

"I'm not rude. I've always been . . . polite. That's it." She drew herself up to her full, if somewhat limited, five-foot, three-inch height and stared at him loftily. "I am unfailingly polite."

He snorted in disdain. "Not today."

"And whose fault is that? You don't even have the common courtesy to introduce yourself." She cast him a triumphant glare.

"Quite right, my dear. My apologies. Very well. Allow me to introduce myself." He swept an elegant bow, straightened and caught her gaze with his. "Wizard Extraordinaire and Counselor to Kings, I am Merlin."

She stared for a long moment then laughed at the sheer absurdity of his statement. "Oh yeah, right, pal.

And I'm Glenda, the good witch of the North. Come on."

His eyes narrowed but his voice was mild. "You do not believe me?"

"Well, duh. Of course I don't believe you." Her words were confident but a ribbon of panic curled in her stomach.

"Look at the book, Tessa."

She tried but couldn't resist the gentle command of his voice. Her gaze dropped to the volume she still held in her hands. It opened of its own accord to the page with the picture of Merlin. Tessa drew her brows together in confusion. The image of an old man with white hair and a conical blue hat had vanished. Now the illustration was of a distinguished older man with a neatly trimmed goatee and a herringbone jacket. The book slipped from her hands. The ribbon widened.

"Very good." She struggled to keep a tremble out of her voice. "Nice trick. But any ten-year-old with a magic kit could probably pull off the same thing."

"Do you think so?" Again his brow climbed arrogantly toward the heavens.

"Sure." She lifted her chin in a show of confidence she didn't feel. The ribbon in her stomach grew into a solid, heavy knot and fear clutched at her heart.

"Really? Gracious, I had no idea modern children were so skilled. Do you suppose a ten-year-old could do this as well?" He raised his arms as if reaching for the sky, then allowed them to fall softly to his sides in a motion fluid and hypnotic. She watched and his features changed so slowly it seemed almost natural. The steel-gray goatee whitened and lengthened. The neatly trimmed silver hair grew in waves, snowy and long. The herringbone jacket melted to a smooth, shining silk, blue and intense with gilded stars and planets scattered over the fabric. It looked exactly like a music video. What did they call it? Morphing?

She swallowed the lump that lodged in her throat. "That would be harder."

"Indeed." His eyes twinkled.

"So . . . you're . . ."

"Merlin. At your service."

"Great." The terror that had gripped her earlier returned in a swell so strong it stole her breath. The kind of terror she'd only ever known in bad dreams. Before today. What was going on here? What was this all about? At once the only logical answer flashed through her mind. "That's it! Why didn't I think of it sooner? What a relief."

"What's a relief?"

"Of course. It's so obvious." Her words tumbled out faster and faster spurred by a niggling fear that she might, just possibly, be wrong. "I'm asleep. I fell asleep right there in the library, looking at that stupid book. This is just a dream, all of it. Watch." She stepped to the wall and smacked her hand against its cold, hard, and extremely realistic surface. "Okay, no problem." She'd more than half expected her hand to go right through. "That may have felt real but it isn't."

She glanced at Merlin. He still wore that Disney-character outfit. "If I close my eyes, you'll go away and I'll wake up. Here we go." She squeezed her lids together tight. "One, two, three" —she'd wake up by the time she got to ten— "four, five, six" —was he gone yet?— "seven, eight, nine" —she snapped open her eyes— "Ten."

Merlin stood right where she'd left him, a smile of amusement quirking his lips.

"Damn." She groaned. Merlin opened his mouth as if to say something. "I know, I know, you don't have to say it. It's a chapel. I'm sorry. But it's not a real chapel, so it doesn't matter. It's all in my mind." She cast her gaze around the room. "I do have a wonderful imagination, though. Look at all this." She waved at her surroundings. "The walls, the sunlight coming in the window, even Sir Hunk over there, it's pretty authentic. Especially when you consider I don't even like this time period."

"A disgusting, crowded, filthy, smelly period. Full of plague and pestilence. I believe those were your words," Merlin said in a casual manner.

"Exactly! See. How would you know that unless this was a dream?"

"Or I was Merlin, Wizard Extraordinaire and Counselor to Kings."

"No way, no how. You're not real. This is a dream." She shook her head vigorously. "And even if it wasn't a dream, you still wouldn't be real because Merlin never existed. You are a figment of my imagination. An impressive figment—"

"I try."

"—but a figment nonetheless. The closest you could come to reality would be as a stand-in for Fred Astaire—"

"Taught him everything he knew," the figment murmured.

"—but even that wouldn't count because I'm asleep. Period. So . . ." She shook her hands in front of her as if they were wet, a nervous gesture she'd had since childhood. Her voice rang perilously high. "Why can't I wake up?"

"Well, I'd say the answer was obvious."

"You're awfully smug for someone who doesn't exist," she snapped. "And what do you mean, 'obvious'? I don't think—dear Lord!" She clapped her hands to her cheeks. "I'm in a coma, aren't I? That explains why this doesn't quite feel like a dream. But I don't remember anything? Maybe I was hit by a car—"

"In the library," he said wryly.

"You never know. Cars crash through buildings all the time."

"You were on the third floor."

"Fine." She glared. "Maybe it was the snow. Maybe the roof collapsed and I'm buried under a ton of snow. That would explain why I don't remember anything." She paced the room, stepping around Sir Hunk, who didn't move a muscle. Just her luck. Her mind comes up with a man like this and he's stiff as a board. And not in a good way. "So, the roof collapsed and I—oh damn!" She stared at Merlin and tears welled in her eyes. "I'm dead, aren't I? I'm dead and this is hell. They've sent me to spend eternity in the Middle Ages with a gorgeous man who's frozen solid and you." She widened her eyes in realization. "If this is hell that means you're—"

"I most certainly am not." His voice thundered with righteous indignation. "I quite resent your assumption. Oh, certainly, I have not been perfect in the last few millennia but I am more than confident I shall not be spending eternity, let alone presiding over it, in any-place substantially warmer than perhaps a nice, lush Caribbean island. Aside from that, you are not dead."

"Thank God." She breathed a sigh of relief and absently pulled the clip from her hair, ran her fingers through it, then reclipped it in a low ponytail at the base of her skull. "Then it must be a coma. Maybe I fell? That makes sense. I fell and hit my head on that table. Sure—big, heavy, oak table. I hit my head and now I'm in a hospital somewhere. People are taking care of me. I probably have tubes in my arms and all that stuff. But I can't be hurt! I'm going to Greece in three weeks. What if I don't wake up in time? What if I don't wake up at all? What if—

"Ouch!" Once more the unmistakable pain of a pinch shot through her. "Why did you do that?"

"I suspected it was preferable to slapping you across the face."

"Yeah, if those are the only available options." She glared at the alleged wizard, who returned her stare with a tolerant smile.

"Are you quite finished?"

"No," she snapped and rubbed her arm. "Okay. Now I'm finished."

"Excellent. If you have managed to get your emotional outburst under control, we have quite a bit to chat about."

"I usually don't lose it like that," she muttered.

"I know, my dear. I must admit I was quite surprised."

"You were surprised? Jeez." Her gaze shot to his. "I'm so sorry."

"And sarcasm too. Tsk, tsk." Merlin shook his head and sighed.

Annoyance swept through her. You'd think if she was going to make up a vision as far-fetched as Merlin,

Wizard Extraordinaire, etc., her subconscious could come up with someone a little less irritating. She clenched her teeth. "I know I'm going to regret this but why are you surprised?"

"You are an adult, twenty-six years of age I believe."

"Twenty-seven."

"Indeed? Hmmm. I stand corrected." He raised that superior brow again. "And as yet unmarried?"

Tessa groaned to herself. The tone in his voice was distinctly reminiscent of her mother's whenever the subject of marriage came up. Leave it to her mom to influence even the invention of her subconscious mind. "As yet."

"I believe I had also considered you to be relatively intelligent—"

"Thank you."

"—considering your gender and the times you live in, of course."

"Of course." Terrific. Her figment was a medieval sexist and a history snob.

"It has nothing whatsoever to do with sexism or snobbery, although I freely admit, your era is not one I'm particularly partial to."

"Don't tell me you can read my mind, too?" She smacked her palm against her forehead. "Of course you can. You're *in* my mind."

He cast her a pitying glance. "My dear young woman, this will no doubt be a great deal easier, on both of us I might add, if you would simply accept the truth."

"The truth?" She studied him for a long moment. If she wasn't asleep or in a coma, and she had to admit, nothing had ever seemed so real in her life as this room and this weird little Fred Astaire clone, then she wasn't entirely sure she wanted the truth. Still, what choice did she have? She drew a deep, steadying breath. "Okay. Let's have it. What is the truth?"

"It's really quite simple." His eyes gleamed. "I have pulled you from your moment in time to one of my own choosing."

"You've pulled me through what?" Her breath caught.

"Time."

"Time?"

"Time."

"Time." The word throbbed through her.

"I believe I just said that."

"I've traveled through time?" Her heart thudded in her chest.

"Exactly."

"Like what's-his-name on *Quantum Leap*? Or that one Star Trek movie about the whales? Or H. G. Wells?"

The figment shrugged. "Drivel."

"Drivel?"

His bushy brows pulled together. "We shall never get anywhere if you insist on repeating everything I say."

"Well, excuse me, Mr. Wizard," she said sharply. "I'm having a tiny little problem here grasping this entire concept."

"Very well. I daresay I should have expected this. It happens every time."

"Every time? How often do you do this?"

He released an impatient sigh. "Do sit down and try to remain calm and I shall endeavor to explain."

Tessa glanced around the chapel. Aside from the

altar and colorful wall hangings, the room was bare. "And just where do you suggest I sit?"

The figment didn't so much as twitch but at once a chair appeared before her with the abruptness of a bad film edit. She tried not to flinch and cast him a condescending glance. "Oh come now. A folding chair? A lousy old metal folding chair from a Wizard Extraordinaire and Counselor to Kings? Surely you can do better than that?"

"Please, forgive me. What was I thinking?" Amusement lurked in his eyes. "Is this better?"

The folding chair vanished. In its place stood what could only be called a throne. A seat fit for a king or an emperor or a fantasy. Huge and golden, with jewels encrusted along every carved, gilded curve, and the heads of lions as armrests, the massive chair fairly filled the small room. Tessa gasped, then bit back a giggle. "I think that's a little too much. Can't you do something in between?"

The throne disappeared, replaced by an aged but extremely comfortable looking recliner.

"Hey, that's my dad's." Tessa grinned with delight and plopped into the chair, running her hands affectionately over the arm rests. "I've always loved this chair."

"I know," the figment said smugly.

"Don't you dare try to take any credit for this." She stretched against the faux leather, reached down and pulled the lever that flipped up the footrest. "This is all part of my subconscious. I've made this up. I've made you up. And I've done a surprisingly creative job of it too." She reclined the back of the lounger, folded her hands behind her head and grinned.

"If you're quite ready?"

"By all means." If she had to be stuck in this crazy coma or dream or whatever, she might as well be comfortable. "Please, go on."

The figment rolled his eyes heavenward as if asking for divine guidance then stared at her with a gaze steady and firm. A gaze that would have made her more than a little uneasy if, of course, he wasn't something she'd made up.

"As I said before, I have brought you from your time—"

"Are you comfortable standing there like that?" she blurted, abruptly uncertain that she was at all ready to hear what he had to say.

"Quite comfortable, thank you. Now as I was say—"

"Are you sure? Because you can have this chair. Or maybe whip up another one?" Why did she want to put off his explanation? If she was so confident all this was the product of an injured mind, a hallucination or simply a bad dream then why this overwhelming reluctance to listen to him?

"Very well." A chair similar to her own popped into the space beside her with the figment already seated in it. "Now, may I go on?"

"I suppose," she said in a weak voice.

"As I attempted to explain earlier, I have removed you from your time and brought you to mine."

"Okay." Why did his words strike fear into her heart? Why did she want to cover her ears, curl into the corner of the recliner and hide from him and his whole world? A world she'd made up. A world she'd invented in the deep recess of her mind. A world that couldn't possibly be real.

But what if it was?

He studied her, as if he knew her thoughts. But of course he knew her thoughts. He *was* one of her thoughts. And absolutely nothing more.

"Why?" she said with a sudden resolve to face this illusion or whatever it was head on. "Why did you bring me here?"

"Then . . ." his words were slow and measured, "you believe me?"

"I don't believe you. I don't believe you exist. In fact, I don't believe you ever existed." She snapped the chair into an upright position and bounded to her feet. "If any of this is real, and I still question that whole-heartedly, there's no way you can be Merlin, Wizard whatever and counselor to anybody."

He reclined in the chair and gazed at her idly. "Oh, and why not?"

"Because, there never was a Merlin. There never was an Arthur. There never was a Camelot. There's no evidence, no proof and nothing that you can touch or see. There never was anything but a make-believe story. A myth. A legend."

"What if . . ." An emery board appeared in one hand and he casually filed the nails of the other. "You're wrong?"

"I'm not," she said with far more confidence than she felt.

"But what if there was a Merlin—"

"There wasn't." *Was there?*

"—and an Arthur—"

"There couldn't be." *Could there?*

"—and everything else that goes along with your so-called legend?" He held his hand out in front of him and eyed his nails critically.

"Never." *Maybe?*

"And let us further suppose . . ."—his gaze drifted above his hand to meet and lock with hers—"that Merlin, who is quite accomplished in the ways of magic and what you think of as science—"

"Wizard Extraordinaire," she whispered.

"—wanted the world yet to come to believe that which he had nurtured and helped create and loved with his whole heart and soul was nothing but a fairy tale. A story. A myth. A legend. And worked his magic to make the world so believe?"

His eyes held her spellbound, her question was little more than a breath in the still of the chapel. "Why?"

"To save it from the denigration of history. To preserve what was, for one bare moment in time, the best man had to offer. Not of his science or his knowledge but of himself. His loyalty, his gallantry, his honor." His gaze burned into hers with an intensity that reached inside her and chilled her very soul. "It did not last long. The nature of flesh-and-blood men predestined it to certain failure. But for a moment, it was man at his finest and he has never reached such heights again."

"Sounds swell." Her voice squeaked with fear and a growing acceptance of what she already suspected. This was no dream, no coma-induced hallucination, no fantasy. "So . . . what does that all have to do with me?"

"You? You!" Merlin rose out of his recliner like an avenging spirit and her heart dropped to her toes. She stifled the impulse to cower and forced herself to stand straight with the set of her shoulders firm and her head held high. And prayed her knees wouldn't collapse beneath her. He aimed a long finger in her direction and she wouldn't have been at all surprised to see flames shoot out the tip. "You do not believe."

"So . . . who does?" She cringed at her own flippant words. Not exactly the way to pacify an irate sorcerer. Real or not.

"But they do not go around preaching their lack of acceptance, their doubts, their disbelief with an unwarranted passion, that goes far beyond the bounds of academia I might add, to classrooms full of young, innocent minds."

"Wait, hold it right there, pal." Indignation swept away her fear. "Young, innocent minds? I teach at a university. The youngest I get are freshmen and 'innocent' is not exactly how I'd describe any of them."

"Still, you are encouraging their skepticism!"

She glared at the indignant wizard. "Isn't that exactly what you wanted? You just said you wrapped Arthur and company in your magic to keep them from being seen in the harsh light of reality. To keep them from being judged as real people are judged by history and the passage of time. I don't see your problem. I'm doing exactly what you want."

Merlin flicked an imaginary piece of lint from his shoulder. "I changed my mind."

"You changed your mind? What do you mean, 'you changed your mind'?"

Merlin shrugged. "I am not infallible, you know, I do make mistakes. I'm only human."

"Could have fooled me."

"Well, perhaps *human* is not entirely accurate; regardless, every now and then, with the passage of the centuries, I get extremely annoyed at having my accomplishments, and the accomplishments of Arthur and the others, seen as little more than a delightful story for children at bedtime."

"That's it? That's what this is all about?" Relief surged through her. "No sweat, pal. I'm more than willing to change my line about your little world. In fact, I'll even tell students, personally, I believe in Merlin and Arthur and all that other stuff. Piece of cake.

"Now that we've got that settled," she nodded with satisfaction, "why don't I just close my eyes and you can zap me home? Back to the library or the hospital or wherever. Your choice. However you want to work this is fine with me." She squeezed her eyes closed. "Okay, I'm ready."

Nothing happened.

"Anytime now. You go right ahead."

Still nothing.

She sighed and opened her eyes. "Do I have to click my heels together and say 'There's no place like home' or what?"

Merlin chuckled. "Now that *was* a fairy tale."

"Oh, I see. Don't believe in Oz but do believe in Camelot. Is that how this works?" She fisted her hands on her hips. "You're not sending me home, are you?"

"I'm afraid not. At least not yet."

"Why not? You've already convinced me of at least the possibility of the existence of"—she waved impatiently at the chapel—"all this. Whether it's real or not, I admit, I'm willing to rethink my position. So . . . why can't I go?"

"It has a great deal to do with him." Merlin nodded toward the knight.

"Him? He doesn't even look alive." Tessa stepped to the still figure and peered at him closely. "See, he's not breathing."

"Oh, he is indeed breathing. You simply cannot see it."

She hesitated for a moment than placed her hand flat on his back, just below his broad shoulders. "No, he's definitely not breathing. I don't feel any movement at all."

"You cannot feel it because we are not yet on the same level of existence with him." A thoughtful frown creased his forehead. "Perhaps I have not explained this as thoroughly as I should have."

"You think so, Mr. Wizard?"

He ignored her and continued. "We are, you and I, between moments, as it were. We exist in the space between his last breath and his next."

"I don't get it." She pulled her brows together and tried to make sense of his so-called explanation. "Are you saying we're moving in fast-forward and he's moving one frame at a time?"

"I would not have put it that way, precisely, but I suppose it's a fairly appropriate description." Merlin shrugged. "It's very much dependent on your point of view. Time is relative, my dear. Your own Albert Einstein recognized that."

"You mean the theory of relativity, and the space-time continuum?"

"My, I am impressed." A wicked twinkle danced in his eye. "I would have thought Einstein's theories would have been in the realm of myth for you. After all, they're not something you can touch or see."

"Maybe not but Einstein was real." She smiled smugly. "You are not."

"I taught him everything he knew," Merlin said under his breath.

Tessa groaned. "I give up but I'll play along. Okay. We're between moments. I'm here in the wonderful world of King Arthur and the Knights of the Round Table." She raised a questioning brow. "You haven't come right out and said it, so this is just an assumption on my part but this is Camelot, right?"

"Very good. My faith in your intelligence has not been misplaced."

"Thanks loads. And I'm here, first of all, because you're pissed that history has treated you exactly as you wanted to be treated, as a legend. Right?"

"When you put it that way it does sound rather fickle of me," Merlin said thoughtfully.

"Doesn't it though?" She couldn't resist a satisfied smile. "And the second reason has to do with him." She waved at Sir Hunk. "So who is he anyway? Arthur? Lancelot?"

"My goodness, no, he is much too young to be the king or Sir Lancelot. That, my dear, is Galahad."

"Galahad?"

"Lancelot's son."

"I knew that." She circled the kneeling knight. "He's the one of the knights who found the Holy Grail. Depending on which version of the legend you look at, Galahad and, I think, Perceval and Bors were the only knights to succeed in the quest."

"I am relieved to note that in spite of your disbelief, you are well versed."

"I do my homework." Tessa studied the stationary warrior. He looked as good up close as he had in the illustration but not quite as perfect. Tiny lines creased the corners of his eyes and Tessa wondered if it was from the glare of the sun on the polished blade of his sword or if it was a result of laughter, loud and unrestrained. The set of his chin wasn't merely defiant but resolute, as if this was a man, firm and unyielding, who carried himself with the arrogance born of unquestioned confidence. And she was right about his eyes. They were blue, so deep and dark she thought at once of—

"Velvet? Sapphires? The sea?" Merlin said.

"No," Tessa said absently. "I was thinking more that dark, blue-black color of the sky right before a thundersto—" She glared at the sorcerer. "Would you stop that."

His eyes widened with innocence. "What?"

"Reading my mind."

A smirk creased his lips. "I had no need to read your mind. Only a fool would fail to recognize your thoughts about—" He cleared his throat. "Sir Hunk."

Heat rushed up her face. "If you don't mind, let's keep that one to ourselves. I wouldn't want to embarrass him."

"Or you."

"Or me."

"Although, I daresay, Galahad would not be surprised at the title. Once he understood its meaning, of course." Merlin chuckled. "He's not unaccustomed to a great deal of attention from the ladies of the court."

"I'll bet." She blew out a long breath and met Merlin's gaze with her own. "So what do I have to do? About him that is."

"You know his destiny is to find the Grail. What

you do not know is that he cannot succeed in his quest alone, without help."

She stared into Merlin's black eyes. "You're kidding."

"I am as enamored of a good jest as the next man but no, my dear, I am not kidding."

"Wait a minute." Tessa shook her head. "I'm not going on any Grail quest. Absolutely not. The only place I'm going is home. And then I'm going to Greece. And that's it. Where I'm not going is on a guided tour of the Middle Ages, even with a guy who looks as good as this one does. I'm sure there are dozens of cute little medieval sweetie pies running around Camelot who would just love to spend some quality time with Galahad here searching for the Cup of Christ." She folded her arms over her chest. "Get one of them to accompany your knight in shining armor. I'm not interested in the Arthurian version of *Mission Impossible*."

"To find the Grail he needs what only you can provide." Merlin's voice was mild but his eyes smoldered with a strength of purpose that told her in no uncertain terms she had no choice.

"What's that?" Caution edged her words.

"You must determine it for yourself."

"A riddle?" She groaned. "You're starting this with a riddle? I hate riddles."

"Learn to like them." He smiled wickedly. "I suspect you shall face quite a few during this quest."

"What do you mean, 'you suspect'?" Distrust narrowed her eyes.

"Time, just like life, is not an absolute." He shrugged. "With every spin of the wheel, the outcome may well change. I cannot say with certainty that all will end as it has before. As you, and I, expect."

"What can I expect?" she said slowly. "I mean, if I do this, help this guy, what happens then? Will you send me home?"

Merlin nodded. "That was my original plan."

Tessa eyed the frozen figure. If all of this wasn't real, and she still stubbornly clung to the fast-fading hope that it was simply a creation of an overactive imagination trapped in a comatose mind, then she had nothing to lose by joining Galahad. If it was real, joining in Sir Hunk's quest was apparently the only way to get Fred Astaire a.k.a. Mr. Wizard a.k.a. Merlin to send her back where she belonged. "It looks like I don't have a hell of a lot of options, do I?"

Merlin cast her a disapproving frown. "I would not have phrased it in quite that manner. The chapel, remember? However, your assessment of the situation is accurate."

"Swell." She heaved a sigh of surrender, turned her back on Galahad to face Merlin head-on. "I'll do it but only on the condition that you promise to put me back exactly where you found me when this silly quest is over."

"I promise." He traced an *X* on his chest with his index finger. "Cross my heart and hope to die."

"That's cute." Tessa snorted in disdain. "I had the distinct impression you live pretty much forever."

"I do."

She raised a brow. "Then that oath you just took is relatively worthless."

"Relatively." He grinned and his dark eyes twinkled. "Everything is relative, my dear."

"You really don't play fair, you know. You hold all the—hey!" Merlin's eyes were still plain to see but the rest of him appeared to be fading. She could see the wall of the chapel right through him. Although she did seem to be getting used to the unexpected. The panic she'd known earlier was now nothing more than a queasy unease at talking to an all but invisible magician. "This is really annoying. What are you doing now?"

"I have a few odds and ends to see to." There was scarcely anything left but the amused tone and the gleam in his eye.

"Hey, don't leave me!" She practically screamed the question as if invisible was synonymous with deaf. "What do I do about him?" Tessa flung her hand at the figure behind her in a gesture of impatience.

"I'm certain you two shall hit it off with no problem."

"No problem?" She yelled but it was too late. She was in a chapel in an age she didn't like, stuck in a legend she didn't believe in, by a wizard who didn't exist. Alone. Could life get any more perfect?

"God's blood! What manner of demon is this!"

She winced at the sound of the strong, commanding voice and knew, without turning to face him, just whose voice it was.

Damn, she hated the Middle Ages.

Chapter Three

❧❦❧

Tessa swiveled slowly and swallowed hard.

If she thought Galahad filled the room kneeling it was nothing compared to his awesome presence upright and prepared for battle, his sword drawn, his eyes flashing. He was absolutely magnificent. And more than a little scary.

"Whoa. Hold it right there, Big Guy." Tessa thrust her hands out as if to ward off the knight towering over her, taut with power.

The tension eased out of him. He lowered his sword and laughed. "Hah. 'Tis but a lad. Take care in the future, boy, not to catch a warrior unawares while he thinks he is in the presence of God and none other." A wide grin stretched across his face. "You are lucky this day. A lesser man than myself would have separated your head from your body first, and only then questioned the wisdom of the act."

"I guess I should be grateful." Tessa glared up at him. "Not that I did anything that would warrant getting my head chopped off, mind you, but I suppose if those are the house rules I'll play by them. Talk about arrogant."

Galahad's brows drew together in puzzlement. "You make no sense, boy. Your words have a foreign flavor that is unfamiliar to me and their meaning is muddled." His expression cleared. "Ah, I see. Poor lad. Addle brained, no doubt."

"Addle brained?" Disbelief stuck the words in her throat. "Addle brained?"

Galahad nodded solemnly. " 'Tis a sure sign of a mind befuddled when a youth repeats his words."

"Repeats his words? I don't repeat my words."

Galahad cast her a pitying look as if she were some pathetic creature not worth wasting his time on and slipped his sword back in its sheath. "Now, be gone with you, lad, and leave me to my prayers."

Galahad turned in dismissal and Tessa stared at his broad back. The man not only thought she was a boy but a stupid boy at that. Well, not for long.

"Wait just one minute. We need to get a few things clear."

Galahad turned toward her slowly and his gaze meshed with hers. His eyes narrowed and a warning simmered there. This was not a man used to taking orders. Unease trickled through her. "What do you want, boy?"

"I want quite a bit but we'll start with the basics. First of all, I'm not a boy."

He shrugged. "You are a feeble excuse for a man."

"I'm not a man. I'm a girl—er—a woman."

His gaze traveled over her blonde hair caught in its low ponytail, navy linen blazer, white oxford shirt and jeans, then back to her eyes. "No woman of proper demeanor, nay even a slut, would don clothing such as yours." Sympathy softened the look in his eyes. "Now then, boy, from where do you come?"

"I'm not a boy!" Tessa gritted her teeth. Obviously there was only one way to convince this medieval Neanderthal. She grabbed the edges of her jacket and opened it wide. "See. Look. What do you call these?"

He drew his dark brows together thoughtfully. " 'Tis an unusual garment."

She glanced down and groaned. The oxford shirt revealed none of her feminine curves, exactly why she typically wore it for class, but was not much help right now. Great. No wonder he still thought she was male. "Okay, now watch." She reached behind her back and pulled the fabric tight against her chest. "There. What do you think now? Boobs."

She glanced up to meet his gaze and froze. He stared at her chest with an intensity that brought a rush of heat to her cheeks, as if he'd never seen breasts before. Maybe she'd gone a tad too far. This was the Middle Ages after all. They probably didn't use the word *boobs*, although she was fairly certain he caught her meaning. She snatched the lapels of her jacket and yanked it closed. "That's enough. You got the point."

"Indeed." He swept a low mocking bow. "My *lady.*"

He straightened and the wicked light of a man at ease with casual flirtation and effortless seduction danced in his eyes. "Please forgive my error. I see now how very mistaken I was. I can only believe 'tis the unexpected nature of your presence that clouded my senses. I should well have noted the delicate curve of your cheek, the length of lash shielding your eyes, the full pout of your lip and the firm thrust of your," he grinned, "boobs."

"Oh, jeez." She rolled her gaze toward the arched, stone ceiling and muttered more to herself than to him. "How humiliating."

"Still, 'tis but one certain way to know a wench from a lad." With one, strong arm he pulled her into his embrace. Before she could so much as squeak, his lips crushed hers. She struggled but it was like fighting a tree. A huge, solid, unyielding oak. His arms were tempered steel pinning her tight to his hard, muscled chest, his lips firm and heated against hers. For a fleeting second desire washed over her and she wanted to surrender to the passion in his kiss. In any time period this guy knew what he was doing. How easy would it be to enjoy his knowledgeable touch? He drew back and stared down at her, for the barest moment looking as intrigued and affected by their encounter as she. His grin was a bit lopsided, his arrogance slipping just a touch. "Aye. Indeed you are a female."

"Indeed I am." He released her and without thinking she clasped her hands together, twisted and rammed her elbow into his stomach.

"Ooooph." He doubled over and she smiled with satisfaction.

"St. Margaret Mary's High School. Self Defense 101."

He gasped. "I would not call it defense."

She dusted off her hands in an exaggerated gesture of a job well done. "Don't ever mess with one of Sister Abigail's graduates."

Tessa never even saw him move. One moment he was bent, clutching his stomach and the next she was jerked through the air, turned and pinned flat, her back against his chest. One massive arm encircled her waist, his other wrapped around her just below her neck. Her feet dangled a good three inches above the floor. His grip was surprisingly restrained but left no doubt that this specimen of medieval manhood could crush her as easily as he snuffed out a candle.

His voice growled beside her ear. "And you should not, er, 'mess' with one trained under the guidance of the king's master at arms himself."

"Put me down, you big ape." She kicked out, trying to break free. "What kind of knight are you anyway? Between this and that kiss you laid on me, the age of chivalry is obviously not what it's cracked up to be."

"Chivalrous behavior is wasted on those who do not display courtesy themselves." His breath was warm against her neck and a twinge of excitement shivered through her. "Still, my apologies." He loosened his grip and she dropped to the floor. "Perhaps 'twould be best to begin our acquaintance anew."

"Perhaps it 'twould." She crossed her arms over her chest and glared. "You first."

"I?" Confusion furrowed his forehead. " 'Tis not I who interrupted you."

"Oh, yeah, right." What the hell was she supposed to do now? She pulled a steadying breath and stuck out her hand. "Hi. I'm Tessa St. James. Nice to meet you."

"The pleasure, dear lady, is mine." He clasped her hand and brought it to his lips for a kiss that was barely more than a whisper. His dark gaze never wavered from hers and unexpectedly her breath caught. Merlin sure had this guy pegged, all right. He was a hunk and he knew it. "What is your purpose here, Tessa St. James?"

"It's kind of a long story." His eyes really were something.

"I have naught to do save listen." Eyes that were blue as the night with the glitter of stars scattered here and there.

"I'm not sure where to start."

" 'Tis apparent, fair lady, you are a stranger to this land. Your arrival 'twould seem to be the place to begin." And his voice, deep and resonant with a gentle strength that seemed to seep inside her soul. He was good.

"Well . . ." She stared up at him, caught in the raw power of his presence. Merlin wasn't the only one practicing magic around here. "I was in the—how tall are you anyway? About six-three, six-four maybe?"

"I stand a head above most men but not so tall as my horse. But you . . . how could I not see you for what you are? As tiny and delicate as a rose in bloom." He gazed at her with a look that clearly indicated she was one blossom he wouldn't mind plucking. A look that left her wondering just how delightful plucking might be. He was very good.

And he knew it. Maybe it was the satisfied upward quirk of his lips at the corners or the way he leaned subtly closer to her as if to snatch her, unresisting, into his arms or the tinge of success that shaded his eyes, or maybe it was the whole package presented by the body language of Sir Hunk, but Tessa abruptly realized the man thought he had her in the palm of his hand. He wasn't far wrong.

In the interest of self-preservation, she took a hasty step back and shook her head. "Watch it, pal. That rose business may work like a charm on your typical damsel in distress but I'm made of different stuff. So you can turn off the knight-in-shining-armor charm right now."

His eyes widened with innocence. "I fear you have mistaken my intentions."

"Right."

He heaved a patient sigh, as if used to dealing with recalcitrant females. "I shall watch my words with you in the future. Now, how came you to be here unbeknownst to me? I heard no sound of your entry into the chapel."

"Remember that long story I mentioned?"

He nodded.

"This is part of it."

"I can well imagine what kind of tale would explain your strange garb."

"My strange—oh, my clothes." She glanced down and shrugged. "Actually, where I come from this is considered almost classic, in a terribly casual sort of way."

"Odd leggings." He reached out a long, tanned finger and poked at her jeans. "Why do you not wear a gown? Even in the far reaches of the realm, women do not wear clothing such as this. 'Tis not suitable for a female."

"It's suitable for me. Besides, I didn't have time to pack. I arrived rather unexpectedly."

"Arrived?"

"Yeah, here in the chapel. In Camelot or whatever. One minute I was minding my own business in the library, looking at your picture I might add, and the next I was whisked here, apparently through time and space and—what are you doing?"

Galahad's hand rested lightly on the hilt of his sword. His eyes gleamed.

"Galahad?" Her stomach fluttered at the expression on his face. A look of consideration, speculation and suspicion. "Come on pal, what are you thinking?"

"I am wondering if thou art indeed the demon I believed when first I saw you." His words were slow and measured. "Your talk of time and space is curious and bespeaks of forces best left unknown to mortal man. How do you know my name?" His fingers tightened around the sword.

"I didn't realize you were that sensitive about a little thing like a name but believe me, it's no big deal." Who knew he'd be set off so easily? She'd better watch her step. She had no doubt he wouldn't hesitate to cut off her head with the slightest provocation. "Merlin told me."

His eyes narrowed. "Merlin?"

"You know. Long beard? Blue dress? Tap dances?"

"Tap dances?"

" 'Tis a sure sign of a mind befuddled when a man repeats his words." She tossed him a smug smile. "Confusion and stupidity are not the same thing."

He stared at her for a long, tense moment. Anxiety clenched her jaw. Oh Lord, surely they had a sense of humor in the Middle Ages? Without warning he threw back his head and laughed. A warm, booming, hearty sound that reverberated through the chapel and resounded through her blood.

"I didn't know anybody actually threw their head

back like that when they laughed," she said under her breath. "Must be a macho, medieval kind of thing."

"God's breath, woman." Galahad wiped a tear of laughter from his eye. "You've a clever wit about you, I'll grant you that."

"Thanks." At least he didn't slap her on the back like she was one of the boys. A whack from one of those huge hands would knock her halfway across the room. But his grin was infectious and she returned it in spite of herself. "I think."

"So, you are acquainted with the king's counselor?"

"We've met."

A glitter of speculation shone in his eyes. "Are you perhaps an apprentice to the sorcerer?"

A vision of Mickey Mouse and dancing broomsticks popped into her head. "Not exactly. Apparently, I'm here to be taught some kind of lesson."

"Ah, a student of the mystic arts then."

"No, that's not it. It seems Mr. Wizard is ticked at how history regards all this King Arthur stuff and he's picked me to make an example of." Her gaze skimmed the chapel. "Not that I think this is really happening, mind you. I'm still hoping for a coma."

He leveled her a puzzled frown. "Coma?"

Tessa sighed in resignation. "Never mind, Big Guy. At this point it doesn't matter. Either I'm going to wake up or I'm stuck here until Merlin decides otherwise. He's got a little job in mind for me. A quest, I guess."

"A quest?" Galahad chuckled. "A woman on a quest?"

"Yes." She drew the single syllable out slowly. "Do you have a problem with that?"

"A problem? 'Tis not a problem." He gazed down at her with condescension. " 'Tis simple. Quests are not for fair ladies. 'Tis a man's place, nay his duty, to undertake such an endeavor. A woman would but make any venture of the like more difficult, perhaps even deadly."

"So . . . I guess that means you wouldn't consider taking a woman along on a quest?" She studied him carefully. "Any old quest?"

He crossed his arms over his massive chest. " 'Twould be foolhardy at best. Only a man with half a mind would agree to such an unwise act."

"Boy, are you in for a rude awakening." What would he do when he learned of Merlin's plans? Galahad didn't stand a chance against the magician. Anybody who could travel through time could certainly bend the will of a mere medieval man. Even one as obviously powerful and stubborn and sexist as this one. Tessa grinned. "I think it's time for you and I to get a couple of things straight. And since Mr. Wizard has disappeared, it's up to me to fill you in. You see, you're going on a quest and I'm—"

"Now, now, no need to go into that quite yet." Merlin's voice sounded behind her.

Satisfaction flooded Tessa. It was a hunch, but she would have bet Merlin didn't want Galahad to know of his plans just yet. And she'd further suspected the wizard wasn't far away. Her attempt to explain to the knight had exactly the result she wanted. She turned and smiled sweetly. "Merlin, old buddy, just the guy I wanted to see. Did you take care of your odds and ends?"

Merlin quirked a brow. "Indeed. And I see you two are getting acquainted."

Tessa nodded toward Galahad. "He thought I was a boy."

The big man's face reddened. " 'Twas an honest mistake. The lady's hair is tied like many a youth's and her garb is most unbecoming for a female."

"Excuse me? I wouldn't call it unbecoming." She stretched her arms out wide and glanced down at her clothes. "I think this outfit looks pretty good."

Merlin sniffed. "Hardly."

"Oh, like you're some kind of fashion plate?" Tessa leveled him a pointed glare.

Merlin glanced at his robe. "I see nothing wrong with my attire."

"Come on, Merlin." Tessa's gaze traveled from the tip of the sorcerer's pointed hat to his toes and back to meet his eyes. "Let's face it, pal. Deep blue silk? Stars and planets? Pretty stereotyped I'd say. You looked better in herringbone."

"I do so enjoy herringbone," Merlin murmured. "And Armani . . ."

"In fact" —Tessa went in for the kill, knowing full well this had nothing to do with clothes— "I'd say what you're wearing has no real style. I've seen better fashions for the well dressed wizard in children's books. Bottom line here is that what you have on is . . . well . . . trite."

"Trite?" Merlin sputtered with indignation. "Trite?"

"What was your comment about repeated words," Tessa said under her breath to Galahad.

" 'Tis a sure sign of a mind befuddled." Uneasiness colored Galahad's voice and he laid a hand gently on her arm. "My lady, Tessa, I would beware your words with the wizard. He has been known to smite those who incite his rage."

"Thanks, but his rage isn't the only thing incited." The panic and fear she'd set aside returned in a wave of fury. She glared at Merlin and struggled to hold back angry, frustrated tears. "I want to go home. Now. Send me back or wake me up or whatever. I refuse to play your little game."

Merlin smiled. "But you do agree the playmate I've chosen is one you do not find unattractive."

"I admit it. Galahad here is a hunk."

"A hunk?" A pleased smile quirked Galahad's lips. The man might not know the exact meaning of the word but he obviously got the drift. "The lady Tessa bethinks me a hunk?"

Tessa groaned. "That's great, Merlin. Just what he needs. Another boost to his ego."

Merlin's voice was soft. "Nonetheless, you are here for him."

"He doesn't want me!" Tessa glanced at Galahad who lifted a brow as if to say he certainly did. "Not like that! I know you're interested in *that*. All men are interested in that."

"Galahad." Merlin chuckled. "You devil you. And you've scarce met the lady. I must say I am impressed."

"She is a fair flower, my lord Wizard. Indeed, she has quite pleasing," the knight leaned toward the magician in a confidential manner, "boobs."

Merlin choked back a strangled laugh. "What have you been teaching him?"

"I don't believe this." Tessa buried her face in her hands. "I'm standing here in the Middle Ages with a wizard and a knight and all they can talk about is my chest!" She uncovered her eyes and glared. "This has to be a dream, because real life is not this weird."

Merlin scoffed. "Of course it is."

She squared her shoulders. "Fine. Dream or coma or real life, count me out. I'm not going on a quest with him or anybody else."

"Quest?" Galahad said.

Merlin shrugged. "You have no choice."

"I most certainly do." Tessa lifted her chin. "If you won't send me home I can choose to live happily ever after right here in," she shuddered, "Camelot."

"What quest?" Galahad stared at Merlin.

Merlin's bushy brows arched upward. "You won't be very happy."

"No, but I will have the satisfaction of throwing a monkey wrench into your plans."

"Tell me of this quest." Galahad directed his words at Tessa.

"Hah. If you think the Middle Ages are bad perhaps you'd prefer to live out your life in the dawn of time." A nasty light twinkled in the sorcerer's eye. "The only human being amidst the dinosaurs?"

"Perhaps I would!"

Galahad's brows drew together in confusion. "Dinosaurs?"

"You wouldn't last two minutes," Merlin said smugly.

"Maybe not." Tessa spit the words. "But they'd be a damned satisfying two minutes."

"Really? I'd scarcely call it satisfying. I'd call it," Merlin cast her a wicked smile, "lunch."

"I'd rather be lunch for a dinosaur than a pawn for you in some real-life game of *Dungeons and Dragons*!" Tessa's voice rose with anger.

Merlin's volume matched her own. "You don't have a choice!"

"Enough!" Galahad's voice blared through the chapel, bouncing off the stone walls and vibrating deep inside her. "Cease this infernal quibbling at once!"

Tessa addressed her words to Galahad and glared at Merlin. "Chill, Big Guy. Keep out of this."

Merlin stared back. "It's none of your concern, Galahad."

"None of my concern?" Disbelief underlaid what Tessa could only call a bellow. " 'Tis of great concern to me. My name has been bandied about without care as to my presence. You speak of a quest I know naught of. 'Tis most perplexing and annoying to be discussed by a wizard and a mere woman with no knowledge of the issue at hand." Galahad was a huge, barely controlled mass of righteous indignation. Wow. He really was impressive. Especially angry.

"Mere woman?" Tessa shook her head and directed her words at Merlin. "Am I going to have to put up with that? Can't you turn him into a toad or something?"

"I prefer not to at this juncture." Merlin shrugged. "However, I would not rule it out in the future."

"He doesn't know about the quest, does he?"

"What quest!" Galahad roared.

Merlin ignored him. "Not as of yet. The idea has always hovered in the back of his mind but the time was not right. And until His Majesty returns—"

"His Majesty? You mean Arthur?" Unexpected excitement flashed through her.

"Indeed. The king's return is expected within a few days." Merlin cast Galahad a benign smile. "All will be explained then, my boy."

"I would you explain now, my lord Wizard," Galahad growled.

"Trust me on this one, pal." Tessa tried to put her arm around his shoulders but he was way too tall for her. Instead, she rested her hand on his arm. "You don't want to know."

"Why, Tessa St. James, you surprise me." Merlin clucked his tongue. "Galahad will be delighted by the news. It's what he's always wanted. His destiny."

"Yeah." She heaved a heavy sigh. "But he never expected me to be a part of it."

"So, it's agreed then." Merlin's words were for her alone. "You will accompany him."

"I guess. I don't know why I keep fighting it."

Merlin's gaze bored into hers. "You have a stubborn spirit, my dear. You have a strength you do not suspect. And there is a capacity within you for greatness. It is why you were chosen."

"Swell." She smiled weakly. "So it wasn't just because I don't believe?"

Merlin laughed softly. "That is but the icing on the cake. There are countless numbers who share your disbelief. But you are special."

"Thanks." She glanced at Galahad. "So what's in the works for us until the king gets home?"

"Galahad, Lady Tessa is a visitor to Camelot from a land very far from our own—"

"Takes years to get there," she muttered.

"—I should be grateful if you were to serve as her escort. Show her the castle and the kingdom."

Galahad swept a low bow. "I would be delighted, my lord. I should like very much to know more of the fair Tessa."

"I'll bet," she said under her breath. "It could be worse, I guess. I could be dead."

"That's looking on the bright side, Tessa. You are in for a remarkable adventure, you know." Merlin's black eyes glowed. "One you will never forget."

"I doubt if I've ever had a real adventure." Anticipation trickled through her. Was she actually looking forward to this?

"Of course you are, my dear." Merlin grinned. "And you well should be."

"Okay." She threw up her hands in surrender. "What do we do first?"

"First, I should like you to become familiar with the times and the land you now find yourself in. Acclimate yourself, as it were. Galahad will help."

" 'Twould be my pleasure and honor." Galahad smiled and Tessa stifled a groan at the look in his eye. Middle Ages or twenty-first century, obviously men were all alike. She had no doubt this one had a very definite quest in mind that had nothing to do with the Grail and everything to do with adventure of a far different nature. She'd have to watch him.

"So what's first on the tour?" She smiled up at him. His eyes really were remarkable. A woman of any era could drown in their blue depths and count herself lucky for the demise. Still, Tessa had a job to do.

"I . . ." Distinct discomfort crossed Galahad's face. He cleared his throat and tossed Merlin a helpless look. "My lord, I think . . . that 'twould be best . . ."

"Her clothes?" Merlin nodded knowingly.

"Damn. I forgot about that. I suppose when in Rome . . ." She cocked her head at Merlin. "I assume you can do something here?"

"Certainly, my dear." The wizard straightened the cuff of his gown. "If you are willing to trust my, what was that word, oh yes, 'trite' sense of fashion."

"I'm sorry. I didn't mean to be so nasty. I was just lashing out. Today hasn't turned out the way I thought it would when I woke up this morning."

"Think nothing of it, my dear." A gracious note underlaid his words. "I quite understand. Now, is there a particular color you prefer?"

"I think the fair Tessa would be beyond compare in gold," Galahad said with a quiet intensity. " 'Twould match the flecks in her eyes, deep and velvet as a doe's."

"And I thought they were just brown." She gazed at him and realized she wouldn't just have to watch him. She'd have to watch herself. She jerked her gaze to Merlin. "Actually, all those mustard yellows are really bad on me. They make my skin look sallow and sick. I'd prefer something dark, a jewel tone, green, red, blue, something like that."

"Very well." Merlin's figure grew faint. "Galahad, I shall leave our guest in your capable hands." Only his black eyes lingered. A queasy sensation settled in her stomach. She'd never get used to this. "My dear, I shall see you later." At once, even his eyes were gone.

"Hey," she said to absolutely no one. "What about my clothes?"

"My lady." Galahad nodded. "I believe that has been resolved."

Tessa glanced down and sighed heavily. Merlin

had indeed changed her twenty-first-century attire to something more appropriate for a medieval king's court. A gown hugged her breasts then flowed to the floor in a wide sweep of soft fabric. Embroidered flowers and birds danced around the bodice in colorful abandon. Here and there threads of gold caught the light and winked and glittered. It was in many respects a magnificent gown.

Except, of course, that it was a truly horrible shade of mustard yellow.

Chapter Four

❧❦❧

"Okay, Big Guy." Lady Tessa sighed. "What's next?"

Galahad studied her silently. Only a fool would think her a lad now. Her hair was freed from its bonds and glowed golden in the shafts of sunshine and light reflected like stars in the dark of her eyes. The gown produced by the wizard's hand molded to the curves of her hips and the swell of her breasts like the soft leather of a fine glove. By the heavens, she was a woman to warm the bed of any man.

Her eyes narrowed. "What are you looking at?"

If any man could get past the stubborn thrust of her chin and the defiant gleam in her eye. Still, 'twas said the true thrill of the tigress was in the taming. "The gown becomes you, my lady."

"It's really a bit much." She raised her arm and glanced down at the dress. Abruptly, her eyes widened. "Why that son of a bi—wizard. He took my und—"

Galahad drew his brows together. "Is something amiss?"

"Something is definitely missing, all right. I know this is probably historically accurate and all that but I'm not used to going without any—"

"Without what, my lady?"

A charming blush spread up her cheeks. 'Twas the same when she'd spoken of her *boobs*. Galahad bit back a smile.

"Never mind." Her voice was curt.

"But if I can lend my assistance—"

"No." She shook her head. "Thanks anyway."

Pity. 'Twould be an interesting game to discover what article the damsel did without that distressed her so.

"I'll deal with Merlin when I see him."

"As you wish."

She eyed him curiously. "This doesn't throw you at all, does it?"

"Throw me?"

"Bother you? Upset you? A strange woman pops up out of nowhere, with clothes you've never seen before, using words you've never heard and you just take it all in stride. How come?"

"Your speech is indeed odd, my lady." He shrugged. "As is your manner. Still, when one is used to the ways of wizards, one accepts, nay expects, the unusual."

"Well, I'll never accept it. We don't have wizards where I come from."

"No wizards? But then you must have sorcerers of some kind?"

She shook her head.

"Magicians?"

"Nope. No wizards, no sorcerers and the only magicians I know of get TV specials or play Vegas if they're good, kids' parties if they're not."

TV specials? Vegas? The unfamiliar terms danced in his head. He was not an idiot—nay, he prided himself on his intelligence, yet with every word, this woman muddled his mind. Perhaps he was right to begin with. Perhaps she was addle brained. He chose his words with care. "How can this be?"

She raised her shoulders in a casual gesture of dismissal. "We don't need them."

"Surely in your land ordinary mortals are not bestowed with the gift of magic?"

"Of course not. We don't believe in magic. A card trick or two but no magic." A superior smile quirked her lips.

"I cannot accept such a thing. 'Tis impossible. How can such a land survive without wizards to help slay your dragons or defend your people?" He narrowed his eyes. "From where do you hail?"

"The U.S., United States. Nebraska, originally."

"I have not heard of such a place," he said slowly.

"That's a surprise." She laughed. 'Twas a lovely sound. Not the sound of a woman mad. Still . . . "It's pretty far from here. Head north, hang a left at the ocean and aim toward the setting sun. Eventually, you'll hit it."

" 'Tis nothing past the horizon but the end of the world."

"I know I'm going to kick myself for asking this one, but 'the end of the world'? Are you kidding?"

"Kidding?"

"Joking? Jesting?" She sighed. "If I'm going to have to explain every little word to you, we'll never get anywhere."

"I am not a fool, Lady Tessa." He considered her for a long moment. If indeed she was unused to magic, had her encounter with Merlin left her confused? Would this bewilderment then pass? He certainly hoped so.

The thought was preferable to the idea that the wizard had left him to care for a creature as demented as she was lovely. He resolved to be kinder and gentler to the lady.

" 'Tis a fact, my lady." He spoke with the care he would show a small child. "Beyond the horizon, the world ends. The oceans themselves empty over a great waterfall guarded by the dragons and serpents of the seas."

"Oh, come on, get real."

"No one has ever returned from such a voyage," he said carefully.

"I hate the Middle Ages." She groaned and pulled a deep breath. "Get ready for a shock, pal." She glanced from side to side as if to ensure their privacy. "There is no waterfall. No dragons. No serpents. The earth does not end. The world is round. Like a big ball."

He stared for a long moment than burst into laughter. "Now I know you jest."

"It's no joke. Seriously, the world is a ball, a globe spinning through space, circling the sun. That's it. Period."

"By all that is holy, woman, mad or not, you are an entertaining female." He grinned down at her, crossing his arms over his chest. "So tell me this, fair Tessa, if it is as you say, a spinning ball, why do we not fall off?"

She sighed once more. "It's something called gravity. We're spinning so fast it keeps us on the ball. Er, on the earth."

"Ah hah!" He shook his finger at her. "Now I have you. If we are indeed spinning on this great ball of yours why am I not dizzy?"

"Well, that's because—"

"I must confess, my lady, I have experienced a time or two where the swift turn of a current or the whirl of a sprightly dance after too much mead has made my head reel. Why does it not spin now?"

"I don't know," she snapped. "We're going too fast to feel it I guess. Beats me!"

"Have you proof of this spinning ball?" He cast her a pitying look.

"No. Not really." She clenched her jaw. "I teach Greek lit, not physics."

"Then you have no proof?"

Lady Tessa folded her arms over her chest in a mimicry of his own stance. "I know what I know."

He raised a brow. " 'Tis not an acceptable argument. I know what I know as well. I know the world is flat like a platter. I further know the seas of the world pour over the edge. And I know the waters are watched by monstrous creatures. That is the truth of it."

"Oh?" She smirked. "And where's your proof, pal?"

He scoffed. "No one has ever returned from the ends of the earth."

"Then you have no proof either."

"My dear lady," he leaned toward her, "that *is* my proof."

"Hah! That doesn't prove anything."

He grinned with the satisfaction of knowing he had bested a surprisingly astute opponent. No, Lady Tessa was not insane, nor was she an idiot. And there was indeed the tiniest possibility the people of her land believed this spinning ball nonsense. If so, what other amusing tales might she tell?

"I give up." She shrugged in resignation. "Have it your own way. The world is flat."

"Period."

"Period. When in Rome . . ." she said under her breath.

He laughed. What a pleasant diversion she would be. With luck she was a widow. Her age would dictate thus. Surely one as comely as she was not still a virgin. He'd had his fill of virgins. They wanted wedlock and he would not trod that path again. But he could well enjoy the company of this lady until the king's return. Then he would lay his boon before Arthur and ask, nay demand, the king's permission to fulfill his destiny. He was nearly eight and twenty and it was past time.

"So, are you going to show me around this place or what?"

He held out his arm. " 'Twould be my pleasure, Lady Tessa."

"Would you cut out the 'Lady Tessa' stuff?"

"Cut out?"

"Just call me Tessa. Okay?"

"As you wish." He grinned. "Okay."

She groaned. "It just doesn't sound the same coming from a man in tights. Wait a minute." She turned and snatched up a book from the floor. "Now I'm ready." She linked her free arm through his.

"What is the purpose of that?" He nodded at the book. It was small and odd in appearance, and she held it close against her as one would grasp a talisman or a charm imbued with great magic or power.

"I don't know for sure but I'm not letting it out of my sight." She clutched it tighter. "It might be my ticket home, or at least my passport."

He smiled to himself. He was not at all certain exactly what she meant but her actions spoke for themselves. Regardless of her words, the lady lied.

She did indeed believe in magic.

"I knew it. It stinks." Tessa blinked against the bright sunlight and wrinkled her nose.

"I smell nothing amiss. 'Tis a good, healthy scent." Galahad drew in a deep breath. "The smell of nature, of existence itself. Man and beasts at one with the world."

"Call it what you want but it's horse manure and bodies that don't know the meaning of the word *bath*. It reeks." Tessa scanned the area. She and Galahad stepped from the cool stone confines of the castle into a courtyard. The area was huge, surrounded by a tall wall constructed of the same type of stone used for the building behind them. Some kind of granite probably. Square towers joined each wall to the next. "You have one thing right though, there's definitely a lot of life here."

Activity pulsed around her. The busy scene bore a vague resemblance to all the old movies she'd ever seen that had anything to do with knights or the Middle Ages. Except the director of this flick apparently operated under the principle of quantity instead of quality. The place was lined with sheds, or maybe stalls. Carts loaded with hay or barrels lumbered through open spaces. Mounted riders armed with lethal-looking swords and dogs yapping at their horses' heels maneuvered through knots of chatting women. Chickens and geese, obviously far smarter than they looked, wandered freely, avoiding the oblivious hooves of oxen or the wheels of their wagons. Noise of every type imaginable filled the air. Metal clanged against metal. Goats bleated and roosters crowed. The high-pitched tone of an argument sounded here, the laughter of a child there.

"I have one hell of an imagination." Tessa shook her head. "Talk about sensory overload."

Galahad heaved a long-suffering sigh. " 'Tis not the first thing you've said today, my lady, that muddles my mind."

"Sorry. Sensory overload is . . . well . . . all this." Tessa waved at the scene. "There's so much going on here. It's overwhelming."

" 'Tis life, Tessa." Galahad raised a brow. "Is it so different from your own land?"

"Different is an understatement. There's no way you could understand just how different."

"Perhaps." He shrugged as if he didn't really care one way or the other and started off through the court-yard. Here and there he'd stop to point out an item he thought of interest, the perfect medieval tour guide. From the chapel he'd taken her down a corridor to a wide, winding stone staircase and outside, muttering something about starting from the beginning. The Big Guy probably wasn't used to anything as menial as showing around a visitor and a woman at that. Tessa suppressed a grin. Even in her own comatose mind she managed to create a man who looked like her wild-est dreams but acted like every macho hero in every movie she'd ever really loved. And she, of course, was the heroine who took him down a peg or two.

Tessa refused to give up the ever dimmer hope of accidents, hospitalization and coma. It was easier to accept that she might be fighting for her life in a hospital than all this. Oh sure, everything seemed real enough, from the hard-packed earth beneath her feet to Sir Hunk at her side and the smells and the sounds that blurred around her. But no one, not fate, not Fred Astaire, would really do this to her. She was a decent person. She'd never really hurt anybody. Oh, she was a little bitchy at times but she did not deserve this. No one deserved the Middle Ages.

Galahad stopped and Tessa nearly stumbled into him. He narrowed his eyes and observed a group of young men, boys really, armed with wooden swords and small shields fighting each other in what was apparently some kind of lesson.

"What is this? Knight school?" She stifled a giggle at the double meaning.

" 'Tis important work." He studied the activity, his brow furrowed. "Honing the skills necessary to do the king's bidding takes a great deal of practice. This hour of the day is reserved for those still learning their craft. Excellent, Bartholomew," he called.

A blond youth who couldn't have been much older than thirteen threw a quick grin over his shoulder and turned back to the mock battle he was engaged in with youthful enthusiasm.

"Bartholomew is my squire. He's a good lad. 'Tis like a son to me." He stopped, his expression darkened.

"You don't have any children?" *What about a wife?*

"No." The single word was clipped and sharp. Galahad turned and strode off. Apparently this was not a subject for discussion. She scrambled after him. Was a wife a forbidden topic as well?

"So, um, this is Camelot, huh?"

"No."

"But I thought—"

"Come."

He strode toward the wall and the nearest tower; she struggled to match her shorter stride to his. Galahad pushed open a heavy wooden door and stepped inside. A spiral stone staircase stretched upward. He took the stairs two at a time.

"Hey, wait up." She panted up the stairs. Damn. If she'd used her Nordic Track more for exercise and less for hanging her laundry she wouldn't be in this shape. She reached the top and stepped through the open doorway. "So, what are we doing here anyway?"

"You wished to see Camelot." On the side of the five-foot-wide walkway he stood on, the wall facing the castle reached to about his waist. The outer wall was a few inches taller than Galahad with gaps at regular intervals stretching nearly a third of the way down. *Crenelated.* The word popped into her head. If she remembered right, it was what made a basic fortified mansion a true castle. "See for yourself."

She stepped forward and gazed through a gap to the scene beyond the walls and gasped.

"Wow." The setting laid out before her took her breath away "It's gorgeous." The castle stood a bit higher than the surrounding lands and the ground rolled away beyond the walls a short distance to a fairly good sized village. On the other side of the castle, a meadow stretched to a forest with only a single small tree to break the expanse. Gentle hills and valleys lay beyond the town. Sheep dotted the pastures. The grass was so green it might have been painted, like faded AstroTurf revitalized for a new football season. The sky was the color of a pale sapphire. A few lazy clouds drifted across the blue expanse as if to punctuate nature's perfection. "Spring," she said under her breath.

"That, my lady, is Camelot. This is the king's castle and the center of his rule and his power, but Camelot itself is not Arthur alone nor is it this fortress. 'Tis the king and his people who make up Camelot."

She couldn't pull her gaze away from the sight. "It's so, I don't know, perfect. Peaceful. But of course it would be."

"Would it?" he said softly.

Tessa drew a deep breath and stared at the landscape. "I made it up. I made you up. It's not real. None of it."

"Tessa." He cupped her chin in his hand and raised her gaze to his. "I am reasonably certain you are not mad. Yet your words make no sense." He grasped her shoulders and turned her back toward the view. "What you see now is not perfect but it is indeed peaceful for the moment. Arthur has—"

"I know the story." Impatience edged her voice. "Arthur pulled all the battling factions of England together, united under one king."

He nodded. " 'Twas when I was little more than a lad."

"I don't know it as well as I should. I should have done more research but I really hated that class," the fear she had battled all day crept closer, "and this legend and this era—"

"Tessa," he said sharply as if he sensed the panic growing within her, " 'tis the magic. You cannot accept what is real and what is not because of Merlin's magic. 'Tis nothing more than that. I have heard it said, ofttimes, for some, it leaves a veil of enchantment on those who are touched by it."

"Get off it. I don't believe in magic." Her voice rose.

"Believe as you will. 'Tis naught save the truth."

"It's not the truth. It's a fairy tale. A dream. And I don't believe it. Any of it. Not Arthur, not Camelot—" Damn. She was losing it. "Not you."

"Tessa." His brow furrowed with concern and he stepped toward her.

"Don't come near me!" She thrust her hand out in front of her. If he touched her now, she'd be lost. He'd be solid and warm and real and she'd know what she already knew. What she couldn't deny. What scared the hell out of her.

"Tessa?"

Her vision blurred and the world swirled as if she was caught in a real-life special effect. Nausea gripped her. Galahad faded to a shadow and the vibrant colors of his world melted together to subtle browns and grays and all the dusty hues of the library stacks. Tessa stumbled forward and smacked her hip on the corner of the table, her reference books still arranged neatly in the center. She reached out and her hand flattened on the solid, oak surface. She was back!

Without warning, her hand pushed through the table. The library vanished. Galahad stood before her. She fell into his arms.

"My lady!"

A weariness so intense it was impossible to fight gripped her. She sank toward oblivion. Was this it then? Was her coma ending in death? Or was this the end of nothing more than a bizarre dream? Would she wake back in her own world? Or stay in his?

No! She struggled to keep her eyes open. Her voice was barely a whisper. "I won't give up. I can't. I'm going to Greece in three weeks . . ."

Lethargy overcame her and swamped her senses. Darkness surrounded her, sucking her deeper into an endless void. She slipped into unconsciousness, her last thought oddly practical and far from the man who held her in his arms or the legend who trapped her in its mists.

Her tickets were nonrefundable.

Chapter Five

❧

"*I* simply cannot believe you have dragged me back here again along with another unsuspecting victim!" Viviane pulled her brows together and cast him her most venomous glare. "This Tessa of yours is right, you know. This era is rather disgusting."

"You tried to send her back," Merlin said, an accusing tone in his voice.

"Of course I tried to send her back. I want to go back. She doesn't belong here and neither do I."

"This is where it all started, my dear." Merlin glanced around the cavern chamber furnished with all the paraphernalia needed for a wizard's art and life. "I must say, I miss it."

"Nonsense. You can't mean that." Viviane waved a disgusted hand. "It's a cave, Merlin. A nasty, cold, drafty, damp cave. It's far too deep beneath the castle for even a hint of sunlight and I hate it."

"It has a certain amount of charm," Merlin said defensively.

"It has a certain amount of mold," Viviane snapped.

"It's part of my persona." Merlin's voice had that

lofty, superior tone that even after centuries of cohabitation had not lost its ability to set her teeth on edge.

"I suppose it's also part of your persona to dress like an illustration in a children's book? I have always hated you in that costume."

"Very well." His blue silk robes shimmered and blurred and snapped, replaced by a pair of gray flannel pants and black mock-turtleneck sweater.

Cashmere, she noted approvingly. Very nice.

"Is this better?"

"Much, thank you." At least he'd had the decency to leave her own clothing alone. She did so prefer her modern wardrobe of sophisticated, flowing tunics and pants, chic little designer suits and abundant sequins to just about anything that could be had in this horrible time period.

"I've always rather liked my robes. They suit me. They say *wizard*."

"They say *ridiculous*."

"Besides, that's what people expect of me."

"Not anymore. The world and its people have progressed far beyond needing magicians that live in caves surrounded by the bits and pieces of spells and magic and enchantment."

Merlin sighed. "Pity."

Viviane bit back a sharp response. She should know better than to go head to head with the man. It had never worked before and was obviously not about to work now. Mentally, she counted to ten and struggled to adopt a more conciliatory attitude.

"Merlin, my love, I simply do not understand why you have thrust us, and that woman, back to Arthur's court."

"I told you, Viviane. I am fed up with the modern world believing that we, that all of this, never existed."

"Merlin," she said gently and clasped his hands in hers, "I thought that was the whole idea. I thought you wished to preserve forever the very special qualities of Arthur's reign and not have them sullied by the scrutiny of history."

"Well, yes, I did. Originally."

"And you have succeeded with spectacular results. My dear, you are a legend."

"Yes, I know."

The man certainly had the ego of a legend. Viviane groaned to herself. "A rather impressive legend."

"Well," he appeared a bit mollified, "perhaps."

"Why, the stories of you and Arthur and Camelot and all of it have withstood the tests of time and continue, century after century, to be the stuff children's dreams and adult fantasies are made of."

Merlin chuckled. "Well, I suppose, when you put it that way."

"There is no other way to put it," she said as if there was never any doubt. "The entire world knows Arthur as more than a mere man. You have made him and his kingdom all that a king and a land should be and much, much more."

Merlin nodded modestly.

"And as for you, my love, you are Merlin, Wizard Extraordinaire and Counselor to Kings." She widened her eyes in feigned admiration. "There is no greater figure in all of history or literature that compares to you."

He shrugged in a humble manner that still acknowledged the accuracy of her words. "It's true."

"Why muck it all up for the sake of proving a point to one woman?" She leaned forward and brushed her lips across his. "Merlin," she purred, "forget this nonsense and take me home. Now."

For a moment the familiar light of desire sparkled in his eye. Her stomach tightened. Even after all these eons the man could still do that to her. And thank the fates she still did it to him as well. The enchantment that bound them together had little to do with a wizard's magic and everything to do with a man's.

"You are astounding, Viviane. I want you as much now as I did in the beginning." He whispered against her lips. "But we're staying."

"Merlin!" She dropped his hands and stepped back. "I don't want to stay. I want to go back to modern times where I—where we—belong. I want air-conditioning and ice cream and zippers. I want the yacht and the condo and baccarat in Monte Carlo—"

"Hah! I knew it." He aimed a long finger at her. "You just want to get back to the casinos."

"Of course I want to get back to the casinos as well as the South of France. It's my favorite time of year. It's at once festive and peaceful and devoid of the hoards of ill-dressed tourists that invade in the summer. And I resent having to miss it." She studied her perfectly manicured fingernails. "Besides, I always win handily at this time of year."

"I daresay, you use magic to win."

"I don't need to use magic. I don't need to cheat," she said smugly. "I have a knack for gambling. For knowing when to play and when to cash in my winnings. I'm very good."

"Regardless." His voice rang with a no-nonsense

tone and defeat washed through her. She was doomed. No Monte Carlo. No baccarat. No roulette. Not even a lousy game of blackjack. "We are here and here we shall stay. If I recall, you did like it here once."

"Once, I didn't know any better and furthermore there was no other choice." She sighed in frustration. "I thought you'd gotten this *I am not a myth* business out of your system a century ago when you brought that charming Samuel person to Camelot."

"Charming, perhaps, but he was something of a disappointment. Ultimately, he simply perpetuated the legend," Merlin sighed, "and he was inaccurate as well."

"If your desire is to change the thinking of the world, you will not accomplish it with this woman. She doesn't have the status or notoriety he did. Face it, dearest, she is nothing but a lowly quasi-professor."

"This time my purpose is not to change the attitude of all men," he said somberly.

Viviane narrowed her eyes. "What are you up to? What aren't you telling me?"

"I have brought her here for Galahad."

"For Galahad? What? Like a pet?"

"No. A partner."

"What on earth do you mean? Why would Galahad need a partner?"

"Galahad's driving ambition in his later years was to find the Holy Grail—"

She snorted with disdain. "Now there's a myth for you."

"Not at all. The Grail is and always has been different things to different men. *'Tis decreed for all time: he whosoever shall seek the Grail and believe shall surely find it . . .*" Merlin stared at a distant spot as if his words had transported him to a place she couldn't follow. It drove her crazy when he did that.

"Merlin?"

"Sorry, where was I? Oh yes, Galahad, of course, failed. All that Arthur had built crumbled and his knights dispersed to far corners of the land. I cloaked it all in magic. And the legend began." Merlin fell silent and a tiny twinge of pity stabbed her.

Poor love. Arthur and Camelot really was the high point of his career. Still, that myth of his didn't cast her in a particularly good light.

"I was always fond of Galahad."

"He was a nice boy, dear."

"I always regretted I did not help him more on his quest."

"It wasn't your fate. It was his."

"That's why, when I concocted the legend, I allowed him to be one of the few knights to find the Grail."

"It was a sweet thing for you to do."

"Galahad died an old, lonely, bitter man."

"Your magic may have created a myth but Galahad was destined to live in real life," she said slowly. "There was nothing you could do about that."

"I'm going to do something now." Merlin drew himself up straight and stared down his nose at her. For an instant she was thrown back to the moment she had first encountered the proud, powerful wizard who would become her teacher and her love. "I'm going to change his destiny."

She stared for a long, shocked minute. "You can't be serious?"

"I am very serious."

"But why?"

"I like Galahad. I've always liked Galahad."

She stamped her foot. "And I liked Marie Antoinette—"

"Amazing creature," he murmured. "Threw the most wonderful parties."

"—but I could not change her fate!"

He smirked. "Your magic is not as great as mine."

"Thank you for pointing that out," she said sharply. "It breaks all the Rules, Merlin. Your Rules, I might add. About changing destiny and altering fate."

"Yes indeed, they are my Rules. I made them and I can break them. Besides, it's been a long time since I've even wanted to break any Rules. I daresay I'm quite looking forward to it."

"Well, I'm not at all sure I buy any of this. You've always been a stickler for the Rules. You taught them to me." Viviane turned and paced the room, trying to make sense of his comments. There was something here she couldn't quite grasp. "Regardless of your words, this desire of yours to come back here again is absurd. I know you liked the boy. And heaven knows you love this revolting era—"

He stepped up behind her. "How can you not love it? Why, this is a time of chivalry and honor. When knights rallied to do the bidding of their king and their God. When a man backed his word with his life and women were revered as fair flowers of femininity—"

"I will admit," she said grudgingly, "that part was rather pleasant."

"And the magic, my dear, remember the magic?" He wrapped his arms around her and she leaned her head back against his chest.

"Well, yes . . ."

"It's what brought you to me." His words spun a spell of memory as potent as any enchantment. "People believed in magic then. It was part of the fabric of life itself."

"Indeed." How could she have forgotten?

"Remember, my love, when the world was young?" His lips nuzzled against her neck and shivers of delight coursed through her. "There are few challenges and little excitement in the modern world you so resent leaving. Why, it's gotten so bad any idiot with a credit card can fly. Once," he nibbled at her ear and her stomach fluttered, "flying was reserved for those of us who studied and practiced the ancient arts. Your world is really quite dull, my dear."

"Dull." She sighed.

"Tiresome." He edged her tunic off her shoulder and replaced it with his lips.

What was he saying? Something important, something she should pay attention to, tugged at the back of her mind, distant and obscured in a haze of delightful arousal. Viviane drifted deeper into a familiar, sensual world where all she knew was the touch of his hand and the heat of his lips.

"Boring." His hand caressed her breast through the fabric of her clothes.

"Boring . . ." She could scarcely breathe. She turned her head, her lips met his. Boring. She stopped. *Boring?*

At once the niggling thought at the fringe of her consciousness broke free and surfaced like an air bubble escaping the depths of the seas. She gasped and pulled away. "That's it!"

"What's it?"

"Don't give me that look, Merlin. You are the only being in all of creation itself who can manage to look innocent and guilty at the same time. You know precisely what I mean." Viviane stepped away and glared. "How could I have been such a fool? I nearly fell for it."

"Fell for it?" Merlin's eyes widened, trying to appear as if he had no idea what she meant. And failing.

"You know exactly what I mean." Annoyance rang in her voice. "All that nonsense about how you were tired of history thinking you nothing more than a myth. And that business about giving Galahad a second chance. Shame on you."

"I still don't know . . ."

"Give it up, dearest. I see it all now. I suspected as much the last time you pulled this time travel stunt. Only then I was willing to give you the benefit of the doubt. Willing to accept that my poor, dear Merlin's pride was wounded because the world thinks he never existed. Why I had even nearly forgiven you for casting me in your legend as the wicked witch who imprisons the noble sorcerer."

He clasped a hand to his chest. "You have imprisoned my heart."

"Don't try to weasel out of this. At long last the curtain has lifted. This little jaunt of yours back to the Middle Ages has nothing to do with history or legends or quests."

"It doesn't," he said cautiously.

"You know full well it doesn't." She drew herself up and glared. "You, my darling, are bored!"

"Bored?"

"Bored! You said it yourself. Modern life is simply too convenient for you. Too easy. There are none of the difficulties of this primitive time. There's no need for magic and, therefore, little need for you. You receive none of the accolade you enjoyed here as a wizard—"

"A Wizard Extraordinaire," he said pointedly.

"And Counselor to Kings. Yada, yada, yada—I know. Everyone knows. Now that I think about it, that's precisely the reason you did this before. You miss the limelight. Being a relatively ordinary man in an era in which survival is no longer in question is far too tame for you. What was it that set you off the last time anyway?"

He looked like a sulking child. "Electric lights."

"I can't believe I didn't realize it until now." She smacked her hand against her forehead. "The signs were all there—"

"Steam engines. The preponderance of those blasted telephones—"

"Upon further reflection I noticed a certain restlessness as far back as the industrial revolution."

"—photography, dynamite." He shuddered. "Psychiatry—"

"Enough!" She shook her head. "The nineteenth century was a time of great advances for mankind. I should think you'd be happy for mortals."

He plucked an invisible bit of lint off his sweater. "It wasn't much fun for me."

"Fun? I thought it was great fun then and even better with the progress of another hundred years. And I, for one, love it." She narrowed her eyes. "So what triggered you this time? Microwave ovens? Cellular phones? The Internet?"

He crossed his arms over his chest in a petulant manner. "Computer animation."

"What?"

"Computer animation."

"Are you telling me we've traveled back centuries because moviemakers can create realistic dinosaurs?"

"Something like that," he muttered.

"That's nonsense and I have had quite enough." She clenched her teeth. "We're going home. Now!"

"No, we're not." He set his lips in a firm line that brooked no argument. By the stars above, if only she did have the power to imprison him or at least defeat him at his own game, the man would be a toad right now.

"There is nothing in your modern world that can compare to the excitement and adventure of a great quest undertaken for the glory of God and country. Galahad is going on his quest. Tessa is going with him and you and I shall be rapt spectators right here."

She stared for a long moment. "Why did you pick this woman?"

"Galahad needs help to find the Grail."

"So give him Arnold Schwarzenegger, not a short, blonde schoolteacher."

"He's busy," Merlin muttered. "Besides, Tessa doesn't believe in me."

She raised a brow. "And you think Arnold does?"

He ignored her. "Tessa doesn't believe in Galahad or Arthur or any of this."

"Pick any ten twenty-first-century residents and nine and a half of them don't believe."

"There is nothing more powerful in the universe than the faith of the converted."

"There is nothing more annoying in all of creation than a man who dances around a question." She glared. "What aren't you telling me?"

He sighed in resignation. "There's magic in her."

"Magic?" Viviane widened her eyes. "She's one of us?"

"Not quite. But there is a touch of fairy in her lineage. On her mother's side. Lovely woman. Recognized the value of my book," he said under his breath.

"Even so, they can't possibly succeed."

"She has what he needs to find the Grail." There was that matter-of-fact confidence again, a most annoying characteristic. "Neither of them realize it at this juncture but they will fit together like halves of a whole—"

"More like oil and water." Still, opposites did tend to attract.

"We shall see." A self-satisfied smile quirked the corners of his lips. "I don't suppose you'd care to lay a small wager on it?"

"What kind of wager?"

"I don't know." He paused to consider the possibilities. "If I win . . . we return to this time period as often as I wish for as long as I wish, even permanently if I so desire, and," his smile changed to a definite smirk, "and you can't utter one single word of protest. And if you win—"

"If I win"—the excitement of a lucky spin of the wheel rose within her—"we say good-bye to the Middle Ages forever. We lay the past to rest. And," her eyes narrowed, "you never use the phrase Wizard Extraordinaire and Counselor to Kings again."

He eyed her suspiciously. "You promise not to cheat?"

She crossed her fingers behind her back. "I told you. I don't need to cheat. I'm good."

"It's agreed then?"

"Agreed." She nodded.

Poor Merlin. Cheating was in many ways in the eyes of the beholder. There was no way Viviane would lose this bet, because there was no way Viviane was coming back here again. Not until time itself ceased to exist. And even then under protest.

This may have been Merlin's heyday but she had been a mere inexperienced novice sorcerer, a star-struck girl head over heels in love and not substantially more than his consort. No, she would not go through all that again.

It was a shame that Galahad and Tessa would end up as pawns in this magic gambit but it simply could not be helped. Hopefully, they would survive. It wasn't her problem. Not really. Viviane had never been particularly callous where the lives of mortals were concerned but this was different. This was now a wager.

And at this moment, she'd bet anything she'd beat the summer tourists back to Monte Carlo.

Chapter Six

"*A*waken, fair Tessa."

Tessa rolled away from the voice intruding on the odd dream lingering in her head and snuggled deeper beneath her covers. "Go away."

" 'Tis time to face the new day."

The voice was strong, insistent and way too loud. She ignored it, hugging her pillow tight against her.

"Lady Tessa?"

The voice was a shade more impatient now. And familiar. She'd heard it before but where? Of course. Her dreams. Strange bizarre fantasies staring Fred Astaire dressed in a blue bathrobe and a gorgeous, dark-haired hunk the size of a small oak and a castle built of stone and magic and—

A slap smacked across her rear end through the covers. She rolled over and jerked upright, abruptly awake and annoyed. "Who hit me?"

Galahad stood grinning down at her. He swept a graceful bow. "Good morrow, my lady."

"You!" Everything since the moment she opened that damned book in the library rushed back to her and she aimed a shaky finger at him. "You're real!"

"I should be disappointed indeed, were that not true." He appeared to consider her comment. "Although I have heard of any number of creatures who are not at all what you and I would consider real. Trolls and gnomes and fairy folk and the like. I would not wish to offend any of them by implying—"

"You hit me!"

" 'Twas but a pat to pull you out of your slumber." He shrugged. "Merlin said 'twould take some effort to awaken you. You have lain here for three full days and 'twas past time—"

"Okay, okay, I'm awake. Three days, huh?" She glanced around the room. Spacious with cool stone walls and high coffered ceilings, there was a fireplace big enough for her to stand in, a large wooden chest, table and chair. It looked pretty much like she'd expected a room in a castle to look, although a bit Spartan for her taste. "Where am I?"

"My chambers."

"Your chambers? Then," nerves fluttered in her stomach, "this would be your bed?"

"Indeed, my lady."

She groaned and flung herself backward, pulling the covers over her head. Any dream, no matter how weird, was preferable to this very questionable reality. "Go away! I'm going back to sleep and when I wake up you'll be gone. All of this will be gone. I'll be in some nice, pleasant hospital room with nice, pleasant tubes—"

His laugh echoed around her. "You are indeed a stubborn wench but I think not, my lady."

"Go away! I'll get up if you just go away. I don't have any clothes on."

"You could scarce rest well, clothed as you were." She could hear the grin in his voice.

She sat up and pulled the covers around her. "Tell me you're not the one who took my clothes off."

He shrugged. "I would tell you that if you wish. But 'twould be a lie."

"Don't you people have servants? Ladies' maids? Something like that?"

"Indeed." He stared down at her. "We are a civilized country. 'Twas no one here to wait on you when I brought you to my bed. I thought it best to do the deed myself."

"What about chivalry, huh? Wasn't it some kind of violation of the rules to take the clothes off an unconscious woman?"

"I was quite courteous in the disrobing," he said thoughtfully. " 'Twas nothing untoward in the act."

"I'll bet. And why am I in your bed anyway?"

"You did not complain at the time."

"I was asleep. Passed out. Something along those lines anyway." She shook her head. "Nothing like this has ever happened to me before."

He dropped down on the edge of the bed and she struggled to keep from rolling toward him. "Merlin says your long sleep was necessary to combat the vestiges of enchantment from your mind and clear your head for the task that lays ahead of you. Are you quite recovered now?"

"Recovered is relative. I'm still here, aren't I?" She combed her fingers through her hair. "Did Merlin say what task?"

"No, the wizard keeps his own counsel and a wise man does not overly question the methods of a sorcerer."

He drew his brows together and studied her. "But only a fool would not seek answers where he may."

"What do you mean?"

He leaned his elbow on the bed. "While you have rested, I have considered your presence here. I have many questions, my lady Tessa, and I think you may well have the answers."

"Don't bet on it."

"There is much that is odd about you. Your appearance, your speech and manner, your purpose here." His dark blue eyes were thoughtful and considering. "This land of yours, where men believe the world is a spinning top, where does it lie?"

"I told you." He was way too close. Uncomfortably close. Why, she could reach out and run her hand along the rough, shadowed side of his face if she wanted. Which she didn't. She shifted away, pulling the covers closer. "Over the ocean. Really far from here."

He shook his head. " 'Tis not the answer I seek. It rings of truth yet I suspect there is more to your tale than that."

She plucked at the covers, avoiding his gaze. She had no idea just how much she should tell him but for now, keeping her mouth shut seemed the best thing to do.

"And I further suspect your purpose here, the task Merlin has set you to, is one that I should be told of."

"Oh?" she said as innocently as she could manage. Galahad was obviously far more perceptive than she'd given him credit for and probably a lot smarter as well. Medieval apparently didn't equate with stupid. She was going to have to rethink some of her opinions about this era and its people. But later. Right now there was no way she was going to be the one to tell him about the quest. Not her. That was Merlin's job or the king's or whoever's. It didn't take a genius to realize this specimen of the Middle Ages would not take kindly to the news that his dream of a quest was about to come true but with a mere woman in tow. "I really wouldn't know."

"Hah! Women." He stood and paced the room. "I should have known the moment you appeared. 'Tis obvious the true reason why you have been thrust into my keeping."

"It is? Feel free to fill me in."

Long-suffering exasperation crossed his face. "Do not play the innocent with me. It does not suit you. You are far too old for maidenly manners—"

"Thanks loads."

"I should not have thought it of Merlin but he is perhaps no better than the lot of the court. Meddlers, each and every one. Not content to let a man live his life as he chooses. Why, the king himself has long urged me to take a new wife."

"A wife?" She gasped. "Who?"

He glared in reply.

"Me?" The word squeaked out of her.

"There is no other explanation." His voice was hard. "I had not expected the magician to be in league with those who wish to see me wed but the mind of a wizard is a mysterious thing. He well knows it would take a woman of a unique and extraordinary nature to lure me to wedlock once again—"

"Extraordinary? You think I'm extraordinary?" She grinned in spite of herself. "You're not all bad yourself."

"Nonetheless, I have no desire for a wife!"

"Well, you don't have to be so nasty about it. Personally, while I can see the appeal you might have in the eyes of a more primitive woman, you're not my type either." She smiled sweetly. "I wouldn't marry you if my life depended on it."

He stopped in mid-step. "I can scarce believe that. I am an unmarried man with considerable stature in the eyes of the king. My heritage is noble. My honor unquestioned. 'Tis not for you to turn me down."

"My, we do have an overinflated opinion of ourselves, don't we? I guess you'll just have to consider this a new experience then." She slid to the edge of the bed, wrapped the blanket tightly around her and got to her feet. "Now," she surveyed the room. "I assume my jeans are still in Merlin's questionable care, so where is that ugly yellow dress of mine? Merlin!" she yelled. "Get your butt here right now!"

Galahad smirked. " 'Tis not the way to call a wizard. Besides, he will not come. He said I am to show you the ways of this land and its people and only then will he return." He nodded toward the door. "You will find your clothing in the rooms allotted you."

"Oh, so I'm not staying here?"

He raised a brow. "Disappointed, my lady?"

"Not at all," she said quickly. "I'd rather have my own place anyway, thank you." She hobbled across the floor, the long blanket trailing behind her. "If you'd show me to my room?"

He bowed in an exaggerated manner but not before she noticed the twinkle in his eye. "As you wish."

She stepped toward the door. Her feet caught in the

twisted blanket and she stumbled. At once he was at her side, scooping her up in his arms.

"Hey, what are you doing?"

"Merlin said you would be weak. Since he has placed you in my charge 'tis my duty to see to your well-being. I will carry you to your chamber."

"I can walk, you know." Her voice carried an indignation she didn't quite feel. It was almost nice to be snuggled up against him like this. Almost but not quite.

"I know." He shifted her in his arms and pulled open the door. "There will be a maid to help you dress and bring you food."

"Great. I'm starving." How long had it been since she'd eaten anyway? "I haven't had anything since I grabbed a piece of pizza and a salad for lunch at the student center."

He glanced down at her, his gaze considering. What was going on in that macho little head of his? "I shall return to fetch you shortly but I give you fair warning, Tessa." He strode down the corridor. "I shall not marry you."

"No problem, Big Guy. I don't want to marry you either."

" 'Tis difficult to believe," he said dryly.

"What's difficult to believe is the size of your ego," she muttered.

He ignored her and continued down the corridor without hesitation. Jeez, her weight didn't even faze him. Maybe just a tiny bit of that ego was deserved.

"And further, if ensnaring me in marriage is not your true purpose or that of the wizard's, I shall not rest until I uncover the truth you hide."

"I don't have anything to hide," she lied.

"We shall see," he said with determination.

She sighed. "I just bet we will."

Galahad stalked through the long halls, his smile fading. He'd left the Lady Tessa in the competent, if somewhat brusque, hands of Oriana, one of the queen's own maids and one of many ladies in the castle to cast a flirtatious eye upon him since his return to Camelot. Oriana was usually the worst of the lot. Past an age when she should be wed, she was unrelenting in her determination to make him her own. Galahad grudgingly conceded the damsel's charms were exceedingly tempting but he had no desire to marry. No desire to have a woman's fate, nay her very life, in his hands ever again.

He clenched and unclenched his fists in a restless manner, nodding absently to those he passed, who eyed him with speculation. No doubt word of Lady Tessa's unique appearance had already traveled throughout the castle and possibly the entire kingdom as well. Judging by the knowing smiles confronting him, gossip had concluded Tessa was indeed here to provide him a wife. It was the only explanation that made sense. She had, after all, been placed in his care and in his chambers. But in spite of his comments to Tessa, Galahad did not believe it for a moment.

He pushed through a heavy outer door and strode toward the stables. Oh, in spite of her advanced years, Tessa would make a fine mate for any man. Strong and determined with an intelligence rare among most women of his acquaintance, she would be a match well worth making. He'd watched her sleep these past days, studying the rise and fall of her chest beneath the blankets, wondering at the vulnerability revealed by slumber, a defenselessness hidden when awake by the fire in her eyes. Although not a great beauty she was indeed lovely, with a fine, ripe figure. He couldn't suppress a smile at the memory: a form well made for pleasure.

Galahad nodded at a stable lad and the boy jumped to saddle the knight's horse. The huge, black palfrey pawed the ground, as if as impatient as his master to race across the countryside. Within moments Galahad was astride the powerful beast and headed out the castle gates.

He wielded the horse away from the town and toward the meadow and the woods beyond. Galahad spurred his mount and the animal shot forward, eager for the release promised by the vast stretch of gently sloping fields. They passed within inches of the only tree to break the expanse of meadow, a scant third of the way to the forest. The young oak had marked the finish line for foot races and the target for archery contests and had served the various and sundry other uses imaginative boys could devise for as long as he could remember.

Man and beast melded as one and thundered across the verdant pastures. The fresh scent of spring and promise of summer yet to come filled Galahad's senses, as always cleansing his demons and renewing the life surging through his veins.

He gave the stallion his head until they were nearly upon the line of trees that marked the boundary between the sunlit grasses and the shadowed forest. Galahad pulled sharply on the reins and slowed the animal to a walk. There was no need to guide the horse. He knew, as well as his master, the way.

They wandered for long moments, each step deeper into the serenity of the woods leaving the bustle of Camelot behind, little more than a distant memory. At last they stepped into a slight clearing. A sparkling stream splashed into a small pool. Galahad slipped from his horse and breathed deeply.

Calm poured over him. He'd discovered this spot as a lad and had claimed it for his own. Through the years it had never failed to imbue him with a sense of peace. He'd wondered, in his more fanciful moments, if this tiny glen was a place of magic. It had always soothed his soul. When he was a boy and longed for affection from a father too busy with his own concerns as friend and companion to the king to heed the needs of a child. Or when he was a man seeking to understand the death of a son never known, and the devastating loss of a love. And countless times in between.

He settled himself on a rock overhanging the pool, the stone contours fitting to him like the welcome of an old friend. And indeed it was this very rock that had borne witness to his frustration at the hard, demanding training of knighthood or his confusion at the vagaries of the minds of women or his contemplation of the stars that danced above him in the heavens. Merlin had long ago shown him the constellations, and the mystic lights in the night sky captured his heart as nothing else ever had.

Except for Dindrane.

Had it been ten years since his wife's death? Absently, he twisted the ring on the smallest of his fingers. How swiftly the days had vanished. The stab of sorrow her name had once brought to his heart had dimmed with the passage of time. He had left Camelot when she had left this earth asking, nay, demanding of the king the most perilous missions, the most treacherous tasks. He had executed Arthur's business for two years when his father had joined him and together they'd done the king's bidding, in the process braving adventure and saving each other's necks more than once. It was the irony of his life that in losing one love he'd found another.

His father had returned to Camelot over and over through the years, torn between the needs of his king and the needs of his son. Galahad suspected that such a man chafed at staying overly long in the pleasant, yet too peaceful, world of Arthur's court, and indeed his father accompanied him in his travels again and again. It was not until the spring before this that Galahad was at long last convinced to return to the only home he'd ever known. And returned as well to a king who looked upon him as a son and a queen who took the place of the mother who had died at his birth.

He leaned forward and trailed his fingers through the water. Ripples ran out from his touch to mar the smooth perfection of the pond. Odd. The pain of Dindrane's loss had faded but so too had the joy of their short time together. They had but two full summers before she'd perished in the attempt to bear him a son. He tried to pull her image back into his mind. Vaguely, he could see a girl: tall and slender, skin like cream, hair dark as the night. But her face, her features, sweet as her disposition, shimmered in his mind, as elusive as the water between his fingers.

Why could he not remember? Guilt and frustration surged through him. For so long, the pain was too sharp to bear and he'd tried not to think of her. Now, he could not call her to mind at all. She was his first love, his only love and had stolen his heart forever. But he was naught save a mortal man with all the frailties of such, and only one face lingered in his mind.

Fair and delicate with a resolute expression and sparks that flashed in chestnut eyes.

Tessa.

Dindrane was a long-ago moment in his life. A moment perfect and unique and preserved forever in his soul. Tessa was here and now and he could not deny desire had teased him since the moment he'd realized she was a woman. Still, he had not remained celibate these long years. Indeed, he'd had his fill of comely wenches more than willing to quench the fire of a man such as he.

No, when he looked in the eyes of this maddening woman it was not the pull of his loins that kept him at watch by her bed. Nor was it the pure simplicity of the love he'd shared with Dindrane. This was altogether different. Indefinable. Inexplicable. And it tugged at something deep within him.

"God's breath." He stared into the water, half expecting to see her face gazing back from the cool, green depths of the pool "I am bewitched."

He pulled himself to his feet, pushing the sorcery of this woman's spell on him to the back of his mind. For now, there were other matters regarding Lady Tessa to consider.

He had not believed the absurd notion that she had come to Camelot to be his wife, although, he noted with surprise, it was not an altogether distasteful idea. Nay, he had only said such to her in hopes of igniting the temper he'd already sampled. With anger would come truth.

What was the truth? Merlin and Tessa had spoken of a quest. He would never attempt such a thing with a woman by his side. The very idea was absurd. Yet, if the wizard decreed it, Galahad would have little choice. He clenched his jaw. Even a female as unique as Tessa was still a mere woman. Galahad's journeys and exploits had been solitary or in the company of his father or other knights. Men willing and able to lay their lives down to save a comrade. Men dependable and trustworthy in battle and friendship. Men with a sense of honor and courage. Galahad had yet to meet a woman with the same.

Galahad strode toward his horse, decision firm in his mind. No quest on earth, save the simplest task, could be survived, let alone accomplished, with a woman along. Regardless of the magician's plans, surely Galahad could convince Tessa of the dangers of such a ridiculous notion. She had a keen mind and could not fail to see the logic of his argument.

Indeed, he pulled himself into the saddle, Merlin himself could not argue with Galahad's reasoning. Besides, as much as he wished to better know the infuriating lady and explore the enchantment she held for him, he would not be at Camelot for long.

'Twas past time to beg the king's permission for the one adventure he'd longed for all his days. For one reason or other he'd missed his chance, time and again. He suspected his father and Arthur had long conspired to keep him from the attempt. Misplaced concern for his safety, no doubt. Few knights ever returned, not because they had succeeded but because their lives had been lost with their quest. Those that did come back lived in the shadow of failure.

Galahad would not fail. He knew it in his bones, in his soul. It was he, and he alone, who would find the Grail and thus become its guardian. He did not know precisely what that role entailed but he was prepared. Whatever the cost, 'twould be well worth it. He snapped the reins and the horse started toward Camelot.

And should Arthur refuse? The thought pulled him up short and he stared without seeing at a point far beyond the forest surrounding him. He had not considered the king's refusal. To defy the king was treason, punishable by death. But more, he'd sworn an oath to Arthur as his liege lord and shirking his vow of obedience to his king would be the highest breech of a man's honor and duty.

And what of my duty to myself? Galahad straightened, resolve raising his chin. There was no choice. This was the path he was meant to tread. He knew nothing in his life so much as he knew this. And no one—not his king nor his father nor a wizard, not even a damsel with golden hair and velvet eyes—could dissuade him from fulfilling his destiny.

It was time and he was Galahad, a knight of the realm. He would seek the prize that all men sought for the glory of his king and his country and his soul.

"'Tis not to your liking, my lady?" The maid's pretty brow furrowed with concern.

"It's fine. Thanks." Tessa nodded at the platter of

bread and cheese and restlessly paced the width of the room Galahad had abandoned her in.

"You have not taken but a morsel."

"I'm not nearly as hungry as I thought I was." It was a blatant lie. Tessa felt like she hadn't eaten in years. Hah. Of course, it hadn't been years, it had been centuries. Still, every time she tried to take a bite, she'd think of pasteurization, not developed yet, refrigeration, not invented yet, and germs, not discovered yet. Who knew what kind of disgusting microbes were flitting around on this stuff?

"You can scarce get your strength back without food." Oriana sniffed. "Sir Galahad left strict orders that you should eat." Her mouth set in a firm, no-nonsense line. A pretty girl with light brown hair and amber eyes, she couldn't be much more than sixteen but she had the unmistakable air of a drill sergeant.

"Okay. You're right. I'm not going to be able to deal with any of this if I'm hungry. This is not the best time for a diet." Tessa stepped to the wooden table that bore her questionable meal, tore off a small piece of bread and gestured with it at Oriana. "I'll just think of this as all-natural health food. Very trendy." She took a bite.

"Trendy?"

"Um-hum." Tessa chewed and swallowed. A little dry, a bit tough but palatable. "Trendy. Hot. Popular. The thing to do."

Oriana pulled her brows together. "Your speech is most curious."

"Believe me, if you want curious, you should try it from this side of the conversation." Tessa eyed the cheese. Pale and crumbly, it didn't look at all appetizing but it wouldn't kill her. Probably. She broke off a chunk and took a tentative bite. "Not bad." She studied the cheese. "Kind of like . . . feta." She stared for a long moment. This was the final straw. The other shoe. The last piece of the puzzle. Her stomach twisted.

"My lady? Is something amiss?"

"Yes. No. I guess not." Tessa brushed her hair away from her face. "I just realized people who are unconscious or in comas or whatever probably don't get hungry. They're fed through IVs, with plenty of vitamins and minerals and protein and stuff. I'm still not totally convinced but—damn." She waved the cheese. "This must be real. You're real." She gestured at the walls. "All of it is real."

"Yes, my lady." Oriana's eyes widened and she backed up, inching toward the door.

"Oh, knock it off." Tessa sighed with exasperation. "I'm not going to hurt you. You're the least of my problems." She popped the last bite in her mouth, surprised she was as calm as she was. "I suppose I knew it all along, you know, I just didn't want to admit it. I really hoped this would turn out to be a weird dream." She shook her head. "I should have known food would bring me around. What am I supposed to do now?"

Oriana took another backward step toward the door. "I know not, my lady."

"Would you stop that?" Tessa said sharply. "I promise not to bite."

Oriana clapped her hand over her mouth in terror.

"It's just an expression."

"But did not the wizard conjure you up in the chapel? 'Twas what I heard." The girl's curiosity shone through her fear.

Tessa groaned. "Hardly. He simply provided the transportation. A Middle Ages *beam me up, Scotty* kind of thing." She pulled a steadying breath. "Honestly, I'm harmless. And I'm sorry I scared you. I'm a little tense right now."

Oriana cast her a cautious stare then nodded, mollified by the apology.

"Great. Maybe you can help me think of some way out of this mess." She smiled. "And I could use a friend."

"I could be your friend," Oriana said slowly, "if indeed you do not bite."

Tessa laughed and traced a cross over her heart. "No problem, sweetie. Now." Tessa strode back and forth across the stone floor of the chamber, shaking her hands absently in front of her and staring straight ahead. "I can't just sit around here waiting. I have to figure out what to do next. A plan or something.

"First of all, let's face it, I'm stuck here for now. I could probably escape the castle but where would I go? It's not like H. G. Wells is waiting outside the walls with his time machine."

"Time machine?" Oriana narrowed her eyes in confusion.

Tessa ignored her. "Secondly, Merlin says I'm here for the express purpose of helping Galahad—"

"Galahad?" Oriana breathed a wistful sigh. "Would that the wizard would command me to help such a knight."

Tessa stopped in her tracks. "You like him?"

Oriana stared with an expression of disbelief. "Only a woman long in her grave would not. He is a fine figure of a man. Strong and healthy and noble with the stars of the heavens shining in his eyes."

"Whoa. You do like him."

" 'Twill do me no good now." Oriana gazed at her pointedly. "All of the castle, nay the kingdom, knows you are to become his wife."

"No way," Tessa said quickly. "His partner maybe, his cohort in crime possibly but not his wife."

"Still, 'twould be a foolish woman indeed who would set her cap for a man so obviously enamored by another."

"What do you mean *enamored*?"

Oriana cocked her head. "Do you not know?"

"Know what?"

Oriana rolled her gaze toward the ceiling and stepped to the stool beside the table. She perched on the edge, stretching out the moment, obviously relishing Tessa's growing curiosity. "I have seen the look in his eyes when he gazes upon you."

Tessa snorted. "Yeah, I've seen that look. Lots of men get *that* look."

"No, not *that* look. 'Tis not lust—"

"Could have bet me."

"—'tis something else. Something more." Oriana tapped her finger against her bottom lip thoughtfully. "Did you know, he watched you while you slept?"

"You're kidding. That's kind of creepy." *And kind of nice.*

"Creepy?" Oriana furrowed her brow.

"Um . . . yucky. Scary. Weird."

"Not at all," Oriana said stoutly. "I saw him from the door of his rooms, my presence unbeknownst to him. He gazed at you as if you were a riddle he could not answer."

"Really? How interesting," Tessa said casually. "A riddle, huh?"

"Would that he would stare at me that way."

Tessa walked over to the table, her voice matter-of-fact. "So tell me something, Oriana." She tore off a piece of bread. "Why is it a man as desirable as Galahad isn't married?"

"Many have done all in their power to change that. Myself amongst them." Oriana's tone was wry. "To no avail."

"But he was married once, right?"

The girl nodded.

"What happened?"

" 'Tis a sad tale, my lady." Oriana sighed. "Galahad was wed to the fair Dindrane. Beloved for her beauty and her charms, she was good and kind and all in the land knew he adored the very earth beneath her feet."

"What happened?" Tessa was almost afraid to hear the answer.

"She died birthing a babe stillborn. A boy." Sympathy shone in Oriana's eyes. "I was naught but a child myself yet I can still recall the sorrow that hung over the castle." Oriana paused for a moment. "Childbearing is fraught with difficulty. 'Tis not an unusual occurrence for mother and child to perish. But never have I witnessed a love such as that of Galahad for Dindrane. He refused to stay where her presence lingered and left the kingdom, traveling the world in service to the king. It was not a year ago that he finally returned."

"That explains it," Tessa said under her breath. "Do you think he's over her?"

"I think Galahad is a man with a man's needs and desires. Needs that neither start nor end in the bedchamber. I think and, I am not alone in the thought, 'tis past time he get on with his life." Oriana rose to her feet. "A man such as Galahad should not live his days alone. He should have sons, strong and handsome and plentiful to make him proud. And daughters to bring him laughter and joy. And a woman who would gaze upon him with a look in her eye," she grinned, "as if he were a riddle and she alone held the answer."

"I've never been good at riddles," Tessa murmured.

"Galahad is no more a riddle than any man."

"Some things never change."

"Hear me well, my lady." Oriana rested her hands flat on the table and leaned toward Tessa. "I would cheerfully wring your neck like that of a hen's for roasting to have Galahad look at me as he looked at you. But the very moment I saw him in your presence, I knew my cause was lost. I believe the good knight is perplexed and far more accustomed to recognizing the lust in his loins than the feelings in his heart."

"I don't care. It doesn't matter to me." Tessa shrugged. "I told you: I'm not here to be his wife or anything even remotely like that."

Oriana chuckled and straightened. "Your heart is as muddled as your speech if you try to deny what is apparent even to me." She turned and headed toward the door. "I have other duties to attend to before the return of their majesties."

"Arthur and Guinevere?"

"None other." She pulled open the door. "Do not forget, Lady Tessa, I have promised to be your friend and I shall do all I can to assist you with your knight."

"He's not my knight." Tessa frowned. "Anyway, I thought you were interested in him."

"Once, but no longer. The years are passing by swiftly and I shall soon be too old for a good match." Oriana laughed. "But there is a knight with hair the color of wheat and dimples in his cheeks who has cast his eye in my direction. 'Tis past time to encourage such interest. A wise woman knows when all hope is lost and she should direct her affection elsewhere."

"That is wise." Tessa grinned. "How old are you anyway?"

"I will pass my sixteenth year with the next harvest." She tossed Tessa a determined smile. "But I will be a bride long before then." She stepped through the door and pulled it closed with a thud behind her.

Tessa stared. Oriana was just fifteen but unlike any teenager Tessa had ever met. Of course, here she was considered an adult. What was the life span in the Middle Ages?

Come to think of it: what year was it anyway? She'd have to remember to ask Galahad.

She picked up Merlin's book off the table, walked to the bed and plopped down. She was going to read this thing cover to cover. If there was any possibility of avoiding this medieval treasure hunt, she'd bet it was in this little volume. She leafed through the pages, stopping at the illustration of the Big Guy in the chapel.

Galahad. So he liked her, did he? A shiver of excitement skated up her spine. She was flattered, of course, who wouldn't be? Medieval or not, the man was a hunk and intelligent as well. Their verbal sparring was fun and challenging, even if he was too stubborn for his own good and refused to accept basics like gravity and the shape of the world. He probably wouldn't admit when he was wrong either but she didn't doubt for a moment his honesty or courage or bravery. He really was a legend come to life. And wasn't there a definite spark when he'd kissed her or carried her in his massive arms?

But was he finished grieving for his wife? And not just any old wife but a beautiful, perfect wife? Ten years in this world was a lifetime but was it long enough to get over a true love? Judging from Oriana's version, that was exactly what it was. True love. A stupid, goofy, sentimental expression in her time, yet here it seemed somehow right.

Not that she cared, of course. In spite of the heaviness settling in the pit of her stomach she had no desire to mean anything to him. Oh sure, he turned her on a little. And maybe, if she planned on staying here longer, she'd explore the disturbing feelings he stirred in her somewhere between her stomach and her heart. And yeah, the possibility of a brief but wildly passionate fling with him was not a completely disgusting idea.

But she didn't care and she didn't want to. They were from different worlds and there was no future to be had with him. She groaned at how accurate that word really was. Tessa suspected he would not take any relationship lightly and she hated the thought of hurting him. Almost as much as she hated how much she could be hurt. It didn't take Einstein to see anything between them would be volatile, maybe even fatal. If she let this man into her heart it would be a disaster, plain and simple.

She flipped back to the beginning of the book and tried to concentrate on anything except a big, handsome knight.

No, she was here to do a job. Accompany Galahad on his quest. Find the Grail. And get the hell out. Quick and dirty.

And no one gets hurt.

Chapter Seven

❧❀❧

"There, Tessa." Galahad gazed at the distant horizon. " 'Tis where my fate lies."

"Where?" Tessa tugged impatiently at the long skirt that tangled between her legs. The ugly color wasn't bad enough but when Galahad had insisted on riding out of the castle to the hill overlooking the countryside, she was forced to share his horse, bunching the skirt up between her legs. Two on horseback looked romantic in the movies but in real life it was damned uncomfortable. He'd given her no choice, simply scooped her up and deposited her in front of him. Good thing though. Aside from the occasional pony ride as a kid, she'd never been on a horse in her life. "That hill over there?"

He slid off the horse and helped her down. "Past the hills and the valleys."

"I don't see anything."

" 'Tis nothing to see but the future."

"The future?" She swallowed the lump that formed in her throat. Did he know about her?

"Aye. 'Tis where my future lies."

She exhaled a breath she didn't realized she held. "Okay, I'll bite. What do you mean?"

He studied the horizon for a long moment and Tessa marveled at the strength in his profile. This was definitely a man with a purpose. She hadn't seen him since he'd left her in Oriana's care yesterday and had to admit she'd missed him. What thoughts and dreams lay hidden in that handsome head of his? "When the king returns, I shall ask him for permission to under-take the quest that has always been my hope, nay, my destiny."

"Oh, I get it. You're talking about the Grail."

He slanted her a suspicious glance. "How do you know this?"

She shrugged. "It's not hard to figure out. You're Sir Galahad. A Knight. One of the good guys. This is Camelot. Besides, Merlin mentioned it."

"Merlin?" He quirked a brow. "I spoke but briefly to him while you slept. He said nothing of this to me. The wizard is not a man who reveals information freely. He spoke only of his desire to have me guide you through our kingdom and customs." He narrowed his eyes. "Nor did he speak of the quest you and he discussed in the chapel."

"No?" That annoying lump was back again.

"No." His voice was firm. "I wish you to tell me of his plans."

"I don't think so." She shook her head. "I have noth-ing to do with this. I'm just along for the ride."

"Nonetheless, I—"

"Let's not talk about it right now." She wandered off a few paces and turned toward him. "Let's talk about you."

" 'Tis nothing much to say." He crossed his arms over his chest as if defying her to contradict him.

"Sure there is. Like . . . um . . ." She plopped down on the hillside and patted the ground beside her. "Tell me about Arthur and Guinevere."

"Very well." He sighed and settled down next to her. "Before Arthur came to the throne, the land was—"

"No, no. I don't want a history lesson. I know all of that. Well, enough to get by anyway." She pulled her knees toward her chin and wrapped her arms around her legs. "Tell me about the man and the woman, not the king and the queen. What are they really like?"

He plucked a long blade of grass. " 'Tis difficult to separate the man from the king."

"But you've known them all your life."

"I have. My father has been friend and companion to Arthur since before my birth, at his side in battle and in peace." He chewed on the grass absently. "Arthur is a good man. 'Tis not always an easy thing, to be a good man and a wise ruler. I have seen him struggle within himself over decisions that would not be good for the few yet ultimately best for the many. Even if he were not my liege lord, he would have my respect and my love."

"Love?"

"He has treated me like a son and I love him as one does a father."

She pulled her brows together. "Doesn't he have a son?"

"Mordred." Galahad spit the name out as if it were obscene.

"I gather you don't think much of him," she said with caution. "Not a good guy, huh?"

"In our youth, we were as brothers. But the years saw us choose different paths." Disgust underlaid his words. "Mordred is a weakling and a fool. Greed pervades his very soul. Should he live long enough to inherit, he will no doubt rip the country apart."

"You don't think he'll make it that long?"

Galahad snorted. "Mordred's days are spent in reckless games and hunts for the sport of killing alone. His nights are filled with drink and women. Arthur can't help but look upon him with disdain. When Mordred is king, all of England will rebel." His jaw tightened. " 'Twould be different if Guinevere had borne the king a child. Even a girl would be better than Mordred."

"Don't mince words, tell me what you really think." In the legend, Mordred was the son of Arthur and his half-sister Morgan Le Fay. In this allegedly real-life version everything was different. Better to ask questions than jump to conclusions. "So, Mordred isn't Guinevere's son?"

Galahad threw her a startled look. "No. The king was wed while still a lad to the Lady Morgan, believed to have fairy blood in her. 'Twas a marriage long arranged and there was no love lost between them. She died, drowned in the lake, when Mordred was but five years of age. He blamed his father although Arthur was away at the time."

"No wonder they don't get along."

"Mordred hates Arthur. Arthur looks at Mordred with sorrow and disgust in his eye." He shook his head. "It does not bode well for England."

"What about Guinevere?" she said slowly.

"Ah." Galahad's face brightened. "Guinevere has a good heart and her laughter brings joy to her people. She has a streak of stubbornness and determination ill suited to an ordinary woman but serving well a queen."

The corners of his mouth quirked upward. "I see such a streak in you."

"Oh yeah? Thanks." She smiled with pleasure.

" 'Tis indeed a compliment to compare you to the queen. She has taken the place of a mother to me."

"Who was your mother? What happened to her?" Tessa wasn't entirely sure she wanted to know. In the legends, Galahad's mother tricked Lancelot into thinking she was Guinevere then made love to him and conceived Galahad.

"Elaine, daughter of a noble family. She and my father had little time together." He held out his left hand. The ruby ring she'd noticed in the chapel winked blood red in the sunlight. " 'Twas my mother's. She gave it to my father and he to me." His voice was matter-of-fact. "She died the day I was born."

"Jeez." Tessa shook her head. "Childbirth is a real bitch here. Women are dropping like flies."

Galahad stared in confusion.

"Forget it. Just remind me never to get pregnant in the Middle Ages." She thought for a moment. "The king and queen both treat you like a son. What about your father? What's he like?"

"He is . . . Lancelot." Galahad laughed and flicked away the piece of grass. "Minstrels sing of his courage and his exploits. He is a knight by which all else are measured and is more my companion than my father. He has both my respect and my affection yet I did not truly know him until I was grown. Still, I believe he cares for me with a father's love. He too is a good man.

"His position at court is the envy of all. He is both advisor and brother to the king and friend and confidant to the queen. 'Twill never be three people closer in mind and heart than these."

"Interesting," she murmured. So, did this mean Guinevere and Lancelot hadn't started the affair that would spell the end of Camelot? Or did Galahad's fierce loyalty to all three make it impossible for him to see what was right in front of him? Was this another part of the myth that didn't mesh with real life?

"Now, fair Tessa." He stretched out on the turf, rolled on his side and propped himself up on his elbow. " 'Tis my turn."

"Your turn for what?"

"My turn for questions."

She studied him warily. "For example?"

"I know you are far from home. I have told you of my father. What of your family?"

"My family? Well, my mom's wonderful even though she still treats me like I was twelve. And my dad . . ." Her throat tightened and she couldn't get out the words. Would she ever see her parents again? Or would she live and die long before they were born?

He reached out and took her hand in his. "You miss them."

She nodded and blinked back tears.

"And are there others you miss?" He paused. "Your husband perhaps?"

"My husband?"

"A widow then." He squeezed her hand in sympathy. "I suspected as much."

She started to deny his assumption but bit back the words. Why not let him think she was a widow? It would be far easier to pretend to have a dead husband then explain the dating and mating habits of women in the twenty-first century, especially to people who thought sixteen-year-olds were past their prime. She shook her head.

"No woman as comely as you could reach such an advanced age and remain unwed."

"Thanks." Between *comely* and *advanced age* she wasn't quite sure if that was a compliment or simply a comment. "I think."

"Now then, tell me of your land." Curiosity shone in his blue eyes. "This place where the earth is a ball and there are no wizards."

She shifted uncomfortably. What could she tell him about the future? Apparently he no longer thought she was nuts. But if she launched into an explanation of airplanes and television and outer space he'd change his mind. Or he'd think she was a blatant liar. "Maybe someday but not now. I have a feeling we'll have plenty of time to talk later."

"Very well." Her fingers were lost in the size of his grip and her stomach fluttered.

"What?" She laughed uneasily. "No argument?"

"As you say, 'twill be time enough. Tell me instead," he pulled her hand to his lips and brushed her fingertips against his mouth, "of the quest Merlin has planned for us."

"I already told you." Why were his lips so warm against her fingers? "I can't. You'll have to talk to Merlin."

"But you do know, do you not?" His gaze bored into hers.

Why was it so hard to breathe? "Um . . . I guess so."

His words puffed against her fingers. "But you will not say?"

"Say?" How could she say anything that made sense with those deep, stormy eyes paralyzing her and the touch of his lips turning her insides to mush?

"Will you tell me this then?" He trailed his lips to the center of her palm and kissed it softly. Chills shivered through her. "Why did Merlin say you are here for me?"

"Did he say that?" she said weakly.

"He did." He tugged gently on her hand and pulled her into his arms. She should resist. She wanted to resist. She couldn't. "You said you were not here to wed me." He bent his head to hers. "What did Merlin mean?" His lips whispered across her mouth and she gasped. Desire, strong and relentless, surged through her. "How are you here for me?"

She moaned. "This is such a bad idea."

"Is it, fair Tessa?" He pulled her tighter against him, so close she could feel the taut planes of his solid body through her clothes and his. "I think 'tis an excellent idea."

His lips pressed against hers, gentle yet insistent, firm yet yielding. She sighed with surrender and a rush of unexpected longing. Her mouth opened to his and without warning urgency sparked from his lips to hers, as if his life's breath triggered her own. He held her tighter against him, his mouth plundered hers and she met his onslaught with a need of her own that sprang from somewhere deep inside. Her fingers gripped his tunic. His hands splayed across her back. She'd been kissed before, she'd even had great sex before but nothing in her life had swept away her senses like the touch of this man. This knight. He was a myth she didn't buy. A legend she didn't believe in. How could he do this to her? How could he be so real? How could she be so lost?

He rolled over on his back, carrying her with him to lie on top of his long body. He smelled of leather and musk and heat and in her world it would have stopped her short. But here his scent called to some primeval instinct inherent in man and woman. His hands moved lower to cup her rear end, the heat of his touch searing through the thin fabric of her dress. She wrenched her lips from his and her mouth found the pulse beat at the base of his throat. He groaned beneath her, grasping at her dress, sliding it upward until he touched the bare flesh of her legs and she shuddered. His arousal was rigid between her thighs and she shifted to feel him press between her legs.

A voice in the back of her head screamed for control. This would never work. This was wrong. This could destroy them both. She ignored it, she didn't care. It didn't matter. Nothing mattered but the flame of his desire that met and meshed and burned hotter with her own. She wanted him with a relentless ache that blazed from her very core and the consequences for her or him or the future be damned.

"Tessa." He breathed her name with a tone so intense she jerked her head up and gazed into his eyes. Eyes that smoldered with a dark yearning and more. Confusion and something else. She stared. His gaze locked with hers. What else? Fear? Did he somehow know what disaster this could bring? Did he sense, as she did now, at this moment, this was not simply the joining of their bodies but a merging of their souls? That nothing would ever be the same again? Or was it guilt? Did the power of the pull between them bring back the thought of the woman he had loved? His one love. His true love. Her breath caught and she knew that one thing alone did matter. A lot.

"No." She rolled off him and staggered to her feet, gasping for air.

"Tessa." He scrambled after her.

"No." She thrust her hand out and backed up. "Stay away from me."

"Tessa." He struggled to catch his breath. She turned away and wrapped her arms tight around herself, fighting to pull herself together.

"I did not mean . . . I do not know . . ." There was an anguished note in his voice.

Laugh it off, Tessa. Make a joke out of it. She willed herself to stop shaking and forced a lighthearted tone. "Don't worry about it." She turned and faced him. "A little afternoon delight that got out of control." She grinned with a bravado she didn't feel. "Hey, you're a man. I'm a woman. It's spring. Hormones are probably running rampant. Forget about it."

"Forget?" His brow furrowed with puzzled anger. "I do not wish to forget. 'Twas not a mere—"

"Stop it right there." Her voice carried a slight tremble and she hoped he wouldn't notice. "I'm serious. This was no big deal. It was a mistake. That's all. And it's not going to happen again. I'm not here to relieve the lust of some medieval hunk."

"Lust?" His hands clenched at his sides. He was a towering figure of outrage. " 'Twas not mere lust when I held you in my arms."

"What was it then?"

"I do not know." He ran his hand through his tousled hair. "I—" He shook his head.

"Look, you'll find out what Merlin has in store for us as soon as he tells you and not before." Good. Her shaking had stopped. "And it won't do you any good to try to get it out of—" She stopped and glared. "Was that what this was all about? You thought you could seduce the information out of me?"

A look of distinct discomfort crossed his face. "Perhaps, at first, I may well have considered—"

"You—you—" she sputtered with anger. "You fraud! The noble Galahad. What a crock. What happened to chivalry and honor and all that stuff?"

He drew himself up and glared. " 'Tis not a question of my honor."

She raised a brow. "Oh?"

" 'Tis a question of strategy. Women are well known to reveal much in the throes of passion. You have knowledge that I suspect I should know." He stepped toward her. "And I will learn it."

"Well, you're not going to kiss it out of me. I can't believe I almost fell for it." She whirled and took a step.

He grabbed her arm and yanked her back. " 'Twas the thought in my mind at the beginning but not at the end."

"Let go of me!" She clasped her hands together and twisted, her elbow stopped short of his stomach by a steel grip. "Ouch!"

Sparks shot from his eyes. "Sister Abigail may not have taught you well enough. A knight will be caught unawares but once."

She wrenched out of his grasp and stepped back. "I'll keep that in mind. And we need to get a couple of things cleared up right now."

"Very well."

"You and I are going to be partners in this little adventure of Merlin's. Strictly a professional relationship. That's it. Period. Get it?"

He shrugged. "As you wish."

"It's exactly what I wish." She turned and stalked off in the general direction of the castle. For just a moment she'd thought he had the same feelings she did. A passion so deep it scared her. Emotions she'd never even suspected existed. When she got back to that crummy, primitive castle she was trapped in, she'd have to have a long cry about this.

Could it possibly be love? Her step faltered at the thought. No, of course not. This happened way too fast for love. But even basic lust had never been this strong. No man had ever turned her on this way. Not just her body but her mind, maybe her soul. All she knew was whatever she felt for him was powerful and terrifying. Under other circumstances, sex with him would be okay. All right, it would be great. Fantastic. Fireworks and the Fourth of July and whatever in the hell passed for a good time in the Middle Ages. But there was no way that could happen now without involving her heart. Damned man. It was obvious he was still in love with his dead wife. And not even here, before her world was ever dreamed of, would she allow herself to love a man who couldn't love her back.

His horse pulled up beside her.

"What?" she snapped without looking.

" 'Tis a long walk back, my lady." She could hear the smile in his voice.

"I'm not your lady." She ground her teeth together. "And I'm up for a long walk."

"I think not." He reached down and grabbed her.

"Hey!"

Galahad scooped her up onto his horse and settled her in front of him without the slightest effort.

"You are so annoying."

"As are you." He paused and she knew if she looked back at him he'd be grinning. "My lady."

They rode on in silence for a good five minutes until Tessa gave up trying to sit straight and tall and as far away from him as possible. She relaxed against him. Why did he have to feel so good?

"The king is expected back today," he said in a casual manner.

"So I heard."

" 'Twill be a great feast tonight." She refused to answer. Finally he sighed. " 'Tis then I will ask him a blessing for my quest."

"For the Grail?" She held her breath.

"For the Grail." His voice was even and carried a strength and determination she couldn't help but admire.

"This is it then." Was it excitement that fluttered in her stomach? Or fear? "The start of the adventure."

"I have had adventures aplenty. This . . . this shall be different."

"No duh, pal," she said more to herself than to him. How was she going to go with him and keep her distance at the same time?

"I am sorry we shall not endeavor to perform whatever minor task Merlin has planned but 'twill be no time. I shall leave Camelot as soon as possible." He paused for her answer but she hadn't the faintest idea what to say now. She hated to lie to him but she definitely wasn't about to spill her guts with the truth.

"I shall miss you, Tessa," he said softly and she steeled herself against the way her heart twisted at his words.

"It won't work this time." She shook her head. "Like you said, a knight will be caught unawares but once. There was more to Sister Abigail's classes than physical self-defense."

He chuckled and they rode on in silence. She might as well enjoy it while it lasted. Galahad would go ballistic when he found out he'd get exactly what he wanted but there would be strings attached. And they'd be tied firmly to her. She meant what she said. From now on it was strictly business. Then she'd go home. The Big Guy would be relegated to an occasional class she'd be forced to teach. Exactly where he belonged and she'd be . . . what? On her way to Greece? Funny, even Greek gods paled a bit beside her legendary knight. Of course, he wasn't her knight and he never would be. Not even if she wanted him to be. Which she didn't.

She shifted in an effort to achieve some minimal degree of comfort and he tightened his grip. It was impossible not to let the warmth of his body seep into her own. This was the last time she'd ask him for a ride. This sort of thing couldn't happen in a nice, comfortable car where everybody had their own seat. Damn, she hated the Middle Ages.

She was pretty sure, by the time they got back to the castle, her butt would ache nearly as much as her heart.

Chapter Eight

❦

*W*hat in the hell was she supposed to do now? She was as out of place, awkward and uncomfortable as a nudist at a black-tie affair.

Tessa stood in the back of the great hall, half hidden behind one of the huge columns that rose like redwoods to a soaring ceiling at least two stories high. The columns marked the separation of a gallery bordering three sides of the immense chamber. Huge vibrant tapestries depicting knights and ladies, unicorns and lions and all kinds of interesting things hung from a balcony directly above the gallery. People, equally colorful, mingled and chatted and took their places at long tables. Tessa had to admit, it was as magnificent as an epic movie and just as overwhelming. Big-budget, feature-film perfect.

And it looked like the director had just yelled "action."

Abruptly, all conversation ceased. At the far end of the room, a multi-colored cloth-covered table rested on a raised dais. Two women sat at the table, a man centered between them. Two other men stood poised behind them, as if they had just gotten to their feet.

She recognized Galahad on the right. Even from this distance she could see he was upset, the lines of his body taut with controlled anger. The figure beside him, nearly as tall and dark, laid his hand on Galahad's arm, the action as much to restrain as to calm. In front of the dais, guards flanked a tall blond man, his bearing proud and erect, his stance defiant.

The room was still, tense, attention focused on the confrontation at the head table. The voices of those involved were raised. She couldn't make out the exact words but the tones were unmistakable. Bold insolence rang in the blond man's voice. It was obviously a threat. Galahad lunged as if he was about to vault the table but the knight beside him stepped forward and blocked his move. The still seated man rose to his feet with a measured dignity. Nobility and strength radiated from him like a beacon in the night. Her heart caught in her throat.

Arthur.

The king leaned forward slightly and addressed himself only to the younger man standing before him. His words were too low to distinguish from her place in the back of the room but she suspected, even if she were at one of the front tables, she still wouldn't be able to hear what he said. In spite of the crowded hall, a distinct air of privacy hovered around the two. The king straightened and nodded sharply at the guards. They stepped back.

Arthur and the blond seemed unaware of their audience. Their gazes locked in a quiet battle of will, a wordless struggle, a silent confrontation. Long moments ticked by. Tension in the hall increased until Tessa wondered if the castle itself would explode with the pressure of pent-up emotion. At last, the man before the king snapped something, his voice sharp and hard, turned and strode the full length of the hall. Tessa moved deeper into the shadows cast by the column. She had no idea who this guy was but staying out of his way seemed like a smart idea. He passed within inches of her but so quickly she barely glimpsed his face.

She glanced toward the dais. The king sank down in his chair and lifted a goblet to his lips, apparently a signal for the festivities to resume. The anxiety in the room eased, the murmur of voices increasing.

"Welcome to Camelot." A voice sounded behind her.

"What was that all about?" Tessa glanced over her shoulder. "And where have you been?"

Merlin's voice was grim. "I have been here all along, my dear."

"What's going on? Who was he?"

"Mordred." Merlin looked as if he was about to say more then decided against it. The tone of his words lightened. "Are you quite ready for tonight? You're not nervous, are you?"

"Nervous? What do I have to be nervous about?" It wasn't like this was her first feast with a legendary king and queen in merry old England. She should have come earlier with Oriana for moral support but Tessa had concocted one excuse after another to stall the inevitable, until the girl left without her. The teenager had helped her dress in a gown probably whipped up by Merlin. No, definitely provided by Merlin. This one was more a bronze than a mustard but still in the yellow family that looked so awful on her.

"I think it quite becomes you."

"You would." She studied the scene before her. On the main floor, trestle tables were laid out perpendicular to the dais. It looked a lot like the arrangement of every faculty banquet she'd ever been to, right down to the elevated level of the head table, obviously the king's. Galahad sat at one end, an empty space beside him. "I heard you had a little chat with the Big Guy. This whole thing is driving him nuts, you know."

"He shall get his answers soon enough."

"Tonight?"

"Tonight."

Galahad leaned over and spoke with the man in the next chair, the one who had held him back earlier. She hadn't noticed at first but now she could see a distinct resemblance. "Lancelot?"

Merlin chuckled. "Like father, like son. The family connection is unmistakable. And next to him—"

"Guinevere and . . ." Tessa's voice dropped to little more than a whisper. "Arthur." Regardless of her opinion of the Middle Ages and the Arthurian legend, the presence of this king and queen was awe inspiring. Like coming face-to-face with Apollo or Helen of Troy and finding out they were—

"Living, breathing people," Merlin said quietly. "As real as you are, Tessa."

She couldn't pull her gaze away. Guinevere was the epitome of grace, stately and slender with hair the dark blonde color of gold. Beside her, Arthur chuckled at some unheard remark, every inch a king with a powerful air of command and confidence. Salt-and-pepper hair with a straight, strong posture, he wore a short, neatly trimmed beard that only added to an overall effect of nobility. The king and Lancelot both looked like they were in their early fifties, Guinevere maybe a few years younger.

"I always thought he was a lot older than she was," Tessa said.

"Myths, legends." Merlin sighed. "Do what you will, they tend to get completely out of control. They evolve under their own power, you know. Stories passed down for a hundred years or so change in the telling. Add to that movies and you can well imagine my irritation."

"You asked for it."

"You needn't remind me," he said with annoyance.

"Who's the woman at the other end of the table?" There was an empty spot between Arthur and a dark-haired woman, who looked a shade older than the queen.

"Viviane. My wife, more or less."

"More or less?" Tessa bit back a laugh. "I didn't know you could have a wife who was more or less. Either she's your wife or she's not."

"The term itself is relative. She and I have been together for centuries. Viviane is a lovely creature. Most of the time." There was a wry note in his voice.

"Is she the one who enchanted you and locked you in a cave or something like that?" Tessa grinned at the thought of Merlin being on the receiving end of his own tricks.

"Now, now, none of that. Remember there is a great deal of difference between myth and reality. That portion of the legend was a bit of a joke on my part, not that she ever saw the humor in it. Viviane's magic is quite remarkable but not nearly as strong as mine. As much as she would dearly like to imprison me on occasion, and with Viviane it would more likely be a condo than a cave, she simply doesn't have the power. Not now, not ever."

Viviane tapped her fingers on the table, boredom written across her face.

"She doesn't look very happy."

"You and she share the same opinion of this period in time. She doesn't want to be here any more than you do."

"Wise woman."

"She thinks so."

Tessa's gaze drifted back the length of the table to the one face that drew her attention more than any other. He was gorgeous all right but abruptly, she realized he could have been downright ugly for all the difference it made. It was his character, his soul, that drew her to him. He had a purpose to his life and the strength to see it through to the end. Nothing was more compelling than that.

She turned and leaned against a column. "He's not going to be happy when he finds out about me."

Merlin shrugged. "We all have our crosses to bear. He shall simply have to adjust."

"Tell him that. How are you going to get him to go along with it? With dragging me on his precious quest? All in all, the man doesn't seem to think much of women."

"Ah, but my dear, it shall be up to you to change his mind." Merlin raised a bushy brow. "I gather he already likes you. Quite a bit."

The memory of his lips hard on hers flashed through her mind and she pushed it away. "That was a mistake."

"Was it?" Merlin said softly.

"Yes." Tessa's voice was firm. "It was. And it won't happen again."

"No doubt."

The wizard's tone was noncommittal but she could tell he didn't believe it for a minute. Too bad. She admired Galahad and respected him. She even liked him. And that was as far as she would let it go. She could be his friend but that's it.

"That's all I wish, Tessa. You are here only to help him. I ask for nothing more."

"You ask for nothing more? That's a laugh. Don't try to scam me, Merlin. You and I both know I'm stuck here until he finds the Grail or—hey!" A nasty thought struck her. "What happens if he doesn't? If we can't pull this off? What happens if—wait a minute. He could get killed, couldn't he? We could both get killed."

Merlin nodded. "That is a distinct possibility. Indeed, there is a great deal of risk in a quest of this nature. But it's the difficulty that makes it such a challenge. And such an adventure."

"I could do with a little less adventure and a little more security, thank you," she said sharply. "You didn't answer my question. What if we fail?"

"Tessa, my dear," Merlin said with a slight smile, "while it is always preferable to find what you seek, it is not always necessary. The end is not as significant as the path to reach it. With whole heart and mind, the prize must be well and truly sought. Nothing more is required."

"It's not whether you win or lose that counts, it's how you play the game? Is that what you're saying?" She stared for a long moment. "That's all this is to you, isn't it? Some kind of silly, magical game that you're playing with people's lives. With my life. With Galahad's."

"Does it really matter what it means to me? Isn't the more important question what it means to him?" Merlin directed his gaze toward the hall.

She turned and watched Galahad's exchange with his father. It was obviously a lighthearted conversation but even now there was an intensity about the man that belied his banter.

"It means everything to him," she said quietly.

"He doesn't stand a chance without you."

"I don't get it."

"Frankly, you don't have to." The wizard's voice was cool. "All you have to decide is whether or not you are willing to let him sacrifice his dream if all he needs to achieve it is you."

"This isn't my decision." She shook her head. "You've already made it for me."

"I've set the wheels in motion but without your wholehearted participation there's nothing even I can do to guarantee success."

"You're saying if I really don't want to do this, I can go home?"

"Don't be silly. I'm not saying anything of the sort." Merlin scoffed.

"I didn't think so."

"What I am saying is that victory, Galahad's victory, is contingent not only upon your participation but your enthusiasm."

"More of that how-you-play-the-game stuff?"

"Exactly."

She stared at Galahad. "So it's really up to me?"

"You do play a critical role."

"And he can't do it without me?"

"He never could."

Tessa sighed. How could she let him down?

"I knew you'd see it that way."

Tessa clenched her jaw. "Would you please let me finish a thought before you answer it?"

"Very well." Merlin raised a shoulder in a superior manner. "I simply thought I'd save time."

"Time? You do know how to turn a phrase."

"It's a gift." He grinned. "Speaking of which, you should probably not mention to Galahad precisely where you come from."

"Oh? You don't think he can handle knowing his new partner in crime is a time traveler?"

"Galahad is no fool but even the most sophisticated minds have difficulty with a concept as abstract as traveling through the ages. It is inevitable that at some point in your journey together, it will be necessary to confess everything. I advise you choose that moment carefully. Aside from everything else, Galahad quite values basic virtues. Things like honor and honesty."

"I haven't lied to him." She thought for a moment. Of course, there was his mistaken impression about her widowed status that she'd done nothing to correct . . . "Not about that anyway."

Merlin raised a brow. "Perhaps not directly. But will he agree? Isn't a sin of omission just as dishonest as a outright lie?"

"I suppose."

"Do not look so disheartened, my dear, I am simply advising you to bide your time as to when to reveal the truth. And now . . ." He offered her his hand.

"Now what?" she said, narrowing her eyes in suspicion.

"Now," his voice was annoyingly patient, "place your palm flat upon the back of my hand and I shall escort you and introduce you to the king."

"You're kidding." Something far too large to be butterflies leapt in her stomach.

"He's really quite charming."

"I'm sure." Tessa rested her hand on Merlin's. "What do I do? What do I say?"

"It's just like in the movies, my dear. No script, of course, but feel free to ad lib. Play it by ear."

"You're a lot of help."

"I know." He chuckled. "I am having a great deal of fun."

"Glad one of us is," she muttered.

Merlin started toward the dais. "You seemed to have enjoyed a moment here or there today. That was one bloody impressive kiss."

She released a long exasperated breath. "I really hate the idea of you being able to see everything I do."

"Get used to it." A wicked light glimmered in his eye. "This is just the beginning."

Galahad spotted Lady Tessa the moment she and Merlin stepped from the shadows. He swallowed hard. By the heavens, the woman was a vision. Was he the only one who noticed? The din of the crowded hall receded. All thoughts of Mordred vanished. He had eyes only for her. He rose to his feet. In the flickering torchlight, her hair and gown glowed golden. Like the morning sun or a finely wrought crown or . . . a chalice.

A chalice. The quest. The thought sobered him and he sank back in his chair. 'Twould be best to wait and see what the wizard planned. Besides, nothing could be gained by pursuing her favors. Even if she did make the very blood in his veins race, there would be nothing between them. He had his destiny to fulfill and there was no room in it for a woman.

Merlin and Tessa drew closer to the dais. Her gaze caught Galahad's and a weak smile lifted the corners of her mouth. Surely, nerves did not the trouble the lady? He grinned to himself. Perhaps, she was not as self assured as she appeared. The Lady Tessa could well provide more entertainment this evening than the court's minstrels and jugglers and mimes.

The couple halted directly before the king. Arthur eyed them with an unaccustomed air of curiosity.

"So, Merlin." A thoughtful smile played on the king's lips. "This is the lady of whom you have spoken?"

"Aye, sire. May I present the Lady Tessa." Merlin bowed with a flourish.

Tessa stared at the king, a sickly smile plastered on her face, her eyes wide. Merlin nudged her with his elbow and said something indistinguishable. At once, Tessa dropped into an awkward curtsy. What was wrong with the woman? Galahad drew his brows together. You would think she'd never met royalty before. Even a land without wizards surely had a king? And what kind of strange kingdom would it be that did not teach women manners of deportment and courtesy? Once again, he wondered as to the nature of her curious country.

"Your Majesty." A slight quaver sounded in her

voice. Not unlike the tremor he had noted after he'd kissed her. He sent a prayer heavenward in thanks that she had failed to notice a similar affliction in him.

Arthur studied her for a long moment and Galahad suspected it was difficult for her not to squirm under the king's perusal. He could well sympathize. Arthur's stare had set many a knight's knees to shaking.

"Are you certain of this, Merlin?" Arthur rested his elbow on the table and stroked his beard. "She seems rather frail for such an undertaking."

What undertaking was this?

"Frail?" Tessa glanced around as if uncertain as to whom the king referred. "Me?"

"Trust me, sire." Confidence rang in Merlin's voice. " 'Tis not the strength of her body that is needed but the power of her spirit."

Needed for what?

"Still . . ." Arthur shook his head.

"She appears quite sturdy to me, Arthur." Guinevere considered Tessa carefully in the manner of one woman's estimation of another. What exactly did the queen hope to discover? "What say you, Lance?"

His father's gaze drifted lazily over Tessa and a light of appreciation danced in his eye. Galahad's stomach tightened. Lancelot was never averse to flirtation with a beautiful woman, especially fair-haired ladies. "*Sturdy* is not exactly the word I would use, Your Majesty. I should think enchanting a more fitting term." The queen cast him a sharp glance. Lancelot shrugged as if his appraisal of Tessa was of no real concern. "In spite of the delicacy of her appearance, if Merlin decrees her to be fit for this challenge, I should trust in the wizard's word."

"Thanks loads," Tessa muttered.

What challenge?

Surely, Merlin did not still believe a well respected knight would go on a quest, no matter how insignificant, with a woman? The very idea was preposterous. Galahad had not the time for such nonsense. Unease trickled through him. Whatever the wizard had in mind he had obviously enlisted the approval of Arthur and his father. 'Twould be disrespectful to ask the king to explain the odd discussion. Yet, Merlin had placed Tessa in his care. Did that not make any plans for her his concern? And if indeed this discussion had anything to do with him—

"Your Majesty," Galahad blurted, "I should wish—"

"Later, my boy." Arthur waved away his words.

"But, sire—"

"Not now, Galahad." The king cast him a quelling glance and Galahad bit back an imprudent reply. He'd always been in Arthur's good graces yet even a favorite knew when to keep still.

"Merlin," Arthur narrowed his eyes, "is this really necessary?"

"It is imperative, sire," Merlin said quietly. "Success is impossible without her."

"Very well then." The king heaved a resigned sigh. "Although I daresay I am not at all confident that a mere woman—"

"Excuse me?" Tessa raised an indignant hand. "Mere woman?"

"I suspect there is nothing at all mere about this woman, sire," Guinevere said lightly. "Merlin would not entrust such an undertaking to a *mere* woman."

"Mere woman?" Tessa clasped her hands together in front of her—as if to keep them under control—and leaned toward the wizard. "This is a pretty universal concept, isn't it?"

"Middle Ages." Merlin shrugged. "What did you expect?"

"Enough." Arthur's voice carried a note of command that silenced even Tessa. "She is an impertinent wench, I'll give you that."

Tessa started to protest. Arthur raised a royal brow and she closed her mouth quickly.

"I do not comprehend half of her mutterings, Merlin, nor do I fully understand your reasoning. Still, 'tis only when I disregard your advice that trouble befalls me. I learned long ago to heed your words."

"Your Majesty flatters me." Merlin swept a low bow.

Arthur snorted. "You know as well as I do, old friend, 'tis a truth we both rely on. As you wish then." Arthur glanced at Galahad with a speculative eye then back to Merlin. "Now?"

"Sire, this is Lady Tessa's first sampling of the castle's hospitality. She has taken her meals in her rooms since her arrival. I should think it would be only courteous to allow her to enjoy the evening's festivities first. 'Tis time enough later."

"Just a few centuries," Tessa said under her breath. "Hey!" She glared at Merlin and rubbed her arm as if struck or poked or pinched by an unseen hand.

"Thank you, Your Majesty." Merlin bowed and again prodded Tessa into a curtsy, somewhat less clumsy than the first but still lacking the polished ease of one used to such things. 'Twas a shame Galahad would not have more time to learn about her home. Or about her.

Merlin escorted Tessa to the seat between Galahad and Lancelot. She glared at the wizard and again rubbed her arm. "If you don't knock it off, I'm going to be black and blue before this is all over."

" 'Tis not an entirely unpleasant possibility, my lady." A teasing note underlaid Lancelot's voice.

" 'Tisn't it? I mean, it's not?" Tessa stared at his father.

"No indeed. Why, with hair the color of sunlight such as yours, black would only enhance your beauty. And as for blue . . ."

"Yeah?" Tessa cocked her head in a most flirtatious and unbecoming manner. "I can't wait for this one."

"The blue of the sky would only flatter eyes that have the hue of the good earth itself. Deep and rich and," he took her hand and raised it to his lips, "fertile."

Galahad groaned to himself.

"Whoa. You're as good as he is." Tessa glanced at Galahad over her shoulder. "Now I see where you get it from."

"I have taught him all he knows." Lancelot cast her a wicked smile. "But 'tis said no matter how the student excels he can never eclipse the teacher."

"Really? But surely you don't believe in old sayings? For example, I've always heard it said those who can, do, and those who can't . . ." Tessa fluttered her lashes, "teach."

Galahad sucked in his breath.

Lancelot stared speechless.

Tessa appeared completely oblivious to the insult

she had just hurled at a man who did not take insult lightly. Especially when the subject at hand was his charm with fair ladies.

A grin broke across Lancelot's face. "Well said." He laughed in the manner of a man who could appreciate a good jest even when it was at his expense. "Well said, indeed."

Tessa smiled sweetly and sat down. Galahad blew a relieved sigh and dropped into his seat. His father, still laughing, took his place on Tessa's other side and winked at his son. "Merlin is right about this one, she has a great deal of spirit."

"Spirit, I grant you." Galahad leaned closer to her and whispered in her ear. "But she may not be as clever as she thinks to mock a man she has but met."

"Worse than that," she said out of the corner of her mouth. "I'm a teacher."

"What is that?" Tessa stared in disbelief at the newest course presented to the king.

"What?" Galahad glanced down the table at the platter laid before Arthur. "Oh, 'tis a swan, I believe."

"But it's," she grimaced, "cooked."

Galahad quirked a brow. "Surely, even in your land, you would not eat it otherwise?"

"No, of course not. But it has . . . feathers." Her stomach churned but she couldn't seem to wrench her gaze away. It was like an onlooker staring at the scene of an accident. "Feathers. Stuck on the bird. Yuck."

He nodded approvingly at the dish. "Aye, and a head as well. 'Tis most lifelike."

"Too lifelike if you ask me."

"One does not eat the feathers."

"Well, this one will pass on the rest of it too." She pushed away the chunk of bread that served as a plate. "Anyway, I've had enough, thank you. I think it was the fish that did it. Very tasty." She picked up her goblet and drew a long swallow of some kind of unidentifiable, overly sweet wine. She'd had far too much of the drink already but the fish and everything else she'd tasted in a seemingly endless parade of courses was so heavily salted and seasoned, she needed something to wash it down. The garlic alone in this meal was probably lethal.

Galahad leaned back in his chair and waved away a servant bearing the platter of swan. " 'Tis not to your liking? Any of it?"

Right now, she'd kill for a hamburger or a Caesar salad or grilled chicken, sans feathers. She pulled her gaze away from the bird. "Let's just say we have different tastes."

"I do not understand you, Tessa." He shook his head. "You display no knowledge of the common courtesies taught from birth. You are surprised at the most trivial details of life. You do not pay proper respect to a magician who can destroy you with a blink of his eye. And your demeanor before the king was questionable."

"I thought I was pretty together when I met Arthur."

"And your words grow no clearer with the passing days." Galahad narrowed his eyes and considered her. "You are a puzzle, Tessa St. James. There is obviously some purpose to your presence yet 'tis clear you do not wish to be here. I would offer you my assistance but 'tis impossible as long as you refuse to answer my questions. You are as obstinate as you are lovely."

"Thanks. I think."

His eyes darkened. "Do not jest with me. 'Twas not meant as a compliment."

"I know." She heaved a heartfelt sigh. "And I am sorry. I wish I could throw myself into all this but frankly," she bent toward him, "this is really weird and I'm a little freaked out."

"Speak plainly, Tessa." Frustration colored his face. "Your words make no sense." He reached forward and grabbed her hand. "I would help you if I could."

Her hand looked so small and fragile engulfed in his grip. She pulled her gaze away to lock with his. "What if the situation were reversed?" she said slowly. "What if I could help you?"

"Help me do what?"

"Oh, I don't know." She tilted her head as if she was trying to think of some minor favor she could do for him. "Something significant. Something important."

" 'Tis an odd question." He scoffed. "I am a man, a warrior, a knight. You are a me—"

"Don't say it!"

He grinned. "A woman. Delicate and born to be protected and coddled. A lady could no more assist a knight in matters of importance than a man could fly."

Don't bet on it. "Seriously, would you accept my help?"

"I cannot imagine—"

"Stop it, Galahad." She squeezed his hand. "Tell me. Would you take my help?"

"Very well, my lady." He smiled in a condescending manner as if humoring a small child. Annoying but worth it. "I would accept your assistance."

"Do you promise?"

"I—"

"Promise, Big Guy. On your word of honor. As a knight." She forced a pleading, feminine note to her voice. "Please. For me."

"As you wish." His eyes sparked and he pulled her hand to his lips. "For you."

"Great." She sighed with relief.

"And what kind of assistance will you be offering me?" He brushed his lips over her fingertips and she steeled herself to the unwelcome shiver he aroused.

"Well . . ." She glanced down the table to catch Merlin's eye. He nodded and rose to his feet. It was time.

"Hmmm?"

She pulled her hand from Galahad's. "There's no good way to break this to you." She kissed her finger— "I'm going to help you"—bent closer and touched the tip of his nose— "find the Grail."

Chapter Nine

❧❀❧

Tessa leaped to her feet and took off in her best bat-out-of-hell imitation.

"What!" Galahad's roar behind her echoed through the hall.

Tessa scrambled off the dais, sprinted around the corner and skidded to a halt beside Merlin. She refused to look back.

"Very nice." Sarcasm dripped from the wizard's words. "Did we learn that from the good sisters at St. Margaret Mary's?"

"Not exactly." She scooted around Merlin. It was probably wise to put as much distance as possible between Galahad and herself. "I had a professor when I was a graduate student who wanted to teach me a few little items that weren't listed in the course requirements."

"I see. Hence the formidable agility." He chuckled. "It should serve you well in the coming days."

Tessa peeked around Merlin. Galahad stood like a bronze colossus, his hands fisted at his sides, his jaw clenched. "Boy, is he pissed. If looks could kill—"

"Fortunately for you, his can't. Mine, on the other hand—"

"Merlin." Arthur's voice carried a note of impatience. "If you and the lady are quite ready, I'm certain the rest of us are eager to get on with it."

"We are, sire." Merlin bowed.

"Do I have to curtsy again?" Tessa said for the wizard's ears alone.

"The way you do it, there's very little point."

"Galahad." The king nodded at the knight.

Galahad jerked his gaze away from her and toward the king. "Your Majesty?"

"If you would join Merlin and Lady Tessa."

Galahad nodded sharply. Within a moment he stood on Merlin's other side, towering over the magician. Why did he look so much bigger when he was mad? He kept his gaze fastened on the king and didn't so much as glance her way. He didn't need to. The rigid lines of his stance, the hard thrust of his chin and his clenched fists spoke volumes. Tessa shifted to keep as much of the magician between her and the Big Guy as possible.

Arthur studied the knight for a long moment. "I hope you realize, Galahad, I am not a fool."

Galahad shook his head in surprise. "Sire, I would never suggest such a thing."

"I have long been aware of your desire to seek the Grail."

Galahad stepped forward eagerly. "Then, sire, I—"

"However." Arthur's voice carried a quiet authority that echoed through the hall and caught the attention of anyone who was not already riveted to the drama playing out at the head table, with the possible exception of Viviane, who simply examined her well-manicured nails. "You have not been at my court for any length of time in the last ten years."

"No, sire, but I—"

"Therefore I have not had the opportunity to seriously assess your fitness for such an undertaking."

Galahad raised his chin. "Have I not proven myself worthy through the years of doing your bidding?"

"Indeed, you have carried out my bidding with remarkable success. I could not have asked for more." Arthur leaned forward, elbows on the table, hands clasped together, index fingers steepled. "Now, I do. Much more. Regardless of whether you believe this to be your heart's desire, you do so in my name.

" 'Tis not easy for a king to send a man, any man, on a mission of this nature." The king paused and for the briefest moment seemed older and tired, as if the burden of governing was too heavy to bear. The perception vanished as fast as it had appeared and he was once again the Arthur of legend. "This quest will be fraught with difficulty. 'Twill certainly require some sacrifice and may well cost you your life."

"I am not daunted by the prospect, sire."

"I did not think you would be, my boy." The corners of Arthur's lips quirked upward slightly as if he wanted to smile but restrained himself. "I never imagined mere danger would dampen your enthusiasm."

"Never, Your Majesty."

Arthur narrowed his eyes and stared silently at Galahad as if looking for the answers to unasked questions or assessing his nature or evaluating his very soul. The king's gaze and the knight's fused in speechless communication. The seconds ticked by.

Tessa shifted from foot to foot. How long would this last? It was a contest to see who would flinch first. If she'd ever thought standing in front of a principal or a boss or a judge was tough, it was nothing compared to this appraisal by a king.

Abruptly, Arthur nodded as if pleased by whatever it was he found. A communal sigh of released tension swept through the room. "Very well then. If this is indeed what you wish?"

"It is, Your Majesty."

A rueful smile lingered about the king's lips. "There is much of your father in you, boy."

"Thank you, sire," Galahad and Lancelot said in unison.

" 'Tis not always a compliment for a reckless son to be compared to a reckless father."

"Your Majesty." Lancelot jumped to his feet. "I do not believe *reckless* is entirely appropriate. I should think *fearless* or *courageous* or even *he*—"

"Enough, Lance." The king laughed. "Unless *foolhardy* was the next item on your long list of virtues, sit down."

"Foolhardy? Hah!" Lancelot sank back in his chair with an indignant huff. "I was going to say *heroic*."

Guinevere cast him an amused glance, as if she'd heard his boasting before and it was simply an endearing trait.

"Reckless," Arthur said firmly. "I too shared your brash nature in our younger days. 'Tis past time to let your son carry the standard we once bore."

"I am not ready to join the old men who sit in the market and tell tales of better days yet, sire," Lancelot muttered.

"Nor am I," the king said sharply.

"Let me go with him then." Lancelot leaned toward Arthur eagerly. " 'Twould be a grand adventure for father and son. Think of it, Arthur, together we—"

"No more, Lance." The king's voice rang with a quiet command and a touch of regret. "I need your counsel here."

"But, sire—"

"Lance." Guinevere laid her hand on his arm. "The king depends on your guidance and your wisdom. You cannot deny him that." She stared at him with an intensity that belied the lightness of her tone. Had their affair already begun?

Lancelot started to say something then looked as if he thought better of it. He shrugged and turned his attention back toward his son, his expression at once envious and proud.

Galahad slanted a quick glance in Tessa's direction and her stomach knotted. She'd half hoped he'd forgotten all about her. No such luck. "Sire, regarding the Lady Tessa—"

"Patience, Galahad. I should think you will need that attribute on this journey. Work on it, my boy. All will be revealed to you in due time." The king leaned back in his chair and waved a casual hand at the wizard. "Merlin?"

"Your Majesty." Merlin took a half step forward and cleared his throat in the style of a grand orator or a bad actor. The entertainment was obviously about to begin.

" 'Tis detailed in the writings, ancient and wise, the chalice of the Last Supper was given into the keeping of Joseph of Arimathea for the protection offered by his name and his house and his progeny." Merlin's voice grew stronger with each word. Tessa glanced around the hall. Spellbound, everyone from Galahad to the lords and ladies of the court to the lowliest servant stared, listening to a story they'd probably heard a thousand times. The medieval version of a rerun.

" 'Tis further said Joseph, in his wisdom, carried the Grail to Britain. 'Tis here the mists of time intervene. Did Joseph bury the Grail at Glastonbury, as some would have us believe, or is its hiding place in another location as yet unknown? The trail is lost but for the words of prophets and seers and men of far greater wisdom than the humble servant who stands before you." Merlin bowed low.

"Give me a break," Tessa said under her breath.

"The path to the Grail is fraught with danger and challenges destined to test the courage and spirit of any who dare tread upon it. 'Tis written"—Merlin raised his hand high, snapped his fingers and opened his hand. A flame leaped from his palm then died, revealing a tightly wound scroll. Onlookers gasped. She had to give Merlin credit, he knew how to work a crowd.

He threw her a smug smile over his shoulder. She rolled her gaze toward the ceiling and sighed. She'd never get used to the arrogance of medieval men. Knights or magicians.

Merlin unrolled the aged document. The parchment crackled in the still of the room. The crowd seemed to lean toward the wizard as if with one mind. In spite of herself, Tessa held her breath.

Merlin glanced at the scroll then up at the king. " 'Tis a guide, Your Majesty, to the Grail."

A shocked murmur ran through the assembly. Galahad stepped toward the wizard. Lancelot rose to his feet. Arthur's eyes flashed and he leaned forward. Even Viviane looked interested.

"Merlin," barely controlled anger hardened the king's words, "though it has been many years since I last sent a knight in search of the Grail, I am haunted still by the ghosts of those who departed here never to return. Why have you not shown me this before?"

Merlin's black gaze met and locked with the king's. The wizard's voice was quiet. " 'Twas not the proper time, Arthur."

They stared at each other for an endless moment. "I have never questioned you before, Merlin."

"Then do not begin now, sire."

"No." A shadow of resignation or sorrow passed over the king's aristocratic features so quickly she thought she'd imagined it. "Now would not be the time." He sank back in his chair. "Proceed."

Merlin nodded and glanced at Galahad. "I have already warned of the hazards that lie before you and the trials to be met."

"I am well aware of the obstacles." Galahad's voice was quiet and strong. "I am prepared."

"Excellent. Prepared is indeed forearmed. Here is written the challenges that must be surmounted." Merlin glanced at the scroll in his hands and paused in a melodramatic manner, increasing the tension blanketing the hall.

"When the peril is naught save illusion,
When the infidel comes to the fold,

When the offering can be no greater
Then the truth shall be revealed
and that which each man seeks shall be his."

Stunned silence hung over the room.

"What in the hell is that supposed to mean?" Tessa said in a low tone.

" 'Tis a riddle." Galahad cast her a superior glance.

"I know it's a riddle," Tessa whispered. "I hate riddles."

"I did warn you, my dear," Merlin rolled up the scroll, "to learn to like them."

"Mud is clearer than this, Merlin." Arthur drew his brows together. "What does it mean, the infidel comes to the fold?"

Merlin shrugged. "I cannot say, sire. 'Tis up to them to decipher the meaning."

"Them?" Galahad pounced on the word like a cat on a mouse.

Merlin nodded sagely. "Them."

"Galahad," Arthur said, "I know this will not be to your liking and I well understand your concerns, yet it has been decided." Arthur shook his head as if he couldn't believe it himself. "Lady Tessa will join you on your quest."

Disbelief rolled through the assembly. Hushed voices carried expressions of shock.

"A woman? On a quest?"

"Absurd. She'll get him killed."

"Nay. They'll both be killed."

" 'Tis yet another who will not return."

"Your Majesty." Galahad leveled an unflinching gaze at the king. "Is this wise? I cannot believe—"

"I could not believe it either. 'Tis not my doing. 'Tis Merlin who insists there is no other way." Arthur waved at the magician.

Galahad turned toward the wizard, a stubborn look in his eye. "Merlin, you entrusted Lady Tessa into my keeping."

Merlin nodded. "That shall continue."

"Yet I cannot guarantee her safety in a venture such as this."

Merlin narrowed his eyes. "Safety is no longer a concern. She will accompany you. There is nothing more to be said."

"Pardon me?" Tessa glanced from Merlin to Galahad and back. "Safety's no longer a concern?"

"Safety is nothing but an illusion," Merlin said out of the corner of his mouth. "It's a clever card trick, a shyster's shell game, a special effect."

She heaved a weak sigh. "I like special effects."

"I shall not take a mere woman on a quest." Galahad eyes darkened with warning.

"And I hate the word *mere*," Tessa mumbled.

"Then you shall not go." Merlin's voice was cool.

"Very well," Galahad said evenly. "I shall not go."

"Yes, Galahad, you shall. And in the company of the Lady Tessa." Arthur rose to his feet. "I wish to speak to you privately on this matter. All three of you." Arthur stepped to the edge of the dais, down the few steps to the floor then toward the back of the hall and a series of archways. Merlin, Galahad and Tessa followed.

"I always did hate going to the principal's office," Tessa murmured.

"Quiet," Merlin snapped.

Arthur strode down a short corridor to a large wooden door. A well-trained servant reached the entry a pace before the king, jerked it open and bowed low.

Tessa stepped into a council chamber, about a quarter the size of the great hall. A massive tapestry depicting what might have been Arthur and Guinevere's coronation or wedding hung above a huge stone hearth. One of the largest tables she'd ever seen dominated the room. Big enough to easily seat three dozen or more, its size was eclipsed by its shape.

"It's round!" She gasped. "It's the Round Table!"

Arthur and Galahad exchanged glances. Merlin gazed heavenward.

"Indeed it is, Lady Tessa," Arthur said, his words measured as if he wasn't sure of her sanity. "Round."

She stepped forward and rubbed her hand along the uneven wooden surface, polished only by the hands of the men who sat around it. "You don't understand. In spite of any prejudices I had going into this, I was kind of disappointed. Nobody had mentioned the Round Table, so I was beginning to think it never really existed."

"Sire, perhaps you should tell her why the table is round," Merlin said, an innocent note in his voice.

Arthur cast him an impatient look. " 'Tis no secret. The table is round—"

"I know this one." She grinned at the king. "It's round so that there's no head or foot, no one is above or below anyone else. Everybody who sits here sits as an equal."

Arthur's brows pulled together and he stared at her. "What an interesting concept. I hadn't thought of that. I quite like the idea."

"Thanks." Pleasure flushed through her.

"Very good indeed. I shall have to use that." Wry amusement glittered in his eye. "In truth, my lady, the table is round because a king, above all men, needs to be able to see the faces and the eyes of those seeking to give him counsel to know the veracity of their words and the intention in their hearts."

"Oh. Right." A vague feeling of disappointment touched her. The common-sense reason for the shape of the most famous table in history wasn't nearly as impressive as the myth.

Arthur dismissed the servant with a nod and waited until he left, the door thudding shut behind him. The king stood a bit taller than she'd expected with a noble bearing that left no doubt this was someone special. You could see it in his eyes, clear and as crystal blue as the water of a mountain lake. And the man practically reeked of charisma. He'd make one hell of a politician. Americans would elect him president on the basis of his charm alone. Or maybe on just the square set of his jaw.

"Tessa," Merlin growled.

"Sorry." She smiled in apology. This was not the time to consider the bizarre implications of this particular President Arthur.

Arthur drew a deep breath. "Galahad, my boy, I know this is not as you envisioned it."

"Sire." Galahad stepped forward. "I cannot take a woman with me. 'Twould be folly of the highest order."

"Exactly what I said when Merlin first approached me with this." Arthur glanced at the magician. "Merlin?"

Merlin shook his head. "It cannot be helped. Galahad, I see things others can only dream of. I know much of what the fates have in store for all of us. Do not doubt me when I say without Lady Tessa by your side, you cannot be successful."

"I do not believe that!"

"You must believe," Merlin said sharply.

"And you must succeed." Arthur paced the room. "When last I sent knights, many years ago, to find the Grail, 'twas not much more serious than a lark. An adventure eagerly sought after by men of courage. Oh certainly, it cost many their lives but 'tis a hard, cruel world beyond the gates of Camelot. I have to admit, I rather envied them their demise coming as it did in the pursuit of the most honorable of quests.

"Now, all is different." The king paused as if saying the words out loud gave them a reality he preferred not to face. "The country is at a crossroads, Galahad. Unrest is brewing in the land. Mordred has as much as admitted his hand in it."

"But you had him here in your grasp, sire." Galahad's voice rang with disbelief. "Yet you let him go free."

"He is the heir to this kingdom and to all I hold dear." Arthur shook his head. "His words were at once threatening and vague. As yet, I have no real proof. And while he can stir up the caldron of dissent, I doubt he has enough followers to unseat me."

"Your Majesty." Galahad's jaw clenched. "Say but the word and I would gladly lead your army against him."

"No. He is still my son." A note of anguish, quiet and intense, underlaid the simple statement. Tessa's heart twisted for the pain of a king and a father. Arthur heaved a resigned sigh. "Besides, 'tis no longer enough. This land and its people have always put a great deal of trust in what cannot be seen. Magic, prophecy and the like. Once, I alone was able to give them something to believe in but it appears with familiarity grows dissatisfaction."

His gaze drifted up to linger on the tapestry. He spoke as much to himself as to them. "All I ever wanted was peace and prosperity. A good life for all in a good land. And it has been thus for a very long time. Perhaps 'tis only in the next world where such things last forever."

Arthur rubbed his temple in a gesture of weariness then raised his chin, his voice brisk. "The people need a cause to pull their hearts together, to forge us once again into a country proud and strong. There is no cause more powerful than the quest for the Grail. Although the legend decreeing whosoever finds the Grail shall become its guardian has yet to be tested, should it prove true, the mere knowledge of your success," he glanced at Merlin, "and I assume we shall receive such confirmation?"

The magician nodded.

"The news of your accomplishment will instill pride in every man, woman and child and unify the country once again. And even Mordred's influence will be for naught."

"I vow to you, sire, I will not fail." Galahad's eyes burned with fervor.

"And what of you, Lady Tessa?" Arthur raised a regal brow. "Do you give your promise as well?"

Three sets of eyes pinned her. What would happen if she said no right here in front of the king? Arthur seemed like a good guy. Given chivalry and all that, he'd never make her do something this dangerous if she didn't want to. Merlin's eyes narrowed. Right. She'd be a toad or dinosaur lunch faster than you could whistle the theme to *The Twilight Zone*. She smiled weakly. "I'm in."

Galahad's jaw clenched as if he'd hoped she'd decline.

"Excellent." Merlin beamed.

"Thank you, my dear," Arthur's voice was solemn. He stepped toward her, took her hand and raised it to his lips. His gaze met hers and her breath caught at the look of regret in his eye. The man knew exactly what he was asking of them and she suspected he wished wholeheartedly he didn't have to. "God be with you, my lady. I will pray for your success and the safety of your journey."

"Thank you." She turned to Merlin. "Now that everything's out in the open, I have a few more questions. First of all, what is this riddle business?"

" 'Tis a guide, to lead you to the Grail," Merlin said.

"Don't give me that," she said with exasperation. "It's a riddle. A lousy, confusing riddle. I hate riddles and I don't want to bet my life on figuring one out."

Arthur smiled in a wry manner. "Merlin, are you certain of this?"

Merlin nodded. "Quite, sire."

"And she will not drive him mad in the bargain?"

Merlin spread his hands in an exaggerated gesture of resignation. "One of many challenges that lie ahead for them both."

"Excuse me?" Tessa glared with indignation.

A skeptical chuckle slipped from the king's lips.

"Very well. As always, I defer to your counsel." The king strode toward the door. "Now, I have other matters to attend to, therefore I shall take my leave. You have much to discuss, plans to make and it would be best if it were begun without delay."

He pulled open the door, then stopped and turned to Tessa. " 'Tis not difficult to see Merlin was right about you. You have a great deal of courage, my lady, although I suspect you do not know it yet. And while I am certain he does not know it yet, Galahad is indeed a lucky man. I leave him in your care."

Her throat tightened. "I'll do my best."

"As for you, Galahad, 'tis a sad truth but I fear we will not meet in this world again. I shall miss you, my boy." Arthur considered him silently. "And I envy you. Were it possible, I would go in your place. But my duty lies here. If you fail, I am all that remains between the people and turmoil. 'Tis little enough to offer them but 'tis all I have."

"I beg to differ, Your Majesty." Admiration shone in the younger man's eyes. " 'Tis a great deal."

Arthur acknowledged the compliment with a terse nod and stepped out of the room, shutting the door behind him.

"Wow," Tessa breathed, "now that's a king."

"I have always thought so." A note of sorrow sounded in Merlin's voice.

"He knows, doesn't he?" she said softly.

"Knows what?" Galahad glanced from Tessa to Merlin.

Merlin nodded. "He suspects."

Understanding, abrupt and complete, surged through her. "And nothing we do will change that, will it?"

"Change what?" Galahad snapped.

The wizard sighed. "Only the details can change. The overall picture remains the same."

"What remains?" Galahad's voice rose.

She widened her eyes and stared at him. "Holy shi—" Tessa's gaze snapped to Merlin's. "He didn't make it, did he? In real life, the first time this little story played out, he failed, didn't he? Why didn't I realize this before?" She smacked her hand to her forehead. "It makes perfect sense."

"Nothing makes sense to me!" Galahad's bellow filled the room.

Tessa ignored him. "There are so many little things here that don't mesh with the legend. This is one of them, isn't it?"

"You are astute," Merlin said calmly.

"What legend?" Galahad roared.

"Would you do something about him? That between one second and the next thing?" Tessa waved an impatient hand at the knight. "Freeze-frame him."

"That's probably best."

Galahad froze as if a pause button had just been pushed. The man made a great-looking statue.

"That's a handy trick," Tessa said with admiration.

"I enjoy it." Merlin's manner was casual. "I could teach it to you, if you'd like."

"Really?" She glanced at Galahad. "You think I could do that?"

"Perhaps."

"That would be great." Tessa grinned. "I could just see a couple of people I know frozen in time while I rearranged furniture and strategically positioned buckets of water and—"

Merlin raised a brow.

"—and we can discuss it later," she said quickly. "When this is wrapped up. Right now, we have to talk."

At once her father's recliner and its mate appeared in the room. "Nice touch but I'm not in the mood to be comfortable."

"Your loss." The recliners disappeared. "I rather think you should enjoy any modicum of comfort available." Merlin grinned wickedly. "While you still can."

"I want to know what really happened. I know the legend. Now, I want the truth."

"Does it matter?"

"Yes. I need to know what to expect."

"I believe I have already explained that what was true once may not necessarily be so again."

"I know, I know." Impatience edged her voice. "You said it before. Chance and probability. The spinning wheel and all that."

"The outcome may well change with every spin of the wheel."

"But you said nothing could change Arthur's fate."

"Arthur's fate is the fate of his country. The how and the why can change but not the end result."

"And Galahad?" She chose her words carefully, trying to work out the convoluted idea of what portions of history could change and what couldn't. "He's small potatoes in all this, isn't he? Even if he succeeds this time, it won't really matter will it? It won't make a bit of difference?"

Merlin's lips compressed into a grim line. His voice was low and filled with regret. "No."

"Look. I know that what happened before doesn't

have to happen again but it is possible, right? You can already see that Guinevere and Lancelot have something going."

"Not as of yet."

"Oh, come on. Maybe it hasn't gotten to the point of an actual affair but anybody with an ounce of insight can see there's a definite spark between them. It seems to me like a classic case of a busy husband, a wife left alone too much and a best friend."

Merlin shook his head. "The frailty of man's own makeup will always spell his ruin."

"No kidding." The last thing she wanted was to get into a debate about the deficiencies of mankind, especially when it came to sex. "So history, their history, Galahad's can repeat itself exactly, can't it?"

"Correct."

"Don't you think I need to know what mistakes he made? What problems he ran into?" Merlin seemed to consider her words and she pressed her point. "How can it hurt? I already agreed to go with him. I promised. I gave my word."

Merlin eyed her as if debating how much to reveal.

"It's bad, isn't it?" A cold hand squeezed her heart. "He was killed, wasn't he? He never found the Grail because he died, didn't he?"

"All men die, Tessa, sooner or later. Some breathe their last in service to king and country and some pass quietly to the next world in their beds, their last thoughts filled with the sum total of their lives. Satisfaction or self-loathing. Contentment or bitterness." Merlin paused. "Galahad lived a very long life."

"Thank God." Relief washed through her and she exhaled a long breath. "I thought for sure—"

"He died an old man, Tessa, alone and filled with self-loathing." The wizard stopped for a moment as if gathering unpleasant memories. "Britain was in disarray, Arthur and Lancelot long dead, the world Galahad cherished fading to a distant memory. Forgotten were the triumphs of his youth. He could not put his failure to find the Grail to rest and spent the last years of his life wondering if he had done this differently or that better, would it have made a difference. In many ways he felt responsible for the end of it all."

Tessa gazed at Galahad, frozen in his anger. Even motionless he was a powerful figure exuding strength and confidence. The idea of him spending his last days as a broken old man was more than she could bear. "There's a chance we won't find it, isn't there?"

"A very good chance."

She glanced at the wizard. "Does it even exist?"

"You must believe, my dear."

She stepped closer to Galahad's suspended figure and stared. She'd never met a man like this and wondered if anyone comparable had lived before or since. Probably not. He was one of a kind. "I've always had a hard time believing in anything you can't see or touch. I've always needed proof to believe."

"I know." Merlin sighed. "It's one of your more annoying qualities. However, it's quite entertaining to watch you change your mind."

She wanted to reach up and run her hand along the side of his face. Just to make certain he was real, of course. Not out of any weird need to touch him. "I haven't changed my mind."

Merlin chuckled. "You did not believe in any of this

before we met. Now, you do. There is much more you have to learn about belief and faith and what is and isn't real before your days here are finished."

"More?" She pulled her gaze away from the knight and swiveled to face the magician. "How much more?"

"If I told you"—Merlin smirked—"it would take all the fun out of it."

She widened her eyes. "Fun for whom?"

"Me."

Tessa groaned. "I should have known. I can't imagine I'll be having that great a time. For one thing, in case you haven't noticed, he's really mad about being stuck with me."

"He'll get over it."

"And for another, why a riddle?"

"Riddles, poems, puzzles, that's how these things work. This is a Quest. Grand and noble and virtuous. It's the stuff of tales told through the centuries and sagas related late into the night and epics passed on from father to son. It's not a scavenger hunt. Such a venture requires at the very least a riddle to solve." Merlin stared down his nose at her as if she had an IQ too low to support life. "In your own rather distinctive term—duh, Tessa."

"Well, pardon me for not being up on the rules." Tessa glared. "This is my first quest. I was hoping for something a little more specific than sappy poetic phrases about illusions and infidels."

"I thought it was quite well written myself," Merlin murmured.

"It was charming. But what does it mean?"

"You honestly expect me to tell you?"

Hope flickered. "Would you?"

Merlin sniffed. "Hardly."

"I didn't think so." She considered him for a moment. "But how about a little help?"

"What kind of help?"

"Oh, I don't know. Nothing too significant," she said with a laid-back manner as if she didn't care what he said one way or the other. "Let me think. Maybe something like . . . oh . . . say . . . a map?"

"A map?"

"Sure, a map." She tried and failed to keep the eagerness out of her voice. "You know. Like, say, a treasure map. Something simple. Maybe even a basic road map with a few pertinent details marked."

"Something like *X* marks the spot, perhaps?" Merlin's voice was thoughtful.

Relief surged through her. "That would work."

He drew his brows together. "But is it enough, do you think?"

"Sure, anything extra would be appreciated," she said slowly. What was he up to?

"Perhaps something more along the lines of a Rand McNally atlas than a simple map."

"An atlas?"

"Certainly. With drawings of tiny little knights on horseback pointing the way to the Grail?" His gaze was innocent but a sarcastic twinkle gleamed in his eye.

"Very funny, Merlin."

He ignored her. "Or maybe I should forget about the map entirely and put up road signs instead? *Grail crossing, thirty miles.* Better yet—billboards. I can see it now." He held his hands up as if framing a sign.

"This way to the Grail. Turn at King's Avenue, then ahead two blocks. Clean toilets available."

"Let me tell you, Mr. Wizard, this place could certainly use some clean restrooms. Have you been in what passes for a bathroom here?"

"It's the bloody Middle Ages!"

"I know that! It's hard to miss. I was just asking for help." Tessa huffed. "You don't have to get so nasty about it."

Irritation washed across his face. "It's a quest, Tessa. Not a treasure hunt. Not a game. The answer is not Colonel Mustard in the drawing room with the candelabra!"

"Candlestick," she snapped. "I don't get it. I know you want Galahad to succeed. Why the big deal about giving me a hand?"

"I have given you the riddle."

"Fat lot of help that is!"

"It's an excellent riddle," he said loftily.

"It stinks."

"It tells you everything you need to know."

Frustration raised her voice. "But what if I can't figure it out?"

"You have to work at it."

"My mind doesn't operate that way. I don't understand riddles. And definitely not this one."

"You will." It was as clear an order as she'd ever heard.

She narrowed her eyes in defiance. "I won't!"

"You'd better." Merlin's black eyes gleamed. "It's his only chance. And one last thing, my dear."

"What now?"

"Hear me well, Tessa. From the moment you and

Galahad begin the quest to the moment of its resolution, be that success or failure, triumph or tragedy, win or lose, you are on your own. Totally and completely. I will not be able to help you in any way. Those are the Rules." Abruptly, she realized he was fading. "Do not depend on anyone but yourselves to see it through."

"You can't throw something like that at me then disappear! That's a pretty wimpy way to win an argument!"

"Sometimes, Tessa, it's not at all how you play the game—"

"You're cheating!" she yelled.

"—it's only winning that counts." Merlin's laughter hung in the room.

"Wait, hold it, stop!" She gestured at Galahad's frozen figure behind her. "What am I supposed to with him?"

"Nay, my lady, what am I to do with you?"

Chapter Ten

❧❀❧

Galahad's voice rang hard and cold and 'twas all he could do to keep it under control.

Tessa stiffened. Surely she was not afraid of him? Although she, no doubt, believed she had reason enough to be, as indeed she did. Still, while he was not pleased with her, he would never harm her. Galahad cast a quick glance around the chamber. And where was the sorcerer? No matter. Tessa was the one he wished to speak with and he would no longer allow her evasions.

"Tessa." The command was clipped and sharp.

Her shoulders rose and fell as if she'd taken a breath for courage. She turned to face him, a smile sweet as a morning in spring upon her face. "Galahad."

Past time for pleasantries. "Why are you here?"

"Did you know when you're mad a vein throbs right at your temple?" Her eyes widened with feigned innocence.

"I am in complete control of my faculties. I am, however, angry." He stepped toward her, his hands clenched at his sides, his nails biting into his palms. Better there than around her neck. "Answer me. Why are you here? Who are you?"

She stepped back and thrust out her hand. "Tessa St. James. I think we've met."

"Do not toy with me." His voice was harsh. Perhaps around her neck was not such a bad idea. "I know your name. Now I wish to know your purpose."

Uncertainty flashed in her eyes. "That's kind of hard to explain."

"Attempt it."

"You're not going to like it."

"Hah! What is yet another thing to add to the growing list of that which I dislike. Your answer, Tessa. Now."

"I just hope you can take it, that's all."

Even when her phrases were muddled her meaning was clear. He narrowed his eyes. "I can take it."

"Okay." She glanced about the room as if looking for salvation that was not to be found.

"Tessa!"

"MerlinbroughtmeheretohelpyoufindtheGrail," she said in one long breath, squeezed her eyes closed and buried her face in her hands. Did she indeed expect him to smite her where she stood? If news of this ilk had come from another he would be sorely tempted.

He stared at her, struggling to accept the inevitable. He'd known all along Merlin had a plan in mind for Tessa and himself. He'd thought 'twould be paltry and frivolous, a matter to while away an afternoon but nothing of true importance. Not until she'd whispered in his ear had he suspected the truth.

Tessa peeked at him through her fingers. "Aren't you going to say anything?"

Galahad stared for a long moment. "Why?"

"Why? I don't know I just assumed you'd have something to say about this."

"By all that is holy, woman!" His patience snapped. " 'Tis not what I meant. Why are you here to help me?"

"I honestly don't know for sure." She shrugged. "Something about you not being able to do it without me and my having something you need."

"It makes no sense." He ran his fingers through his hair. "No sense at all."

"I thought it was pretty weird myself. Especially since I've never been on a quest before. Let's face it, I have no practical questing experience. Oh sure, I went camping with my folks a couple of times as a kid but nothing like—"

"Would you cease that infernal babbling!"

Tessa eyed him in a thoughtful manner, quiet for a mere handful of seconds. "Why aren't you yelling at me?"

" 'Twould do no good to raise my voice." Resignation washed through him. He had no choice in the matter. "My king and his counselor have decreed you will accompany me. There is no argument to be had. Yet I do not understand what aid you could possibly render to me. At least not on a venture of this nature."

"That's what I thought but—wait a minute." Her brows pulled together. "What do you mean by that?"

" 'Tis apparent, my lady, as to my meaning." His gaze traveled over her. 'Twas not an unpleasant journey.

"You look like a customer checking out a used Volvo."

A Volvo?

She planted her hands on her hips. "What are you going to do next? Kick my tires? Check under my hood? Take me out for a test drive?" At once a charming blush swept up her face. Galahad wondered precisely what a "test drive" would entail and suspected it might well be a pleasure.

"You are indeed a comely female, Tessa—"

"You're pretty cute yourself, pal."

"—not unlike a flower in summer, lovely and fragile—"

"I'm tougher than I look," she said quickly.

"—but a man risking life and limb for a treasure such as the Grail needs not a blossom but a sword. Why did they not give me a knight to guard my back or an army to defeat the foes that will surely cross my path?" He shook his head in disgust. "Why have they saddled me with you?"

"You know your attitude leaves a lot to be desired," she said slowly. "And it's really beginning to tick me off."

"Hah! If that means what I think it does you are not the only one ticked off." He crossed his arms over his chest. "Tell me, Tessa St. James, why you?"

"I told you, Merlin said you can't do it without me."

"Why?"

"I don't know. I have something you need."

"Oh?" He raised a brow in scorn. "What do you have that I need?"

"Probably humility," she snapped.

"I am humble enough to know that I have no chance to succeed with a woman at my side."

"Well, buck up, Big Guy. You don't have a choice."

"Nay. The decision has been made for me." He studied her for a moment. She was small but appeared sturdy. Aye, she had felt so in his arms today. Sturdy and well made. Would it be so bad to have her by his side? And had he not regretted that he had not the time needed to learn more of her nature and her land and the feelings she aroused within him? "Very well. You may accompany me."

"Be still my fluttering heart."

He ignored the unbecoming sarcasm in her tone. " 'Twill not be easy."

"That's a surprise."

"I will not put up with the delay caused by servants or carts. We will do without such encumbrances." He paced the room, an idea teasing the edge of his mind. "You will ride a horse."

"Fine." She grimaced. "How hard can it be? A horse is just a big pony, right?"

He stared at her. He had no desire to have a woman's, any woman's, life in his hands. This was a woman obviously unused to the deprivations of an undertaking of this type. A woman who would no doubt turn and run at the prospect of the crude conditions this quest would require, let alone the danger. Could she be encouraged to do so before they left? 'Twould be in her best interest for him to make certain the fair lady knew exactly what difficulties lay ahead.

" 'Twill not be an easy venture. We will sleep on the ground. Hunt for food to supplement the minimal provisions we will take. Discomfort is the least of it. Obstacles risking life and limb will confront us at every turn."

"I can handle it." Was her voice a bit weaker? Did apprehension dim the glow of her eyes?

He smiled to himself. "As I will not take Bartholomew, you will perform the duties of a squire. You shall tend to the meals and the camp. You will make certain the horses are watered and fed. You will—"

"I don't think so."

He stopped. Any fear he'd tried so carefully to fuel was gone, replaced by the obstinate look he already knew too well. What had he said wrong?

"I'm not going to play maid, cook and bottle washer in the wilderness." She shook her head slowly. "I'll share in the grunt work but I won't do it by myself. We're partners in this little adventure. Equals."

He snorted in disbelief. "No woman is equal to a man."

"Not physically maybe—"

"Come now, Tessa." Surely, she did not believe this nonsense?

"In fact, I've always figured women were actually superior to men."

" 'Tis true that a woman indeed has some qualities in greater abundance than man." The image of Dindrane flashed through his mind and his voice softened. "Their spirits are kinder, their natures gentler—"

"Oh, get off it."

"—with some exceptions," he said pointedly.

"I rese—"

" 'Tis the truth, Tessa, that a woman's mind is inferior as is her character."

"Inferior?" Tessa's mouth dropped open. 'Twas clear she could not refute his statement. Triumph swelled in his chest.

He favored her with a superior smile. "Indeed. 'Tis well known that the qualities valued in a man—honor, loyalty, courage—are lacking in a woman."

"Lacking?" She stared wide-eyed.

He chuckled. " 'Tis why women are for kissing, not for questing."

"Really? Tell me more." Her voice was cool but anger flashed in her eyes. 'Twas not the look of defeat. His sense of victory faltered. She stepped to the fireplace and studied the tapestry over the mantel as if she was more interested in it than the discussion at hand. Was her manner meant to disarm him? "About these manly, macho things. For example, tell me about honor."

"Honor? 'Tis a man's solemn vow to king and country. Or his word given freely to another. Or—"

"A promise?" she said innocently.

"Indeed." What was the blasted woman trying to say?

"So going back on a promise would not be at all honorable, would it?"

"Nay. A man's word is his bond." Confidence rang in his voice.

"That's what I thought." She turned toward him, a smug smile on her face. "You promised to let me help you."

Success shattered all together. " 'Twas a trick. I knew not what such a vow would entail."

"Too bad." She walked to the table and trailed her fingers over the wooden surface. "According to your own rules, you have to let me help you."

"You may help. You may tend the fire and cook the meals and—"

"Absolutely not!" She slapped her hand flat on the

table and glared. "Look, pal, I didn't ask for this, any of it. I don't even want to be here. But I am. And like it or not, I'm part of it. A big part. I'm not a bit of excess baggage you have to cart along. And I'm not going to be relegated to menial details, up to and including cooking and cleaning. I don't do that at home and I'm not doing it here. No way, no how."

She stepped toward him and poked her finger at his chest. "And furthermore, get that "women are inferior" garbage out of your mind right now. First—I'm not stupid. I have advanced degrees and a fair amount of respect in my field. Secondly, when it comes to country, I'm as loyal and patriotic as the next person. I always get choked up at *The Star-Spangled Banner.*" A jab of her finger accompanied each point. Galahad stared down at her. By the saints the woman was impressive in her fury. "Beyond that, I'm honest to a fault and I've never, ever broken my promise.

"And as for courage," she glared up at him, "when I was a kid, a tornado passed right over my house. I was terrified. Even so, that was nothing compared to how scared I've been by what's happened to me in the last few days and what's coming up. But I'm not crying my eyes out or cowering in a corner or—"

" 'Tis not enough to say you are not daunted by what you have yet to face." He caught her hand against his chest. "You do not understand. You have never called upon the courage of which you speak. You have not yet been put to the test. Women are weak, Tessa. They—"

She tried to pull her hand away but he held it fast. "I don't—"

"If you were a man, if you were a knight, your fortitude would have long since been tried and 'twould be no doubt as to your na—"

"Then test me." Challenge glittered in her eye. "Test me right here and now."

"Test you?" He released her with a scornful laugh. "Test a woman?"

"Exactly." She strode across the floor, determination in every footfall, then whirled and shook a finger at him. "You name it. Whatever kind of test you want. Sword fight, maybe?"

"Do not be absurd. I would never raise a sword against a woman even in jest. You are far too small." In two swift strides, he stood before her and grasped her hands in his, turning them palms up. "Your hands are too delicate to wield such a weapon. You could scarce lift it off the ground."

"No swords then." She jutted her chin out in a stubborn manner, his anger fading in the face of her resolve. She pulled her hands from his and for a moment, loss swept through him. "What about a joust?"

He shook his head, amusement abruptly replacing his irritation. Whatever else, her spirit could not be questioned. "A lance too is a heavy burden for many men let alone a woman. 'Twould be unfair to give you such a test. Besides," he could not resist a grin, "jousting is upon horseback."

She paled slightly, confirming the obvious: the lady knew naught of horses. Still, 'twas no retreat in her eye. "Then you think of something."

Was this the answer he sought? The way to keep her from harm? Would she not be safer if she were in the position of squire? 'Twas no doubt otherwise she would be at his side and in harm's way. "And if you fail my test?"

"You and I both know, whether we like it or not, I'm along for the ride. But if I can't pass your test," she hesitated then drew a deep breath, "I'll do what you want. I'll take care of the meals and," she shuddered, "the horses."

"Agreed then." He grinned. "I shall pre—"

"Wait a minute. I have no intentions of flunking this little quiz."

"Very well." He could not keep the tolerant tone from his voice. "What prize do you claim should you win?"

"*When* I win." A sly smile lifted the corners of her mouth. "You have to treat me like one of the guys. You know, like just another knight."

"But you are—"

"Except for the physical stuff," she said quickly. "I know I don't have your strength or your power but I am fairly well coordinated and relatively agile—"

"Sister Abigail," he murmured.

She nodded. "She taught gym too. But beyond that—I'm smart."

"Indeed." In his anger over her intrusion in his plans he'd forgotten how clever she really was. 'Twas was one of the attributes he found most intriguing about her.

"I'm not about to do anything that will get us killed but you're going to have to learn to trust me."

"Trust?" He stared at the earnest expression on her face. "And do you trust me?"

"Sure," she said as if she were not certain she spoke the truth. "I trust you."

"With your life?"

She paused then squared her shoulders and looked up at him. "With my life."

At once he knew what to do. "I had planned to leave on the morrow at daybreak. 'Twill be the time then to put you to a test of my devising. Succeed or fail, we leave when the matter is concluded."

She met his gaze with a steady, unflinching stare. "Let's go for it."

He looked down at her for a long moment. 'Twas not necessary to put her to any trial. That she was willing to submit to such a test was proof enough of her fortitude. Was it this aspect of her nature that called to him? That nudged at his heart and kept her always at the edge of his mind? He'd not known another woman like her. 'Twould be so easy to take her into his arms and his bed. As his woman. And perhaps as his equal as well. He vowed silently to do all in his power to keep her from harm and prayed he would not have to choose between her life and the pursuit of the Grail.

He stared into eyes deep and dark and timeless and realized he was no longer certain what that choice would be.

"Tomorrow then, Tessa." Galahad reached out and cupped her chin in his hand. "And remember, my lady, courage is not of the body but of the spirit."

"I'm gonna die. I know it. I'm dead meat." Tessa paced across her room shaking her hands in front of her. She threw her head back and yelled. "Merlin!"

Oriana perched on the edge of the bed. " 'Tis not the way to call a wizard, my lady."

"Well, if he had a cell phone this wouldn't be necessary." She continued to stride back and forth across the room, Oriana's gaze following like a fan at a tennis match. "I can't believe what he's gotten me into. This is it. I'm doomed before this damn quest even starts."

"Doomed?"

"Galahad is going to kill me."

Amusement colored Oriana's face. "You jest, my lady. Galahad would not take your life."

"Oh, not directly. It will be an accident. A horrible, horrible accident. Tragic but unavoidable. I might even not die. Sure. That's his strategy. He wants me injured. Just enough to keep me here when he rides off into the sunset." She pivoted and leveled an anxious gaze at the teen. "You should have seen him at dinner when Merlin and the king told him I was going with him. He was furious."

"I did indeed see him but at a distance." Oriana frowned thoughtfully. "I did not note a display of temper."

"You had to be close to see it. Believe me, he was one big, angry knight." She resumed her pacing. "And I can tell he's still mad. He's covering it up, trying to be all charming and considerate. Pretending to be worried about my safety. But he can't fool me. There's no way he wants to drag me along on this little trip. That's why he's come up with this 'test' nonsense."

"But did you not say the test was your idea?"

"Hah! That just goes to show you how clever he is."

Oriana raised a skeptical brow. "Surely you do not truly believe Sir Galahad means to do you harm?"

Tessa stopped and stared at the girl. Was it only this morning he'd kissed her senseless and she'd kissed him right back?

"Do you, my lady?"

"No." Tessa groaned and collapsed on the bed. She stared up at the wooden ceiling high above them. "Of course not. It's just the panic talking. Sheer, unadulterated fear. Besides, Galahad's probably too good and noble for something like that." She glanced at Oriana. "He is good and noble, isn't he?"

" 'Tis no finer man."

"That's what I figured."

"And you are to accompany him." Oriana sighed with obvious envy.

"You say that like I just got a hot date for the senior prom."

Confusion crossed the girl's face.

It was Tessa's turn to sigh. Merlin could have made this a lot easier by providing them all with some kind of instant translator. On the other hand, she could probably watch her words a little closer. And maybe, just maybe it was time to start putting some legitimate effort into functioning in the Middle Ages.

"Sorry, sweetie. How about . . . an invitation to dance?"

The teen's expression brightened. " 'Tis much better than a mere dance. You and he shall be together for months, perhaps years."

"Years?" A queasy feeling settled in the pit of her stomach. "You're kidding."

" 'Tis true, my lady," Oriana said eagerly. "Quests have been known to last for years and years."

"Years and years, huh?"

" 'Tis impossible to predict how long such a venture can take." Oriana studied her curiously. "Did you know you and he are the talk of the castle? 'Tis most unusual for a knight to be accompanied on a quest by a lady. I know not of it happening before."

"That's me." Tessa rolled on her side and propped her head in her hand. "I'm a pioneer."

"Pioneer?"

"Sorry. A trailblazer? An explorer? Um . . . the first to do something?"

"Indeed." The girl hesitated. "Still, 'tis not a thing most females would wish for."

"Tell me about it. It wasn't my first choice either but I guess I'm stuck with it."

Oriana frowned. "You do not wish this?"

"No, I don't wish this. Not even a little. But it's the only way I can get Merlin to send me back home."

"Where is 'home'?"

"Home?" The well-manicured university campus came to mind and her small but pleasant apartment, followed by images of the Victorian house she'd grown up in, nestled in an older neighborhood in a nice all-American Midwestern city. And beyond that, thoughts of laptops and microwaves and flush toilets and every convenience she'd ever taken for granted crowded her thoughts. Along with Christmas trees and Christmas lights and Christmas carols sung in the cold under a starry December sky. "Home is very, very far away."

"Do you miss it?"

At once her mother's laughter at one of her father's bad jokes rang in her ears and brought a rush of longing so strong she struggled against the tears that sprang to her eyes. "I miss it a lot." She sniffed. "You have no idea."

Oriana stretched out beside her. "Tell me of your home."

Tessa laughed softly. "I wouldn't know where to begin."

" 'Tis said," the teenager traced an invisible pattern on the coverlet, "you come from a place where there is much magic. 'Tis why Merlin brought you to assist Sir Galahad." Her inquisitive gaze met Tessa's. "Is it not the truth?"

"The truth?" Digital watches and cars and lights at the touch of a finger. She chose her words carefully. "I imagine anything that you don't quite understand could be attributed to magic. In that respect, I suppose someone from Camelot would think there was a lot of magic in my world."

"Will you need your magic on this journey? To find the Grail?"

"I'll need something all right but my magic is in short supply. Nonexistent actually. Merlin did offer to teach me a really neat trick . . ." She shook her head. "I suppose magic, anybody's magic, wouldn't hurt. I think we'll need all the help we can get."

"Magic would indeed help."

Tessa considered the idea for a moment. "I've never believed in magic before now, you know. I don't believe in anything until it's actually been proved to me. I didn't think Galahad or Arthur or any of this stuff was real until I came here."

Disbelief shone in Oriana's eyes. " 'Tis indeed a strange land you come from not to have heard of Arthur, King of all the Britons."

"Oh, I'd heard of him, I just didn't believe in him."

" 'Twas faith you lacked then," the teen said with a wisdom far beyond her years. "Everyone must have faith. In God and in the king and in man and in yourself. And," her eyes twinkled, "in love."

Tessa laughed. "Why are you bringing up love?"

Oriana shrugged in an offhand manner. "No reason, my lady."

"No, come on, tell me."

Oriana narrowed her eyes and studied Tessa for a long moment. "I told you once, my lady, that I believed Galahad harbored feelings for you. Feelings he does not understand as of yet. Do you not wonder at his desire to keep you from harm?"

"He's just afraid I'll cramp his style. I mean, I'll get in his way," she said quickly.

"I believe that is not all." A smug smile quirked the teenager's lips. "And I believe you suspect the same."

Tessa bit back a sharp denial, remembering the look in Galahad's eyes this morning when they'd kissed. Hadn't she wondered then if his feelings mirrored her own? If he felt the same connection with her that she did with him? A connection so deep it wouldn't take much more than a tiny spark to explode into emotions too overwhelming to even consider? Or handle?

"I would not worry about whatever trial the good knight plans for you." Oriana slid off the bed and started toward the door. "He will not allow you to come to any harm."

"From your lips . . ." Tessa muttered.

"I would instead fear the damage not to your body but to your heart."

"My heart?"

"Lack of faith is as blinding as a hood pulled over the eyes." Oriana shook her head. "You are as stubborn as your knight."

"He's not my knight."

"Is he not?"

"No." Tessa ignored the abrupt realization that she very much wanted him to be her knight and hers alone. Her white knight. Her savior. Her hero. But what she wanted didn't make any difference, not really. Nothing could come of it. Their worlds were too different and she was headed back to hers as soon as this Grail stuff was over. Besides, there was no way she could compete with the oh-so-perfect Dindrane. He'd adored his dead wife. Tessa simply drove him nuts. "He's not my knight and he never will be."

"As you say." Oriana pulled open the door and stepped over the threshold.

"Oriana." The teen turned back. "I just wanted to thank you. For being my friend." Tessa stepped toward her. "We probably won't see each other again."

"I shall miss you, my lady. You are unlike anyone I have ever known." An impish smile lit Oriana's face. " 'Tis not so bad to lose Galahad to one such as you."

Tessa laughed.

Oriana grabbed her hand and squeezed. "I wish you God speed." She started toward the door then stopped and studied Tessa thoughtfully. "But I do wonder, my lady, if there is more here beyond Camelot that you have not believed in.

"That you may soon discover to be true."

Chapter Eleven

❦

"This has got to be the stupidest thing I've ever gotten myself into," Tessa muttered to herself.

She pushed open a wooden door and stepped out into the walled courtyard enclosing the castle. A *bailey*, she thought it was called. Or maybe it would be called a bailey someday. Life was certainly complicated when you didn't know the basics—where and when you were. Regardless, this was where and when Galahad had said to meet him. It was barely past daybreak, not her favorite time of day in any era although it didn't really matter. She hadn't slept a wink all night. Whatever possessed her to agree—no—demand Galahad test her courage? She almost deserved whatever he came up with.

In spite of the early hour, the area bustled with activity. She'd quickly realized the castle was very much an independent, self-sustaining community with each and every resident playing a supportive role. It would make a fascinating sociological study when she went home. If she lived that long.

"Merlin," she whispered with all the force she could muster. Yelling would have been much more satisfying but the last thing she needed was to attract additional attention. She was already the talk of the court. Of course, she could probably scream her head off and not get an answer. Mr. Wizard was apparently leaving her on her own to sink or swim, and to provide him with a little entertainment.

She wandered through the bailey noting the details of everyday life and filing them away for future reference. It was an old study trick and, right now, served to get her mind off her upcoming test and the quest to follow. She'd been rather surprised to realize how much she already knew about the Middle Ages. Oh, she was nowhere near an expert but in spite of her general dislike of the period, she'd picked up a remarkable bit of information through the years, thanks to the osmosis that occurs naturally in the halls of academia and a lifetime of education. Too bad she hadn't paid more attention. Who knew she'd actually need it some day?

The clothes alone would give her a good idea of the date if she'd studied costume at all. Sure, she'd read somewhere that chain mail predated armor but she had no idea of the specific timeline. Besides, she hadn't seen Galahad or anyone in any kind of battle gear yet. All the men she'd met were wearing tunics and tights, or rather, leggings. As for the women, the dresses were simple, long and flowing and not unattractive. Except for the ugly colors that seemed to be assigned exclusively to her clothes. All she really knew from her own wardrobe was this was a time before zippers and legitimate underwear.

She searched the growing crowd for a sign of Galahad. Was he late or was this a reprieve? Had

Merlin helped her out after all and waylaid the Big Guy? She sighed. Probably not. That would spoil the wizard's fun. The sadist. She'd bet the Grail itself Merlin was having a good laugh right about now.

Tessa surveyed the colorful scene. Exactly where did all this fit into recorded history? And how on earth had Merlin managed to hide it so thoroughly? Surely, memories of those who lived here would be passed down in families from father to son, mother to daughter until . . . Tessa smiled wryly. Wasn't that how legends started anyway? And a little selective magic strategically placed to wipe out a bit of physical evidence here, change a too-accurate story there, erase the memories of an individual or an entire family, and Arthur and Camelot would be nothing more than a fairy tale. She had to admit—Merlin did one hell of a job.

Still, it would be nice to know, even in general terms, what the date was. To satisfy her own curiosity if for no other reason. Although, when it came right down to it, did the date really matter? What were a few years, give or take a century or two, in the scheme of her adventure?

Adventure? She skirted a pile of manure and wrinkled her nose. That was the word Merlin had used. What did he say? Something about her being in for the adventure of a lifetime? No, he'd said she was in for a remarkable adventure. It was her visit to Greece that she'd thought of as the adventure of a lifetime. What a laugh. Not even the most adventurous vacation could compare with undertaking a legendary quest with a mythical hero. An undertaking that was quite simply terrifying.

Then why did her blood shiver with anticipation?

She pulled up short and ignored the curious or casual or irritated stares of those forced to step around her. When had her fear turned to excitement? Her hesitation to eagerness? Her reserve to a restless need to get started? She groaned to herself. God help her, she wanted this so-called adventure. This quest. This journey into the unknown at the side of a man who had already touched a chord in her heart.

And if her heart was damaged in the process? Was that yet another of the dangers and challenges and risks that Merlin warned of? When it came right down to it, was that too high a price to pay for the adventure of a lifetime? Maybe not, but she'd just as soon avoid that particular risk, thank you very much.

A grin broke on her face. Let Galahad bring on his test. Adrenaline surged through her. She wasn't one of his typical damsels in distress and she wasn't a *mere* anything. She was a modern female and knew a woman could do damn near everything a man could do. Not that she'd ever tried, personally, but . . . what the heck. She'd lived a relatively low-key, completely normal life before now. Maybe it was her turn.

The refrain of *I Am Woman* echoed in her head. She was ready. No, she was more than ready. Ready for challenges and tests and whatever else lay ahead. And more than ready for him.

" 'Twould give a king's ransom to know your thoughts, my lady." Galahad's voice sounded close to her ear.

She spun around to find him right behind her. He grinned with a look of welcome that nearly took her breath away. She gazed up at navy eyes sparkling in the early-morning light and lips full and inviting and wondered how she'd ever be able to resist him. And why she'd want to.

She laughed. "Good morning. It's a beautiful day, isn't it?"

He returned her smile. " 'Tis a day unusually pleasant. As is your temperament."

"I have been kind of bitchy—er—ill tempered since I got here and I apologize." She tilted her head and caught his gaze with hers, a flirting technique she hadn't used for years. Judging by the expression of mixed surprise and delight on his face she couldn't quite remember why she'd given it up. "Do you think we could start over?"

Galahad cleared his throat. She'd obviously caught him off guard. Good. He beat her hands down when it came to all things physical but there was nothing in her equality rulebook that said she couldn't use every weapon at her disposal to meet and best whatever came along. Including Galahad. As far as she was concerned, flirting was just another weapon.

He swept a low, graceful bow. "Indeed, my Lady Tessa, I am at your service."

"Great." She beamed at him, hooked her arm through his and they started off. She wasn't sure exactly where and Galahad paid no attention to what direction they headed. Instead, he stared down at her with a bemused expression, as if she were a new species he'd just discovered.

" 'Tis an interesting song. I've not heard it before."

"What song?"

"That which you hum."

"Oh that." She hadn't realized she'd been humming. "It's kind of a hymn."

"Indeed. Odd-sounding tune."

"I'll bet you won't hear anything else like it." *Not for centuries anyway.* "So, are you ready for my test?"

"Your test?" He shook his head as if to clear it. His brow furrowed. "Tessa, 'tis no longer necessary to go through with it. Willingness to attempt such a trial, one whose nature is unknown to you, is test enough." He smiled. "I grant your courage to be unquestioned and concede defeat."

"I appreciate that." She squeezed his arm. "And I must admit it's really tempting, but I believe part of all this worthiness stuff involves honor, doesn't it? Keeping your promise, that sort of thing?"

"Aye, but—"

"No buts. I gave my word and that's that. So." She gazed up at him with her newfound confidence. "What have you got in mind?"

He looked distinctly uncomfortable.

"Come on, out with it."

His words came slowly. "Upon further consideration, I fear the test I have devised is not perhaps as fair as it should be."

She laughed. "What do you mean?"

He heaved a heavy sigh. " 'Twas meant as much to scare you as to prove your worth."

"Scare me?" What had he come up with? After all she'd been through lately it would take a lot to scare her. "I can take it. It's not like it could kill me." All right, maybe not a lot. "Could it?"

"Nay." He scoffed, then hesitated as if thinking about it. " 'Tis a slim chance but . . ." He shook his head. "Nay."

"Glad you sound so confident." Maybe not much at all.

" 'Twas conceived to test trust as well as courage."

"Trust?" Did *I Am Woman* fade slightly in the background?

He steered her toward the outer gates. A bow and a quiver of arrows leaned against the wall next to a lumpy burlap bag. He slung the quiver over his arm and picked up the bow and the bag. Archery? At least this was something she could handle. Maybe. It might depend on what was in the bag.

"You swore you trusted me with your life."

"Sure. What's not to trust?" Did her voice sound a bit weaker to him too or was it the blood roaring in her ears that dampened the sound? And where did that damn music go?

"Aye." He cast her an admiring gaze. "I am impressed, Tessa St. James. 'Tis not easy to trust your life to a man who is in many ways unfamiliar to you. You are indeed a woman of rare courage and faith."

"There's that word again," she muttered.

They stepped through the castle gates and his long strides led them from the town and toward a meadow bordered by a distant band of trees. She had to practically run to keep up with him. Where was he taking her? Probably someplace to easily dispose of the body.

Ridiculous. She stared at his broad back and fought back the fear that rose in her throat. She did trust him, more or less. Not that her instincts when it came to men were always on target. Far from it. Still, aside from a little arrogance and male chauvinism that she should have expected anyway, he pretty much lived up to his legend. And Oriana agreed he was a good guy. On the other hand, there were huge discrepancies between the myth and reality.

For one thing, according to some versions of the legend, Galahad was known as the virgin knight.

"What is this?" She stared at the object he pulled from the bag and handed her.

" 'Tis a cabbage." He quirked a brow. "Do you not recognize it?"

"It's kind of small for a cabbage, isn't it?" She hefted it in her hand. "It's not much bigger than a softball."

" 'Tis a good size for our purpose."

"You think so, do you?" Somehow, given the archery equipment, and the fact that they'd stopped at the only tree between the castle and the woods—add to that old scars on the bark—she was fairly certain they weren't here for a picnic. "And what exactly is that purpose?"

" 'Tis the test." He picked up the bow and snapped the line with a sharp *twang*. "A test of courage and trust and skill."

"That doesn't sound so bad." In fact, it sounded like a piece of cake. Good, she could breathe again. Not that she was an ace at archery. But at least she knew which end of the arrow to point. "I'll give it a shot. I tried a little archery in school."

"The good sisters," he said absently, still checking out the bow.

"Yep. Sister Abigail was quite an athlete." He looked up at her. "Sports? Games? Running, jumping, that sort of thing?"

" 'Tis an odd activity for a nun," he murmured,

apparently finding the bow to his satisfaction. He selected an arrow from his quiver and examined it.

She leaned back against the tree. "Not where I'm from. There are Sister Abigails at every Catholic girls' school in the country. I think they breed them in some secret science lab deep in the sub-basement of a convent conveniently disguised as a Holiday Inn in Southern California."

He glanced at her sharply and she laughed. "I'm kidding. Seriously, Sister Abigail was great. There was a hot rumor that, before she became a nun, she'd been picked to try out for the Olympic rowing team but didn't make it. Something about a chromosome problem . . ."

Galahad didn't question the term. In fact, he appeared to have tuned her out completely.

"So, how's the Camelot soccer team doing? They're the Knights, right? Heard they lost that last game to the Vikings."

"What?" His head jerked up, his forehead furrowed with confusion.

"Nothing." She smiled sweetly.

Galahad narrowed his eyes suspiciously then turned his attention back to the arrow. Poor guy. Did he understand even half of what she said?

He nodded to himself then glanced at her. "Ready, my lady?"

"Sure." Her confidence had faltered but was definitely back. It made absolutely no difference how good or bad she shot, he'd already said the test was a moot point. It was only important that she was willing to do it. "Who's first?"

Galahad ran his hand along the bark of the tree, his

fingers stopping at a point about level with her chin. "Hold the cabbage here against the tree, above this notch."

"Okay." Of course. He planned on skewering the veggie to the oak to use as a target. It was a rather small target but—what the hell. This might be fun.

"Hold it thus." He positioned her hand. "Excellent." He picked up the bow. "Now, keep your hand steady." He turned and started off.

"Where are you going?"

"I cannot shoot at this range," he called over his shoulder.

"But how are you going to keep the cabbage on the tree?" she shouted.

"You will hold it." He kept walking.

What did he say? "I will what?"

"Hold it. Hold the cabbage," he yelled.

"I will . . . what!" She dropped the cabbage and hid her hands behind her back. "I will not!"

He stopped in mid pace. She could see his shoulders rise and fall. Was he heaving a sigh of frustration? Or laughing? He turned on his heel and strode back to her.

She pulled her gaze from him to the cabbage on the ground. It was an awfully small cabbage. She swallowed hard. What happened to the fearlessness she'd known just a few minutes ago? Probably hiding under a bed somewhere. Exactly where she should be.

"Let me get this straight. I'm supposed to stand in front of this tree." She smacked the bark. "This little, tiny tree."

" 'Tis a young oak." His gaze traveled upward toward the top of the tree with a mild affection. "When

I was but a lad, it served my friends and myself well for sharpening our skills. We thought it grew here for us alone."

"It's not much of a target. You can practically put your hands around it."

"Aye. 'Tis a challenge."

"So, I'm supposed to stand here, next to your challenging target, holding a pathetic excuse for a vegetable in my hand, waiting for you to shoot an arrow at me?"

" 'Twill not be shot at you." He scoffed. " 'Twill be shot at the cabbage."

"The cabbage in my hand."

"The very one."

"I think we need to talk about this."

" 'Tis little left to say. You asked to be tested, a test of my choosing. Furthermore, within the hour, you insisted 'twould be a question of honor for you to carry out your end of the bargain." A smug smile played across his lips. "I cannot have forgotten such a thing. Do you now regret your words?"

"Regret my words?" she repeated slowly. "No, not exactly. But have you ever done this before?"

He laughed. "As boys, 'twas a favorite game of skill and nerve."

"What about lately?"

He snorted in disdain. " 'Tis a sport for children, Tessa."

"Just out of idle curiosity, how many people are wandering around Camelot with only one hand?"

He stared at her for a moment then grinned. "You've a clever way with you, my lady. None have ever lost a hand here," he bent toward her, a wicked light in his eye, "but many have sacrificed a finger or two."

"Swell." There really wasn't any choice. Either she could renege and have him treat her like a second-class citizen for their entire time together or she could grit her teeth, pray hard and hold the cabbage.

"Well?"

She stared into his endless blue eyes, ignoring the laughter lingering there. Damn, she really did have faith in him. She really did trust him.

"Let's do it," she said faintly.

His grin widened, he grasped her hand and raised it to his lips. " 'Twould be a pity to lose even one finger so lovely as these." He nodded, turned and strode off, glancing over his shoulder. "Trust, Tessa, 'tis all that's needed."

"Right. Hey!" Tessa called to his retreating back. "Are you any good at this?"

He laughed as if the question was too ridiculous to answer. "I am a knight of the realm."

"That makes me feel a lot better! Have you ever hit anyone in this game?"

"None that did not move."

"Great." She bent down and scooped up the cabbage. If possible, it seemed even smaller than before. She glanced at Galahad. He was getting pretty far away. Surely, he couldn't possibly plan on shooting from such a long distance away?

Apparently he could. Finally, he stopped, turned toward her and loaded an arrow.

She breathed deeply, set the cabbage flat on her palm and held her hand against the tree. Was that the tree moving or was she shaking? Had she ever been this scared? It was the medieval version of chicken. If she so much as flinched she'd be coleslaw. Still, even if she lost a finger or two, she'd still have nine others. Or eight.

He raised the bow and took aim. Her heart hammered against her chest. If she was really brave she'd watch the arrow come toward her. Who was she trying to kid? She squeezed her eyes shut tight and prayed. *Dear God, if you get me out of this I'll go to church every Sunday from now on.* Why not? Her credit was probably thin but not gone. This was a deal she'd made before, usually on the top of a roller coaster. *This time I really mean it.*

A *twang* sounded in the distance. *Help!* The arrow thudded into the oak. The tree shook. She snapped open her eyes and jerked away her hand.

The cabbage, the very small cabbage, was skewered to the tree. Tessa stared and pulled great gulps of air. Out of the corner of her eye she saw Galahad start toward her but she couldn't wrench her gaze away from the impaled cabbage. The arrow quivered, centered almost perfectly in the vegetable. Her knees buckled and she sank to the ground. Courage sure took a lot out of you. Galahad was good. Very good. Obviously, there was never any real danger for her as long as she kept her hand still. As long as she had enough courage to trust him. And faith. Still, he had scared the hell out of her.

"Tessa!" He knelt at her side, his anxious gaze searched her face. "Are you unharmed? When you collapsed, I feared—" He glanced up at the cabbage. "But I did not hit you."

"No, you got the cabbage. Perfectly, in fact." She

brushed her hair away from her face with a shaky hand. "Why didn't you tell me how good a shot you were?"

"I said I was a knight. Besides, did it not take greater courage to face someone whose skill was unknown? Did it not require a greater level of trust?" He got to his feet and extended his hand.

"Not to mention fear," she said under her breath and grabbed his hand. "Trust is important, isn't it?" He helped her to her feet.

"Indeed. You place your trust in me and, in return, I trust in your courage." Galahad grasped the arrow and jerked it out of the tree. The cabbage fell in two pieces to the ground.

"It goes both ways then?"

"Most certainly."

"In that case . . ." She picked up his bow and plucked the string. Could he take it as well as he could dish it out? "It's your turn."

"My turn?" Confusion washed across his face.

"It's your turn to . . . um . . . hold the cabbage."

"I think not." Indignation sounded in his voice.

"Why not?"

"I have no knowledge of your skill."

"I didn't know how good you were when I did it."

"But I am a knight."

"And I had Sister Abigail. Trust, Big Guy, remember. You said it yourself—I barely know you. That 'I'm a knight' line might be self-explanatory here but where I'm from it doesn't mean a whole lot. You did nothing to ease my fears. Blind trust, faith—that's what you asked for from me." She bent down and picked up the smaller of the cabbage halves. "Now, it's my turn to ask it from you."

" 'Twas not I who asked for a test. I have no need to prove my worthiness." He folded his arms over his chest and glared. "I am a knight."

"You can say it all you want, but let me tell you a couple of things." She leaned the bow against the tree and carefully selected an arrow, mimicking his earlier actions. She bit back a smile. The man was definitely nervous. "I've been a Girl Scout, I am a member of several scholastic fraternities, hold a VISA gold card and I'm a natural blonde. None of that gives you the tiniest clue about my ability to handle this thing." She tapped the arrowhead on his chest. "If we're going to work together, shouldn't I have as much confidence in you as you have in me?"

"But I am a man!"

"Sorry." She shook her head. "That's not a ringing endorsement either."

"None has ever dared question my courage—"

"I'm not questioning your courage. I'm simply asking for you to have as much trust in me as you expected me to have in you. How did you put it?" She smiled innocently. "Oh yeah, it takes a greater level of trust to face someone whose skills are unknown."

His brow furrowed in frustration. "Since you throw my own words in my face it seems I have no choice. I will submit to this."

"I thought you would." She handed him the cabbage half then paused. "However, big, brave knight that you are, I think it's only right to make this a bit more of a challenge."

" 'Tis enough of a challenge for me," he growled.

"But not for me." Tessa plucked the cabbage from

his hand. "This is the William Tell test," stretched up on tiptoe and placed it on the top of his head.

"God's breath, woman." He grabbed her hand, pulling her tight against him, the cabbage tumbling to the ground. "Only a fool would allow even the most skilled archer to attempt such a target."

"It's only fair. You chose my test. Now I pick yours."

"I do not—"

"Trust, Galahad." She raised a brow. "I'm only asking for you to trust me the same way you asked me to trust you."

"Trust that I will lose my head?" He glared, his nose inches from her own.

"No. Trust that you can count on me to keep you from losing your head."

"That you cannot do." His voice was intense. "I have lost my head already." His eyes darkened. "And perhaps my heart."

Her breath caught. "Have you?"

"Aye." His gaze bored into hers. Time slowed and stopped. Did she feel the beat of his heart against her chest or was it the hammering of her own heart? Did his body strain toward hers with a yearning so strong it couldn't be denied or was it her own body that ached for his touch? Did a sense of wonder at the depth of feelings still unspoken shine in his eyes or was it just the reflection of her own emotions?

Abruptly, he released her hand and she stumbled backward. Disappointment stabbed through her, a counterpoint to the weakness in her knees and the trembling of her hands.

"Very well. Get on with it then." He stooped quickly

and grabbed the scraggly remains of the cabbage, slapping it on the top of his head and clasping his hands behind his back, the cool tenor of his voice in startling contrast to the comical nature of his appearance. "I feel like a fool."

"You look kind of cute." She stifled a giggle. "Cabbage is your color."

Disgust and annoyance battled on his face.

"Whoops. Sorry. No sense of humor in the Middle Ages, I guess." She picked up the bow and turned. Then without thinking she swiveled, stretched and planted a firm kiss hard on his lips, stepping back before he could react. "I'd hate for you to lose your head almost as much as you would." She pivoted and started off.

"I am much relived, my lady." Sarcasm rang in his voice. " 'Twould be a great comfort in the moments to come were it not for the shaking of your hands."

"Trust me, Galahad," she called over her shoulder.

She could hear him muttering behind her and she laughed. He was probably berating himself for getting in the position of being at the mercy of a mere woman. Galahad would never have considered the idea that she would need to trust him as much as he would need to trust her. Sure. The man knew his own limits when it came to bravery or skill but hadn't the vaguest idea what her abilities were. Besides, she was a woman and in his world that didn't count for much. Time that somebody was taught a little lesson.

She stepped off what seemed like a good distance and turned back toward him. It was hard to read his expression from here but it looked relatively unchanged. Still, wasn't the line of his body a bit more rigid than before? Tension would do that to a man. Even a knight.

She waved in a carefree manner then directed her attention toward the bow and arrow. How much more nervous would he be if he knew her archery experience was limited to a six-week unit in gym in her senior year in high school? Or was it her junior year? Even so, this was not an especially tricky weapon. The bow wasn't much longer than the ones she'd used in school, another clue to the date if she knew when the longbow was developed. Which she didn't.

She notched the feathered end of the arrow in the string of the bow, brought the bow into position and sighted along the length of the arrow to the target. Galahad stood unflinching. He was willing to trust her even though she'd given him no real reason to. He was willing to submit to the same test he'd put her through even though he had no idea if she'd ever shot an arrow before in her life. And he was willing to look ridiculous wearing a cabbage, all for a point of honor. What a guy.

She blew a long breath, pulled back the arrow, shifted, aimed at a forty-five degree angle away from him and let it fly.

The *twang* reverberated through the early-morning air. The arrow sailed in a wobbly arc, missing the tree by a good twenty feet. Thank God. She blew a long sigh of relief. Even deliberately aiming away from him she couldn't be absolutely certain, by some freak of nature, she wouldn't hit him. The only thing she'd been worse at than archery was soccer. And she was terrible at soccer.

She grinned and started walking back to the tree.

Galahad swept the cabbage away, shook the last cling-ing bits out of his hair and started toward her, one of his long strides equaling three of hers. Her grin faded. His expression was not that of a man who'd success-fully passed a test. Her step slowed. No, it was more like a man who'd been conned. Or screwed.

Tough. Didn't he do exactly the same thing to her? She raised her chin and marched toward him, stopping with less than a foot between them.

"You have no skill with a bow, do you?" Irritation underlaid his words.

"Nope."

"This was a trick then."

"Not at all." She couldn't suppress a smug smile. "This was a test. You know, for trust, faith, courage and all those noble qualities."

"You did not intend to shoot the cabbage."

"Duh. Let me tell you, there was no way I could hit that cabbage, or for that matter that tree, with an arrow." She shook her head. "I stink at archery."

"Yet you allowed me to stand there, with a cabbage upon my head, believing you would indeed attempt to skewer it." His words were measured.

"You got it." She studied him for a moment. He ap-peared completely under control. What was he think-ing? "It was something Sister Abigail taught. If you weren't the best player physically, then you'd better be the smartest."

"You are a riddle, my lady," he said thoughtfully. "In truth, Tessa St James, who are you? Where do you come from?"

Was it time to tell him?

"I told you, my land—"

He brushed away her words with an impatient dash of his hand. "I know there is something of magic about you. Yet Merlin stands by your side so I know you are no witch."

"You said witch, right? With a W?"

"You will drive me mad before this ends," he muttered.

"Yeah." She grinned. "But it should be one hell of a ride."

Chapter Twelve

❧

". . . And then, when I was in third grade, my dad was . . ."

The cry of the birds and rustle of the wind mixed with the constant chatter of the woman on the mount by his side and he paid it as little heed. Galahad should have known his silence would not still her tongue. In the scant hour they'd ridden from Camelot, Tessa had barely paused for breath. Was the fair lady affected by nerves now that their quest was truly underway? 'Twould not be a mark against her. The bravest of men were known to hesitate before plunging ahead into the unknown.

With every passing moment, he understood more and more of what she said. Not each and every word, but the meaning of her comments taken as a whole was clearer to him. 'Twas difficult to ignore the often intriguing images she brought to mind but at this moment he needed to sort out the myriad of emotions and thoughts in his own head.

". . . It was the Greeks, of course, who originally developed . . ."

Her words droned on like bees, unheeded, her voice

an almost pleasant accompaniment to his thoughts. His gaze strayed to a long, shapely leg, exposed by the tuck of her skirts beneath her. She'd insisted upon sitting her horse astride in the manner of a man and complained of her missing *jeans*, the heavy leggings she'd worn on her arrival. He admitted privately they would have served her well but aloud merely noted the impropriety of a woman clad in such a garment. His comment earned him a quick retort, her words unfamiliar but her meaning unmistaken. He smiled to himself. She was indeed an unusual woman.

But what did she have that he needed? He slanted her a thoughtful glance. She sat straight and tall, her chin high, her firm breasts thrust forward proudly. Aye, he bit back a grin, she did indeed have what he needed. He'd be a fool to deny he wanted her in his bed. And a greater fool still to disregard that the emotions she triggered within him were far deeper than the lust in his loins. 'Twas equal in strength to the love he'd had for his wife yet 'twas as unlike that sentiment as night to day.

He pushed aside a nagging sense of guilt. He could not help but wonder if his attraction to Tessa was a betrayal of Dindrane. Certainly she would not have thought it so and would have expected—nay—insisted he marry again long ago. Yet that knowledge did naught to allay the unease that gripped him when he ventured too close in spirit to the Lady Tessa. Dindrane would not begrudge his feelings for Tessa. Feelings so different from those he'd held for his wife, he was unsure of their meaning even as he struggled with their depth.

Dindrane was the moon and the stars and the heavens. She was as close to perfection as a mortal woman could be. Quiet and yielding and wanting only what he wanted and he had loved her with a fervor that lasted well beyond her death.

And what of his feelings for Tessa?

". . . It was that whole business about not using your hands that I couldn't . . ."

Surely, if this was love 'twas an odd variation of the emotion. If Dindrane was the heavens, then Tessa was the earth: unyielding and stubborn and strong. He knew of no other woman, save perhaps Guinevere herself, who could face his approaching arrow without swooning. Or refuse to temper her opinions to match his own. Or insist on treatment such as he would bestow on few men, as if she were as good as he.

Perhaps she was.

Nonsense. She was naught but a woman.

Then why did every moment with her challenge every belief he'd ever held regarding females and their proper place and their suitable demeanor? And more, challenge his own mind?

What did she have that he needed?

Perhaps the answer lay hidden in the questions that lingered about the Lady Tessa. His was not a curious nature. He'd wanted to know why she was here only because he'd been confident her answer would have a direct bearing on his own endeavors. And indeed, he was right. Now, it may well be time to learn more about the mysterious land she came from. 'Twas exceedingly odd. Most foreign visitors he'd encountered in the past were all too willing to expound in great, and often boring, detail upon the country of their birth, yet Tessa appeared not merely reluctant but uneasy at the topic.

She was a riddle as complicated as that which led their quest. In this they shared a common bond: he too was not fond of riddles. They seemed to dance in his head with neither rhyme nor reason, frustrating his attempts to unravel even the simplest. Although he would never confess such a weakness to her.

When all was said and done, in the privacy of his chambers, in the quiet moments of his life, Galahad considered himself an ordinary man with a firm belief in honesty and integrity, honor and justice. 'Twas was no more than the times he lived in and an admittedly stronger than ordinary taste for adventure, that thrust him into the role of knight and servant to the king. 'Twas not an especially humble opinion, yet 'twas naught but the truth.

". . . But real underwear would probably brighten my entire outlook . . ."

He was in no way a scholar and while he had been taught the fundamentals of writing, 'twas not a skill he found particularly interesting or useful. Not that he was a stupid man. No, he was simply a man of action more attuned to work of the body than the head. He was prone to respond with the first and most direct solution to any problem, drawing his sword as often as not.

'Twas different with Tessa. She obviously was fond of the written arts. Why, she'd even insisted on taking along the small, odd book he rarely saw out of her keeping. Useless, of course, but she clung to it as if it were an amulet for her protection or salvation. He'd not expected such superstition from her. Tessa was clever, with a sharp wit and a keen mind. She would, no doubt, put thought ahead of action.

'Twould serve her well in the days ahead. Would that he was as—

He jerked up straighter and stared at her.

She cast him a sincere smile. "Don't you think so?"

He nodded in silent agreement. What she'd asked was of no real consequence. All that truly mattered was the realization that cut through him with the sharp edge of truth. 'Twas all clear to him now. Why Merlin insisted he could not find the Grail without her. And why the king had supported the wizard's stand.

They complemented one another, he and this strange, lovely creature. Each had what the other lacked. His courage was forged from strength, hers from knowledge. They were halves of the same whole. Complete only when together. And together they could find what they sought.

Then the truth shall be revealed and that which each man seeks shall be his.

'Twas clear this was the truth revealed. His heart lightened. The riddle may not be so difficult as he'd feared.

He glanced at Tessa. If he could unravel one riddle, then there was indeed hope for another.

'Twas yet another challenge. He heaved a silent sigh. He was not at all fond of riddles.

"So what happened to the brass bands? The crowds of cheering well-wishers? The going-away parties?" Tessa shook her head in disgust. "You haven't heard one word I've said, have you?"

"Indeed I have, my lady." Galahad's voice was a long, lazy drawl, the tone of a man humoring a woman.

Was there anything more annoying? "Each and every word."

"Oh yeah? Prove it."

"Allow me a moment to gather my thoughts. 'Twas so much . . ." He furrowed his brow in an exaggerated gesture, probably the Middle Ages version of sarcasm. "You discussed the journey of your family from a land called *Nebraska* when you were engaged in an adventure I believe you referred to as the *third grade*. You further droned on about the contribution of ancient Greeks to various develop—"

"That's enough."

"—at one point, you again noted the influence of the good Sister Abigail upon your life with particular emphasis on your dislike of something—what was the word, ah yes, *soccer*—"

"All right. Stop." She laughed. "I give up. You were paying attention."

His lips quirked up in a small, satisfied smile. Was he really listening or did he have some weird ability to play back everything he'd heard? Like some kind of human tape recorder? Somehow, she suspected the latter.

"So," she tilted her head and eyed him, "answer my question."

"Which question was that, fair Tessa?"

"The last one. Why wasn't there a big send-off when we left the castle? The king didn't even come out and say good-bye."

" 'Tis not the nature of a journey such as this. While our purpose is not a secret—"

She snorted. "From what I've seen it would be pretty hard to keep a secret in Camelot."

"—the king prefers a certain amount of discretion. Those who were witness last night, from noble to servant, owe their allegiance and loyalty to Arthur and him alone. Word of our quest will not travel beyond the walls of the castle." His voice rang with a quiet confidence.

"So, what's the big deal?" Why didn't she want to hear his answer? "Why does he want to keep this under wraps?"

Galahad paused as if deciding how much to tell her. "There are those who would try to stop us."

"You're kidding, right?"

He pinned her with a sharp glance.

"You're not kidding." She shook her head in disgust. "Of course you're not kidding. Everybody has gone on and on about challenges and dangers and risks. I should have known there'd be a bad guy in all this. What's a good adventure without a villain? So who is it? A rival king? Another wizard? Vikings?" The answer flashed in her mind. "Mordred, right?"

He stared at the road ahead, his tone level and noncommittal. " 'Twould be impossible to say for certain. The king has no proof as to Mordred's treachery. It may well be other adversaries do not exist and our concerns are groundless. Or—"

"Or the multiple-choice answer is all of the above." Her stomach lurched slightly. The sway of the horse had already produced that effect several times but this was different. This was fear. "Swell."

" 'Tis no need to worry as of yet. We are barely out of sight of Camelot." He shrugged. "When I spoke to the king—"

"When did you talk to the king?"

"Shortly before we departed. He said—"

"You talked to Arthur without me?"

"Aye," he said with a touch of exasperation. "He said—"

"Why did you talk to him without me? I thought we were in this together?"

"Tessa." He caught her gaze with his. "I am resigned—nay accepting—of your presence at my side. You have proved your worth. I do not doubt your courage. I no longer even question the reasons behind your inclusion in this venture. But I am unused to dealing with a woman as," he shook his head in disbelief, "as I would another man. 'Twill take some time to accustom myself to the idea. I beg your patience with me."

She stared for a long moment.

Galahad smiled. "What? No quick retort? No biting lash of your tongue? I can scarce believe at long last I have silenced the Lady Tessa."

"Neither can I," she said, struggling to digest his apparent change of heart. She must have impressed the hell out of him with that archery business. "It takes a big man to admit when he's wrong."

"Oh?" He lifted a dark brow. "When was I wrong?"

The fire crackled and snapped and sparks escaped into the night.

"I don't think I'll ever be able to walk again." Tessa sat staring into the camp fire, wondering just how stiff she'd be in the morning. Right now her body ached from her scalp to her toenails. There was a lot more to riding a horse than she'd suspected. A lot more pain anyway. She pulled the meager blanket around her shoulders tighter. The coverlet was thin and scratchy and apparently all she'd get in terms of a bed. "You really think it's a good idea? Sleeping in a cave like this?"

Galahad stirred the flames with a long stick. He'd settled on the opposite side of the campfire, about as far away from her as he could get. Ever since they'd stopped for the night, and he'd helped her off her horse, holding her a bit longer than was probably necessary and a bit shorter than she would have liked, he'd kept his distance. Was he scared of her? Or himself?

"A cave is easy shelter to be made use of. We will not be this lucky every night."

"Are you sure there's nothing back there?" She glanced at the darkness that seemed to stretch forever. They sat with their backs to the chill wall, the opening of the cave on one hand, its yawning depths on the other. Creepy. Very, very creepy.

" 'Twas no sign of bears or wolves." He tossed a short, fat branch on the fire. "There is little else to be of concern."

"Lions and tigers and bears, oh my," she murmured. He ignored her, apparently caught up in his own thoughts. Too bad. She needed to get her mind off of what might have lived in this cave once and what could still come back. "So," she groped for a topic of conversation, "worked out the riddle yet?"

He glanced at her sharply. "Nay. Have you?"

"Nope. I told you, I'm terrible at riddles."

He sighed. " 'Tis not my greatest skill either."

"Maybe we can figure it out together?"

"Aye." He stared at her from across the fire. Was it

the reflection of the flames that burned in his eyes? His voice rang with intensity. "Together."

"Aye," she said softly. Exactly what did *together* mean? What did he want it to mean? What did she? She shook her head mentally, pushed away the images of *together* that crowded her mind and tried to concentrate on Merlin's puzzle. "I really wish I'd written that damn riddle down somewhere. I can't remember exactly—"

"When the peril is naught save illusion, when the infidel comes to the fold, when the offering can be no greater, then the truth shall be revealed and that which each man seeks—" Galahad's dark gaze bored into hers. His deep tones echoed in the cave, "—shall be his."

"Wow." She wanted to melt into a small puddle. Why did he have to look at her that way? Why did he have to sound so good? And why did she want so much more? She struggled to pull herself together. "I mean, that was fantastic. I don't believe it. We only heard the riddle once. How did you do that?"

He shrugged. " 'Tis an odd quirk of my nature. I have but to hear a thing a single time and it lingers in the back of my memory always. 'Tis both a great annoyance and a great value."

"I'll bet. Can you do it with visual images too? Things you see, I mean?"

"Would that I could." He shook his head in obvious regret. What sight couldn't he remember?

"I was right, you're a human tape recorder." She eyed him suspiciously. "When I said you weren't paying attention to my conversation today, I was right about that too, wasn't I?"

For the first time since they'd stopped for the night, he grinned. "I would not admit such a thing even if it were true. I am no fool, my lady."

"I didn't think so." She laughed. "I'll let you off the hook on this one. Now, back to the puzzle of the day. Any ideas how this thing is supposed to work?"

"Within the words of the riddle are the challenges we must meet and best in our path to the Grail. Once we have succeeded, the Grail shall be within our reach."

"You make it sound so simple."

" 'Twill not be easy."

"No kidding. What I don't get about all this, though," she leaned forward, "if we don't understand exactly what the challenges are, how do we find them?"

"We do not find them, they find us."

"What?"

" 'Tis an odd circumstance for you, my lady, and I know not how to explain." His brow furrowed in thought. " 'Tis no ordinary journey we have undertaken. A quest of this nature is ruled as much by forces we cannot see as by those we can."

"Those we can't see? Like what?"

He raised a casual shoulder as if the answer was obvious. Maybe in his world it was. "Forces of magic. Of the darkness of men. Of our own souls."

"This sounds better and better all the time. Lions and tigers and bears are beginning to sound tame compared to this." She studied him for a moment and hoped she was wrong. "Have you ever been on a quest like this before?"

"Not like this." His voice was quiet. "No."

"Just what I wanted to hear." She sighed. "Even with this riddle, there isn't much to go on. We've been riding all day but how do you even know what direction to head? I mean, do we just take off and wait for things to happen to us?"

He raised a scornful brow. " 'Twould be a foolish thing to do."

"Then how—"

"The king advised—"

"In that little chat you boys had without me?"

"Aye." A firm note colored the word. "Have I not begged your forgiveness already?"

"Fine." She huffed. "I won't say another word about it." *Maybe*.

"The king and I agreed the best way to proceed was to travel toward Glastonbury."

"Where Joseph of Arimathea allegedly hid the Grail?"

"Aye. From there, we will see what information can be gathered and what new direction that may take us." He paused. "You should know, as well, the king gave me this." He pulled a small jeweled dagger from a sheath at his waist. She hadn't even noticed it.

"Very stylish but it doesn't look very effective."

" 'Tis a token from the queen." He replaced the knife. "As much or more for luck than protection."

"We'll need it." She pulled her knees up and wrapped her arms around her legs. "Lots of it. You know, none of this sounds very clear-cut."

" 'Tis yet another challenge."

"You guys are really fond of saying that." She shook her head. "I'd better memorize that riddle myself. Just in case. Let me have it."

Galahad recited the lines over and over until she was fairly sure she had it down.

She gazed into the flames. "We need to make sense of this—the peril, the infidel, the offering." . . . *the peril, the infidel, the offering* . . . The words repeated themselves over and over and over in her head like a mantra. The flames danced in rhythm with the words . . . *the peril, the infidel, the offering* . . . Her lids drooped, her eyes closed. Had she ever been so tired?

"Tessa?" Galahad's low voice sounded beside her. He must have joined her. She wanted to look but it was too much of an effort to open her eyes.

"Hmmmm . . ." She leaned toward his voice and found the solid warmth of his body beside her.

"Tessa?" Was that unease in his tone? Was he uncomfortable with her against him like this? She'd be willing to move. In a minute. As soon as she could open her eyes. She snuggled closer against him.

"You should lie down and try to sleep. 'Twill be another long day tomorrow."

"Um-hum." She was so tired. And he felt so wonderful. She was barely awake. He heaved a heavy sigh, his chest rising and falling beneath her head and his arm wrapped around her. Contentment flowed through her. This was so . . . right. Why?

Why not?

Sleep crept closer. All thoughts of perils and infidels and offerings faded, washed away by the solid heat and tender strength of the man who held her. At long last she surrendered to oblivion. His voice drifted through her dreams and warmed her soul as well with words not meant for her.

"Forgive me, my love. I did not know such a thing could happen twice in the same lifetime. Yet, once again, I am bewitched."

Chapter Thirteen

❧❀❧

"Tessa."

Galahad's voice echoed through her dreams. She shifted on the bed. He called her again and she reveled in the sound of her name on his lips.

"Tessa." Still, his tone wasn't at all like the caress of a lover. It was more in the attitude of an order or a command. And why was this bed so damned uncomfortable?

"Tessa!" His whisper rang hard and urgent against her ear, as irritating as a morning disc jockey on a radio alarm clock. Not a great way to wake up. Where was that snooze button?

Right. How could she have forgotten? Even asleep? Her eyes blinked open. There was no snooze button. No disc jockey. Worst of all—no bed. Just this damp, dark cave in the middle of nowhere.

She yawned and sat upright, pulling herself away from the warmth of his body. Nice. She'd apparently slept cuddled up next to him all night. Is that why he sounded so cranky? "Good morning to you, too, Sunshine."

"Be still!" His voice rasped.

"Well, you don't—"

"Shhhh!"

He didn't look at her. His gaze focused on the entry to the cave. Slowly, he drew his arm from around her and got to his feet, keeping to a low crouch, his every move cautious and deliberate. He inched away from her and toward the meager assortment of saddlebags, provisions and miscellaneous items they'd brought with them, now resting on the other side of the still smoldering campfire.

"What in the hell are you doing?"

"Quiet!" His tone was hushed but intense. His gaze never shifted.

"What's going on? What are you looking at?" she said in a fierce whisper.

He didn't answer. Every line of his body was rigid with tension. A hard light glittered in his eyes and his jaw was set and unyielding. He looked every inch the experienced knight, the consummate warrior, ready to do battle. A shiver ran up her spine. Something was definitely wrong here.

She turned her gaze slowly to the mouth of the cave. Pale light lit the sky in advance of the first true rays of the sun. Smoke from the still smoldering fire floated lazily toward the ceiling of the cave. Another plume drifted by the entry. She glanced at Galahad. He reached their baggage and quietly drew his sword from its sheath. She still didn't get it. The only things moving were the wisps of smoke from last night's fires, here in the cave and outside. What did he see that she didn't? What was going on? What—

She sucked in a sharp, hard breath.

They'd only built one fire.

Tessa scrambled to her feet, ignoring the screams of protest from every muscle in her body. "Galahad, what is it? Is there a forest fire or something? Is somebody else out there?"

"I am not yet certain." His voice was soft but firm. "Get behind me, Tessa."

"No problem. You're the knight." She scrambled around the remains of their campfire to his side and struggled to keep the panic from her voice. "Just for the fun of it, what do you think's going on?"

He held his sword before him and stepped in front of her, with his free arm pushing her firmly behind him. The man would make one impressive windbreak but right now she wanted to see what was up.

"Stay back." He stepped forward, toward the sunlight.

"I don't think so." She matched his movement step for step, grabbed a fistful of his tunic and held on. "You're not going anywhere without me. And there's no way I'm staying in this cave by myself."

"Tessa," he growled.

"Forget it, Big Guy. We're in this together. Not that I don't appreciate the thought but—"

"Quiet!"

"Okay." They stood staring for an endless moment. "What are we looking for?"

"I fear . . ." He paused as if afraid to say the words out loud and her heart hammered in her chest. "I fear 'tis a dragon."

"A dragon?" Something that sounded like a cross between a snort and a laugh broke from her. She let go of his tunic. "You're kidding."

He kept his gaze on the mouth of the cave. His tone was level. "I do not jest about such things."

"But a dragon? I'm sure. I don't believe it." She pulled her brows together and eyed him. He really meant it. "There are no such things as dragons."

"Are you so certain?" he murmured.

"Yeah, I'm pretty confident about that one. This is ridiculous. Have you ever seen a dragon?"

"Nay."

"Has anyone you know ever seen a dragon?"

"Nay. But there is much in this world I have not seen for myself or have proof of that I know in truth exists."

"Trust me on this one—dragons are not on the list." She stepped toward the cave entrance. He grabbed her arm and jerked her back beside him. "Hey!"

"Where are you going?" He glared down at her.

"I'm going to check this out." She shook off his hand. "Are you coming?"

" 'Twill get us both killed."

"I don't think so." She started off again and once more he yanked her back. She heaved an exasperated sigh. "What now?"

He clenched his teeth and pinned her with an angry gaze. "If indeed you are correct and 'tis not a dragon then 'tis something as yet unknown. Do you grant me that much?"

"Oh. I hadn't thought of that."

"Think of it then and stay behind me."

She shook her head. "Nope." Funny how her fear had vanished once she realized exactly what he was so worried about. "By your side but not behind you."

"Very well," he snapped. "We shall survive or perish together."

She shrugged. "Works for me."

He threw her a look that said without words what a pain he thought she was and started toward the front of the cave, each step measured and careful. They edged closer to the sunlight. The fear she'd thought was gone returned. He was right. Even if there were no dragons, there were lots of unpleasant people wandering around the Middle Ages. She groped for his free hand and found it. He wrapped his fingers around hers and squeezed and a tiny bit of confidence returned.

They inched toward the mouth of the cave. With every step she could see more of the surrounding countryside. Their overnight shelter was at the edge of a small clearing surrounded by forest.

"I see naught," Galahad said quietly.

"Good." Relief surged through her. "Me neither. Let's check it out." She started forward but he pulled her to his side.

"Take care, Tessa."

Together they stepped over the boundary line between the shadows of the cave and the early morning light. A soft mist hung low to the ground casting a hint of magic over the setting. It was lovely and perfect. Almost too perfect. Tessa shivered. If there was the possibility of dragons, this would be the place for them.

"I don't see anything."

"Then perhaps," he said softly, "you do not know where to look."

He stared at a point slightly off to her right. Her gaze followed his. There was nothing out of the ordinary. She started to tell him just that but a slight movement caught the corner of her eye. Slowly an image took shape. Disbelief meshed with terror and she couldn't have moved if she wanted to. Whether just emerging from the fog and the trees or materializing out of thin air she wasn't sure. The *how* didn't matter. The *what* was overwhelming.

"By the bones of the saints." Galahad crossed himself.

"Holy shit." Tessa followed suit. She hadn't been to church in years but if ever an occasion called for divine intervention, this was it.

It probably wouldn't help.

The creature stood a good ten feet tall and looked suspiciously like a cross between a lizard and a bat. A very nasty lizard and a very big bat. Its skin was definitely reptilian, scaly in appearance, a greenish-gray color overall. It stood on well-muscled back legs, its white underbelly exposed, smaller front legs with clawlike hands or paws or whatever. All in all it bore a vague resemblance to a dinosaur. Except for the wings. Huge paper-thin appendages, they were folded close to the beast's body. Tessa refused to consider just how big the wing span would be unfurled. And the head, much smaller proportionally than the head of the T-rex in *Jurassic Park*, looked a little like an alligator or some kind of bird of prey or . . . No. The only thing this looked like was exactly what was pictured in every fairy tale she'd ever read. Or every nightmare she'd ever had.

" 'Tis indeed a dragon," he said, awe in his voice.

"I admit it. I was wrong, you were right." Her voice was barely more than a squeak. "My mistake. Sorry."

"We will discuss your apology at another time." He held his sword ready before him.

"What are you going to do?"

"Slay the beast." His voice was grim and determined.

"Why?" She stared at the huge creature. Its eyes were slitted like a serpent's and its head swayed back and forth slightly like a cobra watching a mouse. If the options here were fight or flight, flight had her vote. "Can't we just go around it and get the hell out of here?"

As if in answer to her question, the dragon stretched forward its head, opened its mouth and belched. A roar echoed through the clearing and flames shot out toward them.

"I think not," Galahad said.

"Another few feet and we'd be toast. Literally." She edged behind Galahad.

He glanced at her over his shoulder. "Perhaps it was another lady who said, 'by your side but not behind you'?"

"That memory of yours is not going to make you any friends." She peeked around him. Was the dragon waiting for them to make the next move? She shuddered. "Besides, you have the sword."

"And I know well its use."

The dragon seemed to be sizing them up. Probably for breakfast. She swallowed the lump in her throat and willed her knees to stop shaking. How did she get into this?

Galahad stared at the dragon for a long moment, one combatant taking the measure of another. "Tessa, when his attention is fully upon me, I want you to move slowly and quietly to the horses and take your leave."

"No way. I'm not about to abandon you to that thing."

" 'Tis not a question of abandonment." He glanced at her quickly. Concern flickered in his eyes. "Should I defeat the beast, I shall find you. If not, you must continue the quest. You must find the Grail on your own."

"No. It's not my quest, it's yours."

"Swear it, Tessa. On your honor. 'Tis all I ask. Give me your word. Now!"

"I promise." The words caught in her throat. How could she leave him? What if she never saw him again? What then? "I hate it but I promise I'll continue your quest." *If I have to leave you, which I won't!*

"In the movies, this would be the place where the hero pulls the heroine into his arms." She sniffed and glanced at his upraised sword. "Okay, maybe just one arm, and kisses her long and hard before sending her off and sacrificing his own life to save hers."

"I know naught of this 'movie' of which you speak," he snapped. "God's blood, woman, at this moment 'twould be nice to understand all you say! But know this: I would kiss you long and hard if I had a moment, yet 'twould not have the meaning you suggest. I have no intention of sacrificing my life for yours unless it is unavoidable."

"You don't need to be so snippy about it." Indignation sounded in her tone. "Talk about spoiling the mood."

The dragon lowered and raised its head in an odd rhythm, its viperlike eyes glittering with an almost hypnotic effect.

"Go, Tessa, now!"

"Not without you."

"Tessa!"

The creature reared back and lunged forward,

flames spewing toward them. Something inside her snapped.

"And I'm not going to argue. Come on." She grabbed his hand and ran toward the woods to the left of the beast, Galahad hard on her heels.

"Tessa!"

If they could make it a few more feet—

At once the dragon materialized directly in their path, its head low and on a level with theirs. Its eyes huge and yellow and split by black, slitted centers. Her heart lodged in her throat and she bit back a scream. Galahad yanked Tessa hard against him. As one they wheeled and ran toward the other side of the clearing.

Instantly the dragon appeared before them, pulled back his head and roared. Flames shot toward them. Panic gripped her. Galahad jerked her around. For a split second fire flashed, surrounding them, engulfing and deadly. They broke free, stumbling back to the cave entrance, exactly where they'd started.

She threw herself against Galahad and buried her face in his chest, panting for breath, struggling for control. He held her tight.

"Tessa! Are you harmed?"

"No." The word was a terrified sob. She stared up at him. Worry and confusion creased his face. "Are you?"

"No." He shook his head, bewilderment in his voice. " 'Tis indeed a creature of magic. We should be little more than cinders."

"I don't get it. This doesn't make sense. Dragons don't exist." Her mind outraced her fear. "They've never existed. Nobody's ever found dragon bones or fossils. There's no proof that they're real. None. Zippo. Nada."

"The proof lies before us."

"No!" Her words tumbled out faster and faster. "There's evidence of dinosaurs. There are a few species of overgrown lizards like the Komodo dragon, and lots of people believe in the Lock Ness monster but that's it."

"Must you question what is right before you? I fear I am a simple man. I see a brute with evil in its eyes and hellfire spewing from its jaws and I have no doubts as to its veracity."

She shook her head. "Look at him, Galahad. Anything in the knight handbook about this? Have you ever seen anything like it?"

"Nay! And should we survive this encounter I would prefer never to see such a monstrosity again."

She gripped his tunic. "There's something wrong here."

"There is a great deal wrong! How can I impress upon you the very real danger before us?" His gaze burned into hers. " 'Tis not the time now to discuss the nature of reality and existence. When this challenge is met, then—"

"This is a challenge, isn't it?" she said slowly. "A big one."

"Aye, 'tis at least as great as the challenge of dealing with a female's constant babbling and stubborn manner! 'Twas a foolish act, Tessa, to try to run from—"

"No, no." She ignored his reprimand, pulled away from him and stared at the dragon. It stared back. "This is one of the challenges in the riddle, isn't it?"

"I . . ." He shook his head. "It may well be."

"Which one?" She racked her brain. "There's the peril, the infidel, the offering and—"

"The truth," he said with a hard, firm voice. " 'Tis the truth of your own eyes, Tessa. The beast is real."

"Maybe not. Maybe . . ." She furrowed her brow. "There's something I'm missing here."

"And maybe 'tis the offering that can be no greater," he said quietly.

"When the hero or heroine gives up his or her life for the other?" She shook her head. "Too obvious. Besides, don't these clues have to go in order?"

"I know of no such requirement."

"The peril, the infidel, the offering . . ." She narrowed her eyes and studied the beast. "That's it. He's the peril that's but an illusion. There's no other answer. He's a special effect. A computer animation. Something whipped up by a medieval Stephen Speilberg. A hologram maybe."

Galahad cast her a quick confused look. "I know naught of this Hall of Grahme but . . ." He trained his gaze back on the beast. "You are wrong. He is as solid as the earth beneath my feet."

"He looks solid but . . ." She only wished she was as certain as she sounded. If she was wrong, they were dead. Period. If she was right . . . "He's not real. He can't be. He's some kind of trick. Nothing but smoke and mirrors."

Like the smoke that drifted from the beast's snout and faded away. Or the smoke that drifted upward from the remains of their fire.

Smoke and mirrors?

"That's it!" Adrenaline surged in her veins and she grabbed his sleeve. "The smoke, Big Guy, look at the smoke!"

"I see naught save the tendrils from the creature."

"No, no! Watch the smoke." She shook the material clutched in her fist. "Where does it go?"

"It vanishes on the wind."

"There is no wind." She grit her teeth. Why didn't he understand? "Shouldn't it be going up? Doesn't smoke rise?"

"Indeed. I—"

"You said it yourself. How could I have been so stupid?" She smacked her hand against her forehead. "We should be dead. Burned to a crisp. The flames surrounded us but we're not even singed."

" 'Twas at our backs. I did not see—"

"It engulfed us. Did you feel any heat at all?"

"No," he said slowly.

"That's because it wasn't real. I know I'm right about this. You have to believe me. Everything I've ever learned about nature and history tells me this is the illusion."

"Each has what the other lacks," he murmured. "My courage from strength, yours from knowledge." He stared at the creature. "How are we to prove such a thing?"

"I don't know. I suppose we could just walk away and nothing would happen."

"A knight does not retreat."

"I figured as much." She scanned the clearing. "Throw something at it then. If I'm right, it will pass through."

Without a word he pulled Guinevere's dagger from its sheath, hefted it in his hand and hurled it at the creature. The jeweled knife winked in the sun and vanished in the scaley green folds of the monster's skin.

The dragon showed no reaction.

"See." She wished she was as confident as she sounded. "I knew it."

He shook his head. "We did not see the dagger land. We do not know for certain that it passed through the beast."

"Only one way to find out." She drew a deep calming breath. "I'm betting we can walk right up to it."

He raised a brow. "And if you are wrong?"

She smiled weakly. "Barbecue."

" 'Tis an odd word and I do not like the sound of it." He eyed her for a moment as if debating the pros and cons of her theory. "You are either a woman of exceptional courage and perception or you are a complete and utter fool. 'Tis yet another test for me, no doubt. I vowed to trust you." He held out his hand. "With my life."

She put her hand in his and stared up at him. "I'm ready if you are."

He pulled her against him and bent to crush her lips with his in a swift kiss that would have left her breathless at any other time and even now helped ease the cold touch of fear. " 'Twould be a pity not to taste your lips again in this lifetime."

"You got that right." She wanted to cling to him. If they made it through this—when they made it through this—she'd tell him everything. True confessions. About her past and his future and the only time they could share together.

He released her with a nod but her fingers stayed entangled with his. He held his sword high, ready to strike in case she was wrong. Not that it would do them any good.

"I hate to tell you," she said out of the side of her mouth, "but I'm so scared, I can barely move."

They stepped forward, closer to the illusion. Or to death.

" 'Tis not the sentiment a man whose life you risk prefers to hear at a moment such as this," he said under his breath.

The dragon raised his head, drew it back then thrust it forward.

What if she was wrong?

"Oh please, oh please, oh please." Tessa squeezed her eyes shut and braced herself for flames to shoot out of the dragon's mouth and right though them, exactly like before. But what if it didn't happen again? What if this was a horrible mistake? What did she know about a world filled with magic anyway?

Galahad gasped. "By all that's holy!"

She snapped her eyes open. They stood within inches of the beast's belly, white and thickly lined with pale red veins. He towered above them. Galahad lowered his sword. Amazement stamped his features.

"The flames, Tessa." Awe and disbelief sounded in his voice. "They passed through us as if they had no more substance than the air we breathe. 'Twas no heat of the fire nor breath of the wind."

He dropped her hand and held his out in front of him tentatively to touch the beast. His hand pushed through the skin without resistance and disappeared into the creature. He jerked it back against his chest.

Exhilaration bubbled through her and she laughed with sheer relief. "I was right. Look." She stepped forward and walked straight into the dragon. There was no resistance. In fact, from this side there was nothing at all to see but the clearing and the forest.

"Tessa!" Galahad's frantic call sounded behind her.

She whirled and stared. She could see him but apparently he couldn't see her through the illusion. He raised his sword and charged forward, skidding to a halt beside her.

"Hi." She grinned.

"Where is the beast?" His cautious gaze scanned the area.

"I'll show you." She grabbed his hand and led him back the way they'd come. Two steps and the dragon reappeared. "Now you see him." Again, she pulled him through the creature. "Now you don't." She retraced their steps and once more the dragon reappeared. "Now you see him."

He stared in shock at the evidence of his own eyes. "What manner of magic is this?"

"It's not magic. Or maybe it is to you. But to me it's high tech." She cocked her head and studied the image. "It looks three-dimensional, but when you get right down to it there's only height and width, so I'm not even sure if it's technically a hologram or not. I don't know enough about special effects or computers to figure it out. I just watch a lot of movies. And this guy's an Academy Award winner."

The edges of the dragon shimmered and sparked and without so much as a *poof*, the beast vanished.

Galahad's eyes widened and he stared at the spot where the dragon had stood. His voice was unsteady. "There is much we must speak of, Tessa St. James."

"No kidding." For the first time since she'd opened her eyes today, they were safe. The danger, real or not, was over.

So why were her legs like rubber? And her stomach knotted? And her teeth chattering? Why did she want to laugh and cry and scream at the same time? Her head swam and her knees gave way and she sank toward the ground, her thoughts spinning wildly.

Adventure of a lifetime, my ass.

Viviane drummed her fingers on the desk and stared at the monitor as if the computer was at fault. Ridiculous, of course. She reached forward, flicked the power switch and rose to her feet. The fault was completely hers. She was far and away too softhearted.

A real dragon, created through traditional means, basic down to earth magic, would certainly have sautéed Galahad or Tessa or both and that would have been that. But there was something quite lovely and wonderfully ironic about employing the same type of technology that had put Merlin in such a snit in the first place to thwart his plans. Pity it hadn't worked. Aside from that, the blasted man seemed genuinely fond of both Galahad and the woman. Should Viviane cause them real harm, Merlin would no doubt not hesitate a moment to exact revenge. She shuddered at the thought. All in all, they'd lived these past thousand years or so in relative harmony or as well as could be expected given the rather strong personalities of each of them.

Viviane strode across the cavern room to Merlin's library. Mahogany shelves as wide as they were tall covered the stone walls and stretched onward into the bowels of the cave, fading away into the shadows. Merlin did so appreciate a good book as much for the craft of the bookbinder as the contents. He never thought of himself as such but he was a collector. The first editions on these shelves would have a library—no, a museum—green with envy. Here was Dante, a charming creature in his own right but then Italian men usually were, and Rabelais, Chaucer and, of course, Malory. Merlin was exceedingly fond of Sir Thomas's *Le Morte d'Arthur* although Viviane personally had never particularly cared for it.

Her gaze fell on *A Connecticut Yankee in King Arthur's Court*. Nicely written and extremely entertaining yet not at all accurate. At once her mind returned to the problem at hand. Enough of this sentimental nonsense. She liked a good book as well as the next person but unless she wished to spend another few centuries living through the Middle Ages she needed something a bit more practical. Surely, in all these tomes, ancient, antique or new, there was some information that could help her. Failing that, perhaps the Internet would provide an answer. Some way to stop Tessa and Galahad.

Oh, certainly, she could simply sit back and wait for them to fail. The dear boy had failed the first time. But she knew with an unerring instinct that it would be a far different story with Tessa by his side. There were, in the universe, rare couplings of souls meant always to be together yet all too often missing one another through the vagaries of time and space. Viviane had no proof but she had a distinct suspicion this was the case with Galahad and Tessa. Such a bond was indeed a force to reckon with.

In addition, the bloody woman had magic in her she didn't know existed. Merlin had said Tessa had what Galahad needed. That he could not find the Grail without her. Was this what he meant? Magic untapped for a lifetime could prove a powerful weapon once called upon. Oh, certainly, it was insignificant under other circumstances. Yet, in Viviane's experience, the first use of such ability was often quite extraordinary, producing results that could neither be expected nor duplicated.

Just what was needed to find the Grail. Or save their lives.

Or return home?

Viviane paused to consider the intriguing idea. Could she enlist Tessa's own dormant power to end this farce and return them all to the twenty-first century where they belonged? It was unlikely, given Merlin's strength. Still, if there were perhaps some way to mitigate his power or turn it just the tiniest bit against him . . . Viviane sighed. The answer obviously wasn't here. Nor did she expect to find it on the Internet even if one could find bloody well anything else there. There wasn't so much as a single bit on the Web or a single volume amidst the thousands resting on these shelves that could tell her what she wanted to know.

But—a thought stuck her and she drew her brows together. Perhaps the answer lay not in a book that was here but in one that was not? A book with a touch of magic of its own.

Perhaps . . .

Viviane smiled, slowly and with a great deal of satisfaction. It may not be the complete solution but it was indeed a place to start.

Monte Carlo had never seemed closer.

Chapter Fourteen

❧

"Tessa!" Galahad caught her before she could hit the ground.

"Did you see that? He just disappeared." Hysteria raised her voice. The panic she'd conquered earlier now clawed at her and she teetered on the brink of complete surrender. *Delayed reaction*, she thought somewhere in the rational depths of her mind. *Shock.* Whatever the clinical name, it held her in jaws as strong as any dragon's.

"Tessa!" Galahad gripped her shoulders and shook her. "Listen to me! 'Tis over. The beast was not real! 'Twas nothing save magic!"

"Not real?" She laughed, the high-pitched sound of a woman on the edge. "Of course he wasn't real!" She wrenched free and struggled to pull in great huge gulps of air. "How could a dragon be real when nothing else is?"

She waved in a sharp cutting gesture at the rolling countryside. "See the trees and the hills and the sky? It's not real, none of it! This is all something I made up! Me! Tessa St. James. Every bit of it comes straight from my subconscious! From Puff the Magic Dragon right on down to the tiniest blade of grass!"

Worry drew his brows together and he stepped toward her. "I beg you—"

"Hold it right there, Big Guy." She thrust her hand out to ward him off. "This will come as a shock, I know, and I hate to be rude, but you don't exist either. You're a myth, a legend, a story for kids! There was no Arthur, no Camelot, nothing. Hell, you people didn't even know about the Round Table until I told you! Not only are you no more substantial than a dream, you're an inaccurate dream!"

"Please, allow me—" He reached for her but she eluded his grasp.

"Stay away from me." Tessa wrung her hands together, the simple action giving her something tangible in a world whose edges were blurring fast. She stalked back and forth across the clearing, ranting as much to herself as to him. "Assistant professors do not go on quests in the Middle Ages with arrogant knights. Nobody uses cabbages for target practice. And wizards do not tap dance!"

"Tessa!" He grabbed her and held her firm against him.

"You're not real, you're not." She sobbed and pummeled her fists on his chest. "None of this is real! It can't be."

She pounded against him over and over and he stood as steadfast and unflinching as a rock or a champion. She wept out her fears and frustration and confusion until exhaustion crept through her and she sank against him. And still she cried, tiny sobs, until all that was left were odd little hiccups that jerked through her body and the quiet, soothing sounds he made while he held her close and stroked her hair.

And his body against hers was solid and warm . . . and real.

"I don't care how you feel," she wiped at the tears on her face, "you don't exist."

"A lesser man would take your words as an insult."

"It's not an insult, it's the truth. I'm in a coma or a nightmare or maybe I'm dead. One way or another, you're not—"

"Enough!" He voice rang sharp and firm and she jerked her head up to stare into his eyes. Dark as the night, they simmered with anger and something more.

"I am real, Tessa." He grabbed her hand and placed it on his cheek. "Is my flesh not warm beneath your touch?" She stared up at him.

He moved her hand to the side of his neck. "Does my life's blood not pulse beneath your fingers?"

He pulled her hand to his chest. "Does my heart not beat beneath your hand?"

"Yes, but—"

"What is it you fear, Tessa? Is it the reality of the world around you? Or of me?" He bent to place a kiss in her palm. Panic and terror dissolved at his touch. His gaze burned into hers. "Does this scare you?"

"Oh . . ." Desire rushed through her veins and she breathed the word. "Yes."

He brushed his lips across hers and she strained upward to meet him. "My life's breath against yours. 'Tis real, Tessa. Are you afraid?"

"Yes." The word was little more than a sigh.

He pulled her into his arms and whispered a kiss across the sensitive flesh of her neck, just below her ear. Her breath caught. "And this, Tessa, are you afraid of this?"

"Yes." His lips wandered in a sensual exploration to the hollow of her throat. "Oh, yes. That. Definitely that."

"And now?" He trailed his tongue along the neckline of her dress then lifted his head to stare into her eyes.

"Terrified." She reached up and caught his bottom lip with her teeth and tugged gently. "What about you? Are you scared?"

He pulled his head back and his gaze locked with hers. "I too am afraid. Of what may not be real." A question flashed through his eyes. "And what may."

His lips met hers and for the briefest moment his kiss was tenuous, searching. Her hands rested on his chest and she could feel his hard muscles beneath his clothes. His kiss deepened. Her mouth opened and his breath mingled with her own. At once all restraint shattered.

She gripped the fabric of his tunic and strained toward him. He pulled her tighter against him and they sank to their knees. Need swelled within her. She fumbled at his clothes and he swiftly removed hers. Within moments, their garments were scattered about them on the ground and she noted vaguely his skill in disrobing her refuted forever the title "virgin knight."

Even on their knees he towered above her. She ran her fingers through the coarse hair trailing over his chest and down his stomach. He looked as good naked as he did dressed. No. Better. She leaned forward and flicked his nipple with her tongue. He sucked in his breath and wrapped his arms around her, tumbling them both to the ground.

"What manner of wench are you?" he growled in her ear.

"Yours." She tunneled her hands through his hair and pulled his lips to crush hers. He tasted of passion and power and she wanted nothing so much as she wanted him. He wrenched his mouth from hers and ran his lips down her chin and her throat and lower. He cupped her breasts in his hands and circled her nipples with his thumbs until she moaned and arched upward, her fingers digging into his shoulders. He took one breast in his mouth, teasing with tongue and teeth until she cried for release and only then did he shift his attention to the other.

They rolled over on the unyielding earth until she lay sprawled on top of him. He splayed his hands across the small of her back and lower until he held her buttocks and pulled her tight against him. Her mouth ravaged his with an aching desire she'd never dared dream of. All that mattered was his body, hot and hard and demanding against hers.

She felt him, rigid and erect and throbbing between her legs and she slid lower to rub the slick, swollen need of her arousal against his solid heat. He reached a hand between them and touched her and pure pleasure pulsed through her. She gasped. "Galahad."

"My lady." Hunger deepened his voice and he crushed his lips to hers. With a proficiency she should have suspected, he smoothly shifted their positions and once again, she lay on her back and he towered over her, poised between her legs. She stared up into eyes smoldering dark with desire and knew they mirrored her own need. She pulled him lower and he slid into her with a slow ease. Possessing her body. Claiming her soul.

Carefully, as though he thought she would break, he moved within her. Impatiently, she urged him faster. She clutched at his broad shoulders and ran her hands down his back, reveling in the feel of every muscle and sinew flexing with his thrusts. Her rhythm, her body, her spirit meshed and mated with his and they moved as one, as two halves never together before now and at long last joined and whole. The tension within her spiraled upward until she wondered if she'd die of the pure joy of giving herself with a fiery abandon she never knew possible and receiving the same in return.

Waves of ecstasy exploded inside her and she jerked and screamed. He shuddered then stilled, holding her so tight against him she didn't know where he began and she left off. And didn't care. He was her knight, her legend, her myth.

And here and now, even she could believe.

For a long moment they lay on the ground, too exhausted to move, to think. Finally, he eased to his side, propped himself up on his elbow and stared, a bemused smile on his lips. "My Lady Tessa, I believe you have done much to alleviate my fears."

"My pleasure." She giggled with tired satisfaction. "You know I've never done this before."

Shock widened his eyes. "But I thought . . . you said . . . that is . . . you have never done this before?"

She laughed. Someday she'd definitely straighten him out about her marital status. But not now. "Of course I've done *this* before." Relief flooded his face. "I've just never done it outside. On the ground. Naked." She stretched her arms over her head. "It's a wonderful sense of freedom."

"Indeed, my lady." He grinned wickedly. "I did note your lack of restraint."

"You weren't terribly restrained yourself. And I thought you were going to drop that 'my lady' stuff?"

" 'Tis a habit born of a lifetime. A term of respect in acknowledgment of one's rank. In truth, Tessa, I like the way it sounds when I speak of you."

"It's kind of possessive, don't you think? Like I belong to you?"

" 'Tis nothing of the sort." He leaned forward and circled her nipple with his tongue and she shivered. " 'Tis you who has possessed me."

"Oh yeah?"

He chuckled. "Yeah."

"In that case." She shifted to her side, propped up her head with one hand and ran the tip of her finger down his chest to his stomach. She traced a lazy ring around his navel and let her touch drift lower. He tensed beneath her fingertips. "Want to be possessed again?"

Much, much later she lay snuggled up against him with a sense of peace and contentment that could only be found in a fairy tale. Once you got rid of the dragon, you won the hand of the princess. She smiled to herself. And all the rest of her.

Galahad had complained, for the purposes of appearance probably, that they didn't have the time to lie around here. But it had been a halfhearted protest and a few well-placed kisses had convinced him another day, more or less, wouldn't matter. They'd moved back into the cave and tried to possess each other over and over again. And succeeded nicely.

She turned on her side and he wrapped his arms around her and held her close. She could feel the rise and fall of his chest with every breath and nothing had ever been so real.

Tessa closed her eyes and drifted off to sleep.

And to dream.

Of a cavern beneath the earth, lined with books and all the accoutrements of a practicing magician, and a woman with remarkably well-manicured nails.

Chapter Fifteen

❦

"*I* can deal with this." Tessa stared at her very real surroundings. She was in a semi-prone position halfway between sitting up and lying down. And more comfortable than she'd been in a long time in spite of the frantic beating of her heart. "Logically, rationally, I can handle this.

"First there was the dragon that wasn't real. Then I lost it completely. Followed by really great sex and falling asleep in the Big Guy's arms. So far so good. Now . . ." Her fingers tightened on the arms of the chair. She glanced down. She was in her dad's recliner. At once her apprehension vanished. "Merlin! Where are you?"

"As much as I adore modern times I must say, proper etiquette is simply not taught as it should be. It's ever so much more polite to issue a request than bark an order."

Tessa pushed herself up straight and turned toward the voice. The woman she'd seen at the feast lounged in a graceful wing chair beside a small, highly polished mahogany table. A glass of wine dangled carelessly from one hand. "Viviane, right?"

Viviane nodded. "I am impressed, my dear, since we have not been formally introduced."

"Merlin pointed you out to me. Besides," she nodded at the chair, "the recliners were a dead giveaway. That's Merlin's touch or somebody close to him."

Viviane wrinkled her aristocratic nose in distaste. "I can certainly see where a man might enjoy one of those things but it is a shade too . . . well . . . comfortable for me. Especially when I have business to discuss."

"Business? What kind of business?" Tessa struggled to sit upright but she kept sliding back on the slick faux leather of the recliner. "I see what you mean about the chair. I appreciate the thought, memories of home and all that, but could you whip up something with a little less comfort and a little more traction?"

"Certainly." Amusement quirked the corners of Viviane's lips. At once the recliner morphed into a wing chair to match her own. "Better?"

"Much, thanks." The weird sensation of the chair changing around her left her just a tad queasy.

"Wine?" Viviane nodded at the bottle on the table. "It's a rather lovely little Pouilly-Fumé. Very light. Quite refreshing."

"Great." A glass appeared in Tessa's hand and she stared at it. "I gather the bottle is only for appearances."

"Of course."

Tessa sipped at the wine carefully. "This is good."

"Indeed it is. It's from a charming little vineyard in the Loire Valley owned by the same family since the first vine was planted. This was Marie Antoinette's favorite, you know." Viviane held her goblet up at eye level and perused the golden liquid thoughtfully. "I remember saying to Marcel just after the revolution that he shouldn't be at all concerned about—"

"Viviane," Tessa said quickly. "I hate to interrupt but where am I and what am I doing here?"

Viviane lowered her glass and rolled her gaze heavenward like a queen trying to be tolerant with the peasants. Probably something she picked up from Marie. "You are sadly lacking in patience, Tessa."

"I just want to cut to the chase, thank you. Now, what's going on? Where am I?"

Viviane heaved a sigh of resignation. "Very well. First of all, you are in Merlin's quarters."

Tessa's gaze skimmed around the chamber. "It looks like a cave to me."

"It is. Tacky, isn't it?" Viviane cast a disgusted glance around the cavern. "I absolutely hate it. I have always hated it. There's simply no way to create even a modest amount of elegance or refinement or simple style when the primary feature one has to work with is rock. Unfortunately, Merlin adores it."

"Men." Tessa saluted with her wine and took another sip. "Wizard or mortal, they're all the same."

"You can't live with them and," Viviane's eyes narrowed, "and you can't turn them into—"

"Toads?" Tessa said helpfully.

"My dear, I haven't turned a man into a toad in a long time. I much prefer small domesticated pets like white mice or hamsters."

"Hamsters?"

"Indeed. Think about it. Confined to a tiny cage. The only sport available, as a participant or a spectator, is a wheel where they can run forever and never get anywhere. Wonderfully appropriate and extremely satisfying when you consider their masculine egos, don't you agree?"

"Sure. But it's not all that different from a treadmill."

"It depends on one's point of view. Consider it from the perspective of a hamster. Caged. Trapped. Quite at the mercy of the whims of a being much bigger and more powerful. A god, if you will."

"I see what you mean." Tessa grinned at the thought of any number of guys she'd known working up a sweat on a hamster wheel.

"And how do you like Galahad?"

Tessa started at the abrupt change of subject. Just the thought of Galahad warmed her insides. Maybe Viviane couldn't read her thoughts the way Merlin could, but given where she'd been when the lady had so rudely snatched her away, the answer seemed so obvious. "Oh, I like him."

Viviane raised a brow.

"I like him a lot."

"My dear," Viviane's gaze over the rim of her glass meshed with Tessa's. "You love him."

"I do not." Tessa scoffed. "I mean, he's a great guy all right and I will admit the sex was fantastic, but love—I don't think so."

Viviane cast her a pitying glance. "Come now, Tessa. Push aside all that nonsense about how you're from different worlds and have no future together and yada, yada, yada and answer me honestly. Do you love him?"

Tessa stared at the older woman for a long moment. Viviane already knew the answer and Tessa was sure it had nothing to do with reading her mind. Tessa knew the answer, too. She'd probably known it from the moment he first bellowed at her in the chapel. Did Galahad know?

"I thought so." Viviane smiled in a "just us girls" kind of way.

"Why do you ask?"

"It may make a difference." Viviane swirled the wine in her goblet with a studied casualness. "Do you miss your home?"

"Home?" The word cut like a sword. She'd tried to avoid thinking about home and her family and Christmas. Fortunately, events here had moved much too quickly for quiet moments of reflection and self-pity. She'd barely managed to squeeze out time for a small nervous breakdown or two. But damn, she did miss her parents. And Angie. And her friends and her life and her world. And what about those she had left? Were they worried? Frantic? Surely, by now somebody had reported her disappearance? How long had she been gone anyway? She wasn't sure. And what if time in the future moved differently from time in the past? She could return to the day she left or a hundred years in the future. Or maybe not at all. Her throat burned and she fought unbidden tears. "Yeah, I miss it."

"Do you wish to return? Now?"

"I'd kill to return now."

"Excellent." Viviane beamed.

"But Merlin said—"

"Don't give what Merlin said another thought. I believe working together we can accomplish this."

"How?"

"It will take very little on your part. You may refer to your contribution as psychic energy if you wish. Oh, by the way." Merlin's book appeared on Tessa's lap. "You may have this back."

"You took my book? When did you take my book?"

"I believe you were otherwise engaged," Viviane said wryly.

"Oh." A rush of heat swept up Tessa's face.

"At any rate." Viviane waved a dismissive hand. "I had hoped to find an answer, or at the very least a clue, on how to end this ridiculous game of Merlin's and send us all home."

"I gather you didn't find anything?" Tessa paged through the volume absently.

"Unfortunately, no. I suspect unless it is directly in Merlin's hands, or perhaps in yours, there is nothing to the book beyond simple stories." Viviane shrugged. "At least, nothing of significance. Frankly, it's not even especially well crafted."

"I suppose not." Tessa flipped the volume closed.

"The book will not get us what we want. However, you may."

"Me?"

"If I'm correct, we both may well be able to go back to where we belong. I need only your wholehearted support and faith."

"Faith? That seems to be the currency of the realm here. Why are you so hot to send me home anyway?"

"It's quite simple. I find this particular moment in time primitive, uncomfortable and boring. You and I have something in common on that score."

"It's really not as bad as I thought it was," Tessa murmured.

"Oh, come now. It's at least as bad as I remember,

perhaps worse. However, together we can end this travesty and return to where we both belong."

"Sorry. It's tempting," Tessa heaved a heartfelt sigh, "but I can't do it."

"Because you love him?"

"Probably," she said slowly, realizing the truth even as she spoke it. "I love him but I also respect him and I like him. He's arrogant and stubborn but he's also gentle and kind of sweet in his own way. He's got a solid set of basic beliefs in things like honor and honesty and he's got a sharp, twisted medieval sense of humor. And aside from all that, I promised I'd help him. I gave him my word."

"That's all well and good but . . ." Sympathy shone in Viviane's eye. "It simply won't make a whit of difference, you know."

Tessa held her breath. "What do you mean?"

Viviane shrugged. "He did not find the Grail once; he will not find it now."

"No." Tessa shook her head. "Merlin said—"

"Merlin is a dear man and I have loved him for eons but he is a creature who deals in magic and illusion. He is quite literally the eternal optimist when it comes to things he wishes. But even Merlin cannot control the fates." Pity colored Viviane's face. "Galahad is fated to fail and spend his days bitter and alone."

"Not if I can help it." Tessa's voice rang with determination.

"Of course you can help it, Tessa." Viviane smiled pleasantly. "That's precisely why you're here. I suspected you would have a certain amount of loyalty to Galahad's cause but I am extremely pleased to see you care more for the man than his quest."

"Your point?"

"Tessa." Viviane leaned forward, sincerity in her eyes. "Galahad's pride, his sense of self if you will, shall never survive a failure of this magnitude. Why not spare him the entire ordeal?"

"Spare him?" Just the idea of Galahad defeated tightened her stomach. "How?"

"If, as I suspect, we can return to modern times if we pool our collective energies, then I see no reason why we cannot bring him with us." Viviane raised her glass in a triumphant toast.

"Bring him with us? Bring Galahad into the twenty-first century?" The very thought of Galahad confronting modern America or even present-day Britain was enough to make her laugh. Or cry. She pulled a deep swallow of the wine. "He'd be a fish out of water. A living, breathing anachronism."

"Nonsense."

"Nonsense is just the beginning. Where would he go? What would he do?"

"I suspect he would go where you go. As for what he would do," Viviane shrugged as if this really wasn't her concern, "he's a knight."

"That's not in many job descriptions unless he wants to be a waiter at a medieval theme restaurant."

"Sarcasm does not become you, my dear, I was not suggesting any such thing." Viviane drew her brows together in annoyance. "Menial labor would not suit Galahad, although he is an extremely physical man. One can see that quite easily by the breadth of his shoulders and the—"

"Drop it, Viviane, I've already noticed."

"So you have." Viviane leaned back in her chair.

"Galahad is not an unintelligent man. The times he lives in have simply never called for the development of his intellect. In a more stimulating environment, he could, no doubt, manage great things. That is precisely where the very qualities that have made him a shining example of knighthood will serve him well."

"Maybe, but . . . no." Tessa shook her head firmly. "I couldn't do that. Not without asking him."

"Then ask him."

"He'd never agree. He's waited his whole life for this quest. And Arthur is counting on him."

Viviane laughed, a hard unpleasant sound. "Galahad's failure or success will not alter Arthur's fate."

"Galahad doesn't know that."

"No, but you do."

"It doesn't matter." Tessa placed the wineglass on the table that had appeared beside her and stood. "I appreciate your offer but I'll try it Merlin's way. You don't know for certain we won't find the Grail, do you?"

"My dear." Viviane sighed. "You are deluding yourself."

"Maybe. Maybe not. Now, if you could just put me back where you found me." Tessa hugged the book to her chest. "Do I have to tap my heels together or what?"

"Sit down, Tessa." Viviane's voice was cold.

"I'd really rather—"

"Sit down." Viviane's sharp order echoed in the cave. She obviously wasn't as powerful as Merlin but the woman did have a few tricks up her sleeve. Tessa sat.

"I do wish you'd reconsider. At least about going

home yourself." Viviane eyed Tessa with a thoroughness that made the younger woman want to squirm in her chair. "There are a few things you should understand about Galahad before your decision is irrevocable."

"I'm not going to change my mind."

"We'll see." Viviane paused, as if choosing the right words. "If you are staying here out of some romantic idea about Galahad you need to face a few rather unpleasant facts. He shall never love you, not as you love him. He is a man, with all the imperfections of his gender. He will use you to slake his physical desires. He will enjoy your company. He may even whisper terms of endearment in your ear. But his soul died with his wife. I watched him then and I see him now and he still carries that sorrow. There is not a place for you in his heart." Viviane's voice softened. "I am sorry, Tessa, but can you live with that?"

Could she? Could she love him selflessly without expecting his love in return? "I don't know."

"Furthermore, how do you think he'll react when he knows where you're really from? He'll feel betrayed that you haven't confided in him before now. Remember, you did mention honesty among his dubious charms. And, if you can get him to believe you, he'll want to know what happens in the future. What becomes of his king, his country, his world? What is his fate?"

Viviane's voice hardened. "Can you tell him the kingdom falls to ruin? Arthur and his knights are reduced to tales told to children? Can you tell him only in fiction does he succeed in what he wants most in life? Can you tell him the world knows him not as a great knight, not as a flesh-and-blood man but as a character in a bedtime fable? A minor character?"

"I don't know," Tessa whispered.

"And even if by some quirk of cosmic forces you and he do indeed find the Grail, what then? The Grail falls under the protection of he who finds it. If Galahad is successful, he will be its guardian."

"Arthur mentioned that possibility, but so what? It sounds like an honor."

"You have no idea what you're dealing with, do you?" Disbelief colored Viviane's face. "The Grail, if it exists at all, is not some sort of treasure to be brought out at parties or become part of a collection or placed in a glass case at a museum. It stays where it is hidden. Be that a cathedral or a cave. A castle or a cottage. And Galahad stays with it. Bound to the Grail," her eyes smoldered, "forever."

"Forever?" Tessa hadn't once thought about what would happen after they found the Grail. She expected to go home but she hadn't faced the idea of actually leaving him. She'd never considered what his fate would be. Her heart thudded at the thought.

And what if they never found the Grail? Would the quest go on for years until they were both too old to climb up on the back of a horse? Or distinguish a fake dragon from a real one? Or make love on the hard ground? Would she spend her life in an endless search for something they—he—could never have? Would she watch him grow bitter and resentful? Would she grow to hate him as well? Would he hate her? Blame her for his failure?

"It's your choice, Tessa."

Which was worse? Hell with him in a world she could do nothing to improve or change? Or hell without him in her own empty life at home?

Viviane was wrong. She had no choice.

"Thanks for the offer but I'll pass." She got to her feet. "I don't think Merlin would bring me here if there was no chance of finding the Grail. Galahad is one of the good guys and he deserves this shot at his dream. If his success means ultimately I lose him . . ." She shook her head. "I guess I really do love him because I'm willing to risk it.

"As for Galahad never loving me . . ." She shrugged. "I honestly don't know if I can live with that. We'll see. I'm not self-sacrificing enough to say it doesn't matter, because it does. But right now, he likes me and I think he actually respects me. That'll do for the time being."

Viviane's jaw tightened. Tessa knew she'd just made a powerful enemy. "Very well. But do take care the next time you meet a dragon. It may well be real."

Tessa gasped. "You?"

"I had hoped merely to frighten you into agreeing to my proposal. Unfortunately, I failed." She raised her glass. "Pity."

Before Tessa could so much as blink she was lying in the cave, curled up beside Galahad.

Hoping her encounter with Viviane was a dream.

Knowing full well it wasn't.

"Bloody stubborn American!" Viviane glared at the crystal in her hand then turned and hurled it at a rock wall. It shattered in a nicely satisfactory manner. Another appeared and followed the first.

Three smashed goblets later and Viviane was once again calm and composed.

And frustrated.

Tessa St. James was not nearly as smart as Merlin believed. What kind of idiot would pass up the chance to get the one thing she really wanted? And for what? To help Galahad on a futile quest? A fool's errand?

She sipped the wine in the new, intact glass in her hand and pushed away the touch of guilt that nagged at the back of her mind.

Certainly she hadn't needed to be quite so blunt about Galahad's emotions although everyone knew Galahad had loved his wife with a passion beyond measure. Whether that passion existed as anything more than a memory was an inference that could easily be drawn. Why, implying that Galahad could never feel for Tessa what he had felt for Dindrane was really only meant to save Tessa from inevitable heartbreak. Add to that the inescapable fact that Tessa did not belong here anymore than Viviane did, and you could say Viviane was simply trying to help the woman.

Although Merlin would never see it that way.

"Bloody hell." Viviane heaved an irritated sigh and threw her glass against the wall. Immediately, another took its place. She sipped thoughtfully.

She could simply kill them and be done with it. Another dragon, perhaps, real this time, of course. Or something more in line with Tessa's academic expertise. Something Greek, maybe. A hydra or Medusa or some other suitably nasty creature. That would be nicely ironic.

Merlin would never approve.

Merlin will never find out.

Merlin always finds out. She started to throw the glass in her hand, stopped and drained the last drops of wine then helped the goblet meet the fate of its brothers.

She was just damned lucky Merlin didn't know about the dragon. Although she really couldn't be certain of that. Maybe he'd simply let her get away with a threat that was no real danger.

The peril is naught save illusion.

"Bloody hell." Realization flashed in her mind and she flung the glass in her hand with a vengeance. Two more followed in quick succession. She was set up. Of course. There was no question about it. One did not live with a man for more than a thousand years without knowing how his fiendish little mind worked. Worse yet, he knew her equally as well. All he had to do was plant one tiny seed and sit back and watch it grow to fruition. Certainly, she could have caught on and ignored his ire at computer animation, but if he was as much a gambler as she, he would have laid a substantial wager on her picking up the bait. And won.

To add to the insult, she'd actually helped Tessa and Galahad meet the first challenge in the riddle. Helped them on their way to the Grail. And Viviane's way to a permanent stay in the Middle Ages.

She raised back her hand to let fly yet another glass and paused. Somehow, after the third glass, or was it the sixth, or perhaps the twenty-eighth, even the shatter of fine crystal didn't provide a respectable level of satisfaction. The glass vanished.

No, she needed a plan. And possibly a partner. Tessa was the obvious choice but even if Viviane had succeeded in making Tessa realize the futility of a relationship with Galahad, the woman was still far too attached to that "word of honor" nonsense. By the stars, she was as much a sanctimonious knight as Galahad himself.

Allies were few and far between in this day and age. Viviane had never been particularly social in this era. Merlin had been her world. It wasn't until the Renaissance that she'd come into her own, positively blooming in Georgian times. But nothing was as good as the twenty-first century. Determination clenched Viviane's fists. One way or another she was getting back there. For good.

Surely there was someone she could call on for assistance? Or rather, someone she could assist. Subtly, without attracting Merlin's attention. But Tessa had no enemies here. As for Galahad, he was respected and beloved and damn near perfect. It made one want to retch. Not that she didn't like the dear boy herself. She did, in spite of his, well, goodness. Galahad didn't have an enemy in the world. Everyone liked him.

Not everyone.

Viviane pushed the thought away almost as soon as it popped into her head. She'd sooner make a bargain with the devil himself than deal with that nasty, despicable creature. He had a vicious cruel streak, no sense of loyalty whatsoever and probably cheated at every wager he'd ever made. No, he could not be trusted.

Still . . . perhaps just this once such an alliance was permissible. He harbored a great deal of resentment toward Galahad. It would hardly take any effort at all to fan the flames of bitterness to full-fledged hatred. And if things got out of control, and Galahad or Tessa did not survive, it certainly wouldn't be her fault. Not really. Merlin would be annoyed, perhaps even angry, but ultimately any fatalities could not be laid to rest at her feet.

This was a far better idea than that ridiculous faux dragon. This time the game would be played for far greater stakes.

This time, the danger would be real.

Chapter Sixteen

❦

"*Y*ou are remarkably quiet, Tessa St. James." Galahad's comment was offhand, but worry shone in his eye. "Are you certain you are quite ready—"

"I'm fine, really." They rode side by side at a relaxed easy pace. "I just wish you'd stop looking at me as if I was a fragile piece of glass. I went a little off the deep end but I'm all right now." She smiled wryly. "It's probably going to take me some time to get adjusted to the kind of adventures I'm learning are standard issue on a quest."

His eyes twinkled with suppressed amusement. " 'Twas not your, um, fit that concerned me."

"Oh." She bit back a grin. "Then it must have been the sex."

"Indeed." He too stifled a smile.

"It was great."

"That was not in question." He flashed a quick grin, then his expression sobered. "I referred to whether or not you now had regrets as to—"

"No way." She widened her eyes in amazement. "It was perfect." She paused. "Do you? Have any regrets I mean."

"Nay." He shook his head. "But it has been a long time—"

"Don't tell me you haven't done this since your wife died?" *Maybe he was the virgin knight after all.*

He laughed, a full deep sound. "Tessa, it has been more than a decade. I am a man in the prime of life. I am a knight."

"Is that the answer for everything with you?"

"Aye." He laughed again. She could listen to him laugh forever.

"That lecherous chuckle of yours says it all." She eyed him suspiciously. "I thought only the pure of heart could seek the Grail."

"My lady." He swept his arm out with a flourish and bowed his head. "The purity of your heart has naught to do with the lust in your loins."

A sharp laugh or snort exploded from her. "You are really something."

"As are you." A smile lingered on his lips and he directed his gaze toward the barely defined road before them. Long minutes went by. She was going to have to say something soon. With that nasty Viviane on the lose, Tessa didn't have a choice. Who knew what the bitch would do next? Besides, now that Tessa realized love was involved, at least on her side, she wanted to be honest with him. He deserved that much. This little revelation would be much better coming from her than somebody else. Then why couldn't she find the right words?

"What is it that troubles you, Tessa?"

What if he didn't believe her? "Why do you think something is bothering me?"

"I have noted your silence."

What if he thought she was crazy? "I thought you'd enjoy it."

"I have found when you are ill at ease you chatter at a ceaseless pace."

Or a liar. "Thanks."

"But your speechlessness has an air of worry about it. 'Tis most disconcerting."

"If you think this is disconcerting . . ." She sighed. "I don't know where to begin."

His voice was mild. " 'Tis said among the tellers of tales at the king's court that 'tis only one place to start a story."

"Oh?"

"At the beginning."

"The beginning?" Where exactly was the beginning? Merlin popping up in her class? Her mother's package of books? The university library? "Remember when we first met? In the chapel?"

"Indeed. I thought you were an impertinent boy."

"Right. Remember what I was wearing?"

He nodded. "Peculiar garments. I'd not seen their like before."

"Exactly," she said with a note of triumph.

"Nay." He shook his head. "In truth, they were suited more for a man than a women. 'Tis why I was confused. The clothing concealed your true nature until you deigned to correct my incorrect impression with a display of," the corners of his lips curled up in a wicked smile, "boobs."

She groaned. "You're never going to let me forget that, are you?"

"Never, fair Tessa."

"All that aside, didn't you ever wonder where I came from?"

"Merlin said you were from a distant land."

"But didn't you want to know more?"

"I am not a curious man, Tessa, yet I will concede I had hoped to learn more about your home." He chuckled. "Where the people have no sorcerers and believe we live on a ball spinning in the heavens. 'Tis a story to rival that of the greatest bard."

"It's true, Galahad."

He snorted with disbelief. "No one in all of Britain believes such a thing."

"Not today." She braced herself for whatever reaction would come. "But someday they will."

"You make no sense." He slanted her a teasing smile. " 'Tis no longer a surprise to me."

"I'm serious, Big Guy. Someday, everyone in Britain, everyone in the entire world, will understand the earth is a planet spinning through space."

"I do not—"

"Centuries from now, men will circumnavigate the globe and prove the earth is not flat. But that's just the beginning." She leaned toward him. "There are lands beyond England that man hasn't even found yet. Whole continents to be discovered. And there will be inventions. Amazing things to do anything you can imagine. There's the industrial revolution and then steam engines and trains and cars and all kinds of things. And man will fly someday, Galahad. Not just to the sky but to the moon."

He reined in his horse and stared. "Tessa, are you certain you are recovered?"

"I'm fine, really. You have to believe me."

"Such things cannot happen. If you are not mad—"

"I swear I'm not crazy."

"Nay. 'Twould be too easy an answer to believe you daft." Suspicion narrowed his eyes. "Are you a prophetess then, Tessa. A seer?"

"No." She shook her head. "I'm just an ordinary person." *Just a plain old ordinary time traveler.*

"Then how do you know these things?"

She swallowed hard and caught his gaze with hers, willing him to accept her words. "I'm from the future."

"The future," he said carefully, as if trying the concept out in his mind. "The future has yet to happen."

"Actually, I think it has. Kind of. In a parallel sort of way."

He stared and shook his head. "You tell a remarkable tale. But 'tis impossible to believe."

"You believed me when I said the dragon wasn't real."

" 'Twas proof."

"Not much."

"Enough."

"Damn it, Galahad, I don't have any proof." She reached out and grabbed his arm. "Believe me. I'm from the future."

"Nay, Tessa, that cannot be," he said sharply and shook off her hand. " 'Tis no future yet to be from. Indeed, there are the days that have passed. We remember them, sometimes clearly, sometimes not. They are gone. Still, there is no question of their existence. And there is today as we live it and breathe it. But the days beyond this have yet to happen. What you claim is impossible."

"I don't understand it myself. All I know is one minute I was minding my own business in good old two thousand . . ." Maybe an exact date would be too much for him. "Never mind. Let's just say centuries from now, and your buddy Merlin picks me up and drops me in the chapel."

"Merlin had a hand in this?"

"Duh. This whole little adventure, and I use the term loosely, was his idea. Think about it. This scheme has Merlin written all over it."

Galahad brows drew together thoughtfully.

"Whose idea was it for me to come along on this quest?" She pressed her point. "Your quest?"

"Aye," he said softly.

"And with Merlin involved the sky's the limit, right?"

"He is a wizard of extraordinary power."

"I'll give you that." She nodded. "Now, listen carefully, this is the big one for the all-expense-paid dream vacation to the Virgin Islands—"

His eyes widened. "Now I know you jest. 'Tis no islands for virgins."

She ignored him. "Aren't I completely different from anybody else you've ever known?"

"You are a woman of unusual character," he said slowly.

"And have you ever heard one single, solitary person talk the way I do? Or dress the way I did? Or do anything the way I do?"

"Nay."

"So, in a strictly logical sense, doesn't that leave traveling through time as the only thing left?"

"Perhaps . . . Nay!" Anger snapped his words. "I cannot accept this fable of yours."

"But—"

"Quiet!" His tone softened. "Forgive me." He ran his fingers through his hair. "What you've said is inconceivable to me. To the way I understand the nature of the world." He shook his head. "I would have some time alone with my thoughts." He nodded and spurred his horse to pass hers, then settled on the road in front of her. Her mount followed his in an easy walk.

"Take your time." She forced a casual note to her voice but her heart sank. She'd had no idea how he'd take her story and no idea what to expect. This actually wasn't as bad as she'd feared but it wasn't very good either.

They rode on in silence. She stared at his broad back in front of her. What was he thinking? How was he dealing with this? Was he upset? Confused? She shook her head in disgust. No kidding. She'd just done her level best to shatter his beliefs about the very world he lived in. Confusion was probably his mildest reaction.

Without warning he wheeled his horse and rode back to her side.

"Why did you tell me this now?" His gaze simmered with a dark intensity.

She stared at him for a minute. What could she say? *Because I love you and I want you to know just how precious the time is that we have together.* No. She might be able to handle love being one-sided in this relationship but she'd rather he didn't know of her feelings. If she couldn't have his love, she definitely didn't want his pity. "We're in this together, remember. I didn't want there to be any secrets between us." She shrugged. "I thought you should know the truth, that's all."

His gaze searched her face as if looking for the

answers to a thousand years of questions. He nodded abruptly, then spurred his horse and returned to ride ahead of her.

Now what? Galahad struck her as the strong, silent type. He obviously needed time to digest all this. But how much? An hour? A day? A hundred years?

She'd give him a while but eventually he'd have to talk to her again. Until then she could wait.

For an hour, a day, a hundred years. One way or another, she had all the time in the world.

God save them all. It was absurd. Ridiculous. Utter nonsense. It could not be true.

Could it?

Indeed, Tessa believed it. Was there not a ring of truth in her words? Merlin's power was undisputed. If such a far-fetched prospect were possible, would it not take a wizard of remarkable strength? Galahad's mind whirled with conflicting thoughts.

She was unlike anyone, male or female, he'd ever known. Her speech was similar to his own yet oddly flavored. Not like a language unknown to him but more an unfamiliar dialect of his own tongue. He'd already noted how she'd not discussed her home and had wondered at her silence. It was apparent from the look in her eye that she missed her land and her people. Now that he considered it, there was much about Tessa he did not know. Their talks had consisted mostly of her questions about him and his life, his family and friends.

Was he as arrogant as she'd claimed? Is that why he'd paid so little heed to her plight? Hot shame flushed up his face. All he'd concerned himself with was her involvement with his quest. He'd watched her outbursts born of terror when he'd first shown her the castle and after their defeat of the dragon. Each time she'd railed against the reality of the world around her. Of Camelot. Of Arthur. Of him. How had he been so selfish to disregard her fears? And so foolish? To attribute her ravings to the instability of a feminine nature and fail to even wonder why 'twas the very nature of life around them that scared her most.

How had he dared question her courage? The thought struck him like a splash of icy water. He pulled his horse to a stop. Aye, she had succumbed twice to hysteria; yet was that not minor given her predicament?

In her place, would he do better? Could he face a world unknown with the same determination and fortitude? A world in which he was completely alone save for the influence of a wizard and the company of one lone man?

"Are you okay?" Her horse pulled up beside him. Her troubled gaze met his. "Galahad?"

"Aye, Tessa, I am . . . okay." He stared down at her and his heart twisted. She was so fragile and tiny, yet her spirit burned as brightly as any man—as any knight—he'd ever known. And he'd called her a mere woman. There was naught *mere* about the Lady Tessa. "And you?"

"Swell."

He urged his horse on but made no effort to leave her side. " 'Tis time to talk."

She heaved a sigh of relief. "Great. So . . . do you believe me?"

It was his turn to sigh. " 'Tis an odd idea, this traveling from a future that does not yet exist. 'Tis difficult to comprehend or accept."

Her expression fell.

"Yet, I find the notion grows more and more likely with continued thought."

"Really?"

"Indeed. It explains much. About Merlin's insistence on your company here as well as your nature. I should have pressed you for answers about yourself long ago. Yet I was too concerned with my own plans to pay you any heed." He cast her an apologetic smile. "My pardon, Tessa. 'Twas unforgivable."

A soft smile played about her lips. "You had a lot on your mind and time travel probably isn't something that comes up very often."

" 'Tis the first I have heard of such a thing and no doubt 'twill be the last."

"Yeah, I'll bet there's not a steady flow of visitors to the Middle Ages. It's not even one of those nice-place-to-visit kinds of things."

He rolled his gaze toward the sky. Even now, suspecting the truth of her charges, his lack of understanding at all she said would surely drive him mad. But already he had learned to ignore most of her ramblings. "I cannot say I fully understand nor can I believe without question, yet I have come to know you in our days together. You have held my life in your hands as I have held yours. There is trust between us."

"This is a lot to ask for in terms of trust."

"Perhaps. Perhaps it is no more than the sure and certain knowledge than we can depend on one another in times of great trial." He chuckled. "Of course, I would not depend on your prowess with a bow—"

"Wise move."

"—but you have earned my confidence and my loyalty. Now . . ." He reached over and took her hand. "I should like to hear more. Tell me, fair Tessa, of the future from which you come."

"There's a lot to tell." She shook her head. "I don't know . . ."

"Begin with the ball spinning through the heavens."

"Okay." She hesitated as if gathering her thoughts then launched into a saga too fantastic to be believed. Yet every word she uttered rang with the conviction of truth. She spun a tale of seafaring adventurers defying the wisdom of their day to travel ever onward in the same direction and at last reach the point where they'd begun. She spoke of carts and wagons moving without need of horses or oxen. She talked of fantastic devices to allow men to fly like birds through the sky and higher yet, beyond the clouds to the moon.

Minutes flowed to hours and they traveled on, hands clasped between their mounts, her voice bringing visions to his mind he didn't dare accept. Yet, how could he not? He'd venture a query now and then but mostly he absorbed all she said like a parched man drinking at a spring. The wonders of her world enchanted him and cluttered his head with all he'd never dared to dream of. He marveled at her knowledge. Knowledge he grew more and more confident was indeed the truth. Knowledge of what was her past and would be his future.

And what of his fate?

The question hovered at the edge of his mind. She had not said a word about his destiny. Or his king's.

Or his country's. She had not commented on their quest. Would they decipher the riddle and meet its challenges? Would they find the Grail? Why, in all her discourse, had she said naught about that which concerned him most?

The sun drifted low in the western sky. They approached a small stream set in a clearing.

"Here, Tessa, we shall stay the night." He slid off his horse and turned to help her dismount.

"What, no cave tonight?" she said lightly, reaching down to him. "Where's a Hilton when you need one?" He set her on her feet and released her quickly.

"Wait a minute." She studied his face. "What's wrong?"

"I do not know what you mean." His manner was curt. Why had she not told him what he most wanted—nay—needed to know? He pivoted on his heel and busied himself with preparations for the night. He pulled their bedding and bags from the horses, removed their saddles and hobbled them close to the stream, a short distance from where he would build a fire.

She stared at him silently for a long moment then turned to the bags with their provisions. Within minutes, he had a fire laid and sat before it, staring at the flicker of flame growing brighter. She settled beside him and handed him pieces of the bread and cheese they'd brought along.

"We didn't bring much of this." She eyed the meager meal with a skeptical smile. "But I'm actually starting to acquire a taste for it. Have I told you about pizza yet?"

He nodded absently but kept to himself. Did she not

know the answers to the questions raging in his mind? Would she keep such knowledge from him if he was to ask? A direct, forthright question? His mouth could not form the words. Why not?

Fear? God's blood, what nonsense. He was a knight. He had naught to fear from the truth.

Or was it truth itself that brought the rush of fear to his belly?

"I am not hungry." He tossed the bread and cheese aside, pulled himself to his feet and strode to the stream. His mind was muddled with questions and accusations and confusion. Galahad leaned his shoulder against a gnarled oak and stared at the brook bubbling past until the sun slipped below the horizon and the moon shone bright as day on the waters.

Tessa came and stood silently by his side. "Time's up. Spill it, Galahad, what's the matter? What's bothering you?"

" 'Tis naught—"

" 'Tis too! You've been here sulking or thinking or debating for a good hour now. What's going on?"

"Very well." He turned to face her. "Tell me the rest of your fable, Tessa."

"What do you mean?" Caution edged her words.

"You have told me much about what will happen in the centuries to come. Yet you have not uttered a single word about tomorrow or next day or the day to follow."

"I haven't?"

"You know full well, on this alone you have remained silent." He struggled to keep the anger out of his voice. Was he upset with her or himself?

She stepped back and raised her chin in the stubborn manner he knew all too well. "I didn't think it was a good idea."

"Not a good idea? By the fires of Satan, Tessa, why not?"

"It might . . ." She shrugged helplessly. "I don't know. Change things I guess."

"I do not understand."

Her words came slowly as if carefully chosen. "If I told you that you find the Grail, wouldn't that affect how you acted from this point on? Wouldn't you be more likely to take risks knowing everything will work out in the end?"

"Is that my destiny? Do I find the Grail?" He held his breath.

"Wait, I'm not done yet. What if I said you didn't? Would you want to keep going or give up? What would be the point?"

He clenched his teeth. "Do I find the Grail?"

She stared him straight in the eye. "I can't say."

"You will say!" The words exploded from him. "By all that is holy, Tessa, tell me! Now!"

"No!" Her voice trembled. "Not now! Not ever! Besides, Merlin told me what happened once may not necessarily happen again. The major pieces of history, turning points, I suppose, can't be changed. But smaller events, like your quest for the Grail, can."

The truth of what she refused to say surged though him and settled in the pit of his stomach. "I did not succeed then."

"I didn't say that." Denial rang in her words. "And whether you did or didn't in some other version of this timeline doesn't mean anything. Zip. Nada. All that matters is here and now." She reached up with both hands and grabbed his tunic. "Don't you understand? We're reliving these days, you and I. Together. Whatever might have happened before has been erased, the slate wiped clean. This is the opportunity you've waited for all your life. Don't blow it because you think that, one way or another, it's already determined. It's not!"

"Are you to be my savior then, Tessa?" The words came out with a bitterness he did not intend and she jerked her hands away as if burned.

"It's not like that!" She stepped back but he grabbed her shoulders and forced her to look into his eyes.

"If you will not tell me of my fate, tell me this then: what becomes of my king and my country?"

"I can't—"

He shook her sharply. "Tell me! If it is as you say and Arthur's destiny cannot be changed by finding the Grail, 'twill make no difference to know. What does the future hold, Tessa? How does history speak of them? Of all of us? Are the deeds of Arthur and Lancelot remembered by man or is all lost in the mists of time that stretch betwixt your world and mine?"

"Stop it!" She wrenched out of his grasp. Her chest heaved with angry breaths and the moonlight reflected sparks of anguish in her eyes. "Why do you want to know? What difference does it make?"

"It makes a great deal of difference. To know my life and the lives of my king and my father have not been for naught. To know history has remembered us. To know my accomplishments and those of others I hold dear are not forgotten!"

"You're not forgotten." She shot the words at him like an arrow, unerring and straight for the target.

"Everyone knows the story of Arthur and Guinevere and Lancelot and Galahad and all the other Knights of the Round Table. Everyone knows all about Merlin and Camelot. There are vast libraries filled with books about nothing but your exploits. You're a damned legend!"

"A legend?"

"A myth! A fairy tale! But you're not history! History is real life and you and Arthur and all of it aren't included!"

Her words slammed into him with the force of an unseen blow, knocking his breath away, chilling his soul. Shock coursed through him. "What are you saying?"

"I'm saying . . ." She pushed her hair away from her face in a weary gesture. "In my time, nobody believes that you were real. That you ever existed." She hugged her arms to her chest and refused to meet his eyes. "You're a story in a children's book."

"How can this be?" he whispered.

"Merlin didn't want your time spoiled by the scrutiny of history, so he made the world believe none of it was real." Regret touched her voice and her gaze meshed with his. "I'm so sorry."

He stared at her. 'Twas no doubt as to her words: the truth was revealed in her eyes. " 'Tis no wonder you have questioned the reality of the world around you since our first meeting."

"I didn't want to tell you."

He laughed softly. "As you have said, I am a stubborn man. I would not let the question pass unanswered."

He leaned his back against the tree and stared at the

water. 'Twas a great deal to think about, this revelation of Tessa's. "You have called me arrogant, as well." An ache tore at his insides. "I have not thought of myself as such. Only as who I am for good or ill, yet I must be."

He bent down and pulled a tuft of grass from the earth, crushing the blades in his hand. " 'Tis an odd notion to learn you will live and die with naught to mark your passage on the earth save tales told in the night around a fire." He opened his fist and sifted a few blades through his fingers. "Only an arrogant man would find such a fate distasteful."

"You and Arthur and everything all of you did is re-membered." There was a desperate note in her voice.

"Aye, but not as real men." He shook his head. " 'Tis a difference."

"Why?"

" 'Tis better to be known for the fact, no matter how feeble, than the falsehood." His hand dropped to his side and the last pieces of grass drifted to the ground.

"Do you hate me for telling you?" Fear shadowed her voice.

"Hate you?" He stared at her in the moonlight. *I could not hate you, Tessa. You may well be my soul.* "Did Merlin not say I could not find the Grail without you?" She nodded. "Then I was right." He spoke more to himself than to her. "You are my savior."

"Is there anything I can do to help? Do you want to talk or something?"

"I think not, but thank you." He smiled wryly. "I do not find the same pleasure in speech as you do." Even in the pale light, he could see the worry on her face. "Go to sleep, Tessa. It has been a long day. 'Twill be fine in the morning."

She stared at him in the dark. "Promise?"

"You have my word."

She nodded and walked back to the fire. He watched her for a moment or an eternity. He was right when he'd thought himself bewitched by her. Even now, stunned by the prospect of his fate, he could not help but wonder if her presence was worth any price. She did not believe in magic, yet did she believe in love? Surely not. She believed in only those things she could see and feel. 'Twas odd that he should wonder such a thing now. Still, wasn't Tessa and the quest, the future and the past all entwined together like a vine climbing toward the sun?

He settled his back against the tree and stared at the sky. The moonlight had faded and the first wink of the stars appeared. Would it be so bad to have his life remembered as more than it was? The deeds of mortal men were never as good as the stories woven around them. He should not mind. He would not be around to witness it.

Would Tessa?

Would she return to her world when their quest was done? Would he lose her forever to a land so far away he could not truly imagine it? No. Resolve clenched his jaw. By the heavens he would not.

And he would not cease his quest for the Grail. Regardless of what may have happened in another time, another life, he would persevere. He would fulfill his destiny with the woman he loved by his side. And in the process, find a way to keep her beside him where she belonged.

He laughed bitterly to himself.

What else could a legend do?

* * *

What was he thinking?

Tessa pulled the blanket tighter around her and rolled over in a futile attempt to find comfort. Was the ground harder in the Middle Ages or was her twenty-first-century body just not used to sleeping on dirt and grass? Probably both.

Not that even a bed would make a difference right now. How could she have been so stupid? How could she have told him anything about his future, let alone that her world didn't think he ever existed? She groaned to herself. His reaction was a classic case of shooting the messenger and she couldn't blame him. She'd shoot herself if she had the chance.

Still, she'd managed to keep her mouth shut about his quest. She didn't tell him he failed in reality but succeeded as a legend. Oh, he'd love to hear that.

She sighed and gazed up at the heavens. Weird to think these were the same stars she'd stared at all her life. Everything would change through the centuries but aside from a minor alteration here and there, the night sky would remain the same. She rolled to her side, wrapped her arms around the leather saddle-bag she used as a pillow, closed her eyes and wished for sleep. Everything would be fine in the morning. Galahad had given his word and, just like the stars, that she could count on.

Minutes or hours passed and she felt him settle beside her. She opened her eyes and glanced at him. He lay on his back with his arms folded under his head, gazing upward. She ached to cuddle up next to him and offer what little comfort she could but what could she say? *It's all right, Big Guy. Better a legend than nothing at all*. No. He'd let her know when he needed her. If he needed her.

"Tessa?"

"Yes?"

"Is it a good children's story?"

She smiled. He was all right. "It's a great story."

"Does it tell of honor and courage?"

"And loyalty and love."

"And magic, Tessa? In this world of yours that does not know magic, does the tale tell of that?"

"Yes, and so much more."

" 'Tis not so bad then," he said softly, "to be part of such a saga, real or not."

"Not at all." She swallowed the lump in her throat.

He paused as if pulling together his thoughts. "Tessa, was this the truth revealed?"

"I don't know. Maybe."

He blew a long breath. " 'Tis not the first truth revealed between us."

"No," she said quietly. "It's not."

"Tessa?"

"Hmmm?"

"Tell me of the stars." He put an arm around her and pulled her close and she told him everything she'd ever learned about the stars, from Greek legend to science. And when sleep finally claimed her, she noted vaguely how, even when all its secrets were known, the night sky still held a touch of magic.

And so did his arms.

Chapter Seventeen

❧

"Tessa!" Galahad's hard tone jerked her from a restless sleep.

"What is it this time?" She snapped her eyes open. "I'm getting really tired of waking up this way." She sat up and glared at Galahad towering over her. "Don't you ever think about sleeping in? What is it today? Another dragon?"

" 'Twould be preferable, I think." His voice was even.

"Preferable?" She followed the direction of his gaze. Six or seven men, all armed with swords, stared back at them. Three stood, the rest were on horseback. She scrambled to her feet. "Oh, this looks good. Who in the hell are they?"

"Mordred's men," Galahad said softly. "This does not bode well."

"I figured that much," she said under her breath. Give these guys Harleys and they'd look exactly like the motorcycle gang from a bad movie she'd watched late at night a few months ago. Hell's Angels on horseback. "How did they sneak up on us? Weren't you supposed to be keeping guard or something?"

He narrowed his eyes in annoyance. "I am but a man, Tessa, not a legend."

"Swell," she muttered. "Never a legend around when you need one."

The tallest of those standing stepped forward, obviously the leader of the pack, the head minion. Dark and grubby and dangerous. A chill shivered up her spine and she stepped closer to Galahad. The biker swept a curt bow. "My Lord Galahad. I bring you greetings from Prince Mordred. He requests the honor of your presence and extends the hospitality of his home to you and your lady."

"Send Mordred my thanks and my regrets," Galahad said, his voice cool. "But we must decline his gracious invitation."

A nasty smile curled the lips of the prince's biker henchman. "Perhaps I did not make my meaning clear. The Prince insists on the pleasure of your company. My orders are to escort you. You may accompany us in the manner of a knight of your rank, as an honored guest, or . . ."

"Or?" Galahad's eyes darkened.

"Or I fear we shall have to take measures to insure your cooperation." His gaze slid to Tessa and slithered over her like a lustful snake. "And that of your lady."

Galahad tensed at her side.

"What does that mean?" she said out of the corner of her mouth. "Insure our cooperation?"

"You do not wish to know," he murmured. He nodded to the gang's leader. "Then by all means, we shall be delighted to accompany you."

"Sounds like fun. Do we have to leave right now or can I have a few minutes to freshen up?"

The minion's eyes squinted as if he didn't understand her question. Or possibly English.

"You know? Wash my face? Brush my teeth?" She smiled sweetly. "Pee in the woods?"

Galahad snorted. Even the biker had the grace to look embarrassed. "Very well," he snapped. "But not alone. I shall go with you."

He moved toward her. Galahad took a step in front of her to block him. "The lady deserves a semblance of privacy. I shall accompany her."

The minion studied him for a moment then nodded. "As you wish. She may go but you must stay where I can see you. Forgive me, my lady, but should you attempt to escape our company—"

"Escape?" Galahad raised a brow. " 'Tis an odd word to use for such a cordial gathering."

"Pardon me, my lord, a slip of the tongue. Perhaps I should have said depart. Regardless . . ." He directed his gaze to Tessa. "I shall be forced to take whatever measures necessary to subdue both you and your knight."

She didn't like the sound of that. "What kind of measures?"

"My lord prefers his guests still breathing." Their captor grinned, a scraggly, yellow, gap-toothed parody. "But 'tis not always possible."

"Thanks for clearing that up. Now," she tilted her head at the stream, "can I go?"

He nodded. Tessa and Galahad turned and walked quickly toward the brook.

"What do we do?" she whispered.

" 'Tis naught we can do, for the moment." Concern creased his forehead.

"These are really bad guys, Galahad." She glanced over her shoulder. The pack leader and two of his sidekicks watched them intently like wolves sizing up lambs. Were they hoping she and the Big Guy would make a break for it? Her stomach churned. Probably. "Really, really nasty."

"Is Mordred, too, spoken of in your legends?"

"Oh yeah."

"And?"

"And there are a lot of differences between the myth and real life. But from what you've told me, Mordred's character is not one of them. Real or fairy tale, he's a definite villain."

They reached the stream and she bent down and splashed water on her face. "I hope you're coming up with some kind of plan."

" 'Twould be nice," he murmured.

" 'Twould be, 'twouldn't it?" Fear sharpened her words.

"Get on with it." The biker's voice cut through the morning like a sword. She shuddered. Bad metaphor.

"Chill out," she yelled. "I'll be done in a minute. I really do have to pee," she muttered. "I'll go over there, behind that tree. You just keep those goons away, especially the big one. I don't like the way he looked at me."

"Nor did I. I shall keep all the *goons* at bay." He stifled a smile then sobered. "Do not worry, fair Tessa. I will not let any harm befall you."

She gazed into his eyes. "I'm counting on that. And I'll do my best to watch your back. I've already figured out one thing."

"That is?"

She headed for the tree. "These guys are real."

Maybe Mordred wasn't that bad after all.

Tessa closed her eyes and sank back in the tepid water of the wooden tub in her room. They'd ridden all day and well into the night before reaching Mordred's castle. Castle Le Fay. Nice fairy-tale name but she hadn't gotten a good feel for it in the dark. She'd expected to be tossed in a dungeon as soon as they'd arrived. Instead, she'd been taken to a chamber similar to her quarters back in Camelot. Best of all, there was a bed. A real bed. She'd collapsed exhausted and slept a dreamless sleep. When she woke up, it was evening and a steaming tub was waiting for her. She had no idea how long she'd soaked and didn't care but she'd never again take for granted the simple pleasures of life. A hot bath and a real bed.

A sharp knock sounded. Before she could say come in, the door swung open and a vaguely familiar figure, nearly as tall as Galahad with dark blond hair and a rather nicely built body, strolled into the room as if he owned the place.

"Hey!" She scanned the room for a towel and curled up in the tub, trying to cover all her most exposed parts with her hands. "What in the hell do you think you're doing?"

"Ah, the fair Lady Tessa." The blond's gaze raked over her and he smiled in appreciation. He really was awfully good-looking in a too-smooth, too-slick, time-share-salesman kind of way. "I was warned you were quite lovely but your reputation does not do you justice."

"I don't have a reputation," she snapped. "Do you mind?"

"Not at all." He shrugged. "A lady's reputation is of no real consequence to a man unless he is considering marriage. Which I am not." He smiled wickedly. "Unless you would care to change my mind?"

She groaned. "No. I didn't mean that. I meant do you mind—I'm naked here."

He shook his head. "I do not mind that either."

"Would you just hand me that"—she waved at something laid across a chair that looked more like a sheet than a towel—"that cloth over there."

He plucked the sheet from the chair and started toward her.

"Wait. Stop. Don't come any closer."

"If you wish this." He dangled the linen from two fingers. "I either have to bring it to you or you must fetch it from me."

"Great." She heaved a resigned sigh. "Bring it here." He stepped to the tub and held out the sheet. "Can you turn around? Or at least close your eyes?"

"I could, I suppose, but 'twould not be as much fun."

"Fine." She pulled herself to her feet and snatched the sheet from his hands, wrapping it around herself and climbing out of the tub. He smiled with obvious enjoyment.

"You're Mordred, aren't you?"

"Indeed I am." He took her hand and brought it to his lips. She was right—he did own the place. "I am honored to have you here."

"It's not like we had a choice." She withdrew her hand and resisted the immediate impulse to wipe it on the sheet.

"No?" He drew his brows together. "Was not Oscar courteous and respectful in issuing my invitation?"

"Oscar?" An image of the chief biker flashed in her mind. "The leader of the pack's name is Oscar?"

"Oscar is the captain of my guard. Does his name displease you?"

"I kind of thought he'd be more one of those single syllable guys. You know, something simple and basic like 'Ugh' or 'Grunt.'"

He chuckled. "I was warned your speech was unusual but your meaning is apparent. Oscar is perhaps not as cultured as he could be."

"Cultured? Try civilized. It must have been the leer that gave him away."

"He does have an eye for the ladies. Nonetheless, he is extremely loyal, obeys orders and is far more intelligent than he appears."

"The perfect goon," she murmured.

"But I have not brought you here to discuss Oscar's virtues—"

"Before we get into that, would you mind if I got dressed?"

"I think you are most lovely clad as you are."

"I'll bet." Her gaze skimmed the room. "Do you have any idea where my clothes are?"

"If you refer to that rag you arrived in," he raised a shoulder in a dismissive shrug, "I ordered it burned."

"You burned my dress!" She glared. "What am I supposed to wear?"

"Do not despair, my lady, I have ordered a new gown to be found for you." He walked back to the door, stepped into the corridor and barked a command to an unseen servant. Within a minute he returned, shutting the door firmly behind him. " 'Twill suit you, I think." He held out a garment.

"Thanks. My old one was looking pretty ratty anyway." She took the dress, glanced at it and grimaced. "It's yellow."

"A lovely color for one with your fair hair and dark eyes."

"It's great, if you like the jaundiced look. Now, turn around so I can get dressed."

"If you are certain you do not need my assistance?"

"I'll manage somehow."

"Very well." He turned and she dropped her sheet to struggle quickly into the gown.

"When you are ready, I wish to speak to you."

"You know, I don't think that's such a good idea without Galahad." She'd always wondered why everyone had servants in past eras. Now she knew. The clothing here wasn't particularly complicated but she could use a little help.

"Without Galahad is precisely how I wish it." His words had a hard edge.

She adjusted the gown and frowned. This wasn't exactly what she had in mind. "You can turn around now."

He turned and gazed at her for a moment, a sleazy sort of admiration on his face. "I do envy Galahad your company, my lady. Your charms are quite obvious."

"They'd be less obvious if there was more to this dress." She tugged at the bodice of the low cut-gown in a futile effort to pull the dress higher.

He laughed. "And as witty as you are beautiful."

"Thanks. Can we sit down?"

"Be my guest."

"I already am," she murmured and glanced around the room. Aside from the bed there was a single stool near the fireplace, a wooden chest and a long, armless bench. The bed was definitely out. The stool was too awkward so that left the bench. She moved to it with as much dignity as she could muster and sat down, keeping her spine rigid, sitting as straight and tall as possible. The last thing she needed was her chest hanging out. Now . . ." She narrowed her eyes. "What do you want?"

"And direct as well. Excellent." He strode to the bench and sat down beside her. She wanted to inch away but held her ground. "I have a proposal that may interest you."

"I doubt it. What kind of proposal?"

His tone was casual. Too casual. "First, you should know I am well aware of Galahad's quest. I would much prefer that he fail."

"That's a surprise." He raised a brow at her tone. "Want to tell me why?"

" 'Tis no secret there is no affection lost between Galahad and I." A nasty light glinted in his eye. "I quite despise him and he cares little for me. 'Twould provide one of the pleasures of my life to do away with him without a second thought."

"Swell." Her stomach clenched. "So, what's the problem? I thought everybody liked Galahad."

" 'Tis exactly why I do not." He rose to his feet and sauntered across the room. "I know you are from a far-off land and are therefore not well versed in the intrigues and histories of my father's kingdom." He stopped and slanted her a pointed glance. "I am his heir, you know. Next in line to be king of all the Britons."

"That's what I hear."

"He will, however grudgingly, pass on to me his crown, but his affection is reserved for Galahad." His voice hardened. "He regards Galahad as a son and myself as—"

"Scum of the earth?" she said sweetly.

" 'Tis an odd phrase but well said, my lady."

"Thanks." She rose to her feet and folded her arms over her chest. "I can see why you don't like Galahad but what does his quest have to do with you?"

"I do not wish to wait for my father's death to achieve my rightful place."

Unease crept up her spine. "I still don't get it."

" 'Tis simple enough to comprehend." His tone was cold and downright evil. How could she ever have thought he was cute? "My father is counting on the Grail as a symbol to pull the country together. I will not allow that to happen.

"Even as we speak, I have loyal followers in every corner of the kingdom. Supporters who agree with me that Arthur is not the man he was once. 'Tis past time to wrest control from him and place it in the hands of someone who will do for this land what he can do no longer. Someone with the courage to smite our enemies. To conquer, not compromise. England was once a country of proud warriors. My father has turned it into a land of weak old men. Arthur's day is nearing an end and before it is too late, before we are crushed at the hands of our foes, the people need—nay—they demand a new king."

"And that would be you?"

"Arthur is the past." He straightened his shoulders and raised his chin. All he needed was a cape billowing out behind him to complete the picture. She'd bet he had one too. "I am the future."

You are one crazy, loony tunes prince.

"What do you want me to do?"

"I wish you to convince Galahad to cease his quest for the Grail."

"Is that all?" She scoffed. "I thought it was something hard."

"Do not jest with me." His voice was low and controlled. "He will do it for you."

"What planet are you from, pal?"

His brow furrowed with confusion.

"Forget it," she snapped. "What could possibly make you think Galahad will dump his heart's desire just because I ask him to?"

" 'Tis love that will bend Galahad's will to yours." Mordred smirked. "The man is besotted by you."

"Besotted? Hah! Get real." She snorted and crossed the room. "Where did you get a stupid idea like that?"

Mordred frowned. "I was led to believe—"

"Led to believe Galahad loved me? Don't believe everything you hear. It's a crock." Even as she said the words she wished they weren't true. "Who in the—" She stopped and stared. "Viviane! I'm right, aren't I? That's who fed you this line, isn't it?"

"It matters not, if it is untrue." He studied her for a long moment. A crafty smile spread across his face. "Perhaps I was simply mistaken. Perhaps it is you who love him."

She shrugged. "So what?"

"So, my lady, if you do not convince him to end his quest I will kill him."

"I don't think so."

"Oh?" He raised a brow. "And why is that?"

Beats me. Hopefully, the prince couldn't tell a bluff when he saw one. She swaggered over to him with as much confidence as she could manage and poked her finger at his chest. "Because your daddy, the king, wouldn't like it."

He paled and grabbed her hand. "I care not what my father does or does not like."

"Maybe, but it wouldn't be a smart move to piss him off before you're ready for this big revolution, would it?" She smirked up at him and tried to pull her hand away but he held it fast. Her heart hammered with fear but she refused to let it show. *Fake him out, Tessa.*

"You are indeed as clever as I suspected." He stared down at her with icy blue eyes. Arthur's eyes without the warmth. Creepy. Very creepy. "But I do not need to kill him at once. A quest of this nature is of undeterminable length. I could simply throw him in my dungeons and forget about him. His absence would not be cause for concern in my father's court for years. Eventually they would assume the noble knight has gone the way of so many before him, slain in a quest to save king and country. None would ever know he lives his days in foul stench and darkness on a diet of rats and spiders and whatever else he may find."

She stared, praying her defiance hid her frantic efforts to come up with something. She'd already saved the Big Guy from an immediate death only to condemn him to something slower and torturous. How much worse could she do? "No way. It won't work."

"Why not?" He yanked her harder to him. A muscle ticked in his jaw. This was one dangerous guy.

"He doesn't come back and he's a hero. They'll make him a legend. They'll sing songs about him and tell stories about him." She smiled a wicked smile of her own. "Think about it, Mordred. His name will live forever."

"Stop!" He shook her hard.

"Anyway you look at it, you're screwed. You can't kill him now. You can't kill him later." A note of triumph sounded in her voice. "Now let me go. You're hurting me."

"I think not." His words were slow and deliberate. "I don't think I shall let you go at all."

"What do you mean?" Could he hear the fear in her voice?

"She said you have something he needs. He cannot find the Grail without you."

"Viviane is full of it."

"I believe her."

"Then you're full of it too."

"Am I?" His eyes gleamed and her breath caught. "Galahad's quest would be doomed to fail and I would not be involved if you were to, how shall I put it, suffer an unfortunate accident."

"You wouldn't kill me." She forced a conviction she didn't feel to her voice.

" 'Twould be a pity." He glanced down. Her chest was crushed against him and he could see right down her dress. "A very great pity. Perhaps there is another way." He grabbed the back of her head with his free hand and forced her face to his, crushing her lips beneath his mouth. Real fear shot pure adrenaline through her limbs. She struggled against his iron grip with a strength she never suspected she had. Would he rape her? Right here? Right now?

"St. Margaret Mary's High School. Self Defense 101."

His grasp eased slightly. She pulled away and launched Sister Abigail's premier move, the steps automatic in her mind: *hands clasped, quick turn and jab.* Her elbow rammed into his stomach.

He groaned and doubled over. She gulped and tried to pull air into a body too terrified to breathe on its own.

He gasped and straightened. Rage colored his face. Terror gripped her. "Whore!"

He pulled back his hand and cracked it across her face, knocking her backward. Pain swept through her. Stars crowded her vision. She stumbled and fell to her knees. He stepped to her, grabbed her hair in his hand and yanked her to her feet. She swung her arms wildly in a futile effort at defense.

"You fool." He spit the words. "You do not understand. One way or another Galahad's quest is at an end." He released her hair and thrust her away. She staggered but stayed on her feet.

She lifted her chin and glared. "Don't bet on it, pal. He's the good guy in all this and the good guy always wins."

He stared in disbelief then laughed. A vicious, mirthless sound that echoed through the room. "Do not wager on that, my lady. When all is said and done, Galahad and his ilk rarely understand that victory requires more than noble virtues and holy morality. Victory goes to he who has strength and power and the will to use it to his gain. To do whatever it may take to triumph."

Her face throbbed with pain. "He won't give up. He'll never give up."

"He has no choice." Mordred turned abruptly and strode toward the door, yanking it open with a vicious force. He turned back toward her. "I will however, give you both the chance to save your miserable lives. If Galahad wishes to continue his quest for the Grail he may do so but he leaves you behind."

"He won't do that."

"I will give him my word no harm will come to you."

"Your word?" She laughed in spite of herself. "Your word doesn't mean a damn thing."

"Nonetheless—"

"And what's your definition of no harm anyway?"

"I will not kill you." His gaze drifted to her breasts and she resisted the immediate impulse to cover her chest with her hands. "Nay, I quite think I should prefer to keep you alive. For a very long time."

She clenched her teeth. "I'd rather die."

"I will be happy to grant your request." He raised a wicked brow. "Eventually."

"Galahad won't go for it."

"Then it is up to you to convince him, my lady. In spite of your observations about my father's reactions, I am more than willing to kill him now and be done with it. If he refuses my offer, I will do so. If, however, he leaves without you, both your lives will be spared. For now. I do not know what you possess that he needs but I have no doubt he cannot find the Grail without you. I want Galahad's failure more than I want his life."

She shook her head. "He won't do it."

"We shall see. Whether he loves you or not he has sworn to protect you. He can ensure your survival only by leaving you in my hands." He smiled slowly. "I must say I am quite looking forward to having you in my hands." He stepped out of the room, the door clanging shut behind him.

Tessa stumbled to the bed and dropped onto it. Her face throbbed where he'd smacked her. All the fear she restrained in Mordred's presence threatened to overwhelm her and she sobbed for a moment then angrily swiped at the tears on her face. This was not the time to cry. She had to think.

How were they going to get out of this one? The only way she could see to escape Mordred's clutches was to accept his offer and let Galahad go on alone. But surely, he'd never agree to leave her behind at Mordred's mercy? Leave her to a fate she could only imagine. A fate that would leave death the only escape. Would he choose the Grail quest over her?

When the offering can be no greater.

Was this the sacrifice of the riddle? Did she have to give up her freedom, condemn herself to a life, however short, with Mordred to save Galahad? In spite of the gutsy facade she'd adopted since her trip through time, she wasn't really very brave or courageous. She'd spent her entire time here bouncing back and forth between sheer terror and hysteria. The bravest things she'd ever done before taking on the middle ages involved challenging the speed limit to beat a yellow light. She talked a good game but she was basically a wimp. Wasn't she? Maybe she was braver than she thought. Maybe not, but her character had never been tested before. She'd never had her own life or anybody else's on the line.

Until now.

Somewhere in the back of her mind, through all of this, she'd believed Merlin wouldn't let anything bad happen to her. That this was just a game and he'd whisk her away before the bell rang for Final Jeopardy. In spite of all the talk about challenges and dangers and how they could only depend on themselves, she really thought Merlin would protect her. It might have been the dragon or the encounter with Viviane or the very real threat in Mordred's eye or all of it together, but she knew now she was wrong. Survival, Galahad's and her own, depended on her.

How could she find the courage to sacrifice her own life to save the life of the man she loved?

How could she not?

Chapter Eighteen

❧

*W*here was Tessa?

Galahad paced the width of the room that served as his prison. 'Twas no use to try the door: he'd heard the unmistakable sound of a bolt thrown when he'd been cast in here. Odd. Why did Mordred not throw him in his dungeons? In truth, 'twas no difference. 'Twas no way out.

Was she hurt?

His jaw clenched. He'd tried to rest as soon as he realized escape was impossible but his sleep was fitful. His mind was too crowded with dreams of Tessa and fears of what may have befallen her.

Was she dead?

His stomach tightened at the thought and he pushed it from his mind. He would know if she was dead. Somehow, he would know.

The door swung open with a loud creak.

"Galahad. Such a pleasure to see you again." Mordred stepped into the room.

" 'Tis not the word I would have used," Galahad said coolly.

"We never were very much alike." Mordred glanced around the chamber. "How do you find my home, Galahad? If memory serves, you spent some time here as a boy, did you not?"

"Aye, when this castle was home to Arthur and his court."

" 'Twas not in truth Arthur's. 'Twas my mother's and her kin's." Mordred's voice was hard. "And now 'tis mine."

Galahad raised a brow but kept silent.

"So," Mordred narrowed his eyes, "do you not wonder as to the fate of your delightful companion?"

Galahad carefully kept his expression blank. 'Twould not do to let Mordred see how much Tessa meant to him. 'Twould be as foolish as handing the man a sword and aiming it at his own heart. "Nay. I have had much else to consider since my arrival. I assume she is well?"

"She is quite well. For the moment."

Galahad released the breath he had not known he held. "What do you want of me, Mordred? Why am I here?"

"Say but the word and you shall be free."

"And after you've taken such pains to bring me here." Galahad arched a brow. "I can scarce believe 'tis that simple."

"Oh, 'tis indeed simple." Mordred crossed his arms over his chest and leaned insolently against the door frame. "You have but to give me your word that you will give up your quest for the Grail and you, and your lady, may leave."

Galahad snorted. " 'Tis all you ask?"

"Not entirely. I shall provide you with an escort to

the sea and a ship and you, with the fair lady by your side, shall sail away from England. Forever."

"Why would I accept such a proposal?"

"To save her life." Mordred's eyes glittered with malice.

"And if I refuse?"

" 'Tis not the only offer I have made this night." Mordred held out his hand and studied his nails. "Your lady is even now considering a somewhat different proposition that would ensure your safety."

"This is between you and I, Mordred." Galahad clenched and relaxed his hands by his sides. "Tessa is naught but a woman and plays no part in our differences."

Mordred scoffed in disdain. "My dear, Galahad, she plays a very big part. 'Tis my understanding that without her you cannot find the Grail. Still, as you said, she is nothing but a woman and so I find her importance difficult to believe. Yet I have offered to allow you to continue your quest if," a satisfied smile quirked his lips, "she stays behind."

"Never," Galahad said softly.

" 'Tis your choice and that of the lady's. Which you choose matters not to me. Abandon the quest and the two of you leave together, never to return to this land. Or leave her here and go on without her. Regardless of whether or not she is indeed necessary to your success, I would wager that noble sense of honor you prize so highly would undermine your efforts to find the Grail. Abandoning the Lady Tessa to pursue your own desires would destroy your very soul. Either way, victory is mine."

"So it would appear."

"I care not which you choose." Mordred shrugged. "I care only that you fail on your quest."

Galahad grit his teeth. " 'Tis not difficult to determine why."

"Nay. 'Tis obvious. I cannot have the people rally around the Grail. I will not give my father that advantage."

"You cannot defeat Arthur."

"Oh but I can. With your assistance."

Galahad narrowed his eyes. "You will receive no help from me."

Mordred laughed. "Think long and hard before you declare yourself, Galahad. I have given you two choices. There is a third. I can simply kill you now and still keep the lady for my own."

Anger surged through him. His voice sounded level and cold with a threat even a fool would understand. "I swear by the saints above, Mordred, you touch her and I will not rest, dead or alive, until I see your face twisted in agony."

"Well said." Sarcasm dripped from Mordred's words. "You are as noble now as you were as a youth. 'Twill do you no good but 'tis impressive nonetheless." He stepped through the open door and spoke in low tones to a guard in the corridor. "I will give you some time to make your decision. And some assistance as well." Mordred nodded and snapped the door closed.

She was alive. Relief washed through him. But for how long?

He paced the room and tried to think. He'd not been here in more than twenty years. But Castle Le Fay was not invulnerable. There were tunnels, hidden in the dark bowels of the fortress, that led to the forest outside the castle gates or to hiding places within the castle walls. The perfect places for young boys to explore on long-ago winter days. And all led to freedom.

Did they still exist? And if so, did Mordred know of them? Even as a child he had not often joined with the other youth. If indeed he knew of the existence of such passageways perhaps the details had long ago passed from his mind, replaced by his burning ambition for the crown and his appetite for power. 'Twas indeed a glint of madness in his eye. And madmen were never as shrewd as they believed themselves to be. At least, he prayed 'twas true.

If they could not escape he would have to accept one of Mordred's offers, even though he suspected the prince would never allow either Tessa or himself to leave alive. 'Twas a choice no man should have to make—loyalty to his king and his life's ambition or the salvation of the woman he loved.

He was wrong.

'Twas no choice to be made at all.

The door opened abruptly. Rough voices sounded in the corridor. Tessa stumbled into the room.

"Tessa!"

Her head jerked up. Her eyes widened. "Galahad!"

At once she was in his arms. He greeted her with a frantic relief and a need to embrace her, touch her, kiss her as if, for once, 'twas he who questioned the reality of that before his eyes. He could not hold her close enough and he could not let her go.

"Galahad!" She pulled back and her gaze searched his. "Thank God. Are you okay?"

"I am . . ." He stared at her face, one side swollen and discolored. "Who did this to you?"

"It doesn't matter."

Fury burned within him. "Who did this?"

"Who do you think? Prince Personality. Our gracious host."

He gently pushed her hair away from her cheek. "I shall kill him for this."

"Normally I'm not into violence but go for it. Although, I gave as good as I got."

He smiled in spite of himself. "The teachings of the good sisters?"

She grinned. "Sister Abigail would have been proud."

"As am I." He released her reluctantly. "We have a great deal to talk about and I fear Mordred will give us little time."

"No kidding. That is one cranky prince." She lowered her voice. "I think he's nuts. You know, crazy. Daft."

"I agree, there is madness in his manner."

She touched the side of her face carefully and winced. "And everywhere else. So." She stared at him with an expectant look. "What's the plan?"

"The plan?"

"Right. How are you getting us out of here?"

"Tessa." He chose his words with care. " 'Tis not exactly a plan."

"But you do have a plan, right?"

" 'Tis more . . . an idea?"

"You're asking me?" She wrapped her arms around herself and rubbed her forearms as if chilled. And well she might be. He'd not noticed it before but she was wearing a different gown. One that provided an all too revealing view of Tessa's all too appealing charms.

" 'Tis a bit, um . . ." He waved his hand at her dress and frowned. "Bare, is it not?"

Tessa glanced down then back to him. "Mordred gave it to me."

" 'Tis most immodest. I do not care for it."

"Good." She grinned. "Now, don't change the subject. What are we going to do?"

He did indeed have a glimmer of an idea but he did not wish to raise her hopes. "I am not entirely certain."

"Just what I wanted to hear. In that case," she pulled a deep breath, "Mordred offered me a deal."

"Tessa, I—"

"No." She thrust out her hand to stop him. "Listen to me and then we can talk, but I figure we don't have much time to work anything else out and I've got to warn you." She paused. "I've made up my mind."

She pulled her gaze from his and paced, shaking her hands in front of her in that odd manner she had. "Mordred has learned about that stupid business of Merlin's. That I-have-something-you-need-and-you-can't-find-the-Grail-without-me stuff."

"How could he have learned such a thing?"

"Let's just say there's a leak in the castle."

"Only when it rains," he murmured.

"It doesn't matter how he knows," she said sharply, "only that he knows. Anyway, he says you can go if I stay here. So . . ."

She fell silent. He wanted to say something but could do naught save stare. She turned toward him. Her gaze met his. *By the heavens, she is a stubborn wench.*

"I'm going to stay." She couldn't quite hide the hint

of fear in her eyes. *And courageous. She would have made a fine knight.*

"Then I will not leave."

"You have to." Her voice quavered but held firm.

"Nay."

"There isn't—"

"Nay, Tessa." He shook his head. "I can be as obstinate as you and I will not go without you by my side."

"Are you sure about this? This is your chance to continue on your quest exactly the way you planned. Without me."

"Without you?" He smiled. "I cannot conceive of continuing my quest, my life, without you. 'Twould be like cutting out my heart."

For a long moment, she stared as if afraid to believe him. Then she heaved a relieved sigh or a sob and buried her face in her hands. "Thank God. I was so scared." She dropped her hands and cast him a shaky smile. "I have a confession for you. I'm a wimp. I don't have a brave bone in my body. And I really don't want to die before I'm even born. It's not how I planned on spending my sabbatical. I don't want to think about what it would be like here with that slimy, sleazy, obnoxious creep. What he was planning to do to me or with me before he finally killed me. And I'm pretty sure—hey!" Her forehead furrowed thoughtfully. "Did you say something about your heart?"

He raised a brow. " 'Tis not an opportune time to discuss matters involving my heart."

"It may be the only time we have," she said slowly. "What did you mean?"

His gaze meshed with hers. Was it hope he saw in her eyes? Or unease? What if she did not share his feelings? His world was so different when compared to hers, how could he dare—

"Galahad?"

He shrugged and held his breath. "I love you, Tessa St. James."

"I don't . . ." She shook her head in disbelief. "What about your wife?"

"My wife is long dead."

"But you still love her."

"Aye." He nodded. "And I shall love her forever."

"That's what I thought," she said quietly.

"Tessa, my heart and my mind have wrestled with this since I first suspected the truth of my feelings. I vowed to love Dindrane always and indeed I will." He paused. How could he make her understand? " 'Tis not a question of her or you. My love for you does not diminish what I felt for her."

"But she was perfect."

"And you are not." He couldn't resist a wry smile. " 'Tis one of your charms."

Tessa shrugged helplessly. "I can't compete with perfect."

" 'Tis not a competition. 'Tis difficult to explain." He struggled to find the right words. "Dindrane possessed my heart. You, fair Tessa, are my heart. It is as if I am incomplete without you."

"I don't understand."

"I do not fully comprehend it myself. I know I would have gladly given up my life for my wife if given the choice. I would have protected her with my strength and my sword and my last breath but I would not have wanted her by my side in times of trouble."

He gazed into her eyes. "I would have you always

by my side. I would die to save you but if I could not, I would die with you."

Her eyes widened. "You'd die with me? No kidding?"

"No kidding."

"I . . ." She raised her hands in a helpless manner. "I don't know what to say."

" 'Tis a miracle." He grinned. "I love you, fair Tessa." He took her hand and placed a kiss in the center of her palm. "And I will feel thus forever."

"Forever?" She laughed weakly. "Kind of a relative term given the circumstances, don't you think? Forever doesn't seem like much of a possibility right now."

"I wish to have forever with you." He adopted a firm tone. " 'Tis why I have decided to accept the offer Mordred made to me."

"Mordred offered you a deal too?" She withdrew her hand and raised her brow. "I'll bet this is good."

" 'Tis indeed intriguing." He paused for a moment. "He wishes us to abandon the search for the Grail and leave England, never to return."

Her eyes widened. "No way."

"Aye. Way," he said, his manner steadfast. " 'Tis decided."

"Not by me."

He stared down at her. " 'Tis not your decision to make."

"Oh, 'tisn't it? Listen to me." She raised her chin and he knew any objection he would make was for naught. "You wouldn't let me take Mordred's deal. You wouldn't let me give up my freedom—"

"And no doubt your life."

"So what makes you think I'm going to let you give

up what you've wanted for as long as you can remember, and break a promise to your king in the process, to save me?"

" 'Twould be no greater offering."

"My sending you off without me would fulfill that part of the riddle too and you didn't go for that either."

He should have known she would not allow him to accept Mordred's offer. Still, 'twas her life he risked as well as his own and he had to give her the choice. Pride swelled within him at her refusal. "Tessa—"

"First of all." She planted her hands on her hips and indignation sparked in her eyes. "You'd never forgive yourself for breaking your word to Arthur and eventually you'd resent me for causing that. Secondly, get on a ship and go where? In this day and age the options aren't all that appealing. And third, and frankly this is major and I can't believe it just now dawned on me." Her gaze caught his. "There's no way Mordred's going to let us out of here alive. Is there?"

"I think not," he said softly. "Mordred has always enjoyed playing games by his own rules. Games he can win. I fear this is yet another."

"It figures." She drew a breath, no doubt to steady her nerves. He could well use a draught of ale himself. "Do you want to rethink that 'die with you' stuff?"

"Never." He pulled her into his arms. "I could not live without you. I could not take a breath, my heart would cease to beat without you."

"Wow." The word was not much more than a breath upon the wind. She gazed up at him and his heart soared at the look in her eye. "Works for me."

The lock rattled on the door and he released her.

'Twas obvious Mordred suspected their feelings for each other. Still, discretion in his presence would be wise. Galahad shuddered to think what cruelties Mordred could inflict on Tessa to repay some long-forgotten slight by Galahad.

The door swung open. Mordred swaggered into the room, the captain of his guard and two other ruffians right behind.

"Galahad. My lady." Mordred nodded. "I do regret not being able to give you more time but alas," he shrugged in an offhand manner, "I am an impatient man."

"Too impatient to wait for your father to die of natural causes?" Tessa smiled innocently. Galahad groaned to himself. Why couldn't the woman hold her tongue?

"Aye." Mordred's eyes narrowed. "Too impatient to wait for a natural death," a sly smile touched his lips, "for anyone."

"We all have our faults, I guess," she said under her breath.

"What do you want of us, Mordred?" Galahad leveled the prince a steady stare.

"You know well what I want." Mordred's gaze shifted from Galahad to Tessa and a hungry light glinted in his eye.

"I would see her dead first," Galahad said with a smile.

"I could arrange it." Mordred returned his smile.

"Whoa. Excuse me?" Tessa glanced from Galahad to Mordred and back. "Do I get a say in this?"

"In truth, my lady"—Mordred's lascivious gaze swept over her and she stepped closer to Galahad— "you do not. But now and then, I may well let you have your say on any number of minor details. If you are well behaved."

"I don't do well behaved," she snapped.

"How delightful." A note of anticipation underlaid Mordred's words. "I shall have to teach you. Or punish you. 'Twill be a pleasure."

"I will not leave without her, Mordred." He groped for Tessa's hand hidden in the folds of her skirts.

Mordred raised a brow. "In truth, I did not expect you to." He glanced at Tessa and shook his head. " 'Tis a great pity."

"And I won't let him give up the quest." Quiet defiance colored Tessa's words. Her hand squeezed his.

"God's blood." Mordred laughed with disdain. "The lady is as noble and loyal and all the other qualities one searches for in a good dog as you are. Very well then. You have had your chance. You deserve your fate."

Mordred gestured at his men and they stepped forward. Tessa inched closer to Galahad.

"I don't like the way that sounds," she said out of the side of her mouth. "What does it mean?"

"My dear lady," Mordred said. "It simply means my hospitality will continue but unfortunately, 'twill be a slight change in your accommodations."

She glanced at Galahad. "Accommodations?"

" 'Tis simpler yet, Tessa." Excitement stirred inside him but his voice was even. "We will no longer be imprisoned above ground."

Unease clouded her expression. "Above ground? There's a below ground?"

"The dungeons, Tessa." His gaze never left Mordred's. "The infamous Castle Le Fay dungeons."

"Infamous? You flatter me." Mordred laughed. "It

has been years, in truth before either of us were born, since the dungeons have seen so much as a single, shall we say, guest? But I am certain 'twill meet your needs." He nodded at his guards, who quickly surrounded Galahad and Tessa and marched the couple out of the room. Mordred called after them. "My offers remain on the table. Should you change your minds my door is always open. Of course, yours will be barred." A wicked laugh echoed in their wake.

" 'Twill be . . ." Galahad leaned toward her and he flashed her a quick grin. "Okay, Tessa. Trust me."

She heaved a sigh. "With my life, Big Guy, with my life."

He prayed her faith was not misplaced but with every step closer to their prison his heart lightened.

The infamous dungeons of Castle Le Fay.

The perfect place to play on a long winter day.

Chapter Nineteen

❧

"So how's that plan coming?" Tessa said through clenched teeth.

Her ankles were tied, her hands bound together, stretched high over her head and tied to an iron ring attached to a rough beam. A small bale of hay or straw or weeds for all she knew had been shoved underneath her feet. A concession to what? Comfort? Hardly, but an inch shorter and she'd be on tiptoe. Galahad was a few feet away in the same predicament sans bale. Even so, thanks to his height, he looked a lot more comfortable than she was.

The guards had brought them down an endless flight of stairs and through a long, narrow corridor lined with thick, rough-hewn doors, each one probably leading to the latest in medieval torture chambers. Mordred's men had tied them up and left immediately, leaving a torch burning in a holder on the wall. Could have been worse. At least she didn't see a rack in this little hellhole. Not that she knew what a rack looked like. Probably similar to a Nordic Track. Still, it was shadowy and damp and very creepy and Tessa could swear she heard endless scurrying sounds. She didn't want to think about exactly what those sounds meant.

"I guess they don't call it a dungeon for nothing," she muttered and glanced at Galahad. "What are you doing?"

Galahad stared upward at his hands. "I am attempting to untie these ropes."

"Good luck. I can't even move my fingers."

" 'Tis not necessary to move a great deal." His brow furrowed.

She watched him for a minute. "You don't seem to be making any progress."

"And you do not seem to have any patience," he said mildly.

"I'd have a lot more if I wasn't trussed up like a side of beef in a meat locker."

He ignored her, too intent on focusing his efforts to divide his attention. She heaved a heavy sigh. Between the distance and the dim light she couldn't see any headway. "What are you doing now?"

"The same as I was doing a moment ago." His voice echoed the concentration on his face.

"Oh." It wasn't bad enough she was dangling here but he wouldn't even give her the satisfaction of listening to her. "So, what are you—"

"When I was a young boy," he said, his tone patient as if explaining something complicated to someone not too bright. "A traveling magician came to Arthur's court. Oh, his was not true magic, not like Merlin's—"

"Merlin." She ground out the name. "If I ever see that son of a—"

"—but entertaining nonetheless. Sleight of hand,

minor illusions, that sort of thing. But, and perhaps this was indeed true magic . . ." He worked steadily at the bonds. Did she actually see a bit of give in his ropes? "He could untie any knot, even those binding him. And he told me exactly . . ." The ropes loosened. "How he did it." In a moment he held the ropes in his hands.

"Way to go, Mr. Human recorder! All right!" She bounced slightly. "Now me."

He bent and untied the ropes around his ankles. "I think not."

"What do you mean—you think not?"

" 'Twould be a mistake." He straightened and grinned. "You will be safe and out of harm's way here for the time being."

"I don't want to be safe and out of harm's way." Her voice rose. "I want to be with you."

" 'Tis not wise." He stepped to her and kissed her, her mouth for once on a level with his.

She jerked her head away. "Don't think you can make everything all right with a lousy kiss." He kissed her neck and she shivered. "Or a couple of kisses." He trailed his fingers along her side in a long line from her elbow to her hip and she bit her lip to keep from gasping out loud. Her voice sounded a lot weaker than she wanted. "Or . . . um . . . that."

Her trussed-up position and the low neckline of her dress left her chest thrust forward like an offering to a pagan god. He bent his head and kissed a point deep between her breasts and she stifled a groan. Here she was all tied up and all she could think about was sex. His voice murmured against her. "We shall have to try this again someday."

She sighed. "You think so, do you?"

"Indeed I do." He brushed his lips across hers. "But I still do not like this gown." He turned to leave.

"Galahad, get me out of this!"

" 'Twould be my pleasure to rip it from your body but I fear there is no time."

"Not the dress." She grit her teeth. "Untie me."

"Nay, not now." He stepped carefully to the door, pushed it open and glanced around. "Odd, there is no guard."

"Of course there's no guard. We're supposed to be tied up. Both of us. Now, get me—"

"Tessa," he said sharply. " 'Twill be easier for me if I am alone."

"Where are you going?"

" 'Tis not easy to entertain children at court. And young boys find great fun in escaping the watchful eyes of their elders, choosing their own sport and making up their own games. Ours were down here."

She cast him an exasperated glare. "You didn't tell me you've been here before."

He raised a brow. "I did not have the chance." He glanced down the corridor. "Castles are fortresses, Tessa. More often than not designed to keep people out, not imprison them within. Long ago, there were escape routes and passageways down here. This castle is like a comb of honey. I can best determine if the tunnels I remember are still passable if I am alone."

"But if you're alone, I'm alone." A pleading note rang in her voice. "And I really don't want to be here alone."

"You are quite safe." He nodded and stepped through the doorway. "I shall return shortly." The door closed gently behind him then quickly swung open. "I give you my word." He grinned and shut the door.

"Don't you leave me here! Damn it, Galahad!" It probably wasn't a great idea to yell but she couldn't help it. Fear did that to her. Besides who was going to hear her down here? Nobody home but us rats. "Galahad! So help me, Mordred won't have to kill you I'll do it myself!"

The hay shifted beneath her and she stilled. This was not the sturdiest support in the world. If she moved too much, she'd probably knock away the damn thing away. Then she'd really be in trouble.

She strained to hear something, anything that would tell her he'd changed his mind and was coming back. He'd already been gone a good thirty seconds. Wasn't that enough time? How could he leave her here alone? Tied up. She sighed. Safe.

"I love you, fair Tessa."

In spite of her annoyance, the memory warmed her. She smiled to herself. He loved her. And she loved him. Of course, she hadn't told him yet but she would.

When?

When he came back.

If he came back.

Of course he'd come back. Then she'd tell him. No, it would be better if she told him after he untied her. Or when they escaped. Or when they found the Grail.

Or when she had to say good-bye?

Her smile faded. How could she leave him?

How could she stay?

This was not where she belonged. She could never adjust to the Middle Ages. Oh sure, she'd gotten along fine so far, if she wanted to overlook minor inconveniences like capture by a crazy prince and left to hang by her wrists in a dungeon, but this was just temporary. She was going home.

Maybe it would be better if she didn't tell him. He hadn't asked if she loved him although she'd bet he probably assumed his feelings were returned. After all, what woman in her right mind wouldn't be in love with Sir Galahad? He was a knight.

And maybe, if she didn't tell him, he wouldn't hurt quite so much when she left. He'd chalk it up to one more challenge to be overcome and whatever pain went along with it was simply the price to pay. He'd go on about his life with honor and courage, whether that involved the Grail or simply a nice little castle with a picket fence and someone like Oriana. And he'd forget all about Tessa.

And maybe, if she didn't tell him, she wouldn't hurt quite so much when she left. She'd return to her modern life and all its wonderful conveniences and all her thoroughly contemporary ideas and figure the pain of leaving him was the cost of the adventure of a lifetime. She'd file their days together in a safe little compartment in the back of her mind and go back to not believing in myths or magic or love. And she'd forget all about him.

Her throat ached and she sniffed away tears. What good would it do to tell him? For once, it was probably best to keep her mouth shut. But even as she agreed in principle she knew she was lying to herself.

How could she ever forget him?

Every time she looked up at the stars on a warm spring night she'd be back in his arms. And he'd be in her heart.

* * *

" 'Tis as you ordered, my lord."

"Excellent, Oscar." Mordred raised a brow. "Is all else in readiness?"

Oscar nodded, seemed about to say something then changed his mind. No doubt the wise thing to do, yet . . .

"What is it, Oscar?"

The soldier hesitated. Mordred sighed and leaned back in his chair. Galahad's wench was right—Oscar was not a prime example of the best man had to offer. Still the creature was loyal as a dog and ruthless as the devil and, better yet, would slash a foe's throat upon Mordred's order without a second thought. "Spit it out, man."

"I was just thinking, my lord—"

"Tsk, tsk, Oscar. You know the trouble you can get into when you think."

An embarrassed flush swept up Oscar's face and Mordred smiled. At this moment, the guard probably hated him. Unlike his allies across the land who conspired with the prince against Arthur, Oscar and all of his compatriots in Mordred's employ had no noble sentiments about their purpose here. Plain and simply, they were brutes. Their allegiance was provided in return for shelter and clothing and food plus a few coins on a regular basis. And all lived in the hopes that one day he would reward their faithfulness with power or land or wealth. Perhaps he would. Perhaps not.

"I was wondering, my lord, why you did not have them chained instead of tied."

Mordred cast him a pitying look. "If I had them chained, Galahad might never get free."

Oscar's brows pulled together in confusion. "I do not understand."

"Nor is it necessary for you to do so."

"But, my lord—"

"Are their horses within easy reach in the stables?" Oscar nodded. "And their possessions suitably at hand?"

"Aye, my lord."

"Then we are ready." Anticipation surged through him. He had waited for this moment for a long time. "Gather your men and I shall meet you at the castle gates shortly."

Oscar stared, then abruptly, comprehension lit his face. "I see, my lord."

"I thought you would, Oscar." He waved toward the door. "Now."

Oscar nodded and left the room. Mordred reached for the goblet of wine on the table beside him. This was it then. At long last he and Galahad would cross swords without Arthur to interfere.

He drew a long swallow of the wine and noted a shade of reluctance lurking in the back of his mind. 'Twas nonsense. He had waited for this day for years. Had wanted it since the first moment Galahad had bested him in a game or a fight or in the ongoing competition for the king's affection. No doubt Galahad had never even noticed Arthur's expression of pride when Lancelot's son had performed well or honorably. But Mordred had. And had noted further still how his father showed not the same interest in his heir's accomplishments.

He took another sip of the wine, its taste now oddly bitter to match his memories. 'Twas not his father's part in his mother's death that drove such hate between them. In truth, Mordred knew 'twas not Arthur's actions but rather his indifference that caused her death. The king did not care for, nor did he dislike, his first wife. She was the queen and whether she lived or died seemed to matter little to him. As it did to her son.

But, by all the fires of hell, he—Mordred—was Arthur's son and deserved to be treated with the respect and—aye—affection accorded such a position. His hand tightened on the metal goblet. Affection Arthur preferred to bestow on Galahad.

Still, perhaps he owed all he was to the good knight. Growing up side by side, 'twas the desire to beat Galahad that spurred him on. But the king's favorite was always a moment faster and a touch stronger. Mordred could triumph over the other boys and later, other men, but not Galahad. Never Galahad.

And did the competition not continue to this day? Should Mordred not have been the one Arthur sent on the quest for the Grail? Should it not be the heir of the kingdom sent on the mission to save it? Arthur knew of his son's treachery, only his misplaced sentimentality kept the old man from acting upon it. Yet, even if it were not so, Mordred had no doubts his father would never ask him to pursue such a quest. Nay, such a noble venture would be reserved for the king's favorite.

Now, 'twould be different. Now, at long last, he would triumph. And Galahad would die. Oh, the lady's arguments rang true enough. Arthur would be furious when he learned of Galahad's death at the hands of his son. Mordred would not keep such a tragedy from him. Nay, he looked forward to the well-chosen moment when he would tell his father the man Arthur had always preferred to his own son was dead at his son's hand. 'Twould be the very moment before Arthur and Lancelot and all else still loyal to the old ways joined Galahad in death.

And what of the woman? He drew his brows together and considered her. She was indeed fair of form and would provide interesting entertainment. Yet, once Galahad was dead, 'twould not be the same. He had relished the idea of sending Galahad off and keeping the woman, knowing with every step away from her, the knight's head would be filled with anguished thoughts of exactly how Mordred was enjoying the fair lady. With Galahad dead, he no longer cared about her. Until then, she may well be Galahad's lone weakness.

'Twas no question though—Galahad would be dead. Mordred swallowed the last sip of wine and got to his feet. And soon. Mere ropes would never hold a knight. Especially not one who long ago explored the escape routes of the castle he was imprisoned in. And when the knight and his lady emerged with the intoxicating rush of freedom in their blood, Mordred and his men would greet them.

'Twould be the last competition between the two. The final battle. The ultimate game. 'Twas almost a pity to end it. Yet, he would have it no other way. Mordred strode toward the door. In spite of the decadent life Galahad so looked askance upon, Mordred's days were spent as much in sharpening his skills with a blade as in debauchery. He was ready to meet his rival in one last engagement.

Indeed, Mordred smiled to himself, 'twas no doubt he would triumph. For the sake of his pride, he would prefer to depend on his skills alone. But should that fail, he would still best Galahad. This time, Mordred would emerge victorious. After all, he knew the knight's weakness.

And he would not hesitate to use her.

"I may never forgive you for leaving me alone in this pit." Tessa rubbed her wrists briskly in an effort to get some circulation back.

"I was not gone long." Galahad knelt at her feet and untied the ropes binding her ankles.

"Seemed like forever."

" 'Twas only a short time." He stood, grabbed her around the waist, lifted her off the bale and set her gently on the floor. His brow furrowed. "Can you walk?"

"I think so. It's not my feet, it's my arms." She rolled her shoulders and stretched her arms. "How do we get out of here?"

"There is a tunnel that will lead us to the forest behind the castle. I have located our horses as well as my sword, our provisions and the queen's dagger." He patted the knife at his side. "I would give it to you but," his gaze swept over her costume, "there is no place for you to carry it."

"I'd rather have a can of mace anyway," she muttered. "Besides, Guinevere gave it to you for luck. Did you find my—"

"Aye."

"You did get a lot done. I'm impressed."

He strode to the door, drew his sword and cautiously glanced into the corridor. " 'Twas easier than anticipated. The tunnels are as I remember them. The horses were stabled in easy sight. Our belongings were nearby. Even leading the animals through a little-used gate was not difficult."

Tessa crept to Galahad's side, peeking around to see into the empty corridor. Nothing. She breathed a sigh of relief. "Let's go then."

He nodded and stepped into the passageway. She grabbed his hand and trailed on his heels. So far, this was easy. A piece of cake. Maybe . . . too easy. "Don't you think it's kind of weird that Mordred doesn't have any guards down here?"

"Shhh. Lower your voice."

"Well, don't you?" she whispered.

" 'Tis extremely odd."

Her sense of relief dwindled. "When you were checking things out, did you see anybody?"

Galahad stopped by steps leading upward, removed a torch from its metal holder high on the wall and ducked beneath the stairway into a narrow passageway. "Nay."

"Nobody?"

"Not a soul."

"Wait, hold it, stop." Tessa pulled up short and yanked on his tunic. "Look, I know you're the knight and all that but I think we've got a problem." He halted and turned to face her. "This has all been a little too easy." She drew a deep breath. "I think it's a trap."

He stared at her for a long moment then grinned. "Duh."

"Duh?"

"Is that not what you say to express the obvious?"

"Yeah." She shook her head. "But coming from you it has a different ring to it." The light from the torch flickered off his features and gave a surreal effect to the moment. So what else was new? If escaping from the dungeon of a crazed prince wasn't surreal what was? "If you know this is a trap, why are we heading straight for it?"

His grin vanished, his lips compressed to a resolute line. " 'Tis typical of Mordred's games. He has left us no other choice. But a trap loses its effectiveness if the quarry knows of its existence. 'Tis the element of surprise that gives a trap strength. Knowing what we face, we will not blunder ahead blindly. We are prepared."

"And outnumbered," she murmured.

"Perhaps." His tone was somber. He turned and started off.

"We've been through a lot together, haven't we, Big Guy?" she said softly.

His low laugh echoed in the stone passageway. "Indeed we have."

"Do you think we can make it through this one?"

"Trust, Tessa, have faith."

"Right." A heavy weight settled in the pit of her stomach. How many times had she known real, genuine fear since that night in the library? A hundred? A thousand? Could anything in her world come close to the terrors she'd known here? Or the joys? "I'm not the same person I was when I came here."

"I too have changed." He glanced at her over his shoulder and smiled. " 'Tis for the best I think."

"I think so too." She followed silently for a few feet. "I don't know what I'd do if anything happened to you." She swallowed the lump in her throat. Oh, what the hell. She loved him and regardless of how this relationship would inevitably end, maybe he deserved to know. "You've come to mean a lot to me. I—"

"Be still, Tessa." Galahad whispered firmly. "The outer opening is ahead."

Galahad slowed his pace. He approached the exit, caution in every step. At least she thought it was the exit. In spite of his torch, she couldn't see more than a yard in front of them. Eventually, she made out a wall directly before them, thickly covered with vines and weeds. Her heart hammered. The tunnel stopped here. There was no way out.

"Galahad." She clutched his arm. "What do we do now?"

"Hold this." He thrust the torch at her. She grabbed the beacon and held it out before her. He stepped to the wall, pushed his way through the growth and vanished.

"Galahad!" she called in a fierce whisper. "Don't leave me!"

She heard the faint swish of his sword against the vegetation and within seconds Galahad had cleared a path back to her.

"Come, Tessa, quickly." He sheathed his sword, grabbed her hand and led her through the irregular arbor he'd carved. She lowered the torch and pushed her way through the underbrush.

They stepped into a small clearing bounded by the ivy-covered castle wall and the woods. The moon shone nearly full and bright enough to see. Tessa bent and rolled the torch on the ground to extinguish it. She could hear the shuffling and whinnying of their horses hidden just behind the trees.

"I don't see anyone," Tessa said cautiously. For the first time since they'd encountered Mordred's men, that light at the end of the tunnel might not be an oncoming train. Would they actually make it out of this mess alive?

"Nor do I." His grim tone told her more than his words. They weren't out of danger yet. "We must be swift."

"Maybe we lucked out." Tessa refused to give up the slim hope up dangling elusively before her. "Maybe Mordred figured we'd take another way out. Or maybe he thought—"

"Or perhaps he preferred you to come into the open to ensure there would indeed be no escape."

Chapter Twenty

❧❦❧

$\mathscr{M}$ordred stepped from the shadows of the trees, sword in hand.

Tessa's heart plunged.

Galahad calmly drew his weapon and positioned himself between her and the prince. "My lord, 'tis so good of you to bid us farewell."

" 'Twould be impolite of me to allow you to leave without bidding you a safe journey." Mordred nodded, apparently the signal for his small army of biker guards to emerge from the trees.

The two rivals circled each other. Galahad's voice was cool. "As ever, the gracious host."

Mordred's eyes gleamed in the moonlight. " 'Tis nothing more than common courtesy."

Tessa wanted to scream. This was like some kind of macho ritual dance. Two wild beasts stalking each other. Sizing each other up. Waiting to strike.

"Ah yes, but while I would not wish to offend you, I must say the accommodations were not up to your usual standards." Galahad shook his head. " 'Twas a disappointment."

"My apologies, Galahad, I shall try to do better the next time."

"The next time?" Galahad raised a brow. "Will there be a next time, Mordred?"

Mordred laughed, an evil sound that shivered through her veins. No doubt about it, Mordred was out for blood—Galahad's and probably hers as well.

"Alas, sir knight, I regret this meeting shall be our last." Mordred thrust his sword at Galahad.

" 'Tis a shame," Galahad said through clenched teeth, parried and the fight was on.

Tessa had never seen a sword fight outside of an old movie. These weren't the thin, elegant, Three-Musketeer–type swords. No, these were heavy and wicked-looking and required each man to use both hands. This was real. There was no dramatic, adventurous music setting the scene in the background, just the terrifying clang of metal against metal and the grunts and gasps of two men reaching the limits of their strength and beyond. And the thudding of her own heart. It was a battle to the bitter end and tension hung in the humid air like the specter of death.

The seconds stretched to minutes and the minutes stretched endlessly. Mordred would strike out. Galahad would counter. The Big Guy would take the offense. The prince would defend himself. They hacked at each other and with every blow of sword against sword she held her breath, certain one or the other would draw blood at any moment. Hatred glinted in Mordred's eyes, determination in Galahad's. As much as she didn't want to admit it, Mordred's skills were damned near equal to Galahad's.

The combat took its toll on both men. Sweat trickled

down Mordred's face. Galahad's muscles strained with every thrust. They were too evenly matched to predict a clear winner. This would go on until they both dropped. Galahad needed the odds tipped in his favor. She was his partner. She was supposed to watch his back. Keep him safe. She had to do something.

The two warriors battled on, blades slashing through the night air, oblivious to Mordred's men encircling them. Thank God they made no effort to help their prince. Would they stand by him if he was wounded? Would they take their revenge on Galahad if Mordred was killed? Or would they scatter without a leader?

Sooner or later exhaustion would claim Galahad or Mordred and give a slight edge to the other. Fear clenched her stomach. Would it be Galahad? Not if she could help it.

She searched the clearing for something, anything. Why hadn't she taken the dagger? Her gaze fell on the abandoned torch. It was about the size of a good, old all-American baseball bat. She lunged and grabbed the potential weapon. A spilt second later, burly arms held her in an iron grip. She glanced over her shoulder and into Oscar's gap-toothed grin.

"No way, pal." She struggled in his grip and his hold eased just enough for Sister Abigail's premier move. Tessa shifted and spun and jabbed only to find her elbow meeting thin air. Her momentum flung her to the ground. She scrambled to her knees and jerked her head up. The point of Oscar's sword rested at the hollow of her throat.

"Tessa!" Galahad's roar echoed through the forest.

She snapped her head toward him and his gaze caught hers. Terror, not for himself but for her, colored his face. The moment she met his eyes she knew it was a mistake. A fatal mistake. The world slowed to the speed of a dream. Galahad's gaze shifted back to Mordred but it was too late. The prince's sword struck home, driving deep into Galahad's torso, just below the breastbone. His head was flung back, his sword dropped from his hand and he jerked like a rag doll on a skewer.

"Galahad!" Tessa screamed and, without thinking, pushed aside Oscar's sword, knowing only that she had to get to Galahad. She scrambled to his side and pulled him into her arms.

"No!" Frantically, she felt for a pulse in his throat. There was none. "You can't do this to me!" Blood soaked through his tunic and onto her lap.

"I knew she would be his downfall." Mordred's words struck her as deeply as any sword. God help her, he was right. Horror swept through her. This was her fault.

"My Lord, what would you have us do with her?" Oscar said in a low tone.

She could hear the shrug in Mordred's voice. "Leave her to her noble knight and the wolves. I no longer care. She's of no interest to me now."

Tessa pulled her gaze from Galahad's blood-soaked body and stared at Mordred with all the hatred in her heart. Her voice rang like the voice of doom. "You'll pay for this, Mordred. You think you've won but you haven't. Till the end of time your name will be synonymous with evil and treachery. And he . . ." She glanced down at Galahad's still form and struggled to keep from choking up. "He'll be a hero. In the centuries to come, when kings and princes and wise men and even fools speak of things noble and good they'll speak of him. He'll be loved. Always. And you'll be . . ." she spit the word, "nothing."

Even in the moonlight she could see Mordred pale. "Your curse does not scare me. You are naught but a mere woman and whatever quality you possess that would have helped him in his quest is useless to him now." He scoffed but there was a vague note of unease in his voice. "I was right. You and he belong together. He saw the world and the men in it as honorable and just and fine. He never would have struck home when his opponent was distracted. 'Tis why he is dead. He was a fool."

"No." She raised her chin. "He was a knight."

"As you wish."

"I won't let him die! I won't!"

"My dear lady," Mordred's voice dripped with false pity, "you already have."

"No!" She turned her attention back to the man in her arms. Mordred muttered something to his men and they disappeared into the woods.

"Come on, Big Guy, don't leave me." Tears slipped down her cheek. "We're in this together, remember? You and me. The quest isn't over yet. You can't give up. Not now." She pulled him tighter against her as if to share her life with him. "You know I love you, don't you? Sure, you know. What woman wouldn't love you? You're a knight." Her tears fell faster. She smoothed his dark hair away from his face. "A legend. Legends don't die like this. I don't know what to do. I would do anything, anything to save you."

"There is little anyone can do now."

Tessa raised her gaze and hope leaped within her. Merlin stood a few feet away. "Merlin! Do something. You can't let it end this way."

An expression of utter sadness passed over the sorcerer's face and for the first time he didn't look anything like a tap-dancing movie star or even a wizard. Just a very tired old man. "I did not expect this." He shook his head. "There's nothing I can do."

"No!" She screamed until her voice echoed in her ears. "I don't believe that! I won't believe that! Use your magic, Merlin. You can move people through time and space! Why can't you do this?"

"There are rules, Tessa, that govern even beings like myself. What you ask . . ." He hesitated. "No, it's impossible."

"What? What are you thinking?"

"It would never work." He stroked his beard and paced the clearing. "Would it?" He stopped and stared at her, his eyes narrow, his voice level. "How badly do you want him to live?"

"What kind of question is that?"

"Answer me, Tessa."

"I don't know." *I offered once to sacrifice my life for his. Even so there was always the chance I'd survive Mordred's hospitality.*

"And if there was no chance for survival?"

"I . . ." *No chance at all? Could I give my life to save his?*

"Could you?"

She gazed down at his beloved face, his head cradled in her lap and calm flowed into her. It didn't matter that he was long dead before she'd been born or that her world didn't think he'd lived at all or anything else. "What do I do?"

"I was right when I chose you, Tessa St. James." Merlin's voice was quiet. "You have a great deal of strength in your soul."

"What do I do, Merlin?"

He heaved a heavy sigh. "There is no turning back."

"I know."

"What do you believe, Tessa?"

She shook her head in frustration. "What do you mean?"

"What do you believe in, Tessa. Now, at this moment?"

"Damn it, Merlin, not another riddle. Not now!"

"Tessa!"

She tried to think. What did she believe in? "You. And Arthur. The story, the myth, I believe it. All of it."

"More!"

"I don't know!" *Think, Tessa, think!* "Honor and loyalty. I don't know. Trust and faith and . . ." *What else?*

"And?"

"Magic!" Her breath caught and she gazed down at Galahad. "Love."

Merlin's voice filled her mind. "And by all that you believe in, all that you know, would you give your life for his?"

"And by all of that," her voice broke, "yes. For him."

"No!" Fire flashed white and hot and Viviane stood in the clearing. "It's over, Merlin!"

"Viviane!" Merlin swiveled to face her. "Tessa may be able—"

"Stop it, Merlin!" Viviane's voice rang in the night. "There is nothing that can be done. They've failed. It's time to go home!"

"But Tessa is willing—"

"So she says. Words, Merlin, it's nothing but words."

Viviane's tone was hard. "You know as well as I do, the words alone are not nearly enough. Proof is required. Those are the Rules, Merlin, your Rules."

"I know them better than you." Anger colored Merlin's voice. "Do not try my patience, my love. I taught . . ."

"Words alone are not nearly enough . . ."

The edict exploded in Tessa's mind and she knew Viviane was right. She stared down at Galahad. It wasn't enough to say she was willing to die for him. Not enough to simply say she believed.

"Proof is required."

But how? How could she prove something like that? How . . .

The jewels on Guinevere's dagger winked in the moonlight as if in answer to her prayer.

Guinevere gave it to you for luck.

She reached out and pulled the knife from its sheath, now covered with Galahad's blood. She gathered him close to her with one arm, gripped the dagger in her other hand and held it against her chest, right below the breastbone.

"I do believe," she whispered. "My life for yours."

She squeezed her eyes closed tight and concentrated her will, her love, on the man in her arms. Tessa pulled a long, hard breath and plunged the dagger into her flesh. Pain seared through her but she refused to let her mind falter. She could feel the rush of her own blood on her hand mingling with his on the knife and still her focus on him did not waver.

I believe.

The pounding of her heart sounded in her ears. The blood pulsed in her veins. Or was it his heart she heard? His blood she felt? Her soul reached for his, her life merged with his, who and what he was meshed with who and what she was until she no longer knew a difference. And her spirit soared with his. In reunion. In joy. They were together, whether in his world or hers or another never known.

And then . . .

Nothing.

It was as if a power switch had been flicked off. Her pain vanished. Around her were the sounds of the night and the rustling of the forest. Was she dead? She opened her eyes and glanced down.

The dagger was gone. The blood had vanished. Her blood and his.

His eyes flickered open.

"Oh, God, you're alive!" Her eyes widened and tears blurred her vision. She flung herself over him, touching him with her lips, her hands, to assure herself he was really living and real.

"Tessa," Galahad whispered. "I—"

"You're alive. And I'm alive." She gasped for breath. "I—" She glared at Merlin, afraid this was a horrible mistake, afraid it wasn't. "What the hell happened here?"

The wizard smiled. "You were truly willing to give your life for his because you now truly believe in love. I know it sounds simplistic but there you have it. It's one of the basics of life, if mortals would just accept it."

" 'Twas an odd dream . . ." Galahad murmured.

"You are so full of it, old man." Tessa studied the wizard suspiciously. "Now tell me the truth."

"Go on, tell her. You might as well. It's over now. All of it," Viviane snapped. "I never should have come here. If I had kept my mouth shut she never would have—"

"Keep it shut now, my dear." Merlin threw Viviane a pointed glare. She huffed and in a blinding flash of light, vanished. Merlin shook his head. "She can be rather unpleasant at times."

"Now then." Merlin studied Tessa for a moment as if wondering how much to say. Finally he sighed. "You're right. In spite of what poets say, love alone, even eternal love, is not powerful enough to restore life. More is needed. Somewhere in your lineage, back so many generations you could never trace it yourself, you have a touch of magic within you."

She snorted in disbelief. "You're kidding."

"Or rather you had."

"Had?"

"It was something of a one-shot deal actually. You see, my dear, magic never used accumulates like a good investment. It can eventually be employed in one fell swoop for something that closes the account, as it were. As long as you truly, deep in your soul—"

"Believe," she whispered and gazed down at Galahad and her voice softened. "How you doing, Big Guy?"

"In truth, I am not certain." He sat up and shook his head. " 'Twas as though I was here yet not here. As if I floated somewhere above you watching and waiting. A dream, I think, or a vision."

She stared at him. "Are you okay?"

He smiled and got to his feet. "I am quite refreshed."

"That's one of us." She reached up to grab his hand and he pulled her to her feet. "We've got to get out of here. Mordred—"

"I must return to Camelot, at once." Determination hardened Galahad's expression. "I must warn the king—"

"The king will have his warning," Merlin said firmly.

"Then I shall go after Mordred." Galahad's eyes narrowed. " 'Tis my duty to my king."

"No, Galahad. Your duty now lies only in your quest. As does your fate. Mordred will not bother you again. You will have safe passage under my protection for the remainder of your journey." Merlin shrugged. "It's the least I could do. I never expected it to go this far, you know. But these things happen."

Tessa stepped closer to Galahad and he put his arm around her. "So what now, Mr. Wizard?"

"I do hate that expression . . ." Merlin considered them for a long, silent moment then smiled, his eyes twinkling in the moonlight. "I cannot believe you didn't realize it, Tessa, or you either, Galahad, but you've met all the challenges in the riddle." Merlin's image faded slightly. "Simply put the pieces together" —now only his eyes remained, like stars in the night— "and the truth shall be revealed," and then even the stars were gone and his voice alone lingered, "and that which all men seek shall be his."

"What does he mean?" Galahad's brow furrowed in confusion.

"Who knows?" Tessa brushed her hair away from her face. "But if he said we've done it, we've done it."

"It should not be difficult to determine." Galahad paused. "The illusion was the dragon."

"That one was easy. What's an infidel?"

"An infidel." Galahad shrugged. "A heathen, a heretic, a disbeliever."

She drew in a quick breath. "Then that would be me. I didn't believe in you or magic or . . ." Her gaze met his. "Love."

"And now you believe in love?" he asked softly.

"And everything else."

" 'Tis the infidel coming to the fold."

"And the offering that can be no greater?" She smiled wryly. "It seems like we should get extra points for this one. Let's see. You were willing to give up the quest for me. I was willing to give up my freedom—"

"And more, Tessa." His voice was quiet. "Your very life."

"It was worth it."

"Was it, Tessa?" His gaze met hers. His eyes were troubled. "You offered your life and were spared. But you lost a wondrous gift to save me. Do you not regret that?"

"You can't regret losing something you never knew you had." Amazing. He really didn't realize how much she loved him. "Especially when you save what you value most."

"Tessa." He brushed his lips across hers. "You are my soul. 'Tis a truth revealed."

"We get bonus points for truths revealed too I think." She nibbled at his lips. "There was the whole time-travel bit."

"Indeed." His arms wrapped around her waist and pulled her closer. His lips whispered against the side of her neck. " 'Twas the truth of what you possess that I needed."

"Oh?" She closed her eyes and her head dropped back. His mouth traveled to the hollow of her neck and she gasped. "And what was that?"

" 'Twas simple. I act from strength." His tongue trailed lower to the cleavage between her breasts.

She sighed. "Yes?"

"And you act from knowledge. Together, we are whole." He cupped her breasts through the fabric of her gown and teased her nipples with his thumbs. " 'Tis why you keep that book close at hand."

"Uh-huh." Why was he doing this to her? Why wasn't she stopping him? Why did she want to drop to the ground right here and make mad, passionate love to him? And why wasn't she doing exactly that?

" *'Tis why you keep that book close at hand.*"

She snapped her head up. "What did you say?"

"I?" he murmured, turning his attention back to the overly sensitive skin exposed by the low-cut dress. "I cannot recall."

"No, wait." Desire evaporated and she pushed him away.

A bemused smile quirked his lips. "Wait?"

"The book! Did I tell you about the book?" She turned and glanced around the clearing. "Why it's so important to me?"

"Nay." He shrugged. "I assumed 'twas a keepsake."

"More than that." She spotted their bags and dropped to her knees, pawing through the contents of the first one she grabbed. "It's Merlin's book. It's how I got here in the first place."

"I do not understand."

"It's the title of the damned thing." She grabbed the second bag and dumped its contents on the ground. "Here it is. Look." She held the book up to him.

He knelt beside her. "I still do not—"

"It's not an ordinary book." Excitement rang in her

voice. "Things change in this. Pictures, text, everything. When I first got this, the title said *My Life and Times, The Story of Merlin* and then some PR stuff. But the next time I looked at it, and now, it says *My Life and Times, the True Story of Merlin*. Don't you get it?"

Understanding washed across his face. "Do you mean to say this will tell us where to find the Grail? And we carried it with us from the beginning? Surely, 'tis too simple an answer?"

"I don't know. We'll see." She angled the book to catch the light from the moon. It fell open of its own accord and despite the pale illumination, the words were easy to read.

And the Grail shall rest where the journey begins. Deep beneath the castle of the king, concealed by mists and magic, revealed only to those who truly believe and have met and bested the challenges laid before them. There shall they find that which all men seek.

His gaze met hers and they stared for a long moment. "Let us return home, Tessa."

"Home." The word lingered on the air between them.

"Aye." He took her hand in his. "To finish what there began."

Chapter Twenty-one

❧✦❧

$\mathcal{W}$hy was he not eager to return? To fulfill his destiny and find the Grail for his king and his country? Why did he not urge his horse onward? Why did he not strain forward with anticipation? Why instead did a weight lie heavy in his gut and an ache grip his soul?

Tessa.

She rode quietly beside him. Often enough through their days together he had wished for peace from her aimless chatter, yet today 'twould ease his heart to hear her voice. He had no need to ask what troubled her. 'Twas the same for him. When they had ridden away from Mordred's castle last night his spirit had rejoiced at the prospect of ending their quest and at long last finding the Grail. 'Twas not until they'd stopped to rest and he took her in his arms that he'd realized exactly what that would mean. Until that moment, he'd not considered the steep price of success.

"So, how long will it take us to get back?" Tessa stared straight ahead.

"Another day, perhaps two."

"Not much time, is it?"

"Nay," he said softly. " 'Tis no time at all." An awkward silence fell between them. 'Twas so much he wished to say to her. Yet, the words would not come.

"What happens when we get there and find . . . it?" She glanced at him with a look in her eye that said she must ask but did not wish to hear the answer. "Do you really become the guardian?"

He shrugged. " 'Tis what I have heard."

"And this is a permanent position? Forever, right?"

"I . . . aye." He paused. Long moments went by. "And what of you?"

"Me?" She glanced at him in surprise.

"What becomes of you, Tessa, when this is at an end?"

She blew a long breath as if she expected his question yet still was unprepared for it. "I guess I go home."

"Home?"

"Back to my own time." She met his gaze. "Merlin promised to send me home if I helped you find the Grail."

"I see." He studied her carefully. "I know well you miss your home. Are you eager then to return?"

Pain flashed through her eyes and she pulled her gaze from his. She lifted her chin and he wondered why his heart did not crack at the obstinate gesture that was such a part of her nature. Her voice was low and controlled. "It's where I belong."

Of course, 'tis where she belonged. This was not her world and he could not expect her to remain. Hers was a world of wonders where men could reach to the moon and beyond. 'Twas still difficult for him to believe her stories were real. Yet, did she not have to accept the same about his world? 'Twas hard for her but she'd survived and triumphed.

How could he survive without her?

Odd. Did he now regret their quick success? 'Twas what he'd always dreamed of. But a quest such as theirs could well last months and years. He could have heard her laughter and held her close to him for much of a lifetime. Yet still, at some point, she would have had to return. Perhaps it was better for them both now rather than later. Before they'd shared too many joys and too many memories.

If he were free . . .

He tightened his grip on the reins. 'Twas a vow as sacred as any spoken aloud. The finder of the Grail is sworn to protect it till time itself crumbles to dust. Nay, he was not free and 'twas better that she return to her home where he would not have to fear for her safety. Or wonder at the strangeness of her words. Or feel the rise and fall of her breathing as she lay against him late in the night.

And he would be no more than a story to be read aloud to children in the last moments before they succumbed to sleep.

"Galahad." She stared at the road before them. "Talk to me."

"What? Has my lady depleted all topics of discussion?" In spite of his teasing manner his words fell flat.

"I want to know all about you." Her voice was even. "I want to know about your childhood and your friends and your father. I want to know about Arthur and Guinevere. I want to know about your wife."

"I do not know where to begin."

The corners of her lips curved upward. "Begin at the beginning."

He smiled. "My mother was the daughter of . . ."

He told her of his family and his boyhood and his adventures and eventually, his feelings and hopes and dreams. Now and again she would ask a question but for the most part, she remained silent as if she was trying to remember every detail of every tale, every word of every recollection.

And every word brought them closer to farewell.

". . . 'Twas not a difficult contest for the . . ."

Every fall of the horses hooves carried them one step closer to good-bye. Tessa concentrated on his words, needing to memorize every story, every anecdote, every adventure. She focused on his voice, the tone, the nuances, the interesting rustic lilt of his accent. And she tried to burn forever into her memory the way he smiled or how he'd raise a dark brow for emphasis or the sound of his laugh drifting on the breeze. For long moments she'd succeed until the dull ache of knowing what was ahead would return with a vengeance.

How could she live without him?

She didn't have much of a choice. No more choice than she'd had when Merlin had tossed her through time and interrupted the Big Guy's prayers. Or when she'd been told she'd go on his quest or be dinosaur food. Or when she fell in love with a legend.

Oh, there had been a few choices along the way. None of them especially great. Mordred's of course. And Viviane's. The woman's offer to join forces made a lot more sense with the revelation of Tessa's own magical abilities. Of course, that was a moot point now anyway. She'd used up whatever power she'd had to bring Galahad back to life. And well worth it. But Merlin's wife had proposed sending them both to the modern world. What if she'd accepted Viviane's deal? Would they right now be sharing a pizza and watching TV? No. He'd never forgive himself if he abandoned his quest. She couldn't do that to him. He'd given his word. Besides, Galahad would no more fit in her world than she did in his.

". . . But my father did not think such a thing . . ."

Still, hadn't she managed to make it here? And maybe, just maybe, if he wasn't bound by his responsibilities and his promises, it might work. Surely, he'd be able to adapt.

She sighed to herself. Thinking like this would get her nowhere. None of it mattered. This was his destiny. Destiny. Hah. More like a sentence. She couldn't get the image of the ancient crusader from the third Indiana Jones movie out of her head and she couldn't bear the thought of Galahad living for eternity in some cave beneath the castle.

She tried to ignore the ache in her heart. It was a stupid waste of time to cry again. She'd already wept enough tears during this so-called adventure to last a lifetime. They had so little time left and she didn't want to spend it sobbing and red-eyed and puffy. She wanted to spend it in his arms, making love to him over and over until neither of them cared about duty or honor, the past or the future.

". . . And in truth, he was never, by the standards that men set for such things, especially . . ."

In a few days she'd be home. And he'd remain in the world in which he belonged. The world that sent men such as he on impossible quests where success meant forfeiting your own desires and even your life for a nobler purpose. She'd leave far behind the pungent smells of man and beast that pervaded everything and the awkward clothes and the strange food and all the discomforts of the Middle Ages. She'd leave the magic and the man who taught her to believe in it all. And heaven help her, she'd miss it. All of it. Oh, she'd go on and live her life but she'd die a little every time she had to teach a class on the Arthurian legends. Or caught a glimpse of a tall, well-built, dark-haired man striding across campus. Or gazed up at the stars.

Or told a story to a child at bedtime.

"We shall break our journey here this night." Galahad slid from his saddle to the ground. The forest had opened up into a clearing where a bubbling stream flowed into a small pool. The sun was low in the sky and filtered in through the leaves of the trees casting patterns of flashing light and muted green.

Tessa caught her breath. "It's beautiful."

"Indeed it is." A note of pride sounded in his voice. "I have come to this place since my boyhood."

"Oh, I see." She swallowed hard. "We're close then, aren't we?"

"Aye." He reached up to help her dismount and she slipped into his arms. He set her on the ground but kept her in his embrace. " 'Tis but a short ride to the end of the wood. Beyond lies the meadow and the tree where your courage was tested—"

She smiled up at him. "And yours."

"Aye." He laughed. "And mine. Was there a more dangerous moment in our journey than that?"

"Nope." She grinned and stepped out of his embrace, wandering over to the point where the stream splashed into the pool. A large rock hung over the edge of the water and she sat down in a hollow that formed a perfect chair. Her smile faded. "So, we'll be there tomorrow, right?"

He nodded reluctantly.

She couldn't bear to look at him. Tessa leaned over and trailed her fingers in the water. "Are you ready?"

"Tessa." He knelt on the mossy ground beside the rock. "I would change it all if I could."

"Would you?" Tiny waves rippled out from her fingers. "How?"

"I do not know." Anguish sounded in his voice.

"It's my fault anyway although I suppose Merlin gets some of the blame. Make that all of the blame." She struggled to keep her voice steady. "If I hadn't come into your life—"

"If you hadn't come into my life, I would be dead and not of Mordred's blade alone." He raised her chin to meet his gaze. "I would not have the life renewed that you have brought me. Nor would I know my heart could feel such things again. I would not know that a woman's courage can be as great as a man's. And I would not know that love can strike more than once in a lifetime."

"Then . . . I guess it all works out."

"Perhaps." He smiled and she gazed into his eyes, dark and blue as the sky before a storm. She could lose herself in his eyes. She'd already lost her heart. Sorrow, intense and primitive, washed through her and she jumped to her feet. She needed a little distance between them or she'd lose it.

"Funny." She hugged herself tightly and walked along the edge of the pool. "I don't seem to know what to say."

"Ah, the Lady Tessa, at a loss for words?" His manner was teasing and she knew he was trying to make her feel better. Instead, his consideration intensified the ache threatening to overwhelm her.

"Go figure." She gazed into the water. Her reflection stared back. Galahad appeared behind her. They looked like an illustration from a fairy tale. The one where the prince and princess were forced to go their separate ways and no one lived happily ever after. She leaned back against him and watched their image on the water.

"I will miss you, Tessa St. James," he said softly and kissed the top of her head.

She nodded, her voice was barely a whisper. "Me too."

"I wish . . ." He shook his head as if it was futile to speak of wishes and desires and dreams.

"Me too."

They stared into the water for a long time. There was so much she wanted to say but just being here in his arms was enough. It would have to be. The sun dropped behind the trees and the moon rose to cast its spell upon them.

"If all could be different . . ." He drew a deep breath. "I would want you forever by my side. As my wife."

She smiled in spite of herself. "As your partner."

He laughed quietly. "Aye. And my equal." He sobered and turned her to face him. "Tessa, I would give you a token to bind your heart to mine."

"It already is."

He pulled the ruby ring from his little finger and took her hand, slipping the gold circle over her thumb. He closed her hand in his. "Now, I will be with you always."

"Always."

"And in my heart, I will hold you dear as my," he smiled, "partner."

She choked back a sob. "Your wife."

"My love." Galahad bent to touch his lips to hers. She melted against him and they sank to the grass to touch and taste of each other with a bittersweet passion and a desperate need to remember. And together they reached one last time for the magic she'd never dared hoped for and found in the embrace of a man she'd never dreamed existed. Until finally, they lay savoring their last moments in each other's arms with a joy and a sorrow that would mark their souls through time itself.

For once Tessa had nothing to say. And nothing that needed to be said. Together they gazed toward the heavens and watched the stars move across the velvet night and waited.

For the new day.

And the end of the quest.

And good-bye.

Their horses walked out of the forest with a slow, measured step, swirling the ground fog with their hooves, mirroring the reluctance of their riders. It was barely dawn and for once he hadn't had to jerk her out of a sound sleep. She hadn't slept at all. Neither had he.

They approached the skinny, young oak tree that had marked his games as a boy and her test of courage and he reached his hand out to her. She took it and held his hand and slowly they approached the castle. There was no one in sight. Not even a breeze stirred the early morning mists. Tessa wondered if maybe Merlin had pulled his freeze-frame trick to protect them. She wouldn't have been surprised. One of the perks for solving the riddle, probably.

They drew closer to the castle and Galahad pulled up short. "Tessa." He nodded. "There."

She followed his gaze. A rock formation loomed midway between the castle wall and the oak. The mouth of a cave big enough for a man to stand upright yawned in the morning light. This was it then.

An odd note of excitement rang in his voice. "I have not seen that before."

"I don't think it was there."

He slid off his horse and started toward the cave like a man in a dream.

Panic gripped her. "Wait, hold it right there!"

He stopped and turned. She practically fell off her horse and ran to him, frantically trying to think of something—anything—to stall him. "You can't go without saying good-bye."

He had the calm demeanor and serene look of a man who has made his decision and is prepared to live with it but a touch of sorrow shaded his eyes. He smiled and lifted her chin. "I will love you always, my Lady Tessa."

He turned and started off.

"Wait!" He stopped. Desperation gripped her. She had to stall him. "I haven't told you everything yet!" *What? What hadn't she told him?* "There's something you have to know." *What? What did he need to know?*

Of course. She raised her chin. "I haven't said it. I haven't told you. I love you, Big Guy, I love you."

He smiled over his shoulder. "I know."

"How can you possibly know?"

"You offered your life for me. Besides," he flashed her his grin, at once sweet and arrogant. "I am a knight."

Tears welled in her eyes and she wanted to laugh and cry at the same time. He strode toward the cave. Leave it to him to have the last word with the one thing she couldn't refute. He was a knight. Her knight. She would love him forever. In her time or his, how could she live without him? How could she let him go?

"No!" she screamed and started toward him. She couldn't do it. "I'm coming with you!"

A warm breeze drifted past.

He turned back to her. "Tessa!" He shook his head. "Nay, 'tis my life, my choice. I will not condemn you to my fate."

"You're not. This is my decision! I want to stay with you." The breeze stiffened.

Hope washed across his face. "Do you know what you offer?"

She could barely hear him over the wind. "Yes!"

"In truth, are you certain? Once done, there is no turning back."

"I don't care. I'd rather spend forever in a cave with you than the rest of my life or a hundred lifetimes or all the time in the world without you."

"Think, Tessa, of what you'd give up!"

"Think of what I'd have!"

"Come then, my love!" He reached out to her as if to urge her onward or pull her to him.

She struggled to walk toward him but the gale force of the wind kept her back. When had this sprung up?

"It's his fate, Tessa. Not yours." Merlin's voice sounded in her head.

"No!" Galahad was getting farther away. She wasn't making any progress at all, like some kind of awful dream. "My fate is with him!"

The wind whipped around her, disorienting and familiar. Only it wasn't wind at all. Nausea swept through her. Galahad's figure grew smaller in the distance.

She screamed. "No, Merlin, no!"

"It's what he was always meant to do. The whole point of this lifetime." Merlin's voice rang firm.

"I don't care! I love him! I—" Her voice was lost in the void of the force hurtling her through time and space, stealing her breath and gripping her soul. Galahad and his world faded in the wake of an image that grew ever larger until she screamed and buried her face in her hands.

Abruptly, the tempest around her stilled. She didn't want to look. She knew what she'd see. Long moments passed and she waited. Maybe Merlin would change his mind? Maybe he'd send her back? Maybe . . .

At last she drew a steadying breath, dropped her hands and stared. At a scarred, library table and a stack of reference books. And an antique volume, its gilded title gleaming in the harsh light.

My Life and Times
The True Story of Merlin
Wizard Extraordinaire and Counselor to Kings

Chapter Twenty-two

Tessa struggled to catch her breath. Was she really back? Right where she left? And more importantly—right when she left? Everything from the research volumes to Merlin's book looked exactly the same. Untouched. Only she had changed.

She sank down in the chair beside the table and stared at the book that had led her though an impossible adventure. She knew without doubt it was just an ordinary book now. Any magic it once possessed was gone. It wouldn't take her back.

Galahad!

The pain of his loss slammed into her with such force she gasped out loud and braced her hands on the table. How could Merlin have done this to her? She was willing to stay. No. She wanted—needed—to stay with him. Forever if that's what it took. She'd give up anything to be with him. For him. Hadn't she already proved it? Instead, she was ripped away. Left empty. Devastated.

Shock and anguish rooted her to the spot. Was she supposed to go home now as if nothing had happened? As if this was just another night in the library? As if she hadn't spent weeks on a quest for the Holy Grail with Sir Galahad? Obviously, no time had passed here. Merlin had done just what he'd promised—put her back exactly where he'd found her. She had no way to prove what had happened to her.

If it had really happened to her.

What if it hadn't? What if she was crazy? What if she'd had some sort of awful breakdown right here in the library and everything she'd been through was a product of her imagination? What if the adventure and the danger and the love all took place only in her mind?

"Excuse me." A work study student poked her head around a corner of the shelves. "We're closing in a few minutes." She smiled. "Nice dress. Costume research, right? Theater department?"

Tessa glanced down. Of course, her dress! Excitement shot through her. The too-yellow, too-low dress Mordred gave her would prove her story! She glanced up at the student and her heart dropped. Dress or no dress, nobody would buy this one. Tessa wouldn't believe it herself coming from someone else. "Right," she said with a catch in her voice, "research."

The girl nodded, warned her of the library closing once again and disappeared. Who would she tell anyway? Angie? Her parents? They'd all think she was nuts. And what would be the point? Nothing was going to ease the overwhelming grief that held her in a viselike grip.

Tessa forced a few calm breaths. She had to pull herself together long enough to get out of here. The fact that she'd returned to the same moment she'd left was too much to take. She had to get to her apartment before she started screaming hysterically. She reached for the beat-up bookbag that doubled as a purse. A ruby ring sparkled bloodred on her thumb.

"I will be with you always."

Tears sprang to her eyes. How could she have doubted even for a minute?

He was real.

And he loved her and she loved him. And that was real.

Slowly she got to her feet and picked up Merlin's book. She paged through it with trembling hands until she reached an illustration of a knight kneeling in prayer before an altar. A ring glittered on his little finger. His ring. Her ring. She gazed at his well-loved profile and wished just once more to see the deep blue of his eyes lit with annoyance or laughter or love. She tried to swallow past the hard lump in her throat and slowly closed the book.

It was over. The adventure of a lifetime, a love for eternity—gone. As if it had never existed. As if it was simply a story in a children's book. A fairy tale. In this world, in her world, whatever the Big Guy might have been in real life didn't matter. He was Galahad. A Knight of the Round Table.

A legend.

And all she had left of him was an ugly yellow dress, a ruby ring and a heart shattered into a million pieces.

And nothing had ever been so real.

"Okay, I'm here." Tessa and Angie stood in the long line of holiday travelers waiting to check in. "Happy?"

Angie smiled sweetly. "Ecstatic."

"You can leave now, you know."

"No way." Angie shook her head. "Not until I see you walk through security on your way to that plane."

"Whatever." Tessa sighed, slipping back into the listlessness that had been her faithful companion for the last few weeks and toying absently with the ring she wore on a chain around her neck.

Angie narrowed her eyes. "What's that?"

"What? This?" Tessa glanced down. "It's a ring."

Angie crossed her arms over her chest. "I know it's a ring. Where'd you get it?"

Usually the ring was concealed by her clothes to avoid questions just like this. Today, in the frenzy of last-minute packing, she'd forgotten to hide it. Not that much of anything really mattered anymore. "It was a gift from a friend."

"What friend?"

"Somebody I knew a long time ago."

"Who?"

"A knight in shining armor," she snapped. "Are you happy now?"

"Knock it off, St. James. Why are you so touchy about a gift from an old friend?" Angie raised a brow. "Unless this friend is back in your life?"

"No," Tessa said softly, "he's not. I haven't seen him for . . . years."

"It's pretty. A ruby, isn't it?"

"Yes." Tessa stepped closer and held the ring, still on its chain, up for her friend's inspection. Angie took it and studied it for a moment.

"Very nice. Can I get a closer look?" She grinned. "Try it on?"

"No!" Without thinking, Tessa jerked back. The

chain snapped and the ring flew in a short arc and hit the floor. "No!" Tessa's heart stopped. She pushed aside another passenger and lunged for the ring, snatching it a split second before a foot would have crushed it into the floor. She scrambled back to her feet and slipped the ring onto her thumb, the only place it would fit. She turned back toward the line, barely glancing at a series of international travel posters.

"Tessa, I'm sorry about your ring. I—"

Tessa swiveled sharply and stared.

"Hey, are you okay?"

Angie's concerned voice, the sound of chattering travelers, the ever-present Christmas music and all the noises of the busy airport faded into the background. Tessa couldn't tear her gaze away from the poster. It was a scenic shot of rural Britain, the Britain she remembered. But it was the text that caught her attention and tugged at her heart.

Britain. The land of Arthur . . . where the legend continues.

"Oh, my God." Tessa gasped.

"Tessa?" Angie's voice rose in alarm.

"I hadn't even thought of that! I am such an idiot."

"I won't argue with you on that one," Angie said slowly. "But in which way of many do you mean?"

"I mean . . ." Hope surged through her blood and her spirit soared. She picked up her bag and left the line. "I'm not going to Greece."

"Of course you're going to Greece." Angie hurried after her. "You've always wanted to go to Greece."

"Not anymore." Tessa studied the departure boards, found the flight she wanted, marched to the ticket counter and took her place in line. "I don't know how much it's going to cost to trade in this ticket but I don't care if I have to max out every credit card I've got." She handed Angie her tickets and pawed through the items in her oversized purse in a desperate search for her wallet. Her fingers lingered over the spine of Merlin's book, always with her these days. She stared. Did the title glow a little brighter? Was there a tingle in her hand when she touched it?

"What are you talking about?"

She pulled out her wallet and waved it triumphantly. "I'm going to England!"

"England?" Angie's brows furrowed in confusion. "Why?"

"Because." She met her friend's puzzled gaze and grinned. "Maybe, just maybe, he's still there."

"He who?" Angie's eyes widened. "The guy who gave you the ring? The knight in shining armor?"

"Oh, he's a knight all right but he doesn't wear armor. I think he's too early for that. Although I was really never certain. I hate the Middle Ages, you know." She laughed with a giddy exuberance. "I can't believe I didn't think of this before. This might be the stupidest thing I've ever done but if there's any chance, one slim possibility of finding him, I have to take it."

"Tessa." Angie choose her words carefully. "You said you haven't seen this guy for years."

She giggled. "Centuries."

"Then you have no idea if he's still interested in you."

"He will be."

"What if he's married?"

"He won't be."

"Gay?"

Tessa laughed and leaned toward her friend confidentially. "You know, they did call him the virgin knight but it was all a crock. So his sexual orientation is one thing I'm not worried about."

"How can you be so sure about this guy?" Angie's voice rose in frustration.

"Well, there was this wonderful, romantic, star-filled night—"

"No." Angie clenched her teeth. "I don't mean that. I mean how can you be so sure about his feelings?"

Tessa stared at her friend for a long moment. "It's Christmastime, Angie, and now, more than any other time of year, you gotta believe. In miracles and legends and magic and love."

"This isn't like you, Tessa." Angie shook her head. "You've been acting really weird lately. What's going on?"

"Trust, my friend, it all comes down to trust."

"I will love you always, my Lady Tessa."

"And faith." Tessa smiled. "And love."

"Arthur was here. Arthur was there. Right." Tessa glared out the car window. "Arthur couldn't have possibly been everywhere he was supposed to be."

Tessa had studied all the tourist maps and guides, especially those concentrating on the Arthurian legends. Nearly a week of meandering through the countryside in Southern Britain brought her no closer to finding Galahad than when she started. Still, it was New Year's Eve and she was surprised she wasn't a bit depressed at not having found him yet but rather was optimistic that the new year would bring success. It seemed like a good sign. She smiled to herself.

Sure, crazy people were probably always seeing signs. Besides, she had months until she had to go home and no intention of giving up until she'd driven every road and checked out every *Arthur Slept Here* tourist trap.

She leafed through a guidebook with one hand and steered with the other. No problem. This road looked like a little-used country lane. Tessa glanced up and slammed on the brakes. The car skidded on the slightly icy road. The small herd of sheep milling across the road barely even noted her presence. Little used except for sheep anyway.

"Stupid sheep," she muttered and put the car in park. She might as well relax. This would take a few minutes. Tessa reached down to grab her purse. Merlin's book stared up at her, open on the floor. It must have fallen out of her bag. She picked it up and started to put it on the seat but an odd illustration caught her eye.

Her heart thudded with excitement. She hadn't seen this before and she knew this book backward and forward. This was a map. A real map. The kind of map you'd find in an atlas.

"*. . . with drawings of tiny little knights on horse-back pointing the way to the Grail . . .*"

"Well, Mr. Wizard." She stared at the map for a long minute and grinned. She was on the right track. "Welcome to my quest."

She drove on for another hour or two until the sun hung low in the sky. Damn. She was going to have to quit for the night soon. She hated to stop now that she knew she had Merlin on her side but it wouldn't do her any good to search at night.

She spotted a billboard up ahead. Great. Maybe that

would tell her how far to the next inn. She slowed and read the giant advertisement.

> THIS WAY TO THE GRAIL.
> TURN KING'S AVENUE THEN AHEAD TWO BLOCKS.
> CLEAN TOILETS AVAILABLE.

She rammed her foot on the brakes. The whine of screaming tires filled the air. The car skidded, turned a complete circle and shuddered to a stop, sliding just off the shoulder of the road. Tessa pushed open the door, climbed out of the car and ran back to the billboard. Or where the billboard had been.

"Merlin," she yelled. "Stop playing games! I know you're having a lot of fun but the joke's over! I don't need another damn riddle! I need a little help!"

Only the sounds of twilight answered.

She stomped back to her car and tripped over an old wooden sign, apparently knocked down by her car. She pulled the sign upright, brushed off bits of weed and grass and read:

ARTHUR'S OAK

She snorted in disgust. Right. Arthur had almost as many oaks in Britain as he did castles, birthplaces and burial sites. Where was this stupid tree?

She narrowed her eyes, pulled her coat tighter around her and scanned the scenery. A huge, ancient oak dominated a small field. The tree was maybe fifty yards from the road. It looked old enough to have been around in Arthur's time. One of the guidebooks noted some types of oaks in Britain lived for a thousand years or more. She had to admit it was an impressive tree.

" 'Tis a young oak."

No. Impossible. She started toward it.

"It served my friends and myself well."

Her stomach clenched. Centuries ago, his oak was in the middle of a vast meadow, not a little field. On one side was a wild forest, not houses and a few overly civilized trees. On the other, the castle, where a slight rise stood now.

"We thought it grew here for us alone."

She reached the tree and stretched out her hand to touch it. It was massive and strong and real. Maybe she was a complete fool. But maybe . . . if one believed hard enough . . .

She turned away from what was left of the woods she remembered and walked toward a castle that still lived only in her mind. The sun drifted lower in the sky. The hazy light of dusk stretched cold across the brown grass and cast the atmosphere of a dream on the landscape. The air shimmered and waved and grew solid and hard.

She stared straight ahead at a rock formation and the mouth of a cave big enough for a man.

Her breath caught and her knees weakened with the terror of a modern female who couldn't believe such things and the joy of a woman in love who did.

"Big Guy?" A whisper was the best she could do. She cleared her throat. "Galahad?"

She stared at the entrance of the cave for a minute or forever. Finally, a vague movement caught her eye. A moment later a figure emerged. Her heart stopped and tears burned the back of her eyes.

Galahad walked slowly toward her, blinking in the twilight like a man just waking up. She wanted to run to him but her feet refused to move. All she could do was stare.

"My lady." He studied her for a long time then grinned. He looked a shade older than she remembered. "I've missed the sound of your voice."

"Oh, Galahad." She sobbed and threw herself in his arms. "I thought I'd never see you again."

"Tessa, my love." He held her tight as if he could not quite believe it himself. "My life."

She pulled back and a fierce note underlaid her voice. "I won't let you go back. Not alone. I'm never letting you go again."

"Tessa." His brows pulled together and regret simmered in the deep blue of his eyes. " 'Tis not a thing—"

"Don't worry about it, Galahad." A familiar voice rang behind them. They turned in unison. Merlin leaned casually against Arthur's oak. Galahad's arm stayed close around Tessa and they walked toward the wizard.

"Nice coat," Tessa said.

"Armani." Merlin flicked an invisible piece of lint from his shoulder. "I believe someone once accused me of having no sense of style. If I recall, the word that was used was *trite*."

She grinned. "You've come a long way, baby."

"Indeed." Merlin sniffed.

"My lord Wizard." Galahad's voice was grim. "I," he glanced at Tessa, "*we* must know what is to become of us."

"Go ahead, Merlin." Tessa drew a deep breath. "I

can take it. What happens now? Does he go back or what?"

"He can go to Disney World for all I care." Merlin shrugged. "He is free to leave."

"But," Galahad's words were measured, "what of my vow to the king?"

Tessa and Merlin traded glances. "He has no idea, does he?"

Merlin shook his head. "For him, it's only been a handful of years. It's rather hard to explain but think of it as, oh, say, sleep therapy. For the most part, he's dozed through the centuries."

"Brace yourself, Galahad." She gazed up into his eyes. "A lot of time has passed."

"How much time?"

"There's no good way to put this." She heaved a sigh. "Welcome to my world."

"Your . . ." Galahad stared then his gaze strayed from hers and skimmed the landscape. "It seems much the same."

"Believe me, it isn't."

"Now then, if I am no longer needed." Merlin started to fade.

"Nay." Galahad stepped toward him. "I do not understand."

Merlin's disappearing act stopped but he was still a bit translucent. Tessa's stomach clenched against the queasy effect of that particular trick.

"I suppose you do deserve an explanation. Let me think for a moment. It's all very esoteric and philosophical. You see, my boy . . ." Merlin paused. "It's not the prize that's truly important but the quest. Always has been, always will be. Each man seeks the Grail in his own way. And each true believer will indeed find his Grail."

Galahad shook his head in confusion.

"I don't get it either," Tessa said.

Merlin heaved a long-suffering sigh. "Galahad, you pursued your quest in a noble and honorable manner. You succeeded against all odds. You kept your sworn promises in spite of your own desires. All of that accomplishment is, in fact, the Grail." Merlin smiled. "At this point, it is sufficient to simply say your obligations to your king, your country and all in the past have been met. Your life is now your own. Think about it, Galahad, did you ever actually see the Grail?"

"Nay, but I knew—"

"It was your dream and Arthur's and your father's that you sought. And while you were the guardian of the Grail, that in itself cannot be defined." Merlin turned his dark gaze to her. "Tessa, what was the last thing I said to you?"

"You said, this is what he was always meant to do." Her words were measured. "The whole point of this lifetime."

"And that lifetime is at an end. That destiny has been fulfilled." Merlin raised his hands in an all-encompassing gesture made no less magical by the designer coat. "This is his fate now."

"My lord Wizard, I still—"

"Don't worry about it, Big Guy." Merlin grinned. "You'll understand soon enough. The moment you realize your quest was not truly over until now."

"But we solved the riddle," Tessa said suspiciously.

"Did you?" Merlin's eyes twinkled in the dusk. "Did you find that which all men seek?"

"Sure, we found the Grail."

"Ah, but if the Grail is different things to different men . . ."

"Then that which all men seek is not the same." Comprehension sounded in Galahad's words.

"I still don't get it." Tessa sighed.

"He does," Merlin said. Galahad took her hands in his. "His true Grail"—the wizard vanished, only his words lingered—"is you."

Tessa widened her eyes and her gaze locked with Galahad's. She could see the truth in his expression but she wanted—no needed—to hear it. The words choked in her throat. "Am I?"

"Always, Tessa St. James."

She shook her head. "It's not going to be easy for you. Life is a lot different in the twenty-first century."

" 'Tis yet another challenge on our quest." Galahad lifted her hands to his lips and kissed first one then the other. "One that shall last another lifetime. Together."

"Together," she whispered and sheer wonder surged through her. His lips met hers and she knew now that they had all the time in the world; even a lifetime would not be long enough.

And she marveled that she'd ever failed to believe in white knights, myths and magic and most of all . . . in love.

Epilogue

"You cheated, you know."

"Cheating is relative, Merlin." Viviane glanced up with an indignant expression. "And such a nasty word as well. I can't say I'm at all pleased by your use of it. Besides . . ." An emery board appeared in one hand and she filed the nails of the other. "I did not."

"Oh," Merlin raised a brow. "What would you call it?"

"Creative manipulation."

"Creative manipulation?" He snorted. "It was certainly that. You confronted them with a dragon—"

"A mere illusion." She held her hand out and inspected it carefully.

"You tried to make a deal with Tessa."

"And what a disappointment she was." Viviane sighed. "Who knew she'd be that noble?"

"And you joined forces with Mordred."

"I'd scarcely call it joining forces." She shrugged. "I simply gave him a few insignificant pieces of information." She pointed her file at him. "And it did him no good whatsoever."

"True."

"I really don't understand why you're so put out about this." The emery board vanished and Viviane rose to her feet. "They succeeded in their quest, no one was permanently injured and they are, at this very moment, living happily ever after. You won our little wager." She glanced around Merlin's quarters and shuddered. "I, on the other hand, am doomed to relive the Middle Ages."

Merlin studied her carefully. "You didn't play fair."

She crossed her arms over her chest and glared in defiance. "Tough."

"You deserve what you get."

"Very likely."

Without warning the world around her vanished, replaced by a much more contemporary setting. Delight washed through her. "The condo!"

Merlin grinned. "Welcome home, my dear."

She narrowed her eyes. "I don't quite understand. Why are we here?"

"As much as I hate to admit it, Tessa and Galahad taught me a few things during all this. Each was willing to give up what they wanted most for the benefit of other. In spite of myself, I was rather touched. If mere mortals can be so noble . . ." He sighed with exaggerated resignation. "I can do no less."

"What are you trying to say?"

"I will not hold you to your bargain."

"Merlin!" She stepped toward him and eyed him suspiciously. "Do you mean it?"

"We will not relive what was for the most part a glorious time in history."

She bit back the immediate impulse to disagree.

He shook his head regretfully. "It is not always

possible or always preferable to return to what once was. Sometimes, it's best to leave the past firmly in the past."

She wrapped her arms around his neck. "What a wise and wonderful creature you are."

"I am, aren't I?" He grinned.

"Indeed you are. You've brought me home and we should celebrate." She nibbled at the lobe of his ear. He did so like it when she did that. "Would you like to play a little game of master sorcerer and virginal apprentice?"

He laughed wickedly. "One of my favorites." He swept her up into his arms and carried her toward the thoroughly modern bedroom in the totally up-to-date condo and she sighed with contentment. "Although I should tell you I am not completely releasing you from our agreement."

"No?" She widened her eyes in surprise then smiled and reached forward to nuzzle his ear. "Whatever you wish. You are, after all—Merlin, Wizard Extraordinaire and Counselor to Kings. And I will love you until the end of time itself.

"And that, my darling sorcerer, is truly magic."

Don't miss

Desires of a

Perfect Lady

By Victoria Alexander

Coming April 2010
From Avon Books

Savor the delights of Regency love
from *New York Times* bestselling author

VICTORIA ALEXANDER

WHEN WE MEET AGAIN
978-0-06-059319-3
When a mysterious young woman spends the night in his bed,
Prince Alexei finds he cannot forget her.

A VISIT FROM SIR NICHOLAS
978-0-06-051763-2
Lady Elizabeth Effington's life—and heart—are turned
topsy-turvy by the handsome cad from her past.

THE PURSUIT OF MARRIAGE
978-0-06-051762-5
Delicious debutante Cassandra Effington wagers
the Viscount Berkley that she can find him an ideal bride
before *he* finds her the perfect match.

THE LADY IN QUESTION
978-0-06-051761-8
Identical twins, sensible Delia and mischievous Cassandra
Effington were the most delicious debutantes to ever waltz
across a London ballroom. No one ever expected Delia
to be the one to get into trouble . . .

LOVE WITH THE PROPER HUSBAND
978-0-06-000145-2
Well educated but penniless, Miss Gwendolyn Townsend
is shocked when it's discovered a match has been made
between her and the Earl of Pennington.